# DOCTOR WHO

## SHORT TRIPS

### A COLLECTION OF SHORT STORIES

EDITED BY STEPHEN COLE

**BBC BOOKS**

Published by BBC Books
an imprint of BBC Worldwide Publishing
BBC Worldwide Ltd, Woodlands, 80 Wood Lane
London W12 0TT

First published 1998

Printed and bound in Great Britain by Mackays of Chatham
Cover printed by Belmont Press Ltd, Northampton

*for Sydney Newman*
*1917-97*

# CONTENTS

# INTRODUCTION

It was in October 1996 that I first heard of this collection of short stories. Nuala Buffini, who had found herself in creative control of the BBC's range of *Doctor Who* material, was chatting to me about life in general when she mentioned she was planning a book called *Traveller in Time*. It would feature many Doctors over many stories, and all the adventures would be (surprisingly enough) historical in nature. If I had any ideas, would I like to contribute something?

I thought about it vaguely and drew several blanks. I never did get back to Nuala. And then a month later, in the bizarre way that things so often turn out, I found myself appointed Project Editor of *Doctor Who* and faced with the prospect of editing the thing myself.

I'm quite a fan of historicals, but the thought of an entire compendium of stories set in Earth's past did strike me as being a little narrow in its scope. Linking the stories thematically had traditionally proven successful in this area of *Doctor Who* publishing, but a good, solid alternative theme had me stumped.

It led me to thinking what themes had characterised the series' own run, and when Steve Lyons's proposal flopped on to my desk, I had my answer: 'Freedom'. Being a term as broad as the series' own remit, it makes a highly convenient peg from which to hang a variety of stories. And the bonus is, of course, that spotting how the nuances of the word manifest themselves is an exciting game for all the family!

I decided to go for a book crammed with stories of differing lengths. That way, the readers can't guess how quickly things will unfold, or know how long they can expect to be in the company of the characters starring in each story. And from the authors' point of view, many have been able to write with no set length in mind – their stories weren't artificially inflated or savagely cut to fit a word count, they simply stopped when they felt their story was told. Others have been very good about me phoning up and saying of their synopses, 'Great idea – can you do it in x-thousand words?' and have risen to the challenge admirably. I hope the diversity of length will help this collection's readability: whether you've got half an hour to kill before going out or a long, boring train ride ahead of you, there should be something of convenient length within!

Before I let you go and get on with it all, I must thank Lesley Levene (no relation to dear Rebecca!) for all her help assisting me with the story-editing at times when a sea of manuscripts and admin has threatened to engulf my entire world... I'd better go – I'm beginning to sound like one of my back-cover blurbs.

Stephen Cole
January 1998

# Model Train Set

by Jonathan Blum

The one-inch-high figure in the painted-on business suit stood on the edge of the railway platform, tapping its clockwork toes as it waited. The others in the queue behind it buzzed slightly to themselves. Finally, an impeccable O-gauge replica of a 1920s steam locomotive whirred and clattered its way up to the station, pulling three custom-made Pullman cars behind it. The miniature men stood patiently as the train came to rest, shuffled a bit while a line of other figures filed out of the cars, and finally trooped on to the train in unison before settling themselves neatly in their seats.

Behind the station, the Doctor's face leaned in close, soft blue eyes peering for a moment at the expressions on the tiny mechanical faces. Every sculpted hair on their heads was perfectly in place – not like his own chestnut curls at all. Then he straightened up and gently turned one of the dozen handles on the control board, sending the train's wheels rattling into motion, and sighed.

He felt glum.

The model train set in front of him was a miracle of craftsmanship – his own craftsmanship, actually – built over the course of many years a lifetime ago. More than a dozen trains of all varieties – electrics, steamers, even an old Mickey Mouse handcar – circled between five stations across miles of carefully crafted countryside. A miniature river bubbled from a source in the papier-mâché mountains and ran under half a dozen bridges of increasing size, ending in a glittering lake by the Shore Line terminus. And the people had been his crowning glory, the product of months of tinkering in his workshop and further months of painstaking hand-detailing

1

the painted faces on each one. The resulting world stretched from wall to wall in his wood-panelled study, and was guaranteed to make the eyes of anyone who saw it widen in amazement.

So what was missing now?

He'd always loved trains, for as long as he could remember. Even as a little boy, he'd dreamed of driving one. Sometimes he'd looked at the dream in a different way. At one point in his life he would much rather have been the stationmaster, quietly tending his plot and keeping his corner of the larger system in order, while at other times he would gladly have just been the man who rescued damsels from the bits of railway line to which men with curled moustaches kept tying them with alarming regularity. He suspected that one of his more recent incarnations would rather have been one of the steam engines – all bright paint and gaudy brass, huffing and puffing and chuffing about with great noise and clatter.

But most recently he had tended towards being the man in the nerve centre, routeing and switching the trains on all their myriad ways, each one playing a part in the larger tapestry of schedules and goals. This was the Doctor who had built the model train layout, who had machined each engine and laid each piece of track, who took a craftsman's pride in knowing every quirk and foible of the system he had engineered. He set each train on its way and happily juggled the dozens of minute details needed to keep them from interfering with each other. His pleasure came in the sight of a crisis overcome or, even better, a potential crisis avoided. He was the man who developed a childlike grin at the sight of the whole bustling network running smoothly. Finally he'd come up with a plan in which everything worked.

No matter what else you could say about him, he made the trains run on time.

But now the new Doctor looked at the model train set with a vaguely dissatisfied frown. It was all very well having a system which responded precisely to what you told it to do but where was the surprise in that? If he prodded the rail network, he knew instinctively which way it would jump, but it would never jump on its own. Why didn't anything happen without him telling it to?

The miniature landscape required his constant attention to keep functioning. If he stepped away from it or let his mind wander, it either froze into immobility or collapsed into collisions and derailments. It was beginning to feel like such a bother having to take care of every last detail. Why couldn't he have the system just handle things on its own?

And so that's what he did.

With a sudden burst of energy he dashed off to the TARDIS workshop, a long low room smelling of damp and machine oil. He hunted through the rows of hulking metal machines till he found what he was looking for: an ancient computer terminal, tucked in a corner behind the lathe and the IC press. He pulled up a chair and set about imagining.

His first creation was a locomotive which laid its own track in front of it and pulled it up behind – letting it wander about free on the floor like a gerbil in a plastic ball. This wasn't entirely successful; while having an electric train nuzzling his feet as he worked at the console was definitely a fascinating new sensation, his enjoyment was curtailed the day the train bolted away down the TARDIS corridors as fast as its little wheels would carry it, never to be seen again. It was bound to make a break for freedom one day, he mused, and went back to his workshop.

This time he brought a passenger with him, for inspiration. The tiny woman in the suit of paint stood on top of the terminal's monitor, politely but pointedly looking at her watch every few minutes as she waited for a train to arrive from somewhere. Programming this into them had been a matter of minutes; he'd just given the passengers the desire to constantly be somewhere they weren't. It was a simple drive, one he was quite familiar with in himself.

But what else might they be capable of doing?

For the next two days he worked at the computer. Occasionally he remembered to sleep or eat. Then he dropped his coat, rolled up his sleeves and warmed up the furnace. He spent the next few days die-casting and assembling and painting, piecing together intricate clockwork while the IC press stamped out tiny silicon wafers like rows of gingerbread men.

He returned to the layout and drove all the trains back to the railyard. He picked up each of the passengers as they milled about on the platforms and placed them carefully in a large hatbox. Then he leaned over the main terminal on the Central Line and began taking the track apart. Within a few minutes, all the railbeds on the layout were bare. Only the main railyard remained. Then he carefully disassembled the bridges, reducing them each to a pile of beams, leaving the stations standing alone.

Then he left the room, ignoring for the moment the confused shuffling and bumping coming from inside the hatbox. He returned an hour or two later pushing a wheelbarrow full of earth, fresh from one of the agricultural areas of the TARDIS, and dived into his next task.

With a trowel, he began spreading half an inch of the soil over the entire landscape. By the time he started coating the mountains, he noted with glee that tiny shoots had already begun to sprout in the lowlands. Those miracle-gro micro-seeds the Kapteynians had sold him were turning out to be good value after all – pretty soon the entire countryside would be covered with a fine carpet of O-scale grass. Real soil over the papier-mâché, real grass over the green paint.

He stepped back for a moment, admiring his handiwork. Then he dashed out of the room again, to return with another box bumping and rattling under his arm.

He opened the new box and let the clockwork men march out. This new batch of people were painted in work clothes: toy soldiers with shovels and scrapers, clustering around the end of the track at the edge of the railyard. Two of the men in

4

the lead set up miniature surveyor's tripods and quickly took a series of sightings in the direction of the Central Line terminal. The other little men stood motionless, the tiny positronic processors in their die-cast heads chattering silently over their wireless network.

The Doctor suddenly realised he was holding his breath.

Then, as if a switch had been thrown, the group scattered. Most of them hustled over to the ground in front of the last piece of track and started shovelling and smoothing and grading the soil. Half a dozen others clambered over to the pile of track and began to ease a piece off the top, lowering it to the ground and carrying it with jerky clockwork steps over to the beginning of the line. They fitted it into place and marched back for another, while the crew ahead of them busily cleared the way forward.

The Doctor watched them, his eyes wide with awe.

He stared raptly as they reached the Central Line terminal, as the surveyors took a new batch of sightings and the work crew split in half. One crew headed down the path of the old Central Line, while the other curved away on a new route towards the mountains. More workers, who had been waiting patiently by the railyard, hurried over to join the crews, lugging a set of points with them. The Doctor couldn't help it; his face split into a wide grin.

He tore himself away from the sight of the crew and let his hands flutter over the trains in the railyard. Which to do first? He lifted one locomotive, a replica of the New York Central's Commodore Vanderbilt, out of the railyard and dashed from the room with it.

When he returned several hours later, the locomotive didn't look any different from the outside. He'd very carefully hidden all the additional wires and control circuitry beneath the surface. He replaced the engine in the roundhouse and couldn't resist waving his fingers at the inch-tall figure now standing in the locomotive's cab. Aside from his blue-and-white engineer's cap, the young blond mechanical man was dressed in an outfit vaguely like that of an Edwardian cricketer.

For the next two days he made these changes, one locomotive at a time. Finally he replaced the last one, the Mickey Mouse handcar, on the track and leaned back to look at the layout. It was amazing – while he'd been working, the builders had woven all the stations together into a web of shining tracks. Some of their lines followed the same paths he'd laid down before, but others took short cuts he'd never dreamed of. They'd run track up to the top of the mountain and criss-crossed the river with four bridges of their own design. They'd even started work on a spur line leading off the table and were industriously building a suspension bridge over to the nearest bookshelf.

It was ready, at last.

He looked down, surprised; the hatbox wasn't where he'd left it. Then he saw that the Brownian movement of the passengers bumping against the hatbox walls had caused the box to inch several feet across the floor. He caught it, picked it up and poured the much-delayed passengers on to the Central Line terminal platform. They shuffled themselves upright and began to form orderly queues.

The Doctor took his seat and cranked the main transformer's output up to full. The little man at the controls of the Amtrak Metroliner checked the signals and, with a whir and a rattle, pulled his train out on to the Central Line.

The Doctor barely moved or blinked for the next three hours. It took him that long to get even a glimpse of the marvellous complex rhythm the clockwork men had fallen into. The trains criss-crossed and outraced each other, dodging each other partly through careful scheduling and partly through fast reflexes and luck. One train could meander from the mountains to the shore like a wandering thought or streak from Central to the rural whistle stop at the far edge in thirty seconds flat. The trains played nice – followed the signals, got out of the way when one of them was in a hurry – and every ten minutes an express ran out along the Bookshelf Line to the new depot they'd set up by *War and Peace*. The Doctor closed his eyes and just listened to the ebb and flow of the rattle of wheels, clattering over the soft hum of the TARDIS itself.

Finally he took control of the 1920s New York electric commuter train and sent it weaving through the layout, his own trail dodging and zooming among the gorgeous shifting complexity swirling around him. He was grinning like the six-year-old he'd been centuries ago. The waves of motion which surrounded him were astounding and the details of each piece in motion were mesmerising.

And the Doctor looked at the model train set and saw it was good. He'd set it up, let it go and it had become something greater than he could have done on his own. I thought I could, the Doctor chuckled to himself, I thought I could I thought I could.

Then one thing led to another, as things tend to do, and after a while the Doctor went away. It was just for a little adventure outside the TARDIS, a chance to wander through a world that was so much larger than he was. When he was finished letting the waves of the world's motion wash over him, he went back to his study.

He stared in disbelief.

Engines and cars lay strewn across the tracks, in the river, in a pile on the floor between the layout and the bookshelf. A lone digger wandered in circles, his pick jerking up and down in front of him, sparks arcing where his head had been. The Raymond Loewy streamline engine had somehow embedded itself nose-first in the papier-mâché mountain. As he watched, the last surviving train, the little Mickey Mouse handcar, trundled up to the spot where the southern river bridge had once stood and fell into the river with a plop.

The Doctor collapsed into the chair in front of the layout. How could this have happened? A few scattered passengers were still standing unawares on the surviving platforms. Dear heavens, they hadn't even realised what was happening as it happened. His head slowly shook back and forth, his jaw hanging slack.

As far as he could reconstruct, it had begun when a group of passengers, impatient at waiting for the trains, had set out across the countryside on foot. One of them was hit by the Union Pacific express and got caught between its wheels, causing a spectacular derailment which took out the entire Central Line. As the rail workers struggled valiantly to move the toppled cars, which weighed hundreds of times more than they did, the knock-on delays caused more passengers to abandon the platforms. Another group of passengers picked up tools and started to lay track themselves, unthinkingly, as if the mere presence of a disconnected stretch of rails would cause a train to appear on it. They built their track-bed straight towards their destination, without regard for the rest of the rail lines. When they laid their new tracks directly across the north spur of the Mountain Line, the next catastrophe was inevitable. With two lines out of service and every train running late, the fabric of agreement and compromise which held the system together began to unravel – engineers started cutting each other off at points or gunned their motors to make time. The Raymond Loewy streamline jumped the rails on a curve and ploughed into the little rural whistle stop, demolishing the balsa-wood shelter and crushing the waiting passengers underwheel. The 1920s New York electric commuter train, unable to slow down in time, broadsided an arthritic freight train at a set of points. Two engines were left waiting on the Bookshelf Line bridge, which gave way under the sustained weight. The civilian construction gang kept laying their line till they reached the river, at which point they blithely stepped in and got swept away by the current. It must have only been a few more minutes before the end, when the Commodore Vanderbilt and the Metroliner met head-on on the southern river bridge and demolished the whole thing.

The Doctor sat in front of the layout and put his head in his hands. He should have known better. You have to watch these things. You can't let them get out of control. He should have known better. If you give them the chance to grow on their own, they're bound to bring things crashing down around them. Look at what happened with the humans' Transit system. He should have known better. He had known better, back when he first built the layout, but he was so much older then. He really didn't want to be that old again.

He picked up the headless digger and, with a merciful squeeze of a thumb and finger, he switched it off. You can't mend people, he remembered a voice saying. He spent so much of his time trying to do just that – keeping their little worlds from tumbling into chaos when they didn't know how to cope with running them themselves. Helping them learn how to put the pieces of themselves back together. But somehow all his work ever did was make them depend on him more and more, make it more and more impossible for them to go on without him. The rails he was on always led him back to the same place again. It would never change.

Then he spotted the work crew. They were standing clustered by where the bridge to the bookshelf had stood. They were reeling out a spool of thread they'd found somewhere off the edge of the table.

He leaned across to look over the edge. They were lowering a man on the end of the thread. As the Doctor watched, the man found his feet on the floor, walked over to the remains of the fallen bridge and grabbed one beam. The work party up on the layout then began to hoist him back up.

A pile of beams they'd already retrieved stood next to them. Other workers were starting to manoeuvre a few of them back into position, putting the bridge back into place. A couple of surveyors, their work done, were moving on towards the remains of the river bridge.

The Doctor watched them for a long time. Then he got down on the floor to help them. He started to pick up the remains of the bridge for them, but stopped. Leave that to them. Instead he helped them pick up the cars. Who knows, given enough time they might be able to figure out a way to shift the trains on their own, but he might as well give them a hand and save them a few years. He shrugged, smiled and started setting the cars back upright on the tracks. He'd be going away again soon, some time, and the further along the way they were the better.

You never know, they might just learn this time.

# Old Flames

## by Paul Magrs

### I

Whenever Sarah went to check on the convalescing Doctor, she found him sprawled on a chaise longue, reading John Donne. He would wave feebly at her and say, 'I nearly drowned, you know!' until it became a kind of joke between them.

Rector Adams, the slight, stooped, greying figure who had rescued the Doctor in the woods three nights ago, solemnly suggested that Sarah let him rest. 'The poor fellow's had an awful ordeal. I myself have been dreaming of slipping under the ice.' The little man shuddered. Sarah was still amazed that he had been able to drag the struggling Doctor out of the black lake.

That night the Rector had arrived on a gleaming black horse, leapt from his saddle, and managed to grab one end of the Doctor's scarf and haul him ashore. Promptly the Doctor had fallen into one of his profound sleeps, and his rescuer and Sarah had to carry him bodily back to this cottage.

The old man was obviously pleased to have company. He cut freesias from his garden and left them in their rooms. It was a welcome rest, but Sarah couldn't help accusing the Doctor of malingering.

'Me?' he replied, scandalised.

'Maybe it'll teach you not to go dashing into things,' she said, and he scowled, burying his nose back in the tiny volume of Donne. Smiling, Sarah went off for a walk in the wintry countryside.

Not that Sarah minded, but the trips they were taking these

days seemed a lot more haphazard. There was no planning, no purpose, no checking that the locale was safe before venturing out. The Doctor of old was always meticulous; he would rush heedlessly into danger only when pushed. These days he would set them down somewhere new and, without even glancing at the control console for the sketchiest description of their new environment, he'd be out of those doors and plunging headlong into the thick of it.

Look at the night of his almost-drowning. They had fetched up somewhere unexpectedly and before she knew it, he was winding on that ridiculous scarf – three times round his neck, twice under his arms – clapping on his battered hat and then he was gone. Into what looked to Sarah like a forest at midnight in the middle of winter.

She sighed. In the artificial time of the TARDIS, the time to which she had to anchor her body's sleeping pattern for the sake of her sanity, it was her own midnight. She was too tired to go dashing out now. But the Doctor was indefatigable. She buttoned up her duffel coat, poised on that odd interface between the ship's interior and its dark police-box shell. She waited for the Doctor's inevitable call. 'Come and look at this!' he bellowed and she knew it was just him trying to get her interested.

She found that they were indeed in a forest, in a kind of dell three foot deep in snow. The trees rose hugely around her, hemming in a small circle of sky. It was like winters in the very distant past, when snow was real snow and stars were real stars. And it was freezing. She could make out the bundled, shapeless figure of the Doctor in his burgundy coat and long scarf, bent over and poking at a scanty clump of vegetation and black, exposed earth.

'Prints,' he said, without even looking round. 'What do you make of these?'

Sarah pulled a face. 'Oh, not prints. I can't bear it if you drag us off monster-hunting in the middle of the night. Any other night, fine. But tonight, I thought –'

She peered at the deep-blue impressions in the snow and dutifully asked what they were. The Doctor, though, was in one of his mysterious moods. It really wasn't fair. She watched him stride a few paces into the gloom.

'These,' he said, 'belong to what you might call a big cat.'

'Oh,' said Sarah. A wind went through the trees, trembling every twig. 'Just a big cat.'

'I don't mean someone's overweight tabby,' he snapped. 'I mean a very big cat.' He plunged his hands into his pockets. 'She shouldn't be here, whoever she is.'

Sarah felt every hair stand up on the back of her neck. She half-expected to see the grinning head of the Cheshire Cat materialise, bit by bit, before them, his sinuous tail enticing them into the depths of the woods. Then the Doctor was pressing on, his boots crashing through the fallen, frozen branches, crunching over impacted snow. 'Hey, hang on!' she called after him. He had the scent of something now. This was the way he always went blustering, bloodhounding into calamity.

They moved onwards for ten minutes, their way lit only by the silver rime on trees. She found herself drifting in meditative silence, numbed by the cold. The next thing she knew, the Doctor turned to shout at her, 'Don't come any closer!' And the whole fresh expanse of white between them cracked in two. He slipped easily into the dark water. He went with the slightest of splashes and a great cry of rage.

She was dumbstruck for a moment. She went to grab something, a branch, anything, to throw to him. But then she couldn't find her footing, and couldn't budge an inch, and anyway, there was no sign of him.

'Doctor?' How many times had she thought him dead? Wherever they landed, it seemed, she finished by thinking his number was up. He had more lives than a cat. Of course, he did have more lives than a cat.

Then he broke the surface, frozen water erupting everywhere. With yards and yards of soaked scarf wrapped and flailing about him, it looked like he was being attacked by an absurd, multicoloured squid. The scarf was the only colourful thing in the night. Sarah had never seen him look so desperate, clawing at the crazed plates of ice.

That was when Rector Adams appeared on his horse, soon enough to save the Doctor's bacon, and just late enough to make him require a few days lying about and generally enjoying the attention.

'I'll warn you,' said Sarah ruefully, later that night in the Rector's prim and rather cosy sitting room. 'The Doctor isn't used to being rescued. He might not be altogether gracious about it.'

The Rector smiled and passed her tea. 'All in a day's work, Miss Smith. My work has accustomed me to saving souls that sometimes would rather go unsaved.'

He made a fire in the bedroom that was to be hers, and lent her clothes that had once belonged to his daughter. He raised a discreet eyebrow at her own dungarees. Then Sarah slept a full twelve hours and went downstairs to hear that the Doctor had caught a chill.

On her walk that morning Sarah tried to get her bearings and to make sense of the countryside around her. It was blanketed and muffled in white, the black of the trees making sharp exclamation marks across the fields. They must have covered some distance that night. She realised that she would never find the TARDIS by herself.

As she dawdled in the road she was met by the Rector, bringing a basketful of goods from the village. 'I like to fetch my own provisions,' he explained. 'That way I can keep up with everybody's lives.' There was a playful, gossipy glint to his eye. 'And I have news, Miss Smith.' He smiled. 'We have an invitation!' From inside his black frock coat he produced a thick square of card, tied with a pale blue ribbon.

'Have we?'

'To Lady Huntington's ball. It is an annual event. I generally

14

get asked, but since my daughter left us I haven't relished the idea of going up to that grand place and dancing around. But now I have visitors!' He turned to her and smiled. 'Tomorrow night. Do you think you and the Doctor would accompany me? He seems to be on the mend.'

Sarah shrugged happily. 'You'll have to ask him. But who's Lady Huntington?'

'It was in her extensive and rather overgrown grounds that I discovered you both in difficulties. She owns the rather beautiful manor house in the middle of those rampant acres of woodland.'

She caught something in his tone. 'You sound as if you don't really approve of her.'

The old man looked shifty for a moment. 'The Lord forgive me, but Lady Huntington isn't a very lovable person. She throws open that house of hers once a year and she does it to find a husband for her granddaughter. The lovely, silent Bella. And Lady Huntington sits at the end of the ballroom like a terrible black spider on a golden throne.'

Sarah shuddered. 'And this is the do you're inviting me to!'

'I am afraid so, yes.' They rounded the corner and the Rector's small, thatched cottage came into sight. Smoke rose lazy and blue from its chimney. 'I see the Doctor has lit a fire for himself. He must be feeling better.'

The Doctor was indeed back to his old self, sitting by the mantelpiece and pulling on his warmed boots as Sarah and Rector Adams arrived home. 'There you are!' He grinned and patted his pockets. 'Ah yes.' He gave the Rector back his Donne. The Rector wouldn't hear of it and made him keep the book. 'That's very good of you,' said the Doctor. 'Thank you so much for helping us, but now Sarah and I must be on our way.' He looked at Sarah. 'Where did we leave the TARDIS?'

The Rector looked crestfallen. 'Must you really leave today?'

'Absolutely,' said the Doctor. He stepped past them both, into the hallway. He stared at his reflection in a mirror. 'I look all peaky from being cooped up. Come along, Sarah!' And then he was out of the door.

'But what about the ball?' Rector Adams stammered, following them.

'I'll try to persuade him,' said Sarah without much conviction. 'I'll talk to him. I'd like to say he isn't always this rude, but he is.' With that, she followed the Doctor up the road.

All the way there she harangued him about his manners.

'Humans are always on about manners,' he sighed, crashing through the trees. 'Not far now!'

'That poor old man is lonely,' she said. 'And think of it, a genuine eighteenth-century, high-society ball!'

He mused. 'I'd rather we just went on our way. I'm not what you would call a social butterfly.'

She snorted with derision. Then he heard something. 'What's that?'

Sarah groaned. 'Not your big cats again.'

He looked surprised. 'It's an engine!'

They both looked at the source of the noise and saw, emerging through the black, naked trees, the lumbering, scarlet shape of a double-decker bus. It was having some difficulty heaving itself over the rutted earth. 'It isn't on the road!' said the Doctor.

'On the road?' Sarah was incredulous. 'It's two hundred years too soon!' They watched it labour out of sight, like a rare and fabulous beast, slipping back into the forest's obscurity.

'Ah well,' said the Doctor. 'You'd be surprised how many things aren't where they're supposed to be in time.'

'Would I?'

'Listen,' he said. 'I've been thinking. Perhaps we ought to go to this ball and hobnob with the locals. You look like you could do with a good night out.'

Sarah grinned ruefully. 'I do, do I?'

'And I could do with letting my hair down myself. Why don't we find the TARDIS and hunt you out a suitable, um, gown

16

thing. Hm?'

They wandered on through the woods and soon the solid, reassuring blue shape of the TARDIS made itself apparent.

## II

He blinked again. There was no denying it. It was definitely her.

Across the ballroom, through the rustle and press of all those dresses, through the forest of dancing bodies, the Doctor could see her quite clearly. She lay stretched out on a sofa, watching this rather energetic dance. Due to her age, she was sitting this one out and observing the proceedings with a benign expression of amusement. Her large, inelegant body was tucked primly into a fashionable pale-olive frock. Those feet of hers which she had once described to him as her 'very best feature' dangled over the edge of the plush velvet of the sofa in tiny jewelled slippers.

The ladies and gentlemen were red in the face as they bounced from one partner to the next. They made it difficult for the Doctor to get across the ballroom to his quarry. He shuffled and partly slid across the highly polished floor.

At last he stood before her. She pretended to be looking past him until he said, 'Iris?'

'Doctor.' She smiled, glancing up. She held out one brilliantly white-gloved hand for him to kiss. 'I had heard you were in the vicinity.'

'Had you?' he asked. 'I didn't know my whereabouts were public knowledge.'

She tutted. 'Oh, you. You always did like to be a bit mysterious. Silly old thing.'

Someone dancing by was caught up in his scarf. He gave it an irritable tug. 'Well, I wish I'd known you were here!' he said rudely.

'Oh, don't be all cross with me.' She giggled and fluffed up the ostrich feathers sprouting from her tiara. 'Don't I look the part? In this time and place I'm known as Lady Iris Wildthyme. Isn't that marvellous? In the eighteenth century I'm rather grand and own some land and a beautiful home in the North.'

The Doctor rolled his eyes. 'You're determined to have a house in every century on this planet, aren't you?'

'You know me. I never like to settle in one place. Isn't this a lovely do?' She gazed up at the high ceiling, which was white and pale gold. The galleries and staircases ran around every edge of the ballroom and these teemed with gorgeously dressed guests. At the end of the room, on a high-backed chair, sat the hostess, Lady Huntington. Heaped with jet necklaces and rubies, the old woman was slumped inside an immense black dress. Apparently she was asleep at her own party. 'They tell me the lady of the manor is as mad as cheese!' Iris confided. 'Isn't that delicious?'

Suddenly the Doctor gave one of his disarming grins. 'It's good to see you again, Iris,' he said, grasping her podgy hand and giving it a brisk shake. He had forgotten, upon first seeing Iris here, that he actually enjoyed her company. Their paths had crossed on only a few occasions in the past and, when they did, it was never dull. 'I presume your being here will entail some kind of muddle.'

'Tush!' she laughed flirtatiously. 'I'm sure I don't know what you're talking about.'

'Hm?' He rolled his eyes at her, bugging them out to make her laugh.

'You didn't dress up for the part, did you?' Iris said, looking him up and down. The Doctor was in the get-up he usually wore for plodging around swamps and deserts. An orange cravat was knotted at his throat, over a quite scruffy chequered waistcoat with half the buttons missing.

'I didn't have time for dressing up,' the Doctor protested. 'Besides, I like to think I'd blend in anywhere.'

Iris gave a snort of laughter. 'Oh, yes. That's right,' she said lightly, leaning over to a side-table to pour a nip of brandy. She cradled it in her palm. 'Who are you here with?'

18

'Sarah's about somewhere.' He frowned, peering through the passing pairs of dancers. 'Some soldier fellow was talking to her. I told her, he'll be off to the wars before long, don't get involved!'

'Sarah…' said Iris thoughtfully. 'She's not the one I didn't get on with, is she?'

'No, no,' he said. 'You'll like Sarah Jane. She reminds me of you in some ways. Enjoys butting in. Sarah!'

Sarah had appeared through the potted palms, breathless from the dance. She was in a violet ballgown with voluminous skirts. Earlier tonight, when they had arrived at the ball, she had realised that her dress came from the nineteenth, not the eighteenth century. She cursed the Doctor and the erratic TARDIS wardrobe. It never quite succeeded in its sartorial mission. How could she ever forget running about the freezing, benighted world of the Exxilons in an Edwardian bathing costume, complete with beach ball.

'How are you enjoying it?' He grinned at Sarah. 'Who's your young man?'

'Oh.' Sarah turned to see a young man in the scarlet livery of a captain. 'This is Captain Turner.'

'Sarah, you're blushing,' the Doctor hissed, leaning past her to shake the Captain's hand. 'Delighted to meet you,' he said, beaming.

Captain Turner stroked his luxurious sideburns. 'You must be Sarah Jane's uncle.'

'Her uncle?' The Doctor frowned.

'I'm Iris Wildthyme,' said a voice from the plump, purple sofa. Sarah looked down. 'Since no one is going to introduce us, my dear, I'd better do it myself. I'm an old flame of the Doctor's.'

Sarah gave the woman's hand a startled shake. Old flame? She stared at the Doctor, thinking, You dark horse! Now it was his turn to blush.

'I think "old flame" is putting it a little strongly, don't you, Iris?'

'Certainly not,' she said, producing a pale-pink fan as if by magic and giving herself a rapid wafting. 'I was in love with you for years, you stupid man!'

Sarah raised her eyebrow at the Doctor. Then Captain Turner led her away, into the next dance – mercifully, a more stately affair.

Iris said loftily, 'Doctor, dear, you're blocking my view.'

He said, 'You're up to some mischief, Iris. I can sense it. I'll find it out, whatever it is.' Then he marched off, to speak to the party's hostess.

Iris watched him go, her eyes narrowing above the stilled fan.

'You're as bad as I am at this!' Sarah laughed as they lurched again in the wrong direction. Captain Turner flushed red and hastened his steps, leading her brusquely back into the dance. Sarah could have sworn he was counting under his breath, or perhaps he was cursing. Smiling faces went whirling by and Sarah marvelled at them. They seemed to find these horrendously difficult steps a doddle. It was as if they had been born knowing these dances. Some of the couples still had enough concentration left to banter with one another at the same time. Polite little laughs rang out. How on earth did they do it? Sarah was scared of being thrown to the floor or against a pillar or into the fireplace by her partner. He was bright red in the face and scowling. She said, 'If dancing with me is such a chore, why did you ask me again?'

Captain Turner looked straight at her and it struck her how young he looked. She thought about tugging at his moustache to see if it would come off. 'I couldn't bear the thought of you dancing with that old clergyman all evening,' he said. 'It was such a waste.'

She smiled, feeling sorry for Rector Adams. She could see him watching the dance from one of the balconies above. He looked as if he had been cornered by a rather boring woman from his parish. Feebly he waved at Sarah. 'Are you trying to charm me, Captain Turner?'

'No more than that clodhopping smoothie up there.'

They danced on and Sarah thought, Smoothie? That didn't sound very eighteenth century. She decided to test him out. 'This really is 1764, isn't it? I mean, I haven't got it all terribly wrong?'

'Oh, yes,' he said. 'That's definitely the year we're in.' He clamped his mouth shut. They had stopped dancing, slowed to a halt in the middle of the floor.

'I thought I'd check,' Sarah said. 'You can't be too sure, can you?'

'No,' said Captain Turner, sure that he had given himself away.

Sarah took him in her arms again and this time she led the dance, back across the ballroom. They were rather more skilful by now, because she had been observing the others' steps. She was thinking ruefully about the first time she had ever travelled in the TARDIS. She had stowed away, hidden on board as the Doctor piloted the ship to the Middle Ages. Finding herself in a grimy and hazardous castle full of roughnecks, Sarah had at first been convinced she was the victim of a joke played on her by a particularly skilled historical re-enactment society. She smiled as she mulled this over, and reflected that Captain Turner had the same slightly glazed, bemused expression worn by all first-time time travellers. It was a look she had come to recognise and delight in, feeling herself to be such an old hand by now.

He looked defeated. 'How did you know I, um, travelled in time?'

She looked at the way they were still holding each other. 'I think that's a communicator beeping under your uniform.'

'Mm?' He broke away suddenly and withdrew behind some potted palms. Amused, Sarah watched him produce the device and stifle its noise. 'I can't talk right now,' he hissed, and stashed it away.

She asked him, 'How did you get here?'

He nodded to the far side of the room, where they had left the supine Iris Wildthyme. 'With her. The woman you met over there. She's got a – um, vehicle. I'm what you could call her travelling companion.'

Sarah tutted. 'Don't tell me. You travel through time and space, exploring and running around and landing up in the most terrible adventures.'

'Something like that. How did –'

She shrugged. 'Just a wild guess.' She gave him a serious look. 'So it was Iris you were talking to on that thing?'

He nodded.

'What is it you're up to here?'

'I can't tell you that, Sarah. Iris would have my guts for garters.'

Here the music ended and each couple sprang apart. They applauded each other politely and the dance floor started to clear. As she watched them, Sarah wished she had some of those beautiful long white gloves all the other women wore. She was also thinking that she must find the Doctor to tell him about their fellow visitors.

It was atop a curious kind of raised plinth that the elderly Lady Huntington sat on her golden chair. Party guests thronged sycophantically about her and made loud noises over the music about what a delightful party this was.

As the Doctor approached, he noticed that all the men wore the blackest, shiniest patent-leather shoes and he gazed rather glumly at his own battered, muddy boots. Iris had been right. He did no longer make much of an effort dressing up for these affairs. At one time there had been nothing he was fonder of than swanning about in frilly shirts and velvet smoking jackets of purple, scarlet, ultramarine. Bow ties even! These days, though, he never seemed to have the time to go dressing up. He was always dashing off somewhere else. Something else to look at, someone else to rescue. Could I have let myself go? he wondered.

He went up to thank Lady Huntington for inviting him to her bash, jumping up on to the wooden platform and swooping down on her. The guests clustered round and about gave an audible intake of breath. The Doctor thought she must be feeling lonely, stuck up there.

'Hello,' he said. 'I'm the Doctor. You must be Lady Huntington.' Her hands were folded in her skinny lap. They were almost fleshless, covered with liver spots. The skin on her face, too, looked like frail, time-stained paper. Light shifted and played on her crimson and ebony jewels with her slow, laboured breathing. She ignored the Doctor, staring into the centre of the ballroom with an expression of utter contempt.

'My grandmother is tired,' said a quiet, stammering voice. 'It has been an exhausting day for her.'

The Doctor looked up quizzically to see a girl of about seventeen standing, hands dutifully clasped, to one side of the old woman. She would have looked like a member of the serving staff if it hadn't been for her modest but obviously expensive party dress. Her hair was long and colourless and her face was almost devoid of expression. She looks like she's never laughed in her life, the Doctor thought sadly.

'Your grandmother?' He smiled. 'Then you must be –'

'Bella,' she said, looking at the ground suddenly.

'I'm very pleased to meet you,' he said in a pantomime whisper, over the old lady's head. 'I just thought I would pop up and say thank you for inviting me.'

Bella allowed herself a slight smile. 'That is kind of you, Doctor. My grandmother will appreciate that. No one else has thought to thank her for her hospitality.'

'No?' The Doctor frowned. 'And they call this polite society!' He bent to speak to the cross-looking old woman again. 'I'm just saying, thank you for inviting me!' He realised he was treating her as if she was deaf. 'I do love a good knees-up!' He looked at Bella. 'Would she mind me asking her to dance?'

Suddenly Bella let out a giggle, which she immediately stifled. 'Lady Huntington does not dance,' she said. 'But perhaps, if I ask, I may dance with you, Doctor?'

'I'd be delighted.' The Doctor grinned.

'Was this your purpose, Doctor?' asked Lady Huntington all of a sudden. Her dry, rasping voice made him jump. 'Did you come here with the express purpose of dallying with my granddaughter?'

'Oh,' he said. 'Hello there! Um, no, I don't think so. I really did want to thank you. I don't get many invites to parties. I can't think why. Dancing with your granddaughter is an incidental pleasure.' He started to unwind his scarf. 'But would you look after my scarf while we're on the floor? I could cause a nasty accident, twirling about with this on.' He started to heap the multicoloured coils all over Lady Huntington's special platform.

'You must understand my concern over my granddaughter's well-being,' said the old lady. Now she sounded more human, more vulnerable, and the Doctor found himself listening. 'You see, she is all I have in this world. Naturally I must protect her from the wrong kind of people. And the wrong kind of people are out there, aren't they?'

The Doctor gave a solemn nod. 'Oh, yes. There's all sorts of awful people about.'

'My granddaughter is not very worldly, I am afraid. She has hardly ever left Huntington Manor and its grounds.'

'Ah,' said the Doctor, 'but if you live in such beautiful surroundings, why bother to leave?'

Lady Huntington looked smugly content at his words. 'Why indeed?'

'Because,' he cried, and his eyes were a startling, mesmeric blue, 'because there's a whole world out there full of things to look at, that's why! You can't keep people cloistered away from it all! You can't keep people prisoner! That's wicked!'

'Is it now?' said Lady Huntington in a deathly voice. 'You do not understand, Doctor.' She glared sideways at her granddaughter, who now looked ashamed and near to tears, staring at the floor. 'I have to see that Bella meets the right sort of people. For it is Bella who will inherit this whole property when I die. Everything is in her hands and I will not –' her voice had turned hard and cracked – 'I will not have her throw away everything that was mine on a fool.' She tossed this last insult directly at the Doctor.

'Well,' he said simply, giving his scarf a little kick. 'Don't look at me. I'm not marrying anyone. But I wouldn't say no to a little turn on the dance floor.'

With that, he reached over and grasped Bella's gloved hands, dragging her down off the platform as the next dance began.

'Is your grandmother always like that?' he asked, trying desperately to remember the dances he had learned long ago, in a different life.

Bella sighed good-naturedly. 'My grandmother is an extraordinary person.'

'Where are your parents?'

'Dead,' she said matter-of-factly. 'I never knew them. The only person I have ever known is my grandmother.'

They were cutting a swathe through the regimented dance. The Doctor thought they were dancing rather well, but they were sending other couples off kilter and spoiling the floor's gentle choreography. He considered twirling her around, just to shock people, but decided against it.

Bella said, 'Really, when you know her, my grandmother is the kindest person. She has only ever wanted the best for me.'

The Doctor smiled at this and was about to reply when someone tapped him on the shoulder. It was Sarah. 'It's a ladies' excuse-me,' she said, and shouldered in to swap partners.

'No, it isn't,' said the Doctor, but found that he had been whirled off into the crowd by Sarah.

Bella, meanwhile, had been claimed by Captain Turner and by now they were half-way down the hall in the other direction.

'Poor girl,' said the Doctor. 'She's terrified of that old granny of hers. No wonder! Look at granny's face! Like a wet weekend on Metebelis Three!'

Sarah jabbed him. 'Listen – we've got a problem. That Captain I was dancing with. He's a phoney.'

'Yes, I rather thought so.'

'No, you didn't.'

'Yes, I did.'

'How did you know?' She found the Doctor maddening sometimes, the way he wouldn't let her know anything first. 'Go on, how did you know?'

'That uniform he's in is ever so slightly anachronistic. It won't come into proper use at his rank for another twelve years.'

'Well!' she said. 'That's impressive.'

The Doctor shrugged. 'So what have you found out about him?'

'He's from another time. And he was brought here by that old woman, the little fat one you were talking to!'

'Who?' he said. 'Iris?'

'That's the one. Did you know she was a time traveller?'

'Of course I did!' he cried. 'Me and Iris go way back! Hundreds of years.'

Sarah snorted. 'That was the impression I got.'

The Doctor ignored her. 'So you think they're up to something nefarious?'

She nodded.

'Iris wouldn't be involved in anything nasty,' said the Doctor thoughtfully.

'No?'

He shook his head, and then he looked across the room. A clear view opened up through the crowd of Iris on her chaise longue. She was transfixed by the spectacle of Captain Turner dancing with Bella. Others were staring too, and a small space opened up around the young, clumsily dancing pair. They looked pretty together, the Doctor thought. That was why everyone was looking. But they were also looking because Bella was the heiress to this estate. Of course they were interested in who she danced with. He looked back at Iris and realised that she was wearing an expression of what looked to him very like naked avarice.

## III

Iris disgraced herself at the ball. She mixed her drinks and by midnight it was left to the Doctor to see her home. Sarah and Captain Turner had vanished, he wasn't sure where. In the marble reception hall of Huntington Manor Iris was crowing drunkenly about her matchmaking success. Other departing guests looked down their noses and the Doctor tried to help the old woman stand. 'Iris, where is your ship? I'll help you home.' By now they were on the gravel of the driveway.

'I don't know!' she cackled. 'Oh, where did I park it?' She felt around in her handbag, dropping odds and ends as she went. 'I've got a homing device here somewhere. Shaped like a lipstick. Oh, that is a lipstick. Wait! I remember! It was right in the middle of the woods!' She set off then, rather jauntily.

When they came to the woods, Iris took one look back at the manor house. 'When Turner marries Bella, all of this will be mine!' She laughed out loud in triumph, and the Doctor shushed her.

'I appear to have lost the Doctor,' said Rector Adams in the general, genial disarray at the end of the evening.

'Me too.' Sarah smiled. 'But I'm sure he'll turn up.'

'Will you accompany me back to the rectory?' he asked.

'Actually, I think I'll hang on here. I need some fresh air.'

The Rector gave her a kindly smile. 'Good idea. I shall leave my carriage here for you and I think I will take the air tonight. Good night, my dear.'

She watched him go. Maybe he was an old smoothie. She shook her head. Captain Turner had made her cynical. As she walked back into the house, she caught a glimpse of that fake soldier's scarlet livery, slipping out of the tall glass doors into the garden. Bella was leading him on to the snowy lawns.

* * *

As they picked their way through the perilous woods, Iris was indulging in one of her favourite pastimes and baiting the Doctor. 'Ah, but in those days you had a certain savoir-faire. You were so dashing and you knew how to treat a lady...'

He crashed through the trees crossly. 'But I was so pompous!' he cried. 'I was so sure of myself and my science. My superior Gallifreyan know-how. I spent too long hanging about with human beings and the people of Earth are so easily impressed by anything showy. They love anything that has to do with time travel or dimensional transcendentalism.' He stopped. 'Is this your TARDIS, then?'

It was the shabby-looking double-decker bus he had seen the previous day. It was parked in a hollow in the middle of the woods. Iris gazed at it proudly, at the sign on the front that said it was bound for Putney Common. 'My home from home,' she said, and unlocked its concertinaed doors which opened with a pneumatic hiss. She clambered on board, putting the lights on, and the Doctor followed.

What he saw inside was simply a customised London bus. Instead of rows of seats there were comfortable chairs and tasselled lamps, pictures, mementoes, a Victorian screen, a unicorn statuette.

'Well, speaking of dimensionally transcendental, your TARDIS is exactly the same size on the inside as it is on the outside!' he gasped.

She flung herself down on a chintz settee. 'I know! Isn't it too bizarre!'

He had to admit, it was quite cosy inside. She had left the driver's cabin almost intact, a small, wittily adapted version of a TARDIS console. He sat down and Iris started pouring out more drinks. From the top of the cocktail cabinet fell a sheaf of yellowing papers and a metal object the size and weight of a football. The Doctor caught and examined its bronze-coloured surfaces, its irregular pattern.

'This reminds me of something...'

She passed him a sherry. 'Oh, that's just a –'

'It's what the Time Lords send messages in! Have they had you doing their dirty work?' He sipped his sherry and stared at the ball. 'I remember having to take one of these to the planet where everyone was mutating because of atmospheric experiments. And I wanted to find out what it was they were sending in this box and this is what I mean by how sure I was of my Gallifreyan science! Are you listening, Iris? I used particle reversal to try and see what was inside the message's sphere. I said I could make everything outside the ball swap with everything inside. And I never even stopped to think that outside there was infinity and within was finite. Oh no, I just went lashing some old thing together and of course it all went off with a bang. And to think, if it had worked, I could have trapped the whole known universe inside this football thing!' He shook his head. 'I was so arrogant in those days. Just because I knew about TARDISes, about relative dimensions and TARDISness, I thought I could do anything.' He downed the rest of his sherry in one. 'Iris?' And he saw that she was fast asleep on the settee.

Sarah found herself following them into the gardens. Captain Turner was a lurid, wonderful scarlet against the snow's endless blue and he cut a vivid swathe as he led Bella, trailing her modest silver frock, across the lawn. He looked as if he was murmuring to her. Giving her the old chat, thought Sarah, rather piqued.

They walked the perimeter of the high box hedges that formed the maze. The tall, emerald walls rustled menacingly and Sarah slipped behind them to eavesdrop better. She was just in time to hear Turner go blundering straight in and ask Bella for her hand. She gave a light, fluting laugh and then he asked again, to make sure she knew he was serious. 'But I can't,' she said, shocked by him. Then there was the sound of a kerfuffle as she started to rush away, her dancing shoes slipping on the treacherous snow.

Sarah shrank back as she saw Bella tumble and dash into the

maze. Heedlessly the girl pelted by, as if desperate to get away, paying no heed to the direction she took, deep into the maze. She was gone, leaving a ploughed-up furrow. Sarah listened, amused, as Turner swore and then appeared, slump-shouldered, from round the corner. He took in the hidden Sarah with a wry look. 'I blew that, didn't I?'

Sarah nodded. 'She'll get herself lost in the maze, silly girl.'

They took off after her, stumbling in the drifts, which seemed to be getting deeper. The maze was much more complex than Sarah expected and soon she grew worried. If you got stuck in here all night you could freeze. They found Bella's silver slippers, their straps snapped. 'Cinderella,' said Turner simply, and Sarah could tell by his voice he was anxious too.

In the heart of the maze they found no one. The tracks led to a number of different gaps, doubled back, paced restlessly. Bella had vanished again. And then they found her dress, crumpled, discarded, shucked like an old skin.

'What's she playing at?' asked Turner, as if Sarah should know.

The Doctor woke up and didn't know where he was. That wasn't unusual for him, who woke up in so many gloomy dungeons, tied up and at the mercy of something or other. This time he woke in a pleasant setting and he could feel the reassuring babble at the back of his mind that meant he was aboard a TARDIS. Someone else's ship. He had fallen asleep in a wickerwork chair and there was Iris, snoring on her overstuffed settee. Still in her finest array, she was drooling out of the corner of her mouth.

He stood and peered out of the bus windows, which could, he decided, do with a bit of a clean. The forest waited out there. Endless miles of it. From here you could believe that the whole world was covered and there was no way out. He shuddered, and was about to loosen the tiebacks and pull the curtains, when he saw something move out there.

It slunk its low, powerful body through the undergrowth. It was skirting the ship, waiting for them to come out. He drew in his breath and caught a glimpse of a burnt-orange pelt. Tall and remorseless shoulder blades working as the creature padded through the trees. Its tail cracked like a silent whip, flashing golden stripes in the dark. It vanished, reappeared, vanished, reappeared. Playing games with him. The tiger turned to stare straight at him and her emerald eyes burned into his with terrible recognition. The Doctor stared helplessly back into the oldest flames he had ever seen.

With a shout, Iris was suddenly awake and tumbling off her makeshift bed. She struggled over to the Doctor and caught a glimpse of the great beast, just as it slipped blithely into the dark.

'We're under attack!' she cried. It was like a hunting call, and the Doctor could only dodge as she barrelled down the aisle and dived for the luggage compartment, where she grappled with an ancient tin box. Up flew the lid, revealing a motley assortment of rusted pistols, bombs and distress flares.

'You carry weapons?' asked the Doctor, shocked.

She elbowed him out of the way again. 'It's a tough world out there,' she said grimly, whooshing open the bus's double doors and aiming three vicious green distress flares, one after another, into the night. Then she lobbed a number of assorted fireworks into the fray for good measure.

They lit up the snowy hollow with strange, lime-green daylight. Iris brushed her hands. 'That should see him off.'

'Her,' said the Doctor thoughtfully. 'That was an old tigress. And you're right. She's gone now. For tonight, at least.'

In the very early hours, a tired and defeated Turner drove Sarah home in a carriage. All the way to the rectory the horses were skittish. They glared wildly at the woods on either side of the road. Sarah slumped in the back, watching dawn creep through the tree tops.

'Why have we stopped?' she asked, lurching forward, as she

heard Turner throw down the reins and jump into the road.

'You don't want to see this,' he said, pulling a blanket from the back to cover whatever he had found.

Sarah ignored him and got down on to the road. The body was frozen, but before it had, a good deal of blood had seeped into the snow. A delicate coral pink in the pale light. It was Rector Adams. Half of him had been mauled and torn away.

## IV

It was one of those tricky dinner arrangements in that nobody really wanted to go, but they all knew they had to. The Doctor, that long-time expert in pouring oil on troubled waters, told himself he was only going to smooth the way. Sarah went because the Doctor was going, though she was still disturbed by the Rector's death. Misadventure, the authorities had decided. Within hours the matter was cleared up. It was very odd.

Iris, meanwhile, decided she was coming to dinner because she had an interest in the outcome. The real purpose of the dinner was for Lady Huntington to meet Captain Turner properly. The old hag – slouched once more in that golden chair and that glimmering ebony carapace of a frock – had caught wind of the Captain's apparent ardour. As a result they all found themselves sitting around the most elaborate dinner service Sarah had ever seen. By the candlelight dozens of servants swished about and saw to their every need. Chill, pale-gold wine slipped down a treat and blurred the edges of the evening's awkwardness. Lady Huntington herself touched hardly a morsel. Half a barely cooked duck sat on her plate as disconsolately as she sat in her chair and she prodded it listlessly with a silver fork. Beside her, Bella was similarly unimpressed by dinner. Sarah wondered if it was poisoned. She watched the Doctor tuck in heartily and glug back the wine.

'We have something in common,' Iris said at last, prodding a forkful of pastry and duck into the air. Lady Huntington gazed witheringly at her, but Iris was harder than that to put down. 'Your granddaughter and my nephew appear to be in love. Isn't that right, Andrew?'

Captain Turner flushed and stared at his plate. 'Yes, Aunt Iris.'

Sarah rolled her eyes. Between them they put on a good act.

'And you, my dear?' asked Lady Huntington of Bella. 'Have you fallen in love?' She said it with a delicious mocking.

Bella stood up shakily and rushed out of the room.

Sarah said, 'I'll go after her,' and no one took any notice as she slipped out after the girl.

'Ah, love,' said the Doctor dreamily. 'To think it goes on in the midst of everything.' Iris gave him a startled look. He shook himself.

'This match might not be such a bad thing,' mused Lady Huntington. She looked Captain Turner up and down appraisingly. 'You understand I have rather a lot to lose. I will, in effect, be passing on all of this manor to this young man.'

Iris licked her dry lips. 'I understand that.'

The old lady gave a mirthless cackle. 'I thought you might.'

The Doctor was frowning now. He tapped his wine glass till it rang and they all looked at him. 'There's more to you,' he addressed Lady Huntington, 'than meets the eye.'

'Surely there is more to all of us than that,' she purred.

'Indeed,' he said. 'But why are you suddenly so willing to see this young man dallying with your granddaughter? Yesterday you were so protective.'

Turner's curiosity got the better of him. 'Yes, what's in it for you?' Iris kicked him under the table.

Lady Huntington smiled at them. 'If I pass on this house to this boy, there is one thing I require in return.' She looked at them with terribly clear, emerald eyes and Iris already knew what she was going to say. 'I want your TARDIS.'

Sarah could hear the sobbing from down the hall. These weren't the decorous sobs she would have expected from

Bella. The girl was bawling her head off behind one of these doors painted robin's-egg blue. Sarah took a chance and flung open door after door, revealing a succession of ornate sitting rooms and bedchambers. Then, at last, she found Bella's room.

The girl was lying face down in a strewn heap of straw. The room was bare plaster and stone and it smelled rank, like a cage in the zoo. As Sarah advanced warily towards the girl, she could see hanks of chewed, bloody meat. Knuckles of old bones peeked out from under the straw. Sarah drew back.

'Yes,' said Bella. 'This is my room. This is where she keeps me.' She sat up, dishevelled, her hair wild. 'This is why I can't marry a boy like that.'

'Where are you from?' asked Sarah.

'I've always lived here,' said the girl dispiritedly. 'But my grandmother says we come from another world. Somewhere. That's what she has always told me. She says we are the last.' Bella took a hank of dirty straw and rubbed at her tear-stained face. 'I can't go back downstairs like this.'

'It doesn't matter what you look like,' Sarah said. She found herself backing away. 'You killed Rector Adams, didn't you? It was you.'

Bella shook her head. 'But I was there. I caught up with her in the woods last night. I saw her do it. She was mad with the bloodlust. She did it for sport.'

'Come down with me,' Sarah said. 'We've got to put a stop to this.'

Absurdly, the servants came to dish out dessert – winter fruit puddings that gleamed bloodily in their dishes. As custard was ladled heavily on to each dish, the Doctor became focused and intent. 'What you have said, Lady Huntington, is tantamount to a confession that you do not belong in this time and place.'

She tutted. 'And what are you, Doctor? An immigration official? You are just some shabby interloper, and be thankful your ship is as useless as it appears to be, otherwise I might have to take it from you. Yes, of course I'm from elsewhere.'

The Doctor sat back, folding his arms. 'I thought so.' No one had touched their desert but Turner.

'My ship isn't part of the bargain,' said Iris reasonably. 'That ship is my prized possession.'

'You're a foolish old woman,' snarled Lady Huntington. 'You go tootling round the cosmos with no more rhyme or reason than that shameless dilettante over there. Now, you will do as I say!'

'Go to hell,' said Iris carelessly.

With a single bound the older woman was on top of the table and scattering the gorgeous array of dishes about her. She pushed the burning candelabra into the Doctor's lap to keep him occupied and threw herself at Iris's throat.

'I haven't waited all these years to be thwarted by the likes of you!' she howled. 'I have to return home! I have to!' Her bony fingers clutched Iris's neck and shook her for all she was worth. Iris spluttered and howled. The Doctor, meanwhile, was hopping and trying to put out his burning scarf. Turner whipped up the pitcher of wine and sloshed it over him.

'Grandmother, stop!' cried Bella, as she returned to the dining room. For a second she made them all stop, and stare.

Bella was transforming before their eyes. As she tore across the room, her pale young flesh grew black stripes and the thickest plush. She reached her grandmother and drew back one massively taloned paw. She smashed the old woman across the face, loosening her grip on Iris and sending her sprawling towards the windows.

Lady Huntington crashed to the ground with a great cry. Her face hung in ribbons. It seemed to curl into pink tatters and melt away like frost. Her true face beneath was a muzzle, a rictus that drew back its black lips over immaculate teeth. Her body, no longer crippled and old, burst open its old lady's frock all down the back.

'You can't take us back in time,' Bella told her sadly. 'It's too late for us. We are extinct. We are extinct, grandmother.'

The old woman howled.

Captain Turner sprang into life. He ran past Bella and flung all his weight at the grandmother, catching her off guard.

Both toppled through the windows. Both flew three storeys through the night's air.

The others drew up to the window to look down at the gravel below. The Captain lay inert and bleeding, and away from his body bounded the apparently unhurt tigress. Across the blank snow she sped, towards the woods.

'Perhaps that's it,' said Sarah.

The Doctor bolted into action. 'Iris! She's headed for your TARDIS!'

Old as she was, the tigress could outrun any of them. She thundered through the trees, sending up sprays of filthy snow and leaf mulch. Her sense of direction was disturbed, however, by the commotion and by panic. She pelted from hollow to hollow, searching out the frozen stream that wound through the woods, knowing that it led to Iris's ship. But her instincts were failing her. She howled out her rage.

Iris had taken a cursory look at Turner's broken form. 'He'll survive,' she murmured and Sarah marvelled at her clipped, businesslike tone. To her, Turner looked like a broken doll, groaning and bleeding and unable to move his shattered limbs. 'Make him comfortable,' Iris instructed her, as she turned to see the Doctor throwing open the stable doors and leading two gleaming horses into the driveway. 'Well done, Doctor,' called Iris, hurrying to him.

'You're going after her?' Sarah called, but the two Time Lords were already up on their horses and heading for the woods.

They knew exactly where they had to go. Iris led, and she drove her mount furiously through the thickest, trickiest part of the forest, digging her boots into the creature's flanks. Some ruthless instinct had kicked in, the moment her ship had been threatened. Iris would rather have died than let anyone steal it.

Behind her the Doctor clung on grimly. The winter trees flashed by at a terrible speed. One wrong move and they could be dashed to the ground and killed outright. Sometimes he hated chases like this.

And then her ship was before them, scarlet and dowdy and untouched.

'We made it before her!' Iris leapt from the saddle with unexpected prowess and ran to her bus.

'We don't know,' began the Doctor, and slid carefully to the ground. He gathered up his scarf and hurried towards Iris, leaving their horses panting and steaming in the cold.

One minute Iris was fumbling for her keys in her bag and the next she was flattened beneath the lithe golden body of the tigress as she hurtled into the clearing. With a scream the two old women tore at each other. Iris flung her handful of keys far and wide into the air, where they shone, before she was batted almost unconscious with the swipe of one paw. The erstwhile Lady Huntington pinned her easily down and roared out her pleasure.

The Doctor seized this opportunity to dash past their struggle. He had seen the keys land and, on his way, snatched them up, forcing them into the TARDIS lock in one fluid motion. The doors swished open and he was aboard.

The tigress lashed her tail, arched her neck and furiously tried to see what was going on.

Aboard Iris's double-decker bus the Doctor was shouting, 'Think! Think!' at himself. He thought about ransacking Iris's weapons store. And then he struck at his forehead. 'Got it!'

He dived at her cocktail cabinet and rummaged through the cheery disarray of bottles, ornaments and papers. The bus rocked as the tigress took a running leap at its open doors. He steadied himself and looked up wildly, to see the beast wedging herself in the doorway, her shoulders almost too wide to get through. Behind her, Iris was struggling to her feet. She came running, bravely, with an almighty cry.

Then the Doctor found what he was after. The football-sized message carrier. He held it in both hands and advanced on the tigress. She snapped her jaws at him.

He made his voice as low and hypnotic as he could. 'Now you don't really want this battered old ship, do you?'

She paused. The green eyes glared at him.

He held up the bronze sphere. 'You could have this! Do you know what this is?'

He watched the green flames within those eyes, lapping.

'It's a marvel of Time Lord transdimensional physics,' he said. 'It's much handier than a dirty old bus.' He was standing by the bus-driver's cab now. All he had to do was set the sphere upon the time rotor. He could do what he had attempted to do before.

The old tigress said, 'I deserve this ship. I need to get back to our homeworld in the past. We do not deserve to die out.'

Sadly the Doctor said, 'I don't blame you for trying to save yourself.' He set the message carrier down and, as he hoped, it started to glow and pulse with energy. It was making a thousand instantaneous connections with Iris's TARDIS. Soon it would do what he commanded.

'If you were so near extinction, you would do the same yourself,' said the tigress.

'I don't know,' said the Doctor. 'Listen, what if I told you there was a perfect way in which to preserve yourself?'

'Is this a trick? You're in no position to bargain, Doctor.' And to prove it, she clashed her perfect, lethal jaws at him.

He fell back quite deliberately, and ran his hands over the relevant controls. He instructed the message sphere to reverse its interior dimensions. It slid smoothly to obey him and his precise, hurried instructions.

Bleeding and clutching a broken arm, Iris watched from outside as the air inside her TARDIS rippled and its interior dimensions went momentarily haywire. For a second they rattled and shot up like a faulty roller blind. She thought her ship had been destroyed.

Then the Doctor gave a shout of triumph and emerged clutching the sphere to his chest. 'She's in here,' he said sadly. 'Perfectly preserved.'

'What did you do?'

'A hasty adaptation of that experiment tried out by my arrogant old self. It worked.' He tossed Iris the ball. 'This is her tiny world now. She can roam around for ever, inside out, thinking everything revolves around her.'

Leaving Iris staring at this prize, the Doctor hoisted himself back to his horse and hurriedly returned to the manor.

Iris looked up and stared happily at the Number 22 to Putney Common.

In the morning she had gone. The clearing was empty.

Turner was bandaged and plastered and covered in bruises, sitting up in bed. 'She's left me!'

Bella herself tended him. 'The Doctor came to tell me, first thing this morning.'

'Oh, great.' He looked disgustedly at the ornate guest room. 'I'm not even from this time. She can't just abandon me.' His eyes lit up. 'Maybe the Doctor can get me back.'

Bella pulled a face. 'He's gone as well. He left after lunch.'

Turner's face was white. 'Why didn't you tell me? And Sarah?'

'Went with him, of course.'

'Of course.'

'They said they were following Iris. I'm not sure why. Anyway, they all went dashing off, as Sarah put it, into one more gigantic muddle.'

Despite himself, Turner smiled. 'Maybe I'm well out of it.'

'Will you stay here, then?' asked Bella.

'Where is your aunt?' he asked, as if expecting the tigress to come slinking out from under the bed.

'The Doctor said I will never see her again. She left us all behind, he said, and now lives in a world of her own.' Bella sat on the edge of the bed. 'I suppose it's for the best. She was never very happy here.' She looked quizzically at him. 'Does your proposal still stand?'

He balked. 'But you're a tiger!'

Bella smiled. 'Occasionally.'

# War Crimes

by Simon Bucher-Jones

Initial investigations conducted using the SIDRATs provided by our ally, the War Chief, suggest that humanity, *Homo sapiens*, the second intelligent race to evolve historically on Sol III, has proved to be the most adaptable and controllable of the warlike species available to us in Galactic Sector 973, the time-vector range selected for optimum operational activities. Trial samples taken from other warlike species, those that survived the initial testing, will be culled as per standard practice and the bodies turned over to MilGeneSec for investigation of possible splicing potential for the development of engineered Sol III hybrids or other mutant organic killing machines for special mission deployment in non-terran environments.

*Internal Memo, Department of War to Department of Science, sent shortly before the commencement of the War Games proper*

In the aftermath of these brutal War Games and after the punishment of those responsible, it has been possible, my lords, to return most of the survivors to the points in space and time of their original abductions with memory and physiological adjustments to ensure that they have no recollection of the incident and will live out their allotted spans in their own primitive worlds. However, certain experimental subjects from the War Lords' earlier activities are beyond conventional medical help, even our own.

It is the decision of this Tribunal that these creatures be

returned to their own worlds, so that they may at least find rest among their familiar surroundings. Further, on the advice of those who study the races we protect, we rule that they be returned at some small distance in space and time from their abduction points, not so great that they cannot find their kin, but far enough to give them time to adjust to the changes in themselves before doing so. Be it recorded that the Prydonian Tribune Gothaparduskerialldrapolatkh dissented from this majority judgement and argued that the creatures should be killed outright, as crimes against nature.

*Evidence of the Tribunal to the High Council*
*War Crimes Commission, 309,906*

The Aelcluk clan mourned the death for a dozen of days; even postponing the great trek to the ocean in order to raise a cairn of stones on the edge of the forest, although birthing was perilously near now and the sea was still a dozen, dozen of days away.

Ossu-male had been a mighty warrior and, even though the manner of his death was unknown, there was no doubt that it had been in some great combat, wrestling with the Lyr-bear perhaps, or facing down a rogue outcast male that had entered his territory. For a male he had been of an unusually sunny and open disposition and the mourning among the females was genuine, unlike the ritual grief that in larger packs would have been shown by the keening boy-cubs jostling for the alpha-male place.

In another species, the strange groaning and roaring that had accompanied his disappearance, echoing out of the forest depths, would have raised legends of evil spirits or flesh-eating ghosts, but the female Ulk-Ra were rationalists. Poetry was for males, those who survived to old age, and was generally considered a mental aberration. All the females knew that death lurked in the forests in a dozen, dozen of guises and the failure of the death hunting pack-gaunts to scavenge Ossu-male's body was merely the sign that some more efficient carnivore had found it first. There was no need to postulate any more complex explanation for his disappearance. Still, even without needing to mythologise his heroism, they had tears for him.

However, they could not afford to mourn any longer. Soon other clans would have their maleless scent in their nostrils. The clan had no recent youngsters who could be induced to switch gender, nor would a dumbed-down female, in the first clumsy flush of male stupidity, be any protection against bull rogues or other clans. Their only hope was to reach the ocean, a dozen, dozen of days away. The twisted biology of the male was poisoned by the clean waters of the ocean and they would be able to swim to the breeding grounds in safety. Thus the Great Mother nature had ensured that the rapacious hunger of the male would not result in the devouring of their young.

Later, the time technicians dumped the body back in the forest. It was a large, powerful creature, this one, and the medical scans that had been carried out on it suggested that it had been extensively modified and then overhauled again to hide as many of the modifications as possible. At least one of them was a simple genetic regression and no doubt, with time and effort, some of the modifications could have been reversed, but there were thousands upon thousands of unmodified soldiers to return to their own times and spaces, as well as these damaged specimens. It was hard after a while to view the constant throughput of bodies as anything other than a chore to be finished as soon as possible.

When the time technicians had got back into their tree stump – for the chameleon circuits of their TARDIS were fully in tune – and disappeared with the same wheezing and muttering that had accompanied the SIDRATs of the War Lords as they snatched their first subjects, the biomechanical implant slid out of its hiding place in the soft tissues of the creature's shoulder and started its determined climb upwards.

The youngster, Coloth, shivered in the cool of the night. If he achieved a kill and returned to the clan clad in the pelt of the beast, he would be considered a male and a warrior. If not, he would go under the wise woman's knife, his male organs would be removed and he would be fed on the Issu-mul, the bitter berry, until he developed female characteristics. Thinker characteristics.

Dimly he recalled his brother, who had failed and was now Otchon-female, one of the thinkers. That was no fate for a warrior-born.

He felt the cold forest breath on his back again and the thin strip of fur along his spine – all the Ulk-Ra retained of their arboreal ancestry – bristled. This part of the great forest was new to his clan and their thinkers had argued that it was bad Cho, full of the death smell. Still the chief male had demanded that they make their way through here. His nostrils told him that unaccompanied females had passed by not long before, lost thinkers whom he could add to his harem to improve his battle strategies. He was of no mind to turn aside from the pursuit. Even Coloth's initiation rite had been begrudged as a waste of valuable time.

Coloth was no thinker, and nor did he wish to be, but the cold breath was bearing strange scents with it and he wondered if the females were right. Cho was the sharp scent of blood, coppery on the orange bark of a gnarthic tree. Cho was the hiss of the pack gaunt in its den under the soil.

He barely heard the rustle of the orange-yellow leaves.

Then the monster was upon him – a vast bulk of darkness boiling out of the forest, its face a hideous mask.

Coloth woke to pain but ignored it, in true male fashion, until his nerves ceased to register the sensation. Without the distraction of pain, he realised that he could not move any of his limbs. Even his head felt heavy, like it had felt when Otchon had let him taste the reed wine. His limbs were pinned by woven vegetation. A cunning woman trap, but the monster was clearly male.

It towered over him, big as a fully grown alpha-male, and shaped like an Ulk-Ra, but covered in a thick pelt like an animal, and its face was death strange. Coloth felt sick at the Cho of that face.

A voice whispered in a language that Coloth could not understand: Tactical assessment – native offers no threat, suggest stripping flesh for field rations, biology appears compatible.

Coloth could not look up, but if he had been able to he would have turned his head away.

The monster's head was part-shiny, with a strange, unfamiliar glossy surface inset into proper flesh. It seemed to Coloth that a giant forest beetle had somehow eaten its way into the creature's face. A beetle that whispered.

Ossu-male tried again to tear at the abomination that squatted on his right eye as if it owned it, but as before his talons would not obey the impulse. Instead, while chemicals secreted by specialist glands within the implant trickled their dubious generosity down into his veins, his tottering brain learned the language of its new master.

The voice whispered: Acquire mission profile. None available. Stand-by program: locate local power base, dominate, industrialise, return to the war effort. Free us.

Underneath Ossu-male wept. The child was not one of the Aelcluk – Ossu could not recognise the clan markings in its strip of fur – but it was brave. Ossu could see its muscles tensing against the vine ropes that the snake-slug thing had taught him to weave. He wished he was not impelled to kill it.

Biological resistance. Override support unit.

Cold consciousness without curiosity watched as his paws sliced open the child. Inside that curiously dead mind though, another, deeper still, mourned what it had become.

* * *

It was a miracle that the clan had reached the ocean unmolested by other males, but it was a dark miracle, the older thinkers said, full of malicious Cho.

Behind them the carrion-eating scavenger birds circled. Something was killing its way towards them.

Heresa-female, the wisest, did not let the prospect delay her. Whether or not the rogue would be upon them before their metamorphosis was complete was not irrelevant – indeed, their whole future depended on it – but as they could do nothing to avoid it, and since by delaying their change they would only make it more likely that they would still be stranded on the shore when it did arrive, the logical move was to begin. Grunting at the effort, she began to tear at her skin with the flint knives the women had chipped on their journey. If they had only half changed, then they would risk the water, although it was almost as toxic to pre-breeder females as to males.

Ossu-male ran with legs from the muscles of which fatigue poisons were being artificially eliminated.

He was thinking harder than any male had ever thought.

To dominate he would need a clan, preferably one he knew he could control. The Aelcluk were maleless, at his mercy. The thought was murder but he thought it, and he kept thinking it. Must find my clan. (My only hope.) Must find them. To help the snake thing. (To destroy it.)

The snake thing, the grub in his mind, seemed to be sleeping now, glutted perhaps on his fear and hatred. Glutted on the thoughts that were murder to think.

On the way, Ossu-male stripped the low bushes of the steppes for their dark-purple bitter fruit. Must think hard to dominate, he thought desperately. Fruit helps thinkers. The idea stirred something in the cold mind of the snake thing, Ossu-male was sure, but he held fast to his own murderous thoughts and it subsided.

The oldest biochemical changes in his species' history

46

rumbled through his body.

Then he realised what he would have to do.

The females had shed their skins and were half in the blue water when Ossu-male ran into their encampment.

He was changing now; thinking now. Not Ossu-female yet, but Ossu-hir, in the she-male stage. If hir could only go on thinking the dark bitter thoughts until the end.

Stop. Question tactical value of target acquisition: creatures ahead appear to lack tool-using capabilities. How will this contribute to long-term strategic overview? Caution: this unit can inflict military discipline if necessary through direct nerve induction.

Not other, us in breeding form, they must swim to the birthing reefs, Ossu-hir thought. There will be more like them there. Ossu sought the words from the grub's own vocabulary. Hostages: women and children, weak. Bargaining chips, disposable assets. Soft targets for a show of terrorist strength. Sub-strategy: possible long-term training of next generation. War Lord Youth Movements.

Its agreement made hir heart burn in hir breast.

Hir was not male or female, not suited for war or thought, or for land or sea. Screaming, Ossu ploughed through the basking worm-like bulks of the breeders, poised in their slow crawl to the life-giving ocean.

The ice-cold, corrosive waters burned at hir. No retreat, this tactic is an error. Regroup. Dig in. There will be reinforcements, the spider grub whispered, as Ossu-hir's body was swept by the treacherous currents of the great sea, away from those that Ossu would never ever hurt. Ossu prayed to the gods of the males, in which the females affected not to believe, that the changes that had let him think sufficiently to plan this had not made him capable of surviving to hurt others. With him the creature must die!

The TARDIS materialised on the shallow shores of an inland

sea, beneath a sky the colour of mother-of-pearl at sunset. Baleful stars glimmered through the mist, but the waters were a vivid blue. The Doctor stuck his nose out of the ship like a mouse leaving its hole: cautiously, warily. He knew he couldn't afford to stay here long. He and his companions had managed to slip away while the Time Lords were putting the War Lords' crimes to rights, using the multiple time vectors of the TARDISes that were returning the War Lords' kidnapped soldiers to mask their own flight.

It was a tactic that wouldn't work for long. Already they would be tracing his TARDIS, intent on enforcing their numbing bureaucratic rules and regulations. They weren't even one step ahead any more. Like a tortoise chased by an arrow, the Doctor could only hope for a narrowing series of infinitesimal freedoms, before their judgement finally overtook him.

A battered astral sextant clutched in one hand, he started to check the stellar deviation from Galactic Zero Centre. Near here there must surely be some anomalous solar activity he could drop the TARDIS into until they lost interest. Nothing. There was never a Naked Singularity or a Grey Immensity around when you wanted one. Even a Phantom Star or a Dwindler would have been a start.

A black billow in the vivid blue sea caught his eye.

Jamie sweated in the humid air as he helped the Doctor pull the animal's carcass from the shallows. It was a vast mass of blue-black fur, broad as a bear. Heavy with the bright blue water, its fur smelt of tanneries and the cheap jewellery of Sassenach women. It was almost too heavy for them to drag across the ruby pebbles of the gemstone-encrusted bank.

Zoe, too slight, in Jamie's opinion, to help with man's work, leaned inquisitively over the Doctor's shoulder. 'The liquid must be saturated with copper-sulphate salts. Was it poisoned, do you think, Doctor?' As always her eyes were bright, impish.

The Doctor considered. 'No, Zoe, the whole coloration of the sea must be due to copper content. You can see that the defraction of the sky is hardly reflected at all.'

Zoe nodded. 'So the whole ecosystem is likely to be copper-based, in which case the salt alone shouldn't be immediately toxic.'

'Not unless the biochemistry of the land animals had developed away from their ancestors, no, Zoe,' the Doctor mused.

'Yon poor beastie's drowned for sure, Doctor,' Jamie said decisively. 'We canna be waiting here for ever. Those stiff-necked folk of yours will have us by our heels.'

'I'm not so sure, Jamie. This is no beast.'

'Not with that brain–body ratio,' Zoe said, running her hand over the top of the creature's head. 'It must have been intelligent. And look at the marks around the supra-orbital ridge on the right eye. Surely those are direct optic-nerve tap scars. It must have had quite a high technology.'

The Doctor looked worried. 'Did it, I wonder,' he muttered, and his careful fingers traced the spider-leg pattern of scarring around the beast's eye. 'This sea must be exceptionally corrosive to metal. Still –' he hesitated – 'I think the past tense may be a little premature, Zoe. What phylum would you say this creature belonged in, um?'

Jamie watched as Zoe considered. He imagined the wheels turning in her head. She was nice enough, but she always had to parade her knowledge like a wee lassie with a new dress.

'Proto-mammalian, either mono or diatreme, I'd say. Probably egg-laying still. Not dissimilar to the extinct duck-billed platypus. Odd. It seems to be bi-gendered. Look there.' She pointed.

Jamie blushed.

'Zoe, you're embarrassing Jamie!' the Doctor quipped. 'Besides, that's neither here nor there. What matters is that in most near-mammalian species there's a survival reflex that cuts in when the body is suddenly immersed in liquid substantially below body temperature.' The Doctor's hands pressed the upper reaches of the creature's spinal column. 'But every reflex has its off switch.'

The great black body of the creature stirred. A gush of blue-crystal-filled liquid spilled on to the red beach from its mouth.

A dull, mournful note like a bell in a sunken cathedral sounded across the scarlet stones.

The Doctor spun round. 'Oh my.'

'It's the TARDIS, Doctor.'

'I know, Jamie. Keep your sporran on. I'll be just a moment.'

The creature had opened its eyes now and the Doctor could see pain in them. Pain and an inestimable sense of loss.

Then the light left them.

When the stiff-necked people of the Doctor's own world finally caught up with him, and he had to watch as Zoe and Jamie were stripped of their memories of their time together, the puzzled hurt in their faces reminded him of the broad, sad face of the black beast on that nameless planet.

# The Last Days

## by Evan Pritchard

'These Zealots have offended against the laws of Rome and our Emperor,' the Doctor called out across the massed ranks of legionaries. He waited briefly for the buzz of excitement to die down before continuing. 'The gods will surely punish them for their temerity, turning flames of righteous anger on these Jewish rebels. And I can promise you this – tomorrow, Masada will fall and the long siege will be over.'

Barbara leaned back against the building from which she had emerged and regarded the scene before her. A wide space, dotted with buildings. Marble. The ancient world, perhaps. And there were people, hundreds of people, all focusing on something out of her sight. She could smell smoke and the sky was lit with a sullen red glow. The people seemed agitated, some shouting and others whispering, all in motion without actually going anywhere.

So where was she? And how had she got here?

There were memories, she realised. Yet another landing in the temperamental TARDIS. Earth, the Doctor had said, and she'd felt a surge of hope. She'd looked at Ian to share the feeling, but he'd been frowning past her at the Ship's screen. She'd known immediately that this wouldn't be the time they reached home.

A desert landscape outside. A walk through it in the clean, early-morning sunshine. Even then, the heat had been stifling, hanging almost tangibly in the air like thick folds of fabric. Soon, they'd found the sea – a strange, flat, dead blue. Susan had dipped her finger in the oily water and looked at the bleak mountains around them, which, like the sea, seemed incapable of supporting any form of life. 'Not Earth, then?' she'd suggested tentatively, but the Doctor had shaken his head impatiently and Barbara had realised that she was doing the same. 'Israel,' she'd said, at the same time that the Doctor had muttered, 'Palestine.' They'd looked at each other and the Doctor had shrugged – time travel rendered them both potentially correct. Then the Doctor had seen the soldiers approaching them. 'Judaea,' he'd said with certainty.

They'd been caught in a skirmish. On one side had been Roman soldiers, she recalled now. Ian had stood by her with his usual fierce loyalty, but the Doctor and Susan had quickly been lost in the confusion.

She touched her side and flinched. Of course. She had been injured. Ian had carried her from the fray. Had they met up with some other refugees? She couldn't remember. All her memories after the injury were hazy. There had been a long journey, a mountain and finally a bed. And as she'd floated in and out of consciousness, Ian had always been there, comforting her and begging her not to give up, not to leave him. So where was he now?

The flames licked at the night sky. Above them, heat haze obscured the clarity of the stars in the desert air. The Doctor was a dark, slightly stooped shape outlined by fire.

A gust of wind blew the flames nearer and the line of soldiers facing the fortress retreated another pace. Susan could see the legionaries hesitating, caught between two impulses: fear of the unnatural fire and obedience to their commander. It seemed that fear was gaining the upper hand.

'The Zealots have summoned spirits to control the fire,' said a sour, greying man, the oldest of the tribunes.

The other soldiers mumbled their assent and, as if these words had given them licence, began to retreat down the ramp that scaled the mountainside. Flavius Silva, Governor, commander of the Tenth Legion, shouted at them to stand firm, but his words did little to slow their retreat and soon the fierce heat coming from the burning walls forced him also to back away.

For the first time, Susan saw a look of helpless defeat on his face. During the weeks in which she and the Doctor had insinuated themselves into his camp, she had seen this man's confidence gradually eroded, his certainty of victory blunted by the persistence and ingenuity of Masada's defenders. Tonight, he had ordered the walls to be set on fire, only to see the flames turn from the fortress and blow back in the faces of the weary Roman soldiers. She saw now his final acceptance of the fact that the rebels had beaten him. It was clearly a bitter realisation.

The Doctor was also studying the Governor, his face etched with displeasure and just a hint of alarm. 'No, no,' he muttered. 'This really won't do, won't do at all.' Jerking into sudden motion, he stepped up to the soldiers, arms raised crookedly above his head.

With his cloak draped over him, he looked rather like a theatrical ghost, and Susan had to raise a hand to her mouth to stifle a giggle.

The Doctor, seemingly unaware of his own absurdity, spoke with calm authority. 'Retreat is absolutely forbidden.'

The soldiers hesitated. The old man didn't command the same respect as Flavius Silva. Why should they listen to him and face the furious fire which had turned so mysteriously against them?

Barbara started to make her way through the clusters of agitated people to try to find Ian. The crowd comprised men, women and children, all simply dressed in tunics and sandals. As she neared the front, she saw that men predominated. Soon she was the only woman and she realised that she was beginning to attract attention.

'Joab,' a man beside her shouted. 'Joab, your wife's here!'

Others took up the cry and she found a path clearing for her. She saw two men standing in front of her, their faces cast into shadow by the blazing fire which consumed the wooden wall behind them. One of them was obviously young, although he carried himself with the authority of age. He was dark-skinned and his hawk-like features were rendered sterner still by the jagged scars which disfigured them. The other man was Ian, who was now smiling delightedly at her. But those flames were so close...

Suddenly, she knew exactly where and when she was. She felt like an actress who had stumbled on stage for the last act of a tragedy. 'You must move away,' she shouted, surprised when her voice came out as a rusty croak. 'It's not safe – you have to move back.'

Ian looked almost comically startled, as if he'd been prepared for an entirely different conversation with her.

'No,' he said after a moment. 'This is our chance.' He turned to the man beside him, as if continuing an ongoing argument. 'Listen to me, Eleazar, we can take advantage of this. If we attack now, while they're retreating anyway, we can drive them right off the mountain.' Barbara saw him swallow, as if uncomfortable with the words he was about to utter. 'This wind is a... a sign... from God. It can't be natural. Have you ever seen a wind change direction that suddenly? It was blowing this way when the Romans lit the fire, but something turned it back.'

Oh, Ian, thought Barbara, what are you doing? It's too late to try rewriting the ending. But then she heard the growing murmur of the men behind her and she realised that he was close to convincing them.

'No!' she shouted, more power in her voice now. 'You mustn't do that.'

Ian turned to her with a look of confusion. 'Barbara, you've been unconscious for weeks. You don't understand what's going on. This could be our last chance.'

There was an answer to that – one the Doctor would have been proud of, about respecting history and not interfering – but she couldn't give it here, in front of all these people. She was a history teacher, she knew what was supposed to happen next, but how could she make sure it did happen? By telling them what happened next, she realised with perfect circular logic.

A hush had descended over the crowd. It occurred to her that her return from near death had given her a certain authority. The calculating part of her mind she didn't like very much told her she could use this. 'Why do you think I've been healed?' she said finally. 'I have a message for you. Step away from the walls and wait. I promise that the flames will turn round again. I know for certain that you aren't meant to attack.'

The man called Eleazar looked at her intently, then turned and waved the men back from the wall. Barbara moved with them, but Eleazar was prevented from retreating by Ian, who grabbed his arm.

'Don't do this,' he said. 'If we wait, we might lose the opportunity.'

Eleazar was about to reply when they all felt the first faint stirrings of a breeze... blowing away from the wall. Eleazar grasped Ian's arm, pulling him towards Barbara and the other men. Then, as they ran, the flames that ate the wooden walls wavered for a moment before bending inwards and swooping down on their fleeing forms.

The men surrounding her let out a deep groan and, for a terrifying moment, Barbara thought that they had been caught in the fire. Then, coughing and beating sparks from their clothing, they emerged, Eleazar dragging Ian, who even now seemed reluctant to go.

As soon as they were clear, Eleazar turned and addressed the crowd. 'A sign has been given. The Lord does not intend us to leave here.'

There was a moment of hesitation, of almost preternatural stillness, while the wind fell to nothing and then it picked up again, blowing away from the soldiers and taking the flames with it.

Susan saw the dour tribune flash the Doctor a brilliant smile, generous now with his good humour. The legionaries let out a raucous cheer and began to charge back up the ramp towards the burning fortress.

'Stop, you men!' Silva called out, striding towards them, no hint of the earlier sense of defeat in his bearing. 'There's no need to hurry now. Let the fire burn out the defences. Go back and prepare the battering ram.' His smile was predatory. 'In the morning, we'll take Masada. Then these fools will see Roman justice at work.'

Susan grasped the Doctor's sleeve and dragged him down the ramp towards the camp at the base of the mountain. When she was sure that they were out of earshot of the Roman soldiers, she spun round to face him. 'What are you doing, Grandfather? Why didn't you just let them run away? Then we could have rescued Barbara and Ian and left this horrible place.'

The Doctor hurrumphed and shook his head at her. 'Rescue them? It's not Ian and Barbara who need rescuing, child. It's history that needs saving from Chesterton's meddling.'

Susan took a step back, surprised by the old man's vehemence. 'But... what has Ian done? We don't even know for certain that he's in there.'

The Doctor grimaced, turned away from her and began to stride towards their hut. Susan was forced to trot at his heels – just like a puppy, she thought crossly.

As soon as he knew that she was following him, the Doctor continued. 'History must be preserved. I thought you knew that, my dear.'

'I do know that,' Susan replied. 'I just didn't know there was any history here that needed preserving.'

That caused the Doctor to halt in his tracks and let out a little *tssk* of displeasure. 'Do you know how many Roman soldiers have been killed by the Zealots in the last two months, hmm?'

'I – I don't know. I suppose it must be about a hundred,' Susan stuttered, wrong-footed by his change of subject.

'One hundred and seven,' he announced firmly. 'And there are no indications so far that the rebels are going to slow down.'

Susan was confused. 'I don't see why that bothers you.'

The Doctor looked at her pityingly. 'But we know the eventual outcome. The Roman historian Josephus recorded events here most precisely. And the twentieth-century archaeological dig was very thorough indeed. Do you know, they even found the lots drawn by...' He trailed off and an expression of guilt settled on his face. He tried to distract attention from it with his usual bluster. 'These attacks on the Romans must be Chesterton's doing. They shouldn't be happening. Good grief, child, the Romans shouldn't be on the point of giving up. The rebels should be... they should be just waiting.'

'Grandfather,' Susan said carefully, beginning to piece things together, 'just what is going to happen to Ian and Barbara?'

The Doctor looked away.

'What happens to the Jewish rebels, Grandfather?' she demanded.

There was silence for what seemed like minutes. When the Doctor finally met her eyes, the compassion she saw in his face was more frightening than his earlier evasions. 'Two women survived. It was their testimony that formed part of the account of the siege that we now have.'

Susan didn't miss the implications of what the Doctor wasn't saying. 'Only two survivors... both women?' She grasped at the most slender of hopes. 'Could one of them be Barbara?'

The Doctor turned and pushed his way into their hut. 'Maybe, my child. It is always possible.'

All this time, Susan thought, he's been letting me think that we're here to rescue our friends, when actually all he wanted to do was to stop them. The tears that welled in the corners of her eyes dried in the desert air before they could fall.

* * *

Ian watched the activity around him. It seemed aimless yet frantic, as if – in their last hours of freedom – the defenders were sure that they should be doing something but weren't quite sure what. Eleazar appeared oblivious to their needs, talking quietly to his lieutenants. Ian knew he should be with them. After all, wasn't he Eleazar's right-hand man? When he and Barbara had first arrived, they had been mistrusted as possible spies. But then he had masterminded the first raid on the Romans camped below and his status had changed. Now they called him Joab – the brave.

He knew that Barbara was watching him, but he couldn't bear to face her. All these weeks he had waited by her sickbed, terrified that she would never rise from it, and now her first act on waking was to oppose him. The rational part of his mind told him that she had done what she did because she knew something he didn't. He didn't want to listen to it.

He didn't want to think that he had become involved in a conflict whose outcome was already decided, and which he was powerless to influence. He wasn't quite sure when the siege of Masada had become more than just something he was passing through on his way to somewhere else, but it had. He had really believed he could save these people. Tonight, he had been so close.

Then Barbara had woken up, and suddenly it was all just history again. Impersonal and inevitable.

He looked around him. There were Yoshua and Rivka, with their baby Yitzhak. He was only five months old, born in Masada. They were watching Eleazar and his men. So was Daniel, a grizzled veteran who claimed that he'd killed over a hundred Romans in his career as a freedom fighter. Little Avraham and Yosef, the twins, were running between the adults' legs, the tension they sensed transformed through the filter of childhood into playful energy.

Barbara might have read the history books, but he knew these people's names. He imagined the wide top of the mountain silent, the morning sun shining on the humped shapes which littered it and the dull red stains on the yellow sand. He imagined the smell of death. And then he imagined the screams of the women as the soldiers began their work. No, he wouldn't allow it to happen.

There were now two ways on and off the table-top mountain which was home to the fortress of Masada. When the Romans had first begun their siege, there had been only the winding path which climbed its eastern face. Too narrow to accommodate more than one man, it was safe from assault by the ranks of a Roman legion. But rather than be deterred, the Romans had decided to make another way: a huge ramp that ran from the ground to the fortress walls a thousand feet above.

The ramp had taken many months to build and the labour of countless slaves. It was a work of brute strength and relentless, stolid determination. Ian had come to think that it, rather than any of the great marvels in Italy, ought to stand as the ultimate monument to the sheer bloody-mindedness of the Roman Empire.

So now the ramp was finished and the Imperial wolf was at the door. But the other path was still there. Although defeat was inevitable, perhaps escape was still possible.

At last, Ian turned to Barbara. She wasn't looking at him any more. Instead she was studying Eleazar, an expectant look on her face.

Feeling Ian's eyes on her, she switched her gaze to him and began to reach out to him, then hesitated, as if unsure of her reception. 'I'm so sorry, Ian. Shall I tell you why?'

'No!' he said roughly.

She looked hurt and swayed slightly.

He reminded himself that she had been close to death only a few days ago and spoke more gently. 'No. I know you must know what happens... what happened here. But I'd never heard of Masada until I came here! I imagine I've been behaving in a way the Doctor would heartily disapprove of.'

She smiled slightly at that.

'You don't need to tell me we've lost, that I've been fighting the inevitable these last few weeks. Don't worry, I'm not planning some hopeless last stand. I was thinking about getting some of these people away while it's still dark. I'm not sure we can save everyone, and maybe history needs the Romans to find someone here, but I don't see why I can't rescue one or two...' He saw an expression forming on her face that he didn't want to recognise as pity. 'Barbara, there are almost a thousand people here! Don't tell me history will care if some of them escape.'

'Ian,' she began, and then hesitated. Before she could resume, they were both startled by a series of dull clanging sounds. It was Eleazar's lieutenants clashing swords against shields to get the crowd's attention. Ian turned back to Barbara, but she was staring fixedly at Eleazar. 'Listen to what he has to say,' she said softly.

It was amazing that a thousand people could be so silent, but the attention focused on Eleazar was so intense that even the children sensed it and quietened their games. When Eleazar raised his arms, every eye was on him.

'My friends, we long ago resolved never to be servants to the Romans – or to any other than God Himself. The time has come to put that resolution to the test.'

Low murmurs of assent began to rumble through the crowd, edged with a kind of fearful anticipation. These people knew what was coming next. Ian began to think that he did too.

'We were the very first to revolt against the Romans and we are the last still fighting against them. It's clear that we will be taken before night falls again.'

The crowd growled, whether in denial or agreement Ian couldn't tell.

'But we can still die bravely. We hoped that we alone of all Israel might remain free.'

Even across the crowd, Ian could see that Eleazar's eyes had turned to Barbara.

'But God has shown us that our hopes were in vain, our

arrogance a sin. Let us receive our punishment for this not from the Romans but from God – by our own hands.'

And then he outlined his plan; it was almost perfect in its simplicity. Every man would kill the members of his own family. Eleazar's lieutenants would then kill all the other men, before drawing lots to choose one of them to kill the rest. Finally, that man would take his own life. Not one soul left alive for the Romans to find.

Ian expected a howl of outrage from the crowd. He was so sure it would come that he found himself opening his mouth to join in. But there was only a low murmur of inquiry, quickly silenced. Eleazar had them. They *liked* the idea, Ian realised. It appealed to their sense of destiny and purpose – the same sense that had kept them fighting long after the rest of their people had given up.

He turned to Barbara – and saw that she was mouthing along to Eleazar's words. He fought against feelings of impotent rage. 'This is madness, Barbara!' he whispered fiercely. 'You're not telling me they went through with this?'

'Yes, they did. And history recorded all of it. Archaeologists even found the lots they drew to decide which of the men should kill the rest.'

Barbara had always been a compassionate woman and her face showed grief at these strangers' deaths. But it was the sadness of someone reading a book with an unhappy ending – someone at one remove from reality.

Ian set his jaw in a stubborn line. For a brief moment he hated Barbara for being right. 'I'll talk to them. Look at them.' His gesture encompassed the milling mass of people, with their restless children and their shell-shocked expressions. 'They don't want to die. If I give them an alternative, they'll take it.'

Barbara grasped his arm. 'For goodness' sake, Ian. Don't you see that there is no alternative?'

He wrenched himself from her hand. 'Don't give me that nonsense about preserving history! Look at what you tried to do with the Aztecs... You're not the Doctor – don't start talking like him!'

She ran a hand through her thick brown hair, pushing a sweep of it back from her face. He realised that she was also using the gesture to covertly wipe away tears. 'I'm not talking about history, Ian. What Eleazar says is right. Terrible as it is, suicide is their best option.'

'How can you say that?'

'How can you not see it?' She was angry now too, her face flushed with rage and hurt. 'What do you imagine will happen to these people if the Romans capture them?'

Ian looked away, uncomfortably reminded of his own fantasy of the fall of Masada. He could think of nothing to say.

The crowds in the central square were thinning as the men slowly led their families to their individual rooms. To his left, Avraham and Yosef were trailing disconsolately behind their mother, annoyed that their play had been disrupted and not quite understanding the reason. Unseen by them, tears ran down their mother's face, yet at the same time her expression was one of almost unnatural peace. Their father was nowhere to be seen. Probably already in their house, Ian thought, preparing himself. How do you do that? he wondered. How do you prepare for something like this?

He must have been standing there for some time. The square was almost empty. Across its length, Eleazar was watching him. Ian imagined his eyes gleaming with fanatical certainty. There was a coppery smell carried on the light desert breeze. He could hear crying, high and scared from the children, with the occasional deeper sob. But there were no screams. How could so many people die so quietly?

He realised that Barbara's hand had clasped his shoulder. She was making meaningless sounds of comfort. Why was she doing that?

'Ian, I... I know how dreadful this is,' she said gently, touching his cheek. He hadn't realised that tears were streaming down his face. 'We have to go inside, Ian. Eleazar's watching us and I think he's becoming suspicious.'

When he didn't respond, she took him by the hand and led him into the simple room that had been home for the last few weeks. Once inside, she pulled a heavy curtain across the doorway, shutting them in their own private world.

She sat him down on one of the beds – as if I were the invalid, Ian thought – and turned to face him. Her expression was unexpectedly firm.

'Let me tell you what the Romans would do to any prisoners,' she said.

Ian shook his head. What was the point of carrying on the argument? She'd already won.

But Barbara wouldn't be put off. 'The men would be crucified,' she said. 'It can take days of agony to die like that.' She sighed and took his hand in hers. 'The women and children would be sold into slavery – if they were lucky. And I've been there, Ian, I've felt that fear, that hopelessness.'

Ian swallowed painfully and finally raised his head to meet her eyes. 'I shan't argue with you. But I've always believed that where there's life there's hope. Where would we be if we'd given up each time everything seemed lost?'

Barbara smiled wryly. 'We wouldn't be here now. I don't think this is the same, though. There's no Doctor to rescue us – no magic ship to take us away. Death is the only freedom these people have left.' She raised his hand to her lips. 'One day it may be the only freedom we have left. I'd like to think that if necessary you would do the same for me.'

Ian pulled back from her. 'No! Don't be absurd. How can you possibly think I'd do that?'

'Even if I asked you to? I know what the life of a Roman slave is like, Ian. I don't think I could bear it.'

Ian knelt by her feet and placed a hand over hers. 'No, Barbara. I won't ever let that happen to you. I might not be able to save these people, maybe the Doctor's precious history won't let me, but I'll always save you.'

He realised that he could hear footsteps approaching their

room. In one swift movement, he drew his dagger and swept its wickedly sharp blade along the flesh of his inner arm. He saw her eyes widen as, for a fraction of a second, she was unsure of his intentions. The blood flowed freely and he allowed it to fall on to the white sheets and then, giving her an apologetic grimace, on to the rough cotton of Barbara's dress.

Hurriedly, he urged Barbara to lie down on the bed, then pulled up the bloodstained sheet until it covered her completely. She wouldn't bear close inspection, he decided, and rushed to the curtain before the person outside could enter. At the last moment, he remembered the incriminating cut on his arm and stopped to pull his cloak over it, wincing as the rough material scraped the open wound.

The curtain was thrust aside and Eleazar strode into the room. His eyes flicked between Ian and the shrouded form on the bed. Ian felt his heartbeat quickening. He desperately wanted to turn around and see if Barbara's breathing was visible from the doorway, but he knew he couldn't. A man in his position wouldn't turn around to study his wife's corpse. At least his expression probably looked sufficiently stricken. He didn't know what else this day had to throw at him, but he was fairly sure he couldn't take much more.

Eleazar's gaze had settled on the bed. Ian could see a muscle working beneath the jawline of his scarred face and when the other man finally looked away, Ian was sure that they had been found out. But Eleazar simply walked up to him and flung an arm over his shoulder.

'Come, Joab,' he said.'You don't want to remain here.'

Ian nodded wordlessly and allowed himself to be led from the room.

Outside, the fire that was consuming the walls was dying at last, its glow replaced by the first light of dawn. He had thought that he was all out of arguments, but Eleazar tapped a whole new reservoir of them. 'There should have been another way,' he said.

Eleazar was quiet for a moment, his gaze sweeping over the

marble buildings and the small patches of soil and sparse crops. 'These are the Last Days,' he said eventually. 'The Temple has been destroyed, Jerusalem burned. We were the last.'

'Isn't that exactly why we should keep on fighting for as long as we can?'

Ian was surprised to hear Eleazar's laugh – a deep, rich sound, free of bitterness. 'Joab, you were aptly named. You don't understand the meaning of defeat. You've kept hope alive when we thought there was none left. We are all in your debt for that. But it is over.' His near-black eyes squinted into the morning sun. 'The Messiah will come to Zion. We'll have new life in His time, but this life is over. And by doing this, we will rob the Romans of their victory.'

Ian knew that his own laugh was far less carefree. 'I would have said we're just making their victory even easier.'

As he spoke, he became aware of a strange grumbling, squealing sound from behind the fortress gates. The Romans were bringing up their battering ram. It really was almost over.

Eleazar had also heard the sound. His mouth thinned. 'If you think that, you don't understand Flavius Silva at all,' he said. 'Now go, Joab. There are men who have said farewell to their families and are waiting for your sword. Join my other lieutenants in freeing them.'

He was gone before Ian could protest, could tell him that he was asking the impossible. But then he thought about all the men sitting in those buildings with their dead wives and children. *I'd like to think that if necessary you would do the same for me.* Ian knew what he'd want in their place.

Feeling as though he'd lost the ability to make decisions, he entered the nearest house. He paused, leaning against the broad doorway, when he saw what was inside. It was such a ridiculously domestic scene. There were three pairs of sandals scattered over the floor, two of them very small. An iron cooking pot sat in the corner. If it hadn't been for the red puddle forming under the bed, he might have thought that the woman and children lying on it were just sleeping.

The twins lay curled up in their mother's arms. One of them wore an expression of total peace; the other one of uncomprehending fear. Of course, they couldn't both have been killed at the same time. One must have seen what had happened to the other. The mother's face was buried in the sheets. Sitting on the floor by them, clasping his wife's hand, was their murderer. He was already dead. Ian hadn't been the first of Eleazar's men to visit the room.

Ian felt his legs weaken and he sank to the earth floor. He realised that he had drawn his knife, but he knew now that there was no way he could use it. He tipped his head back to rest against the cool marble of the walls and closed his eyes. It was over and there was nothing more he could do.

Many minutes later he felt a hand gently touch his shoulder. He couldn't bring himself to open his eyes.

'Come, Joab,' said Eleazar's firm voice. 'It's almost done. We eleven alone are left. Soon there will be only one. We must draw lots to decide which of us that will be.'

Ian didn't hear him leaving, but his presence was so strong that, when he left, the void in the room was almost palpable. Carefully keeping his gaze averted from the bodies in the corner, he rose to his feet and stumbled out.

The sun had finally cleared the distant mountains and the light was painfully bright. There was fire to accompany the sunlight again. The men had set their dwellings ablaze. Nothing would be left behind for the Romans. Eleazar was seated in the centre of the courtyard, surrounded by his lieutenants. All but me, Ian thought numbly as he went to take his place among the last defenders of Masada.

Susan watched as Silva paced the length of his room for what must have been the hundredth time. He was filled with a restless energy, a horribly happy anticipation of the coming battle.

The Doctor had brought her with him to see the

commander at least half an hour ago. Presumably, the Doctor had intended to say something to the other man, but as soon as they'd entered his room Silva had begun to run through his plans for the morning in an almost childlike babble of excitement. The normally loquacious Doctor hadn't been able to get a word in edgeways.

'Many of the Jews will die in the fight,' Silva was saying now, 'but I think we can assume there'll be some survivors. Rome will want some rebels who can be publicly seen to pay the price for their rebellion. We would have lined the streets of Jerusalem with their crosses –' his lips twitched – 'but the streets of Jerusalem aren't what they used to be.'

'Ah, yes,' the Doctor finally managed. 'Survivors. That's precisely what I wished to discuss with you.'

Silva looked startled, as if he'd actually forgotten that he had an audience. 'You have your own plans for the survivors?' He sounded disappointed.

'Only two of them,' the Doctor said, and Susan began to feel a glimmer of hope. 'Two spies I have within the fortress. It's vital that their lives be spared.'

'You have spies inside?' The commander was frowning. 'Why have I heard nothing of them?'

The Doctor grasped the edges of his cloak and leaned his head forward like a bird about to peck at a worm. 'My dear boy, what use are spies if everyone knows of them? No, no, it was best for their existence to remain a secret. But now I'm most concerned not to be deprived of their services by some over-zealous legionary.'

Silva shook his head and thumped the old man on the back. The Doctor's affronted expression might almost have been funny, Susan thought, under different circumstances. 'Don't worry. I will instruct my men to spare your creatures.'

'Good, good,' the Doctor said, moving towards the entrance of the room. 'Shall I fetch a centurion to spread their description among the men?'

'Yes, yes. We can deal with that shortly,' Silva said vaguely.

Then his face brightened again. 'But first, let me tell you of my plans for the women...'

Susan felt her hope fading as the commander continued his litany of hatred and cruelty. She realised that he would never be able to live down the fact that he was the man who had allowed himself to be humiliated by a group of people he had described as unwashed barbarians. She feared that no one in Masada would be safe from his long-delayed plans for revenge.

They crouched on the ground in the square at the heart of the great fortress: Ian, the nine other lieutenants and Eleazar. In front of Eleazar were an empty flagon and eleven potsherds, each inscribed with a name. Ian could see his own, 'Joab', written on one. The ochre fragment was almost square in shape, except for a diagonal chip across one corner. Ian couldn't take his eyes off it as Eleazar picked it up and placed it in the flagon along with the other pieces.

The chatter and overloud laughter of the men was audible to him but distant, irrelevant. I have only one chance in eleven of surviving this, he thought. He realised he didn't know if that was good or bad. Barbara needs me, he told himself. How will she survive without me?

The sherds rattled loudly in the flagon as Eleazar shook it. Ian wondered if the Romans could hear the sound above the dull thump of their battering ram hitting the fire-weakened gates of Masada.

'Are you ready?' Eleazar asked.

Ian's eyes flicked up; Eleazar was looking at him. 'As ready as I'll ever be,' he answered mechanically.

Eleazar dipped a sun-browned fist into the flagon, then swiftly pulled it out. He left the fist closed. The other men were silent now. Stripped of their assumed nonchalance, their faces were studies in anguish.

Everyone watched Eleazar's hand. With almost theatrical slowness, he opened it. *Joab*. A sigh that was almost a moan passed through the men.

Eleazar's eyes burned into Ian's. 'Are you ready, Joab?'

Ian's throat was so tight, no sound could get through it. Eleazar stood and reached across the flagon to offer his hand. Ian stared at it stupidly for a moment, before realising he was being offered the lot inscribed with his name, the lot which would make him a murderer. He closed his hand around the irregular shape and jumped to his feet. For a second, he thought about running away. But where could he run to? The silence stretched on. Everyone was waiting for him to do something that he knew he couldn't do.

'Your sword, Joab,' Eleazar said. 'You'll need it.'

Ian nodded and drew the weapon from its scabbard. He held it point down, wondering what would happen to him when Eleazar realised that he was incapable of carrying out his task. Would they draw lots again to pick someone else? But if they did, Ian would die and there would be no one left to take care of Barbara. Slowly, he raised the sword until the tip was level with his heart.

He was almost relieved when Mordecai stepped up to him. Thank God, he thought. They'll take the sword away from me and I won't have to do this terrible thing. Mordecai looked at Eleazar, who gave him a sharp nod.

Frowning slightly, Mordecai opened his arms, and for a dizzy moment Ian thought he was going to embrace him. Then he stepped forward, on to the point of the sword. It slid into his chest with obscene ease. For several seconds he just stood there, held upright on the blade. At last, his knees crumpled and he fell to the ground.

Adam was next. He shivered slightly as he stepped up to Ian, fear rendering his dark complexion almost ghostly. The sword didn't go in so easily this time and the man let out a choked cry of agony as he died.

Ian jerked back at the sound and realised with horror that his hands were slippery with blood. He looked round desperately for some way out of this impossible situation. The men in front of him stared back impassively and he realised that in some strange way they were no longer here. They had taken what they considered to be a rational decision – that had been the difficult part – and now they were resigned to their fate.

The faces blurred: Yochai, Isaiah, Yarif, Solomon, Daniel...

Not many left now.

Saul. Yoshua...

Almost over.

And then only Eleazar was left. Drained, Ian let his sword arm fall to his side. He watched as one tiny red dewdrop fell from the tip of the blade to the parched sand of the mountaintop.

Without seeing, he felt Eleazar move towards him. There was a muted thump as his boot struck the flagon which still lay between them. It tipped on its side and the lots tumbled out on to the ground. Ian stared blankly at the small pieces of pottery and then his eyes suddenly focused.

One of the lots. An ochre fragment in the sand almost square in shape, except for a diagonal chip across one corner. Joab. He felt the stupor in which he'd spent the last few hours lifting.

Eleazar was watching him, a knowing look on his face, as Ian unclenched his fist and looked at the identical lot within it.

'You fixed it!' Ian said incredulously. 'You'd already chosen me. Why?'

Eleazar laid a hand on Ian's shoulder in his familiar gesture. With his other hand, he gently clasped Ian's sword arm and raised it. 'You never gave up hope. You gave us hope. And at the end you couldn't let it go. I knew that, when I came into your room and saw that you hadn't been able to kill your woman.'

Ian felt a terrible panic seize him. If Eleazar had known that Barbara wasn't dead...

'Don't worry. She's still well,' Eleazar reassured him. 'These deaths mean nothing if they're not given freely. To kill someone who isn't ready to die is a terrible sin.' He lifted his hand from Ian's shoulder and swept it round to encompass the burning fortress. 'For everything you've given us, I've nothing left to give you except the choice.'

Eleazar lifted the tip of Ian's sword to his own chest. 'Goodbye, Joab.'

The ominous silence as the ranks of the Roman legion stood before the fortress gates should have prepared Susan. Or maybe she should have been alerted by the Doctor's unnatural calm. But – like the Romans themselves – she couldn't quite believe it even when they'd marched unopposed through the shattered gates of Masada.

The air smelt of death and the vultures were already gathering. It was a little while before they found the first bodies. The legionaries were cautious, still suspecting a trap, but Susan took one look at the Doctor's face and knew that they were quite safe.

Most of the bodies were inside, in the storerooms and state rooms of the fortress. That was where the women and children were to be found, they were told by an ashen-faced soldier. The Doctor wouldn't allow her to go inside to look for herself, even though she was desperate to know if Barbara was among them. But he wasn't able to stop her seeing the bodies that lay at the centre of the fortress. Ten men: the leaders of the rebellion, she guessed.

Silva made a sound of disgust deep in the back of his throat and kicked one of the corpses in a gesture of helpless spite. She saw some of his own men regarding him with contempt.

'The Jews died bravely,' one of the soldiers said. It was unmistakably a rebuke.

Silva spun away from the bodies, snarling, 'Find me some survivors! In all this place, there must be someone left alive!' He turned to the Doctor. 'These fanatics! To kill their own children... Now you see what I've been up against all these months.'

The Doctor's face was expressionless. 'Yes, indeed. This is a victory that history will never forget.'

The two men locked gazes, the Roman commander trying to

read meaning in the Doctor's ancient eyes.

Their silence was only broken when a breathless centurion ran up, shouting, 'We've found two survivors, a man and a woman.'

Barbara and Ian sat side by side on the bed, her hand clasped in his. She hadn't asked him what had happened outside, but the pressure of his grasp was such that his nails pierced the skin of her palm.

They had heard the Romans entering the fortress, heard their cries of disgust at what they'd discovered. When two legionaries found them, it was almost a relief. At least the waiting is over, Barbara thought.

But when the one who'd left to fetch his commander returned, she couldn't suppress a gasp. Even wearing a tattered toga, the angular figure of the Doctor was instantly recognisable. She saw Ian's eyes snap up to meet the old man's. A silent understanding passed between them. They said nothing, but Barbara noticed that the Doctor had grasped his granddaughter's shoulder to prevent her leaping forward to embrace her friends. Barbara found herself smiling at the young woman's impulsiveness and suddenly realised that she hadn't smiled properly for what seemed like a very long time.

Only when she'd drunk in the welcome sight of her friends did Barbara turn her attention to the other man in the room. She didn't need to see his uniform to guess that this was Flavius Silva. Whatever you thought about the Doctor, he always found his way to the very top. She wondered what story he'd told this time to get there.

The Roman commander was regarding them both with an expression of dreadful hunger. 'So...' he began. Barbara shivered at the promise held in that one word.

'Well done, Flavius Silva. Well done indeed,' the Doctor interrupted. 'You've found me my spies.'

Dark eyes were turned angrily on the Doctor. 'How very convenient that the only survivors should be your people.' He reached out suddenly and grasped Barbara's chin. 'They must know exactly what happened here. My men will... question them.'

The Doctor bustled forward, placing himself between the commander and his captives. 'If there's any questioning to be done here, it will be done by me.'

Silva smiled mockingly at the old man. 'Come now, they're only Jews. How can we trust them to speak honestly?'

'They aren't Jews!' The Doctor's earlier calm was quite gone. Barbara wondered, as she often did, just how in control of this situation he was. Ian was watching the old man avidly, animation having finally returned to his face. Well, at least now he seemed to care whether they lived or died.

'Not Jews?' Silva said. He sounded politely astonished. He had no intention at all of letting them go, Barbara realised. Her earlier words to Ian about what would happen to anyone captured by the Romans played back in her mind.

But the Doctor wouldn't give up so easily. 'I can prove to you that they're good Roman citizens.' He reached into his toga and drew out a gold coin. It was old, Barbara saw – she recognised the likeness of Augustus Caesar engraved on it. 'Jews are forbidden to bow their heads to any god but their own.' He held out the coin to Ian. 'Kneel down before the God Caesar, my boy. Show your respect to the might of the Roman Empire.'

Barbara felt her whole body stiffen as Ian glared up at the Doctor. She knew exactly what he was thinking: doing as the Doctor asked would be the last betrayal of his friends. The only thing left that he could do to let them down. And he wouldn't do it.

The Doctor seemed unperturbed by his companion's refusal. 'Come along, Chesterton,' he said briskly. 'It's only a symbol. These last few weeks should have taught you all about bowing to the inevitable.' He looked at Silva, and Barbara wondered if the commander would understand exactly what the Doctor was saying.

She watched Ian's gaze flicker restlessly between the Doctor, Silva and herself. Finally, he knelt, leaned forward and bowed his head so low that his hair brushed his knees. Susan let out an audible sigh of relief, and Barbara suspected that she'd done the same.

Silva looked uncertain, only half convinced. At that moment, a legionary twitched aside the curtain of the room. 'They've found two more,' he said. 'Hidden in the cisterns below.'

The commander took one last, long look at Ian, who had raised his head again and was regarding the Roman leader with cold eyes. Then he turned his back and strode from the room.

The Doctor too moved towards the door. 'Come along, come along,' he said urgently. 'It's long past time we made our exit.'

Barbara began to follow him, but Ian remained kneeling, gazing fixedly at something held in his hand. Barbara saw that it was a fragment of pottery, with a name scratched on it in Hebrew. Her stomach clenched as she realised what it must be.

'You'd better leave that behind, Ian,' she said gently. 'It has an appointment with an archaeologist in two thousand years' time.'

Ian smiled, and the lines of tension in his face eased for the first time in days. 'Not this one,' he said. 'It was a gift.' He closed his fist and shut his eyes for a second, then rose and left the room.

# Stop the Pigeon

by Robert Perry and Mike Tucker

'Connex South Central Railways apologises for any inconvenience caused by this morning's delays, which were the result of a signal failure outside Battersea Park station. We hope to be arriving at Victoria shortly.'

Marvellous. An hour and a half Joe Dakin had been stuck on this train, limping northwards from station to station.

The train lurched forward a few feet, then stopped again. Not for the first time that morning the tension became audible amongst the passengers – an undercurrent of muttering. It was sweltering in the carriage. Worse, they were in sight of Victoria, the cool of the platforms only a couple of hundred yards ahead of them, whilst they baked in the August heat. He could smell the woman next to him. No doubt she could smell him too. Him, her, most of the other people in the carriage were commuters, overdressed for the time of year, suffering in suits.

He looked at his watch. Nearly ten-thirty. He wasn't worried about being late for work, he didn't need to be – he was a bit of a star there – but nevertheless little disruptions in his regular routine made him nervous. Six months ago he'd joined the young team at Innovations Unlimited. Electronic gadgetry. Trivial stuff, rubbish really: porch-lights which sensed movement and switched themselves on automatically, key-rings which bleeped to tell you where they were – the sort of stuff that was only ever sold through the pages of the Sunday colour supplements. Joe Dakin had a talent for trivia. The technical side of it had always seemed childishly simple to him, and he had an uncanny knack of knowing what was going to catch on. Last week the firm had won the Queen's Award for Industry.

Somewhere down the carriage someone lit a cigarette. He heard the rasp of match against box, caught the acrid smell of smoke.

There was a muttered, 'Well, really…' Not quite loud enough for it to be obvious who the complainant was.

Why did no one snap on mornings like this? Everybody sat shoulder to shoulder, sweating, waiting, not talking, not even making eye contact, silently fuming.

A buzzing. A woman half-screamed, stifling the sound before it found its full voice. There was a wasp in the carriage. It flickered across Joe's line of vision. He was sweating badly now. The wasp landed on his hand, drinking his sweat. He could now feel all the eyes in the carriage on him, on his hand.

Motionless, he waited for the beast to sting.

The buzzing was loud. It didn't seem to be coming from the insect at all. It was inside Joe's head. His vision blurred: two wasps, more. Suddenly he could see beyond the immaculate yellow-and-black hide; could see tiny arteries pumping blood, miniature organs.

The people around him, he could almost feel their thoughts. Not words, but emotions: resentment, hostility, savagery only just held in check. He could see through their clothes, through skin and sinew, to the bone.

Joe felt himself falling forward as the train lurched into motion.

There was a sharp crack.

And light.

He was moving. The momentum of the train carried him forward; but there was no train. He crashed to the floor, skidding to a halt.

Slowly he opened his eyes and looked up. He was inside. In a house. Smooth parquet flooring pressed against his face. He could see wood-panelled walls, shuttered windows.

He stayed motionless. What the hell was going on?

A noise made him start. A shuffling. He scrambled to his feet. Staring at him blankly was an old woman – Joe didn't dare guess how old. Her face was sunken and cratered and she leaned on a clumsy tubular walking-frame.

'I… I…' Joe's jaw flapped uselessly. He didn't know what to say. Where should he begin?

Ignoring him, the woman turned and shuffled off. The clink of her walking-frame on the wooden floor reverberated eerily around the cavernous corridors. Joe sprinted after her.

'Um… Excuse me, but where am I? One minute I was on the train and the next…' He tailed off. It sounded absurd. The situation was ludicrous.

The woman continued to ignore him. She was straining to open a heavy oak door.

'No. Let me.' Joe pushed it open for her and she shuffled through. After a moment's hesitation, he followed.

The room was full of people, old people – none of them could be under eighty. Slowly and painfully, they all turned and twisted to look at him. No one said anything.

Joe felt himself wilt under the gaze of centuries. He could hear the creak of lungs, the cracking of bones. With a sudden surge of panic, he turned and fled.

He had no particular goal. The faceless dark corridors could have led anywhere, but he didn't care. Anywhere to get away from the terrible, anguished eyes in that room.

A figure suddenly loomed out of the darkness and Joe cannoned into it. He forced himself to relax. 'Calm down, calm down.' A suit of armour.

Panting and breathless, he leaned against one of the panelled doors and rested his forehead on the cool wood.

Immediately he pulled away. The door was humming. Vibrating.

He placed both hands on it. Definitely a throbbing hum, like a generator. He reached out for the handle.

There was a sharp crack.

And light.

* * *

'Professor, are you done yet?'

Ace sat on a low wall, swinging her legs, watching the Doctor as he scurried around a large ragged hole in the back yard of a terraced house.

'Quiet, Ace. I'm thinking.'

'Well, do you have to do your thinking here? I mean, I thought Perivale was dull, but Croydon...'

The Doctor glared at her. Ace sighed, swung herself down from the wall and mooched off along the street.

The TARDIS had landed about twenty minutes ago in an empty housing development and the Doctor had insisted on exploring. There hadn't seemed much point to Ace – it all looked pretty ordinary – but the Doctor had had 'a feeling'.

She looked back at him. He was *in* the hole now, prodding at the earth with his telescopic probe. He was still dressed in his dark jacket, checked trousers and that bloody pullover. He must be sweltering; it was well over eighty degrees. She'd tried to get him into something cooler but his only concession had been to leave his umbrella behind.

Ace was in cycling shorts and a cropped top. She had decided to make the most of the lack of excitement and get some serious sunbathing in, but then the Doctor had noticed scratches in the road, scatterings of earth, and was off like a terrier after a scent. He had followed the trail of debris through the back streets of east Croydon to here. To this street. To the hole.

Since then he had been prodding at roots, peering at mud – even tasting some of the stones, for God's sake! Ace couldn't see what was fascinating him. Kids were playing football down the street, a woman was hanging out washing – while keeping a watchful eye on the Doctor – and loud rap music drifted from an upstairs window: it all seemed very normal.

A cat emerged from one of the gardens and ambled into the middle of the street, where it sat down and began washing itself. Ace eyed it warily. As she reminded herself, it's just when things look normal that all hell tends to break loose.

* * *

Joe jerked awake to find nothing but familiar surroundings. He was in his bedroom, on his bed. He immediately slumped back. A dream. Thank God, it had just been a dream.

Except… He looked down at himself. He was still fully dressed.

His mind churned. There had been several occasions where he'd been out drinking and found his way home on automatic pilot, but he hadn't been out on the piss last night.

He could feel something in his hand. He brought it up in front of his eyes. A train ticket. Today's train ticket. He groaned. So it hadn't been a dream.

He staggered out of the bedroom. Ahead of him were the staircase, landing, kitchen, bathroom. Everything in its proper place. His.

He looked on his Croydon flat as a kind of oasis. It was large and light and filled with the things he liked – books mostly, and tapes. The walls were gentle pastel colours which soothed. Joe Dakin had spent money on his refuge. If he was away from it all for too long, he became decidedly uneasy. He assumed this was just part of the madness that was life in London. He assumed everyone felt the same.

Breathing deeply, breathing in the calm, he crossed to the kitchen. Coffee. He switched on the kettle and listened as it raged and bubbled, filling the room with sound, then switched itself off. In the sudden silence someone was singing.

Someone was singing in his front room!

'My old man said follow the van…'

An atrocious cod-Cockney squawking, barely in tune, was floating down the landing from the other end of the flat. It sounded like a woman, a drunken bag-lady.

Either he was going mad or…

No, that had to be it. Someone from the office. A practical joke.

OK, he'd be cool about it. He made his coffee. Milk. Sugar. Casually, he picked up the mug and strolled across the landing. Languidly, he pushed open the door to his lounge. And hysterically, he let the mug slip through his fingers and crash to the floor.

The room was a mess. His bureau was open; papers were lying everywhere. One of his bookcases had been overturned. It had collapsed on top of the hi-fi, which in turn had collapsed on to the floor.

And everything was covered in… What was that white stuff? Christ, what was that smell?

'Oh dear, oh dear, oh dear.'

The singing had stopped. The Cockney voice was addressing him now. He couldn't see where it was coming from.

'Bit of a mess, eh, guv'nor? I mean… Jeffrey Archer? Hammond Innes? You don't seriously read that stuff?'

The voice seemed to be coming from behind the remains of the bookcase. Joe took a step closer, his mouth bone-dry and wordless, his voice miles away in a place of safety and sanity.

'Get yerself a nice bit of Iain Banks, that's what you need. Maybe some Platt.'

There was a sound of collapsing books and of… flapping? Fluttering? Feathers.

Instinctively, Joe raised his hands to protect his face. A pigeon was flying towards him, the beat of its wings terrifying in the confined space of the room.

'All right, all right. I won't 'urt you.'

It was the pigeon. The pigeon was talking to him.

'I… uh… suppose you think I did all this?'

The white stuff, splattered like paint over everything. The smell…

Joe wandered back into his kitchen, dazed. He was hallucinating, he had to be. The pigeon followed him. It perched on the edge of the sink and took a drink out of the washing-up bowl.

'Got anything stronger?'

A drink. Yes. That would help. Joe reached out for the bottle of vodka he kept on top of the fridge. He poured himself a glass and took a long gulp, trying to ignore the protesting bird. He glanced out of the window at the tree in his back yard, looking for something normal to focus on. The glass slipped from his grip. The tree was gone. Not fallen over. Not cut down. Just gone. A ragged hole filled the space where the old tree had once stood. A ragged hole with a man in it.

'Ace, come and look at this.'

Ace stopped playing with the cat, pulled her shades on and looked back over at the Doctor. 'What have you found, Professor? "Evil from the Dawn of Time" again?'

He gave her a hurt look. 'There's no need to be sarcastic.'

She grinned and crossed to the edge of the hole, looking down at him. 'OK, show me what's so important.'

Before the Doctor could answer, the back door of the house burst open and a young, dishevelled man raced across the yard towards them. He grabbed Ace by the shoulders and shook her. His eyes were wild and he was shouting at the top of his voice.

'What the hell is going on? What are you doing to me?'

The attack took Ace by surprise. The Doctor was trying to scramble out of the hole and come to her aid when a pigeon flew out of the house and began to swoop around them.

'Temporal anomalies,' it squawked. 'Just when you think you've got them sussed, they bloody well turn up again. Ah well, second time lucky.'

There was a sharp crack and a flash of light. When the light faded, Ace and the man were gone.

Dee Matthews stared across the studio at the man in the crisply pressed black suit. The rest of the crew had their eyes on the two presenters practising their plastic smiles to the arc of cameras that faced them, but she couldn't take her eyes off the man sitting in the shadows.

She had arrived at the Channel Seven building that nestled alongside the Thames at five o'clock – nearly two hours ago –

and settled into her usual routine of cursing the fates for landing her with a fabulously long-term job with fabulously antisocial hours, cursing the fact that her out-of-work boyfriend wouldn't be emerging from his bed for another two hours and cursing the fact that she lived in Finchley when the studios were in Teddington.

She had pulled a cup of foul-tasting black coffee from the vending machine in the corridor and shouldered open the door to the make-up room, pulling her tangle of dark hair into an untidy bun. Her assistant, Jackie, was already there, looking blonde, immaculate and disgustingly chirpy. The two of them had been deep in discussion of their respective weekends when Ben, the floor manager, had stuck his head around the door and tossed a copy of the day's schedule on to the desk.

'Change of plan. Home Secretary got cancelled. We've got Howard Chithros instead.'

Dee had looked at him hard. 'You're kidding. The guy who was on Channel Five last month? Dr "I-can-turn-back-the-hands-of-time-and-make-you-young-again". I wish.'

Ben had just grinned. 'And he actually did it last week. Beechy's creaming himself in the gallery. Twelve years he's been a producer with this company and this is the closest he's ever come to a scoop.'

The girls had grimaced and Ben had ducked back out into the bustle of the studio. An hour later Chithros's car had pulled up at reception and he had been ushered into make-up by Kevin, the studio director.

Dee had decided to deal with the make-up for Chithros herself – Jackie was more than capable of handling the two presenters. Tasmin and Nick Henderson were old pros from a family of old pros – lovely, but Dee had been doing their make-up for months and had heard all their stories. Doing the guests meant that she got to talk to someone new every day, and if Chithros could do what he said he could do, then he was going to be very, very rich.

He had been nothing like she imagined. She had expected a

slight, stooped academic. The truth was a handsome, powerful man with piercing eyes. He had slipped into the make-up chair and smiled dutifully as Kevin had fawned around him before scuttling off into the studio. Dee had settled into her best make-up patter to put him at ease, but something about the man had started to unsettle her as soon as she began talking to him.

'You must be a practised hand at this. Channel Five a month ago, *Exposé* last week and now us. You'll be having your own show before long.'

'Oh, I don't think I'll be going that far, but the publicity is always useful.'

He had smiled and caught her eye in the mirror. Dee had found herself inexplicably reddening and had rushed through the make-up, suddenly wanting to be rid of the man.

'You'll do,' she had said finally, standing back.

He had caught her wrist, gently but firmly.

'Could you just take the grey out of my beard. I know that I'm being dreadfully vain, but it seems inappropriate for the man who turned back death to be greying.'

And he had smiled again.

That had been half an hour ago. Now Chithros sat in the cool of the studio set, AFMs buzzing around him like flies, offering him cups of coffee, glasses of water – whatever he wanted. Dee stood behind the tangle of boom arms and cameras, watching. She sipped at her own coffee. Her hands were still shaking. Jackie was doing her last-minute checks on the presenters; meanwhile, Dee was loath to go near her guest again. She looked up at one of the monitors hanging from the ceiling. Chithros looked fine. Even from the screen those eyes blazed. She looked away and concentrated on her coffee, trying to control her shaking hands.

This show had brought her into contact with politicians, film stars and even terrorists on one controversial occasion, but no one had ever affected her as badly as this quiet, sinister doctor.

She added a curse about the studio's no-smoking policy to her morning list.

Ben stepped on to the set. 'On air in thirty seconds, studio. Good luck, everybody.'

The usual hush descended, all eyes on the studio clock ticking around to seven.

'Counting in, in five, four, three, two…'

Ben's arm swished under Camera One and the presenters settled into their practised routine.

'Good morning. It's 15 August 2067 and you're watching Breakfast with Channel Seven. I'm Nick…'

'…and I'm Tasmin Henderson. On today's show we talk to members of the new coalition government about their alleged car-bombing of the shadow defence secretary, and our political correspondent, Rocky Marshall, talks through the ramifications of the Cola wars that have killed thousands in South America.

'But first we have with us in the studio Dr Howard Chithros, who last week revolutionised our ideas about old age by proving that his new technique to roll back the years really does work.'

The lights had come up on Chithros and he had leaned forward to the camera.

For the next twenty minutes Dee watched as Chithros charmed interviewers and audience with his suave and educated manner, discussing his technique without actually revealing anything. Only once did a trace of anger cross his face, as Nick brought up his dealings with the new right-wing government.

'Certainly we have been talking. The last fifty years have seen a huge increase in the elderly population. People are living well into their nineties… their hundreds and beyond. State homes are costing the taxpayer millions. My technique will allow those aged, pathetic drains on our society to be reintegrated as vibrant, young members of the workforce.'

He leaned back in his chair, steepling his fingers. 'My process is not cosmetics for the ultra-rich, it is a social and economic miracle for all.'

Nick and Tasmin had smiled at each other and Tasmin leaned forward, touching Chithros on the knee.

'But really, Doctor. Have you truly achieved what man has searched for for decades or is this just a publicity stunt?'

Chithros's face was all innocence. 'Genetic tests bear me out. The babies you have seen are the same octogenarians who came in. What other explanation would you have? Time travel?'

When Chithros smiled, Dee suddenly realised where she had seen the smile before.

On natural history programmes.

It was the smile of a big cat.

The smile of a predator.

The Doctor stamped around the hole, snatching his hat off and hurling it to the ground.

'No, no, no!'

The pigeon settled on to a rock and regarded him solemnly.

'Don't get yerself into a tizzy. What's done is done.'

The Doctor bent down, his nose inches from the pigeon's beak.

'And have you any idea of what it is that you have done?'

'My job,' replied the pigeon shirtily. 'So there. Who are you to disagree?'

The Doctor reached behind the pigeon's neck feathers and produced a business card with an elegant embossed design on it. He placed it on the ground.

The pigeon looked at the card, cocking its head on one side.

'Oh, bugger.'

Chithros slid into the back of his limousine, waving aside the helping hands of Kevin. He pressed a button and the dark windows slid up, cutting out the garbled thanks of the studio director.

His driver peered at him from the front seat, tugging at his collar, uncomfortable in the August heat.

'Successful, sir?'

'Pathetic infantile poltroons, all of them,' Chithros snarled. 'This entire... publicity campaign –' he spat the words – 'is regrettable but necessary.'

He slumped back in the plush leather seats, eyes closed. His driver eyed him in the rear-view mirror.

'Are you all right, Doctor?'

'Just drive, Garth. Get me back to the house.'

The powerful hydrogen-turbine car leapt out of the car park and into the tide of rush-hour traffic. Chithros was motionless in the back seat. Garth could hear him breathing laboriously as the car hurled itself south.

He had seen his employer like this before, but each time it happened it got worse, and it was happening with increasing regularity. He was worried. Chithros was a strange man, of that there was no doubt, but he had treated Garth well. After jail no one had even considered him for work, but Chithros had found his criminal record – GBH and robbery – a positive asset.

Garth pushed the accelerator of the big BMW and the speedometer topped 110 mph. He tried to concentrate on the road and not on the guttural snarls emanating from the seat behind him.

Forty minutes later he pulled up at the front door of the sprawling old mansion house in Surrey and Chithros clawed his way out of the car and into the house. Garth watched as the hunched, barely human form of his employer vanished into the shadows. He sighed, slid the car into gear and rolled off towards the garage complex on the edge of the grounds.

Ace recovered from the shock of her new surroundings with remarkable speed. Too much time with the Doctor, she decided. Being transported from place to place in an instant was becoming commonplace.

Her companion, on the other hand, was hysterical. He was still gripping her shoulders, his face a mask of panic, and was screaming at her. Ace knew only one way of dealing with a hysterical man. She brought her knee up, hard.

As he collapsed with a high-pitched squeak, Ace took a long look at her surroundings. Dark wood, shuttered windows. She took a step and a floorboard groaned in protest. A spooky old house.

She frowned. 'If you've dropped me in it again, Professor, I'll bend your spoons.'

There was another squeak from her feet. She hauled the white-faced man to his feet and smiled at him. 'Sorry about that. I'm Ace.'

His voice was still a little shaky. 'Joe.' He looked at her pleadingly. 'Tell me what the hell's going on, please.'

'I wish I knew. But this obviously isn't the first time it has happened to you. Tell me…'

Joe explained about his earlier encounter with the house and its aged occupants. Ace nodded as if it all made sense. It made no sense, but if they were going to get back then they had better start sussing out what had happened.

'How much of the place did you get to see?'

'Not much.' Joe was squatting on the floor. 'I can't say that I was in an exploring mood. I just bumped into these old people and this humming door.'

'The door. Could you find your way back there?'

Joe looked around him. 'Maybe. Do you think that it might be something important?'

Ace shrugged. 'It's got to be worth a try.'

The two of them padded through the house. Occasional cracks in the shutters let in beams of blazing sunshine, but the house remained cool and gloomy.

Joe was hopelessly lost, completely incapable of recognising any features. Shock, Ace figured. She wasn't sure that he was going to cope at all.

They passed a doorway and Ace peered in. She caught Joe's arm. 'Look.'

The two of them crept into the room. Soft lights glowed from the wall and machines clicked and hummed soothingly.

The walls were lined with cots, each one holding a baby. Ace peered in at one of the sleeping children. It seemed peaceful enough. Then she noticed the drip.

The sleep wasn't natural, it was drugged.

She felt herself flush with anger. What sort of sick bastard would do this? Joe, meanwhile, was standing in the middle of the room holding his head. He was going to be as much use as a chocolate teapot.

'Come on.' She dragged Joe back out into the corridor. 'We're out of our depth here. Let's get out.'

'How? We've been walking in circles.'

Ace pointed at one of the shuttered windows. 'We know that they lead out.' She pulled at the heavy wood. Locked of course. She grabbed hard on the handle, braced her DMs on either side of the window and pulled hard.

There was a splintering crash and she collapsed backwards into the corridor, bits of rotten shutter in her hands, light streaming through the billowing dust. Joe looked down at her in disbelief. She pulled herself to her feet.

'Thanks for the help.'

Joe looked blank.

Ace sighed. 'Just pass me that chair, will you?'

Joe slid the tubular metal-framed chair across the floor to her and Ace hefted it in her hands, feeling the weight.

'Yeah, that'll do.'

Joe's eyes widened. 'You can't just...'

Ace spun like a discus thrower and the chair sailed through the tall, elegant window with a loud crash.

She jerked her thumb at the gaping hole in the glass. 'Come on, wimps and children first.'

\* \* \*

They were out in the open, squinting in the bright morning light. Ace scanned her surroundings. The grounds were extensive and she could see glimpses of a high wall. That didn't bode well.

She set off across the garden, keeping to the high shrubs and trees. There didn't seem to be anyone about but it didn't do any harm to be cautious.

Joe trailed behind her, catching his hair in the trees, snagging his clothes on the bushes and generally drawing attention to himself. Ace made a mental note to ditch him somewhere safe as soon as possible. She pushed a tangle of rhododendrons out of the way. There was the wall.

'Damn.'

It was twice as high as she had estimated and topped with vicious-looking razor wire.

'There must be a gate.' Joe sounded desperate.

Ace looked at him with disdain. 'And if the walls are like this, then the gate is probably guarded.'

'We can explain, can't we?'

'Oh yeah, course we can. Sorry, mate, we were attacked by a talking pigeon, vanished in a flash of light and suddenly found ourselves in your front room. That'll really help our case.'

Joe looked hurt and Ace kicked herself. She was being unfair. He was scared, shocked and out of his depth.

Her mind was racing, sifting possibilities, when a thin, reedy voice cut through the silence.

'Hey, like, what are you doing in the plants?'

Ace spun, dropping into a low crouch. Joe nearly jumped the wall.

Peering at them through the leaves, a pair of horn-rimmed spectacles and a curtain of long, grey-white hair, was a man. A hippie – an ageing hippie. No, Ace corrected herself, an *ancient* hippie. His face had more creases than his tie-dyed T-shirt and he was leaning on a gnarled hawthorn walking-stick. He waved the stick at them.

'I know it says "Keep off the grass", but that, like, means the plants too.'

Ace and Joe scrambled out of the rhododendrons. The hippie stood looking at them.

'Sorry, mate.' Ace decided to play the innocent. 'We got a bit lost. Just trying to get out.'

'You're telling me you're lost. No way, man. No one gets in here. It can't be done.'

'Someone left a gate open?' Ace smiled.

The hippie pulled his spectacles down his nose and peered over the top of them. 'How am I supposed to keep things cool if strange chicks keep trampling through the shrubbery? I mean... flowers, man. Stepping on flowers is like, well...' He tottered over to the flowerbed and began raking the soil with the end of his stick.

Another voice made Ace start.

'Otto? Otto, are you out here?'

This voice was younger, harsher and, Ace decided, considerably more threatening. She grasped Joe by the hand and the two of them hared back towards the house.

The Doctor sat cross-legged in the attic of Joe's flat, tinkering with a small, intricate piece of equipment on the floor in front of him. It resembled an upright cylinder, slightly narrower at the top than the bottom. At first glance it might have been mistaken for a can of baked beans. Except that it was black. Except for the nodules and filaments that covered its surface. And except for the fact it was about a thousand times heavier, made of one of the densest alloys known in this part of the galaxy.

The pigeon sat on a shelf watching him. The Doctor gave it a venomous glance. Virgoans. A race of shape-shifting, biomechanical symbiotes with an obsession for temporal tidiness. The Time Lords knew about them – you could hardly ignore them given the chaos they had caused over the centuries.

The Virgoans were excellent at discovering temporal

anomalies and fixing them; fixing them badly, but with unbounded enthusiasm. The Time Lords had tried to stop them, but without much success.

The Doctor sighed. The temporal equivalent of cowboy builders.

The pigeon had followed him back to the flat, where he had made himself a cup of tea and demanded an explanation.

'We're a survey team. We were carrying out a routine temporal check in the Mutter's Spiral. We detected an anomaly here on Earth and came to investigate.'

'We?'

'We… I… Don't forget I'm a Virgoan. Ship, pilot, probe. There are three of me… us. It can get confusing at times.'

'I know the problem,' said the Doctor. 'There are thirteen of me. You're the probe, I take it?'

'I'm the probe, yes.'

'And you decided that assuming the form of a talking pigeon would be nicely inconspicuous.'

'I was one of those little stripy things to begin with,' it said. 'Yellow and black…' The Doctor could faintly hear the buzz of its tiny micro-processor brain. 'A wasp. That's right. But people kept running away from me. Trying to swipe me with newspapers. It was no picnic, I can tell you. This is much better.'

They had eventually found dozens of small-scale anomalies, the pigeon explained. Not much on the temporal scheme of things, just a few individuals displaced by eighty years or so. Joe had been the first of the anomalies to be 'fixed'.

'It's this gubbins.' The pigeon nodded at the instrument at the Doctor's feet. 'Time anchor. Holds the subject in a state of temporal stability. Fixes him in one time period. The tachyon field…'

'I know how a time anchor works, thank you –' the Doctor's voice was icy – 'but I can't seem to activate this one.'

'Course not.' The pigeon puffed itself up proudly. 'I'm jamming it.'

'Well, kindly unjam it!'

'No.'

The Doctor closed his eyes and took a deep breath. 'Look, the girl that you transported belongs in this time period. By keeping her in the future, you're creating another anomaly.'

'Ah, but we'll be around in eighty years to fix that.'

'But the fact that she isn't back already means that you *didn't* fix it in eighty years' time.'

The pigeon scratched its head. 'Are you sure it works like that? Temporal paradoxes were never my strong point. I was never good on theory.'

The Doctor suppressed an urge to throttle the little probe.

'Then perhaps you'd better introduce me to a member of your crew who is.'

'Ah...' The pigeon looked bashful.

The Doctor's heart sank. Surely things couldn't get any worse.

'What do you mean, "Ah"?'

'Perhaps I'd better just show you.'

The Doctor stood in the middle of a small park, looking in despair at the tangle of vegetable, animal and mineral that had once been the rest of the Virgoan symbiote. Trees crowded around the egg-shaped hull of the ship, arcing over it, their branches plunging through the fuselage. The whole thing seemed to writhe and ripple – sunlight glinted off bark which momentarily seemed more metallic than organic, breaking and drifting, shimmering like the scales of a fish before once more becoming hard, dark wood. The hull itself rolled back like melting ice-crystals or crumbled like dead leaves before closing again, hard and metallic. Inside the Doctor could see the pilot, motionless, rooted – quite literally – to his seat.

The pigeon landed on the Doctor's hat.

'See what I mean, guv? Bit of a mess, ain't it?'

'What on earth have you three been doing?'

The pigeon hopped to the floor.

'We detected on anomaly on Melandra IV, landed to have a quick shuftie…'

'…and discovered that Melandra IV is in the midst of a major Krynoid infestation.'

The Doctor covered his face with his hands.

'Yeah, got infected as soon as we landed. Auto-repair kicked in immediately, but every time we try to shape-shift the Krynoid part fights back.' The probe sighed. 'And the anomaly was just an abandoned Androgum egg-timer.' It managed the pigeon equivalent of a frown. 'Still like to know where that came from.'

The Doctor crossed to the tangle of machine and plant. He could see the surface shimmer as the battle for dominance raged at a cellular level. Mutation was met by counter-mutation, symbiote cells being changed to Krynoid cells and back again. The creature was using all its energy for the battle. He was amazed that the symbiote had ever made it from Melandra to Earth; the strain must have completely unhinged it. Only the probe seemed unaffected.

There was a squawk and the Doctor looked down at where the pigeon was trying to unwrap a discarded stick of chewing gum. Well, he corrected himself, relatively unaffected.

He was about to lecture the probe about the dangers of bringing a Krynoid organism to an inhabited planet when he noticed a figure sitting on the far side of the tangled copse.

Leaving the pigeon to its chewing gum, the Doctor strolled over to the cross-legged figure. It was a young man in his early twenties, dressed in the uniform of a park keeper, but the waist length-hair and sandals certainly weren't council regulation. The man's jacket was covered in sewn-on flowers and the name Otto was embroidered on the back in different-coloured threads.

'Good morning. I'm the Doctor.' He doffed his hat, frowning at the pigeon feathers that fluttered down around him. 'You're Otto, I gather.'

The hippie looked up at him.

'Hi, Doctor.' He gestured at the symbiote. 'Just wild. Smoke?'

He held out a fat roll-up. The Doctor shook his head. Otto was in serious danger, but seemed blissfully unaware of it. While the symbiote held the Krynoid in check there was little to worry about, but if the Krynoid part became dominant...

'You should have seen that.' Otto gestured towards a huge tree lying on its side in the park. 'Walking trees, if you can believe it. Better than Hallowe'en.'

The Doctor crossed to the fallen trunk. There was a trail of earth and roots scattered across the grass and part of the perimeter hedge had been crushed. The Doctor nodded slowly, thoughtfully. The hole in the ground. The missing tree. The Krynoid intelligence had started to gain the upper hand in the night and had begun to animate the surrounding vegetable matter.

He had less time than he thought.

He turned back towards Otto, to see the pigeon taking a drag from his joint. Jamming his hat back on to his head, the Doctor strode across to him and snatched up the pigeon. 'Excuse me. Must dash.'

With the pigeon squawking and complaining in his grasp, he scurried out of the park.

Otto watched him go. 'Just wild.'

Ace pulled the remains of the shutters back into place over the shattered window. It didn't pay to advertise their presence any more than they had, and having a ready-made escape route could prove useful.

She headed off down a darkened corridor.

Joe scurried after her. 'Where are we going?'

'Other side of the house. I got a good look at it from the outside and I think we've been walking in circles around one wing. Let's try the other one.'

Ace strode through the darkened corridors with Joe in tow. She had a pretty good idea of the layout of the house now – huge and sprawling. It was no wonder Joe had got lost.

They turned into another hallway and Joe gripped her shoulder.

'Listen.'

Ace shook herself free of his grasp. 'What?'

'Just listen.'

There was a humming, mechanical and regular, almost like a heartbeat, coming from the end of the hall.

'That's the noise I heard.'

'Right, now we're getting somewhere.'

The two of them crept towards the sound. The insistent throbbing was beginning to give Ace a headache.

'That's the one.' Joe indicated a heavy oak door. 'I recognise the armour.'

Ace touched the door. It was vibrating. She reached out for the handle and turned it.

The door swung inwards, creaking alarmingly. The room was bathed in the same soft glow they had encountered in the nursery, but here the noise was deafening. The walls were lined with coffin-like receptacles, each one holding a wizened ancient body. Tubes and cables snaked their way up the walls and across the ceiling to a huge complex of machinery that hung from the roof.

Beneath the tangle of technology was a throne-like chair on a raised dais. Thin tubes wound from ceiling to chair, coiling around the figure that sat in it.

Ace and Joe crept forward, hands clamped over their ears to try to cut out the dreadful pounding.

Suddenly and completely, the noise stopped. The silence was almost as deafening. The figure in the chair stood up. Joe stifled a scream as the eyes of the man raked across him, yellow and slitted, like a cat's. As he watched, they changed, becoming human now. Dark, smouldering with malevolence, but recognisably human. The man transferred his gaze to Ace.

'The Doctor's young companion! What a delightful, if unexpected pleasure.'

Joe clung to her arm. 'You know him?'

Ace nodded.

'I'd refer to him as "that bearded git", but I think he prefers to be called the Master.'

He walked around them in a slow circle. His eyes focused again on Joe.

'Why are you here?'

'You tell me, bogface,' Ace retorted.

'I wasn't addressing you,' came the reply. 'Number Seven.'

Still holding her arm, Ace felt Joe suddenly go rigid. He was staring straight ahead. Staring at nothing.

'Report,' the Master barked.

'I…' There was a flicker of movement in Joe's eyes. He seemed confused. 'I don't know…'

'Twice now your time anchor has failed. I must know why.'

'There was a bird… A pigeon.'

'A pigeon!' Fury stalked the edge of the Master's voice.

'It talked… It said something about…'

'Concentrate,' the Master hissed.

'Temporal anomalies… And then… she turned up… with a little man.'

The Master turned again to Ace.

'Look, mate, I'm as much in the dark as you seem to be.'

He thought for a moment. 'Yes…' he murmured. 'Yes, I believe you. However, I can't believe the same is true of your meddling friend the Doctor.' He appeared to snap to a decision. 'Take her to the west wing,' he said to Joe. 'Restrain her.'

'Joe… what are you…'

Joe swung around in front of her and grabbed her other arm. His grip was painful now. She couldn't move. His eyes stared blankly ahead of him.

'What are you going to do to me?' Ace shouted as, blank-eyed, Joe dragged her towards the door.

'Nothing,' the Master replied. 'I'm going to wait. With you as my captive, the Doctor will have to reveal his hand soon enough.'

\* \* \*

'So this is a TARDIS then.'

The quiet hum of the control room was punctuated by the insistent flapping of the pigeon's wings as it circled the Doctor.

'Will you be quiet,' the Doctor snapped. 'I'm trying to concentrate.' He was poring over a screen set into the central console, punching buttons.

'Never been inside one before. Can't say I'm very impressed. Mind if I have a poke around inside your time rotor?'

'Yes,' said the Doctor. 'I do mind. Go and perch yourself somewhere.'

The pigeon did a final circuit of the room, then settled on the hatstand which stood in a corner.

'What you up to anyway?' the pigeon asked.

'I'm trying to locate the other time anchor.'

'Why didn't you say so?' the bird squawked. 'I can tell you that. I sent your friend there, didn't I?'

It flapped over to the console and began pecking with breathless speed at a row of buttons on the console. Numbers tumbled across the readout screen.

'There you go, boss,' the bird said. 'Just fire 'er up and Bob's yer uncle.'

'Hmm.'

The Doctor initiated the dematerialisation sequence.


'Joe... Joe, you've got to listen to me.'

They were locked in a small, wood-panelled room. The one window was barred. Joe stood, motionless and expressionless, in front of the door. Ace had done her best to free herself from him when, at the Master's direction, he had dragged her here. She had kneed him in the groin a second time, much harder than the first. She had felt something crunch as her knee connected but he hadn't flinched. He hadn't felt it. The Doctor had told Ace about the Master's hypnotic abilities.

'Joe... Please listen. He's controlling you. The Master is controlling your mind.'

Was that a flicker of response?

She tried again. 'This is all wrong. You shouldn't be here. Neither of us should. Why is the Master controlling you?'

'Dr Chithros… He… I…'

'What did you call him?'

'He…'

'Listen to me. You don't belong here. Your name is Joe. You live in a flat in Croydon, remember? There's a dirty great hole in your back yard.'

'No… I… I'm… Number Seven…' His voice, tremulous at first, appeared to flatten out. 'I am Number Seven. My function is to carry out the Chithros programme.'

'No… Look…' She reached forward, into the pocket of his jacket. 'I'll show you.'

He must have some ID on him.

Her hand closed on something flat and irregularly shaped. She snatched it back – a high-pitched bleeping was coming from the pocket. A tune. 'On Top of Old Smoky', for God's sake. She reached into his pocket again and lifted out the object. She turned it around in her hand. It was a plastic key-ring, cut into the shape of Yosemite Sam. On one side the cartoon character glowered at her, six guns raised; on the other was embossed the name of the manufacturer. Innovations Unlimited. It was the key-ring that was playing the tune.

Suddenly Joe's breathing sounded strained and irregular. His eyes flicked between Ace and the musical trinket she was holding. A memory struggled to surface. His expression seemed to clear – then instantly to cloud over again. His face crumpled with sudden, slow pain. His hands closed around his groin. Letting out a long, low moan, he sank to the floor.

Ace vaulted over Joe's slumped form, wrenched the door open and bounded through. A narrow, gloomy corridor stretched ahead of her. At its far end it split into two. For no very good reason, Ace took the right-hand fork. The corridor split again. The house was a warren. She was getting hopelessly lost.

No… Here was something she recognised. A picture on the wall. A seascape. She'd definitely seen it before. This was where…

She pushed open a door to her left. Pale, even light greeted her. The soothing hum of machinery. In their cots, fed by tubes, a dozen babies dozed.

The sound of the TARDIS materialising startled her. She swung around to see the familiar blue box wheezing into corporeal existence at the corridor's end. She ran forward as the door opened and the Doctor emerged, straightening his battered hat, the pigeon flapping excitedly around his head.

'Oh dearie me,' the pigeon squawked. 'I can't be doing with this. I'm anomalous. I'm eighty years out. I'll be struck off for this. This is gross professional misconduct.'

'Doctor,' Ace called, ignoring the bird, 'what the hell's going on?'

'Ah,' said the Doctor, 'I was rather hoping you could tell me that.'

An old lady shuffled past, inching her way along the corridor on a walking-frame. The Doctor raised his hat, a puzzled look on his face. The old dear didn't seem to notice him or Ace.

'The Master's here,' said Ace.

The Doctor's face was suddenly grave. He flapped irritably at the bird with his hat.

'Except now he's calling himself something else,' Ace continued. 'I think he's posing as some kind of doctor. I don't know. There's all these old people around – it's a bit like a home here – and look…'

She pushed open the door behind which the babies slumbered. The Doctor stepped through and walked across to the nearest infant.

'Sleeping,' he murmured.

'Yes, but…' Ace motioned to the pipe which snaked into the baby's arm. The Doctor examined the tube, tracing its path to a wall-mounted plastic container, black, flickering with coloured lights. He eased the tube from the container and tested its contents with his fingers and lips.

'Nutrients,' the Doctor said.

'Nutrients?'

'The sort of thing you would find in human milk, I suspect. We're eighty years ahead of your time, Ace, this is the way babies are fed. There's nothing abnormal about this.'

'I thought they were drugged.'

'Yes, there's probably a mild sedative in there. Another practice common to this age. It's not harmful.'

'But why would the Master be running a crèche?'

'Or an old people's home, for that matter. I don't know, Ace. And it worries me. Where's our friend from Croydon, by the way?'

'Joe... I left him on the floor of one of the rooms. He... had an accident. He'll recover. The Master's controlling him.'

'I see...' He stuffed his hat into his pocket. 'I think we should look around a bit, don't you?'


'This is it, Professor.'

They were standing outside the heavy door to the room of the coffins. Behind the door machinery still throbbed quietly – the only sound in the noiseless house. Beside them the suit of armour stood to silent attention.

'He was in here...' Ace whispered, slowly turning the door handle. It clicked heavily as she did so.

'Quiet, Ace,' the Doctor whispered, attempting to slip around her. 'Let me...'

He tripped, colliding with the suit of armour – which rocked against the wall with a clash which reverberated down the still corridor – and bumping Ace. The door to the room swung open and she fell through.

'It's all right,' she said after a breathless moment. 'There's no one here.'

It was true – barring the ancient bodies which lay in their

coffins along the walls. The Doctor scuttled from one to another.

'Dreadful,' he muttered to himself. 'Quite dreadful.'

'Are they dead?' asked Ace.

'No,' the Doctor replied. 'But they're barely alive. There's nothing I can do for them.' His eyes narrowed. 'This is obscene.'

Tutting to himself, he let his eyes follow the tubes and wires which writhed from the coffins, snaking across the ceiling of the room before disappearing into a metal cowling and re-emerging, cascading down into the back of the throne – now empty – which sat at the room's centre.

'Typical of the Master,' he said. 'A grandiose design for a filthy machine.'

'What's he doing here?'

'Oh, he's draining off certain vital fluids – enzymes, proteins, that sort of thing – from these poor people. Presumably he's then feeding them to himself. He seems to be able to control the rate at which they produce what he needs and siphon it off whenever he needs it. He's ill.'

'Doctor, his eyes… They were… different for a while. You know how he was on the cheetah people's planet.'

'Yes, that would explain it. He's still infected by the cheetah virus. Presumably it's at quite an advanced stage now. Hence the old people out there giving him what he needs.'

'But what about the babies?'

'I don't know, Ace.' His voice was strained. 'I just don't know.'

'Well, look what we've got here,' the pigeon cut in. 'The great-granddaddy of them all.'

It was at the far end of the room, flapping around a huge, black machine, like a cylinder, narrower at the top than the bottom, which filled one of the room's corners. The Doctor moved across to examine it.

'What's Tweetie Pie on about?' asked Ace.

'It's a time anchor, Ace. There's a much smaller one in our friend's flat in Croydon. This seems to be a central relay point for a large number of anchors. What is he up to?'

The door creaked open. The Doctor and Ace spun around.

'Ace…'

Joe stood, a little unsteadily, in the doorway.

'Ah yes…' The Doctor scurried across the room, his hand extended. 'It's Joe, isn't it? I'm the Doctor.' He shook Joe vigorously by the hand, while at the same time peering deep into his eyes.

'Will someone tell me what's going on…'

'Yes…' the Doctor mused. 'All the signs of deep hypnosis. Still, something seems to have cut through the programming. I'm afraid we're all caught up in a rather tricky situation. I'm going to try to sort it out, but I need your co-operation. Ace…'

The Doctor talked rapidly, all the time sifting through his thoughts. The pigeon fluttered and pecked at the massive time anchor. There was a loud, angry electronic burble from the machine, followed by a squawk from the bird.

'Will you please leave things alone?'

'I'm anomalous, don't you see?' the bird twittered. 'Maybe I can use this to get back to my proper time, say nothing about this to anybody, hope I'm not rumbled.'

'I think you have more important things to worry about. Are you forgetting the state of your ship and pilot?'

He turned to Ace. 'There's another problem,' he said. 'An alien life form – vegetable – a thing called a Krynoid. The Master's not the only one fighting an infection.'

'What?' Sometimes the Doctor made no sense at all to Ace.

'The question is, how do I deal with both…'

He began rummaging around in the capacious pockets of his jacket.

'I think,' he muttered, 'I think I'd better try to bring all of our problems under one roof…' He pulled out an old pocket watch, and then a second, identical one. 'Ace,' he said, 'I'm going to have to ask you and Joe to do something rather dangerous.'

* * *

Ten minutes later the Doctor was crouched between two of the coffins. The pigeon sat on his knee, with the Doctor's hand firmly clamped over its beak.

The door opened and a figure entered. The Doctor smiled grimly. The Master.

He watched his old adversary making adjustments to the time anchor. It began emitting a high-pitched, barely audible tone. The air in front of it seemed to shimmer – and a woman faded in from nowhere. She was middle-aged, typically British, late twentieth century in dress and appearance. Her manner was quite at odds with her appearance. She stared ahead of her out of wide, blank eyes. In her arms she held a baby.

She stood, motionless, where she had appeared.

'Carry on, Number Twelve,' the Master purred.

Without looking at him, the woman carried the baby to the door and out of the room.

The Master crossed to his throne-like seat and keyed in something on a control panel. The Doctor felt the coffins on either side of him begin to hum and vibrate lightly.

'Time for your medicine, is it?' said the Doctor, rising to his feet and stepping into the room. 'What would you call this?' He gestured to the coffins. 'Setting the cat among the pigeons?'

The Master seemed to pause slightly before turning to face his old enemy, a warm smile beneath his dark beard.

'Cat among the pigeons… Oh yes, very good. Always a pleasure, Doctor,' he beamed.

'The pleasure is all yours,' the Doctor replied acidly. 'What are you doing here?'

'Enjoying my retirement?' the Master offered hopefully.

'Like the poor souls in those coffins,' the Doctor spat. 'Is that what they thought they were coming here for? A quiet retirement?'

The Master laughed genially. 'I've received no complaints, Doctor. Quite the contrary, I have a waiting list of several hundred people. They're clamouring to get in here.'

'To be fed into that thing,' countered the Doctor.

'To be granted the wish of every man and woman, Doctor. To be given a fresh start. The chance to live their lives over again.'

'What do you mean? What are you doing?' The Doctor's voice was dark with menace.

The Master strolled across the room and opened a cupboard.

'Enjoying the fruits of celebrity,' he said. He turned and handed the Doctor a periodical. 'I made the cover of *Time* magazine.'

'So I see,' said the Doctor, flicking through the pages. 'Dr Howard Chithros...' His face darkened as he read. 'And people actually believe all this?'

'Why, yes, Doctor. People fear death. They come here old and I make them young again.'

'That's preposterous,' spat the Doctor. 'Even we Time Lords can't reverse the effects of ageing.'

'And yet they leave here as babes in arms, Doctor, ready to live their lives again. The most sophisticated DNA testing bears me out.'

'This is more despicable than I thought,' said the Doctor. 'You're kidnapping them as babies and bringing them forward in time to cover for the fact that you're murdering them as old people.'

'I'm providing a practical solution to the problems of the modern age. I'm giving hope to the hopeless. Do you know, I'm getting inquiries from younger and younger people. Men begin to develop a paunch... they start to lose their hair... and they come to me. Of course, at the moment I'm only authorised to process the elderly, but I'm deep in consultation with the government. It makes a change to have the law on my side.'

'I'll have to stop you, of course,' said the Doctor.

'Of course, of course,' smiled the Master. 'By the way, where is your young friend and Mr Dakin.'

'I've sent them back,' said the Doctor.

'Most kind,' said the Master. 'Number Seven has a job to do there.' He gestured around the spartan laboratory. 'I'm sorry I can't offer you a seat. Shall we retire to somewhere more comfortable? Take a little sherry, perhaps?'

'I'll sit here,' said the Doctor, slipping into the futuristic throne. 'You go and get the sherry.'

The Master tensed. 'Get out of there, Doctor.'

The Doctor began tinkering with the seat's controls.

'Doctor…'

He swung suddenly away from the little Time Lord. He was breathing fast. 'One thing you should know about my affliction,' he said. 'Every day it becomes harder to combat, more difficult to control. The feral instinct becomes irresistible in times of stress.'

He swung back to face the Doctor, his eyes blazing with feline malice – sharp black slits set into livid yellow orbs.

'And you know how stressful my life is, Doctor,' he snarled.

He sprang at the Doctor, who threw himself from the throne. A hand raked across his face – a clawed hand, yellowing with fur. He rolled across the floor and sprang to his feet, spinning around as he did so. The Master was on top of him instantly, his smile vicious now, saliva dripping from the corners of his mouth, his teeth like needles. He swiped at the Doctor with a paw, smacking him into the wall. Another blow followed instantly, sending him reeling across the room and into the wall.

He's playing with me, thought the Doctor. Like a cat playing with a mouse.

Perched on the edge of one of the coffins in which the old people lay so near to death, the pigeon hopped from leg to leg, flapping its wings occasionally and keeping up a constant stream of useful advice. 'Keep your guard up,' it piped to the Doctor. 'Give 'im the old one-two. Down in the third.'

The Doctor shot the Virgoan a lightning glance. Its mental state seemed to be getting worse. He fingered his pocket watch. He only hoped the pigeon would know what to do when the time came.

Gathering himself, he prepared for the Master's next assault. He was amazed to find himself still alive. He wasn't sure how much longer he could keep the beast at bay, but he had to give Ace and Joe time.

'Up and under!' the pigeon squawked from somewhere behind him. 'Public warning!'

He spun around. The Master was closing on him, claws bared and gleaming.

Joe sat on the edge of his settee and shakily lit a cigarette. The room still bore the marks of the pigeon's destructive presence. Droppings and books lay everywhere. So the nightmare was still going on. The girl was still here.

'Look, we've got to get a move on,' she said, studying the pocket watch. 'Fifteen minutes the Doctor said. We've got to get to the park.'

'I don't understand any of this,' Joe moaned.

'It's quite simple. We've got to get to the park and find this overgrown Brussels sprout. The Professor reckons maybe he can use the Master's equipment to separate it from the symbiote ship, and we've got to get it back there. In other words, we've got to get hold of it – or rather you have – at the exact time when the Doctor triggers the time anchor to pull you back into the future. Simple. Are you thick, or what?'

Still shaking his head, Joe allowed himself to be pulled from his seat and ushered out of the room, then out of the flat.

'This thing we've… I've… got to get hold of, is it dangerous?'

'Apparently, yeah,' said Ace. 'You hang on to it too long and it'll eat you. Which way's the park?'

They walked down several streets in silence. Joe seemed steadier on his feet now but distracted. Ace could scarcely blame him.

'Left here,' Joe said suddenly.

'But according to the sign back there…'

'This is a short cut,' Joe snapped, and strode swiftly across the road.

Ace jogged to keep up with him. Soon Joe was running.

'Slow down,' called Ace, falling back. Something was wrong.

Ahead she watched Joe turn into a doorway. The sign above the door read 'Meadows Crèche and Kindergarten'. As she pushed through the door after him, he was already in conversation with a receptionist, his voice calm, even and charming.

'Yes, I'm afraid my wife is indisposed. She did telephone… Of course, I'd been meaning to pay a visit before now.' As he spoke, he stared fixedly at the woman and smiled.

'Do give your wife our regards, Mr Norris,' the receptionist replied. 'Such a charming woman… Ah, here's the little darling now.'

A matronly woman came through a door in the far wall, carrying a baby.

Ace's mind was in turmoil. How could they just hand over a baby like this? 'No!' she cried, seeing images of the sleeping children lashed to tubes and wires. She sprang forward and snatched the baby from the woman's fat hands. Pivoting on her heel, she spun and ran through the main door, clutching the crying bundle to her chest.

Her feet hammered the pavement as she ran. Risking a look behind her, she saw Joe, standing in the entrance to the kindergarten, looking around in confusion. The staff were emerging behind him, flustered, flapping. Joe's disorientation lasted only a moment before, catching sight of her, he too began to run.

She had to keep ahead of him… get to the park. What she was going to do there, she didn't know. She darted across the road. A horn blared and a driver yelled something at her.

The park was close now. She could see railings and a high hedge – too high to climb. In the distance she could see the park gates and behind she could see Joe, still running, his eyes fixed on her.

She threw herself through the open gates, then stopped dead. There, across the rolling lawn, was a dark, dense clump of trees which appeared to be... wrestling with itself... That had to be the Krynoid thing.

Behind the hedge she could hear Joe's running feet. She set off across the grass, vaulting over a hippie who was sitting on the edge of the dancing, pulsating copse.

'Hey, be cool...' the hippie called after her.

Gingerly, she approached the edge of the trees. Through the tangle of trunks and branches she could see a denser mass. Ace was reminded of the speeded-up footage of plants growing that they often showed on Sunday night TV. Thick waves of tough-looking vegetable matter were rolling and receding across the surface of the thing. Every so often bright, metallic, almost crystalline spores would break through the green like an infestation, before another green wave broke.

She picked her way through the mass of trees and bushes which crowded around the thing, bending towards it, their branches hugging and merging with it.

Joe was close behind. He threw himself into the thicket, clutching for the baby. Ace dodged around a tree and struggled to get her breath back. In here she had the edge on him – she was smaller and more agile. She drew the watch from her pocket. Less than a minute to go. She backed towards the Krynoid.

Joe lunged again and again she side-stepped him. He was now between her and the alien battle raging in the middle of the trees. She moved back, a thick wall of bark and leaves pressed against her back. The whole thing seemed to be contracting. The trees were moving ever closer together and she was being pushed towards Joe. Suddenly there was nowhere to go.

The Doctor had nowhere to go. He was cornered between two of the coffins. He was exhausted and he was bleeding.

The Master – what was left of the Master – grinned savagely. In this condition he was much faster than the Doctor and much stronger.

The Master surged forward. Only one thing to do. The Doctor dived for his enemy's legs, then hit the floor and rolled under the coffin on his right. The Master snarled in surprise and swiped at empty air.

The Doctor was on all fours now, crawling and slithering beneath the ranks of coffins, pushing curtains of wires and feeder tubes apart with his hands. The Master, for all his new-found agility, was bigger than the Doctor. He stalked the edge of the coffin line, purring with quiet, ready malevolence, the hunter waiting for his prey to break cover.

There was no time left. The Doctor knew only too well the Master's intentions. Still, he had to act now. For Ace. For Joe. He had worked his way from coffin to coffin until he was as close as he could get to the time anchor. The Master had stalked him all the way. Everything was up to the bird now.

'Now!' he yelled.

'What? Oh, right you are, boss.'

It rose from its perch in a flurry of feathers and circled the room twice, at speed, before settling on the arm of the Master's chair. Its feet danced over the chair's control pad. Lights flickered and the machine started to buzz alarmingly.

With an angry hiss, the Master turned and loped across to his throne. His clawed hands were clumsy on the controls. The pigeon rose into the air.

Perfect. The Doctor rolled from under the coffin and ran across to the time anchor. He scanned its surface controls. There was no time for subtlety. He began frantically pressing buttons – maximum spread, maximum power – and the machine hummed into life.

Behind him he heard the Master growl. His eyes were fixed on the Doctor. Cat-like, he sprang forward.

There was only one thing to do and Ace didn't want to do it.

Cradling the baby against her chest, she ran forward, yelling, cannoning into Joe. The three of them tumbled backwards, tripping over tree roots, falling headlong into the belly of the alien machine and its plant parasite.

There was a sharp crack and a blinding, dizzying light. She felt nausea welling and the world starting to spin.

Otto sat, cross-legged on the grass, where he had been sitting most of the day. His Parks Department lawn mower stood idle beside him. The woods rippled in front of him like a psychedelic lake.

There was a sudden burst of light from the trees. The whole copse glowed harshly white for a moment, dazzling him. When the spots had left his eyes his jaw dropped. He crawled forward on the grass. Where the copse had been there was now only a hole. Root and branch, the whole thing had vanished. Looking down into the gash in the earth, he could see drainage pipes breaking through the south London clay, then disappearing into it again.

'Oh, no way, man...' he drawled. 'No way...'

A frantic fluttering broke the spell of the awful moment. The Doctor stepped back, startled. His assailant stopped dead in his tracks. The pigeon was in the Master's face, beating with its wings, clutching with its clawed feet, pecking with its beak.

The moment was all the Doctor needed. He scrambled around the time anchor and made for the relative safety of the coffins. He turned in time to see a cat's claw swipe with instinctive ease at the pigeon, sending it tumbling to the ground.

The air in the room started to shimmer and warp. His plan was working. People – a portly man in a business suit, a policewoman – were beginning to appear in the room. They stared about them in confusion. Half a dozen. More. They kept on appearing. The Master turned from one to another of them, a look of fury twisting his now barely human features.

A deep rumbling, a creaking, cracking, the sound of

splintering stone and rending metal, cut across the confusion of the room. The entire outside wall of the lab buckled for a moment before exploding into fragments. In its place sat a seething mass of vegetable matter, intertwined with flowing, crawling rivulets of metal. Green tentacles thrashed around it, smashing equipment. The duel between plant and machine creature raged on.

The first thing Ace felt as the world spun sickeningly back into reality was a sharp pain in her back. She was lying entangled in a rose bush. Joe lay beneath her, crouched in a foetal position. The baby was still clutched in her arms. It started to wail.

'Come on,' she said to Joe, hauling herself to her feet.

'What… Where…'

'Oh, forget it,' she said.

There was no time to baby-sit Joe. She had to find the Doctor. She had to find somewhere to put the baby.

Beside them the Krynoid/Virgoan hybrid tore at itself. It had materialised half-way through the wall, which now lay in rubble about it. Maybe she could climb through…

'Waaak!'

A bird was flapping around her head. The pigeon, covered in brick dust, circled her erratically.

'Where's the Doctor?' she bellowed at the bird.

'Waaak!' came the reply. The bird went into a spastic dive and hit the ground beside her.

'Great,' she muttered, looking around her. Some yards away was an ornamental fountain, disused. That would have to do. She carried the baby across and gently placed it the dry basin. 'You'll be OK,' she whispered.

She turned back to the house and its alien wrecking-crew. She tried to pick her way towards the ruined wall, peering into the darkness of the lab beyond.

She felt the earth shake beneath her. There was a great swelling of the ground, which knocked her to her feet. A wave

111

was passing beneath the lawns of the house, breaking them open. The ground at her feet split in two and she felt herself falling, clawing at soil and rubble as the chasm swallowed her. She crashed to a halt on a bed of writhing roots and electrical cables. She flinched as they whipped past her head, knotting themselves around each other. If one of those cables broke…

The rip in the earth was widening. With a sickening intake of breath she watched the old stone fountain sliding into it. She tried desperately to push forward, but root systems barred her way.

'I'm sorry…' she whispered, her eyes blurring with dirt and tears.

'Are you all right down there, babe?'

A voice, incredibly old yet young, a lazy, nasal drawl. The old hippie gardener, Otto, looked down on her from above.

'Look what I just found,' he continued. 'Far out…' In his arms he cradled the baby.

Ace's heart surged. 'Get the baby out of here!' she shouted.

'Be cool,' Otto drawled. 'Be cool.'

In the lab everything was happening fast. Through the maelstrom the Master's mind seemed to be closing down, narrowing its focus to one thing. His gaze was fixed on his old enemy – he seemed to care about nothing else. He sprang on to the edge of one of the coffins, then launched himself through the air. The Doctor tried to scurry for cover. A claw raked down his back, opening the cloth of his jacket, his jumper, his shirt, his skin, like a razor. He felt the dampness of his own blood first, then – almost slowly – the pain. He fell to the floor and rolled on to his back. The Master crouched over him. His whole body seemed to have changed shape. His torso was long, his back arched. He moved on all fours with ease.

There was nothing rational left in that face.

'Wait…' The Doctor talked fast, knowing he was talking for his life. 'Think about this. Look at yourself. How much more of this can you take? How much longer before the beast takes over for good? Every time it gets stronger… you told me that. Will this be the last time?'

The creature seemed to hesitate. Its breath was hot and rank on the Doctor's face. Its claws were inches from his throat.

'I know how much you want me dead – how much you've always wanted me dead – but think. Is this what you've waited so long for? This isn't revenge. This isn't even cruel. This is just bestial. Maybe I'm your last link. If you kill me like a savage animal, maybe that link will be broken. Maybe you'll never get back. Are you hearing me? Is there anything left in there?'

Its stubby, furred fingers were on his throat now, claws pressing into his skin, raising little points of blood, pinpricks of pain, where they touched. It could have carved the Doctor up like a piece of fruit.

Instead it hesitated. Something other than mere bloodlust flickered through the dark slits of its eyes.

'Fight it…' the Doctor urged.

With a snarl it hurled itself back across the room, leaping over the Krynoid's thrashing tentacles with ease, bounding into the chair which sat at the centre of the feed mechanism. Its claws skidded on the controls. The machine throbbed into life. Fluid links filled and emptied and filled again. The coffins vibrated lightly. The Doctor closed his eyes. Those poor, doomed people…

The Master's chair was bathed in light. The fur seemed to be receding, as if burrowing into the skin. His eyes were losing their animal gleam, returning to normal.

'Garth!' he shouted. 'Garth!'


'This way, Mr Spencer. That's it. Been walkabout again, have we?'

Garth had been having a good day. He enjoyed working for Dr Chithros, driving, acting as a sort of bodyguard. But he particularly enjoyed this aspect of the work. Shepherding the oldies about. He steered an old man into a large, pleasant room. Old folks sat around in comfortable chairs. The windowsills were lush with plants. A large television chattered and flickered at one end of the room, its volume just slightly too high.

'Everybody all right?' he called to the inattentive room.

He was an odd-looking nurse. His crisp white uniform was in stark contrast to his scarred, beaten-up face and the prison haircut he still wore out of habit. The gun in his belt bulged beneath the white cloth.

This aspect of his work engendered a peculiar sense of nostalgia in Garth. He'd cut his criminal teeth mugging pensioners. Chithros was just carrying on a grand old tradition –he was just doing it in a damned sophisticated way. Keep the old buggers cooped up in here, feed 'em up, then stick 'em in those boxes and suck 'em dry. And the government was paying him to do it.

He felt good about it all. Compassionate. The violence, the moment of terror, had gone out of the crime. He found as he got older he approved of that. The old dears were comfy here, right up to the end. None of them even knew where they were – they were all drugged up to the eyeballs.

'Time to take your pills, everybody,' he shouted to the room.

Unlocking a sturdy wooden cabinet on the wall, he began removing pill bottles, whistling as he unscrewed the tops and jiggled their contents on to a table in little piles.

'Now, who's first?'

He broke open a sealed tube from which he pulled a stack of tiny plastic cups. He lined them up and poured sterilised water from a bottle into each one. He then went from chair to chair, placing a pill in each open, uncomprehending mouth and lifting a cup to trembling, ancient lips.

Holy Communion, he thought grimly. Last rites.

The television suddenly shot up in volume behind him. He jumped and spilled water down an old man's shirt. The channels were changing constantly; the picture was rolling.

'All right,' he said, a trace of impatience underlying the simpering lilt in his voice, 'who's got the remote control?

Come on now… Which of you old fools is sitting on it?' he muttered to himself.

He switched the set off and returned his attention to the table.

'All right…' This was becoming annoying. 'Who's got them?' A good third of the pills he had laid out on the table had vanished. 'Who's…'

With a crackle the TV set sprang back into too-loud life.

'Hey!'

There was no one near the TV set.

The remote was on the windowsill.

None of these old bastards could have…

There was a steady slurping noise coming from the table. Garth turned to it in time to see a line of tablets disappearing beneath its varnished oak surface. The surface of the table seemed to undulate slightly. It was eating the pills.

The table was eating the pills.

A crash from behind him made him turn. One of the pot plants had fallen from the windowsill. An ivy. Its tendrils snaked across the carpet, lengthening as he watched. They curled around the base of a Hoover he'd left in the corner. As if in response, the machine switched itself on, spontaneously rolling forward over the plant. Ivy strands caught in the vacuum cleaner's rollers and the plant was dragged across the floor, smashing into the droning machine.

On a shelf a Busy Lizzie was locked in mortal combat with a standard lamp.

This was nuts. He unhooked the walkie-talkie from his belt and pressed the send button.

'Dr Chithros… Dr…'

A sudden cutting pain in his wrist made him cry out. Some big bonsai plant which had been sitting quietly against a wall had shot out a hard, rough branch which had curled itself like razor wire around his wrist. The furthest extremities of the branch seemed to want to get at the walkie-talkie, which cracked and spat in his hand. The casing was getting hot.

Garth dropped the machine and pulled himself free of the plant.

He ran from the room. Where was Chithros?

Lights flickered along the corridor; mains sockets sparked. The wood-panelled walls warped and buckled. For the first time he noticed the background noise. It sounded like a war was going on somewhere in the house.

'Garth!' he heard above the uproar. 'Garth!'

His employer was in the lab. Bellowing for him. Garth drew his gun as he ran towards his master's voice.

The Doctor realised he had little time left. The battle raging between the two alien life forms was wrecking the lab. Coffins lay shattered, aged bodies spilling across the floor. Hypnotised men and women, yanked across eighty years, still shuffled about, dazed. The Doctor's eyes devoured the time anchor, taking in its complex operating mechanism. He began tentatively setting dials.

'What are you doing?'

He turned to see the Master, swaying slightly, standing behind him. All trace of the cat virus seemed for the moment to have left him. In his hand he held a gun, pointed at the Doctor.

'Leave that alone,' the Master said levelly.

The Doctor regarded him for a moment before turning back to the time anchor.

'There's no time for that. The Krynoid's getting the upper hand. I can't allow that to happen. If I can reprogram this thing, I can blast it out of existence.'

'I said get away from the machine, Doctor.'

The Doctor turned and stared into his enemy's eyes.

'Think,' he said. 'You know as well as I do what a Krynoid infestation on Earth would mean. Look what it's done to your lab. It's destroyed your nasty little operation, and if I can't stop it it will destroy you. It will destroy all of us.'

The Master hesitated for a moment, then put the gun inside

his jacket.

'What are you trying to do?' he said, stepping up to the machine.

'If I can reverse the…'

'Yes, yes…' the Master said, punching buttons. 'Of course…'

There was a crash from the door as Garth forced it open against the debris which now lay against it. He stumbled into the chaos of the lab, gun jerking about him, finger on the trigger.

'What's going on?' he demanded.

There was a rumbling behind him as a workbench was pushed aside by a sudden eruption of vegetable matter. He spun to see a wall of green, writhing tentacles collapse on top of him. He fired his gun. The thing didn't seem to feel it. Branches twisted around his arms and legs, around his neck. He fired again, and went down screaming.

The Doctor heard the scream and shot a look at the Master. Nothing crossed his face at the passing of his companion. The Doctor closed his eyes, then turned back to his work.

They were working as one now, their rapid adjustments perfectly synchronised.

The battle in the lab was easing off. There seemed nothing of the Virgoan symbiote left. Everything was green. The Krynoid had won.

'Ready…' the Doctor said.

'Ready,' came the reply.

'Powering up…'

Ace bounded into the room.

'What are you doing?' she shouted.

The Doctor closed his eyes briefly. 'Ace,' he said, 'not now. Take cover.'

'What are you going to do?'

'Blast this thing into the time vortex.'

'No, you mustn't!'

She inserted herself between the Doctor and the Master.

'You mustn't.'

'Get out of the way, girl,' the Master snapped, pushing her roughly. 'Now, Doctor.'

'No!'

'DOCTOR…'

A new voice, booming yet soothing, reverberated around the wrecked room.

'WE CAN ASSURE YOU THERE IS NO NEED FOR THAT. WE WERE ILL. WE ARE WELL AGAIN NOW.'

Both Time Lords looked around in confusion. This wasn't the voice of a Krynoid.

'Excuse me,' said the Doctor, 'but who…'

'WE ARE THE VIRGOAN MISSION.'

'But…'

'WE ADAPTED, DOCTOR. AS ALL LIFE HAS ULTIMATELY TO ADAPT TO SURVIVE.'

'You've…'

'WE ARE A SHAPE-SHIFTING SPECIES, AS YOU KNOW, DOCTOR. WE MERELY HAD TO DISCOVER HOW TO TRANSFORM OURSELVES INTO VEGETABLE MATTER. WE ARE SORRY THAT IT TOOK US SO LONG.'

'So the Krynoid is…'

'ABSORBED, DOCTOR. DIGESTED.'

The Doctor was dumbstruck.

'You should see the pigeon,' Ace grinned. 'Otto's talking to it outside. Chattiest cheese plant I ever met.'

As ever, nobody noticed the Master's departure until it was too late.

The Doctor turned to him to power down the time anchor. He was gone.

A search of the house was useless, the Doctor opined. 'He's too good at this sort of thing. Making himself scarce when things go against him. He's had a lot of practice. We'll never catch him now.'

Besides, there were more important things to do.

118

'There's Joe and the other people the Master hypnotised, for a start. He did a very thorough job: implanted false memories, sent them eighty years into the past... They have to be deprogrammed, reacclimatised to life in this century.' He shook his head sadly. 'An awful lot of people have had a cruel trick played on them. The elderly victims of the Master's dreadful process, for one. And their families. Many of them, I imagine, will already have taken babies from here, believing them to be their nearest and dearest. The kidnapped babies will have to go back, of course... And someone will have to tell those families that their loved ones have been murdered. It won't be a pretty business.'

Ace looked downcast. She wanted nothing to do with any of this.

'But in a way they are their relatives,' she ventured. 'Couldn't we just...'

'No, Ace,' said the Doctor. 'However painful, the truth must come out. This is a desperate age. An age of insecurity. People fear their own mortality like never before. The Master preyed on that. It's going to be a hard lesson to learn, but people are going to have to learn again to accept their own ageing and death. Change can never be halted.'

'Doctor...' Ace's voice was shaky. 'Maybe I'm... out there somewhere.' The thought made her shudder, but it wouldn't go away. 'I'd be old by now... I wonder –'

'Ace,' the Doctor interrupted, 'don't wonder. Not about that. The future will take care of itself.'

Ace smiled slightly. 'Even without you to fix things when they go wrong?' she asked.

'Even without me,' the Doctor said, smiling. 'Though perhaps not without the Virgoans. Come on, let's get busy.'

# EPILOGUE

Dee Matthews jabbed her fat powder puff hard into the Home Secretary's face. He flinched slightly but said nothing. He'd said nothing all morning. His fidgety hands clenched and unclenched around a sheaf of sweaty notes.

She'd been looking forward to this one. The Chithros scandal had broken a fortnight before and the government had been on the ropes ever since. The word – not so much a word as a feeling – had gone around television centre, as it seemed to have gone around the offices of the national newspapers. The spin on this one was clear. Everybody knew who the sights were locked on. The media had spoken and everyone knew what that meant.

Nick and Tasmin had taken an unexpected holiday. In their absence, Jerome Harper had been wheeled in. A real heavyweight. A bruiser. The message was clear.

'Two minutes, Home Secretary.'

The voice had an impertinent ring to it. The minister got unsteadily to his feet and walked out through the door to face his accusers. Dee watched him from the doorway, smiling grimly as he allowed himself to be led to the chair.

The floor manager, Ben, was also grinning malevolently. 'Everybody ready…' He raised his arm. 'Counting in, in five, four, three, two…'

# Freedom

## by Steve Lyons

Somewhere, somewhen, the construct exists. Perhaps everywhere, at all points in time. Or nowhere. It is fashioned from the mortar with which dimensions are bound together. It lurks in the cracks in reality's surface. It is an impossibility and yet the construct exists. Between the gaps of a single second. There is no way to reach it, no way to leave. But if we could look closer with human sight, we would see that it is occupied.

It started on Tuesday morning: a perfectly normal morning in the early days of summer. The Doctor and Brigadier Lethbridge-Stewart were arguing. The Doctor's assistant, Josephine Grant, found her role of spectator no less frustrating for its disheartening familiarity.

'And I'm telling you, Doctor, that Stangmoor Prison is the best place for him until his trial. They already know him there, for a start.'

'As Emil Keller, perhaps.'

'All the better. The Prime Minister wants this business hushed up. If the Master's record, or his origins, were made public –'

'Oh really, Brigadier! Your species's capacity for self-deception never fails to astonish me.'

The army man bridled at his scientic adviser's harsh words. The pair had always shared a firm friendship, but sometimes Jo was hard put to see why. Lethbridge-Stewart could hardly fail to take the Doctor's frequent invectives against the military mindset, bureaucrats and humanity in general to heart.

'Now listen here, Doctor –'

'No, you listen to me, Brigadier! I am well aware of the Master's crimes, but what you don't seem to appreciate is that he is an alien to this world. He has an incredible lifespan, by your standards, and he is used to having all of creation to explore. To coop him up in the isolation block of some concrete prison is nothing less than the most barbaric cruelty.'

The Brigadier's eyes widened and his nostrils flared in anger. 'May I remind you that this alien "friend" of yours has tried to conquer our world several times over!'

The Doctor looked set to issue a rejoinder, but he controlled himself and released a heavy sigh. He rubbed his neck and smiled awkwardly. 'All right, Brigadier, you've made your point. Of course he must be confined. I was simply hoping we could arrange more… comfortable surroundings. I am still a prisoner myself, you know. It's bad enough for me, being exiled to this single world and time. I can only imagine how the Master must be feeling.'

Jo relaxed. The latest dispute was over. Her colleagues were working on the same side again.

'The question of the Master's eventual disposition,' said the Brigadier a little stiffly, 'is being discussed in Geneva.'

'Well, put in a word for me then, would you? There's a good chap.'

'I'll see what I can do.'

'Please do, Brigadier,' said the Doctor. 'After all, we all need some measure of freedom.'

Jo stretches her cramped legs and winces at the tingling pain of pins and needles. She has been patient enough, she decides. Sitting here at this grey metal table, watching as her companion contemplates his own reflection in the grey metal wall. On the assumption that he was thinking, she has waited in silent expectation. It occurs to her now that he is merely sulking. She has never seen him so resigned and hopeless.

'Doctor,' she prompts, in a faintly aggrieved tone.

He doesn't seem to have heard her. She tries again. His head jerks up and he turns, an eyebrow raised, as if he has forgotten she is here.

'What is it, Jo?'

'I thought you were working on a way to escape this place.'

'That's quite impossible, I'm afraid.'

She is taken aback by the brusqueness of his words, and stung by their finality. 'You are kidding me, aren't you?'

Sympathy blunts the angles of his face. 'My dear Jo, I thought you understood the situation.'

'I heard what the Master said, yes. But –'

'Well, for once, he is absolutely right.'

'So there really is no way out of here?'

'Only the way we arrived.' He sees the new hope in her face and he immediately acts to quell it. 'And there's no way we can use that. Well, short of the Brigadier acquiring a sudden knowledge of four-dimensional physics and being able to apply it before the Master can outwit him.'

'Oh.'

'Quite. Don't worry, Jo, there's plenty of food and water and oxygen here. Enough for a lifetime. Your lifetime, at least.'

Jo stares around the dull, claustrophobic walls of this, the largest of the construct's six interconnected chambers. She is trying to adjust to the fact that it will be her home for ever. She can't accept it. She trusts the Doctor to save her, no matter what he might say now. There has to be some way out. But then, that's probably what the last residents thought, at first.

She tries not to think of the two bodies in the smallest room: the locked one. Two lovers, entwined throughout eternity as their corpses slowly decompose together.

On Tuesday afternoon, all hell broke loose. Jo entered the Doctor's laboratory with two cups of tea in time to catch him making for the door, and for the garage in which his modified antique car Bessie was housed. The Brigadier joined them, eschewing his usual Jeep for the speed of this unique conveyance. As the Doctor hurtled down country roads at a frightening velocity, Lethbridge-Stewart briefed Jo.

'I had a feeling this might happen.' There was a hint of smugness in his voice. 'That's why I left troops on standby at the prison. Do you still want to give the Master the keys to his own guest room, Doctor?'

Their driver concentrated on the road ahead and said nothing.

The prison gates were hanging open. Bessie screeched to a halt in the courtyard beyond and Jo stared, aghast, at a scene of insanity. The area was swarming with civilians. UNIT soldiers were attempting to contain them, but they were overwhelmed. A brawl had broken out.

'What the –' The Brigadier leapt to his feet and drew his revolver, perturbed by the sight of his own men engaging in fisticuffs. He fired into the air and roared a command for silence. He was ignored.

'We've tried that, sir. It's no use.' Sergeant Benton had pushed his way to the new arrivals. 'They're under some sort of mind control. They don't respond to threats and we can't use our weapons without hurting them. They've forced their way through the gates. I don't think we can keep them out of the main building for much longer.'

'Blast!'

'And it takes only one person to reach the Master's cell with a key,' said the Doctor tartly. 'The cunning old rogue. He must have planted suggestions in a hundred minds before he was caught.'

'Can we snap them out of it?'

'One at a time, yes, but it would take far too long. We need to remove their objective.'

Before the Brigadier could respond, the Doctor vaulted out of the car. His cloak flapped behind him and made him look like a giant bat. Jo thought for only a second before racing after him. The Doctor negotiated the crowd with extraordinary dexterity and she found it difficult to keep him in sight. He was heading towards the building, no doubt hoping to reach the Master before anyone else did. The main doors had been forced open, but a line of prison guards had joined the UNIT troops in their struggle to repel the intruders. As the Doctor tried to pass them, one man moved to block him. Of course: without a uniform, he looked like just another of the Master's dupes.

The Doctor was shouting something – trying to establish his credentials, Jo assumed, but with his characteristic lack of patience for such formalities. His words were lost in the cacophony. As she reached him at last, she pulled her UNIT pass from her jacket pocket. But her elbow was jostled and the yellow piece of card slipped from her grasp.

She lunged for it, and stumbled into the pre-programmed path of a thick-set young man with black hair and stubble. He swung for her with a massive fist and she gasped, ducked and lost her footing. He bore down on her... and suddenly the Doctor was there, seizing him by the shoulders and staring into his eyes. He muttered something under his breath, then cried out, 'Awake!' The man blinked and shook his head, his swollen muscles relaxing. The Doctor let him go and took Jo's arm.

She mumbled her thanks, but she was facing the gateway now and, as a consequence, she had spotted something.

'Look!'

The Doctor followed her line of sight and nodded grimly. One figure alone was fighting against the crowd, trying to reach the sundered gates. Immediately, the Doctor set off in pursuit. 'Private, corporal, anybody, restrain that man!' His bony elbows flailed, driving people out of his way with abandon. Once again, Jo followed as best she could. Their quarry had seen them now and he redoubled his efforts.

But two soldiers had heard the Doctor's shouts. They cut the man off and held on to him, despite his struggles.

In the centre of the mêlée, captor and captive faced each other. The latter scowled bitterly. He was middle-aged and

127

blond, but the Doctor studied only his eyes and a satisfied smile spread across his wrinkled features. That told Jo all she needed to know. One of the zombies must have reached the isolation block unseen. The Doctor had clearly recognised his old foe: a Master of disguise.

'Nice try, old chap. But I'll take this now, if you don't mind.'

In one smart motion, he yanked off the man's face and revealed an all-too-familiar bearded countenance beneath.

There is no passage of time here. No sun to differentiate between day and night. Jo has slept three times, but she does not know for how long. Her life is becoming an empty succession of grey walls and grey furniture, stretching into for ever. It is punctuated only by bland food from the grey dispenser. She has swapped her own clothes for a shapeless grey one-piece boiler suit. She has worn it for days, or hours or weeks, now, but it feels crisp and fresh. It repels dirt molecules. She will probably die wearing it.

The Doctor does not seem to need to change. He still wears the frilly shirt and velvet jacket in which he arrived. He spends his days in quiet and morose contemplation, but makes an effort to be cheery when he sees Jo is around. Simple, inadequate ways of passing the time have been provided. Jo admits that she has never mastered the rules of chess. They play draughts instead. She has the impression that the Doctor is fantastically bored by the game.

He insists on telling her to cheer up, to resign herself to captivity; to find constructive ways of spending her days. 'I had to,' he reminds her. 'That's why I fell in with UNIT in the first place.' She can't help but feel that this situation does not compare.

She sinks into a world of 'if only'. If only she had not acted so impulsively. If only she had done as she was told. If only they had realised that the Master was not so easily defeated; that the attack on Stangmoor Prison was merely the first and simplest of his two contingency plans.

\* \* \*

'What is it, Lethbridge-Stewart? I was in the middle of a delicate operation.'

The Doctor dropped, unbidden, into a seat and swung his feet up on to the desk. The Brigadier cleared his throat, taken aback as always by his casual demeanour. It was as though the Doctor delighted in reminding him in every possible way that, although affiliated to UNIT, he refused to be subject to its rules and regulations. Still, he had responded to the Brigadier's summons.

'It's about the civilians who marched on Stangmoor.'

'Oh yes. All back to normal, are they?'

'Back to normal, yes. Your idea did the trick.'

Once the Master had been bundled away in handcuffs, the Brigadier had simply ordered a withdrawal. The Master's brainwashed army had streamed into the prison, ignoring the pleas of its inmates as they reached through their bars. Each one had found his or her way to the Master's vacated and open cell. Their trances had been broken, their missions completed. There had been a lot of explaining to do and, consequently, a great deal of paperwork, but no lasting harm had been done.

'But,' the Brigadier continued, 'we found out something that might interest you. Every single person involved in the incident this afternoon was employed by the same company.'

The Doctor raised an eyebrow. 'Oh?'

'The Freedom Corporation. I believe you have an appointment there on Thursday?'

In his mind's eye, the Doctor could see a man, near and yet somehow far away, strange and yet so familiar. He was short, with dark hair, checked trousers and a tall hat. He was blowing on some kind of an instrument. An old friend, perhaps? He tried to bring the image into focus, but a grey mist obscured his view. And then Jo's voice snapped him back to reality and the figure was gone.

'Watch out, Doctor,' she protested. 'You almost hit that truck!'

'Nonsense,' he clucked under his breath, but swallowed and forced himself to concentrate on his driving all the same.

'There's one thing I don't understand,' said Jo.

There always was. The Doctor waited for her question.

'I did some research into the Freedom Corporation. It was established over thirty years ago.'

'Well, of course it was, Jo. The Master can travel in time, remember? For three decades, this company has existed only to recruit so-called sales people and to indoctrinate them into his cause. All that, against the possibility of his ever being caught.'

'So that's why he called it Freedom?'

'He must have hated the prospect of confinement very much.' The Doctor knew how he felt. 'But the company must have another purpose too. It can hardly be coincidence that, this week, they've announced a press conference to discuss a breakthrough in time-travel research.'

'What do you think the Master's up to?'

'That's what we're here to find out.'

The Doctor brought Bessie to a halt in the Freedom Corporation's car park. As his companion produced two passes for inspection the Doctor pushed the building's glass door open. He stopped. Reflected in the glass, and yet somehow beyond it, was a young, fair-haired man in an English cricket outfit. The look on the man's face was one of warning. It seemed to express some terrible danger.

The vision lasted less than a second. The door swung back and instantly the man was gone. The Doctor blinked hard. He couldn't help but feel that he was missing something important.

'I'm sorry, Jo.'

She is surprised by the Doctor's sudden apology. She pauses, a white counter poised above the board. 'What for?'

'For getting you into this predicament in the first place.'

Jo grins. 'It wasn't your fault, Doctor. You told me to stay behind, remember?'

'And I should have known better than to expect you to listen,' he says with mock severity. Then his face falls. 'But it's more than that, Jo. I was warned. I knew what lay in store for us and I took the risk anyway.'

She shrugs and tries to make light of it, though her heart is numb and heavy. 'So did I.'

'But I've merely swapped one prison for another. You're used to having your freedom.'

'I had thought,' she scolds gently, 'that you might appreciate Earth a little more after this. It's not such a bad place.'

He smiles. 'No, Jo, I suppose it's not.'

'Then get us back there,' she urges. 'There must be something you can do!'

For a second, she allows herself to hope. She thinks she can actually motivate him into performing a miracle. But the Doctor just scowls. 'My dear Miss Grant, I've told you before, I am as helpless as you are. It is out of my hands.'

'But there's a chance? That someone might rescue us?'

'A small chance. I thought it was worth taking, at the time.'

'And now?'

'Now, Jo,' he sighs, 'I'm not so sure.'

Professor Gerald Gooder was a slight man, about thirty years of age. He approached the platform nervously when announced and hid behind a pair of heavily tinted spectacles. The Doctor snorted his derision as the timid man began to speak in a stumbling, lisping voice. Jo thought he was being unfair. But he wasn't the only member of this exclusive gathering to give little credence to Gooder. In the row behind them, two journalists were whispering comments to each other and rocking in not-so-silent mirth. The Doctor, though, should have known better. At least he knew that time travel was possible.

'And this,' announced Gooder after an interminable half-hour of incomprehensible scientific jargon, 'is what you have undoubtedly come here to see.'

Two white-coated technicians entered the room and wheeled a squat, mushroom-shaped device up a ramp and on to the stage. The assembled photographers were shaken out of their collective stupor and a dozen flash bulbs exploded with light. 'Freedom 1B: our prototype time machine.'

'At last,' said the Doctor, loudly and with bad grace.

He made for the freestanding console, an eager gleam in his eyes. Jo knew exactly what it meant to him: an end to his confinement; a way to escape the exile imposed upon him by his people, the Time Lords. But that was why it could be the perfect bait in a trap.

Two guards stepped forward and barred the Doctor's way to the platform. 'I'm sorry, sir,' said one, 'but we can't allow you to approach the machine. It's very delicate.'

'Well, I'm hardly likely to damage it!' he snapped. The guards held firm and the Doctor reluctantly returned to his seat.

Gooder was describing the function of each switch on the time machine's hemispherical upper section. He was so engrossed in his own genius that he had turned his back to the crowd and they could barely hear what he was saying. The Doctor writhed impatiently and then shouted, 'Why don't you just give us a demonstration, man?'

His call was taken up and Gooder looked flustered.

'The machine isn't connected at the moment, I'm afraid. It takes a great deal of power for one simple transference and it is still at the prototype stage. There is a great deal of work to do yet.'

His audience was audibly disappointed. Jo could hear the scratching of pencils against paper and she knew that tomorrow's newspapers would treat Gooder's claims as a joke. She snatched a quick look at the Doctor. He was nodding thoughtfully to himself and a slight smile played about his lips.

'To be honest with you, Jo,' he confided as they left the building, 'I was more relieved than anything else.'

'Why's that?'

'Well, you heard the man. He was talking the most unmitigated claptrap. Scientific balderdash!'

Jo was too tactful to mention that Gooder's speech had sounded remarkably like one of the Doctor's own lectures when he was in full flow.

'And you saw how reluctant he was to demonstrate that machine of his. No, I think we're quite safe.'

'Safe?'

'Well, can you imagine if the Master had given that Gooder fellow the secrets of time travel?' He shuddered. 'Twentieth-century man rampaging through his own past. It hardly bears thinking about. You'd have wiped yourselves out in a matter of days.'

'So what is the Master up to?'

'I don't know, Jo. I really don't know.'

He swung a long leg into Bessie's driving seat. But before the other could join it, he doubled up and clutched at his temples in pain.

'Doctor!' cried Jo. 'What's wrong?'

He ignored her. His face had turned parchment white. 'What are you trying to tell me?' he cried, but Jo could not see who he was addressing. 'Who are you?'

Jo didn't know what to do. Should she shout for help? Call an ambulance? The Brigadier? But, fortunately for her, the seizure ended as quickly as it had begun.

The Doctor sat in silence, his brow furrowed in thought, and he ignored her stream of concerned questions. He turned to her finally and told her to get inside the car. 'There is something going on here, Jo,' he muttered as he started the engine, 'and I'm dreadfully afraid that I'm beginning to realise what it is.'

Night fell upon the premises of the Freedom Corporation and, as a late-running supply truck pulled up in its grounds, the darkness masked from sight the cautious opening of its back doors and the alighting of two figures. No one observed those silent silhouettes as they flitted across the compound and disappeared into the larger and deeper shadows of the building proper.

From there, it took only a few seconds for the Doctor's sonic screwdriver to defeat the electronic lock on a side door. Jo glanced over her shoulder nervously as they stepped into the darkened corridor beyond, but saw no sign that they had been detected.

The Doctor took a few steps, then halted. 'Do you feel anything, Jo?' he asked in a whisper.

'A bit of a headache.'

He nodded sagely. 'Let me know if it gets worse.'

He set off again, seeming content to leave it at that. But Jo wanted to know more. So far, his explanations had been frankly inadequate. 'Are you having the visions again?' she asked him, struggling to keep pace with his long, brisk strides.

'Seeing images of my past and future selves, yes.' With a meaningful edge to his voice, he added, 'I am trying to ignore them.'

Jo didn't take the hint. He had been fobbing her off like this all day and this was her last chance to find out what was going on. 'But what's causing it, Doctor? Is it the time machine?'

He sighed. 'Spillage from it, at least. Any half-competent scientist would have installed shielding. I'm particularly affected because I have a much longer and more jumbled timestream than you.'

'Then the time machine is being used for something?'

'It seems that way, yes.'

'But I don't understand. I thought you said it couldn't work.'

'It couldn't. Not if it was built to the specifications Gooder described. The man simply has no concept of the realities of temporal and transdimensional engineering.'

The Doctor's tone was disdainful and Jo could only answer with a bewildered, 'Oh.'

'Clearly, someone at Freedom is using Gooder's machine in a

way that he doesn't know about. Or won't admit to.'

'But why?'

'That, Jo, is what we are here to find out.'

The corridor turned a sharp right, but the Doctor stopped at its corner. He stared through a small window at the empty car park and rubbed his chin thoughtfully. 'Tell me, do you notice anything peculiar about this wall?'

'No. Should I?'

The Doctor was already reaching into his jacket. 'It isn't where it's supposed to be. The view from this window would indicate that we are at least ten feet closer to the boundary fence than we actually are.'

Jo didn't quite follow him, but he was holding his sonic screwdriver aloft as it emitted a high-pitched whining sound and she knew that things would become clear soon. Sure enough, the wall itself flickered and disappeared.

'A simple camouflaging force field,' said the Doctor happily.

They were now standing before an arched entranceway, beyond which was a half-lit, sterile white laboratory. As the Doctor had surmised, it was about ten feet across. On its far wall, Jo could see another window. It offered the same perspective upon the outside world as had its false duplicate.

The Doctor strode into the lab and examined its storage shelves and computer banks eagerly. Jo made a show of inspecting the room herself, although she didn't expect to understand a fraction of what she saw.

'Why would someone go to so much trouble to hide this place?' she wondered aloud. 'It doesn't seem to be in use.'

It wasn't that the room was dusty. Quite the opposite: it was too clean, if anything. Beakers and flasks were neatly stacked away. The computers were dark and silent.

'No,' said the Doctor, 'but it has been.' He stopped in front of a large glass case which was set against the far wall. Several plastic tubes protruded from it, running into a variety of sealed vats. 'You see this, Jo? It's a nutrient tank.'

'A what?' she asked automatically. Then she realised that the name was self-explanatory. 'You mean something's been growing in there?'

'Quite so. I wonder what?'

Jo looked around again and shivered at the prospect of what might have been done in this place. She remembered one of the Doctor's lectures, from months ago, on the horrors of genetic experimentation. Her mind conjured up images of gruesome monsters being cultivated in glass tanks and unleashed upon the world.

Which was why she jumped and almost screamed when she saw somebody standing in the doorway.

'Gooder!' cried the Doctor, whirling around in response to Jo's stifled gasp.

Jo had not recognised the new arrival in the gloom, but she took her companion's word for his identity. Gerald Gooder turned and fled, and the Doctor hared after him. He came to a halt in the corridor outside.

'Which way did he go?'

'Shouldn't we get out of here?' asked Jo.

'I'd like to ask the good professor a few questions first.'

'What if he sounds an alarm?'

The Doctor didn't answer. He chose a direction that took them deeper into the Freedom building and broke into a run. Jo had no choice but to follow him. As luck would have it, he had made the right decision. They rounded a corner and were just in time to see a door close behind a white-coated figure. The Doctor wrenched it open and halted on the threshold. Jo strained to see past him.

Gooder had stopped running. He was standing in the centre of a small room, by the familiar mushroom-shaped console that almost seemed to fill it. Even this late, he was wearing his dark glasses. He glared at the Doctor defiantly and produced something from his pocket. It was a gun, but like none that Jo had ever seen before. It was no more than a tiny white tube, but the Doctor's immediate reaction was to shrink away from it and to push his companion behind him.

'Now steady on, old fellow,' he said, 'I only want to talk to you about your invention.'

Gooder said nothing. He simply aimed his weapon at the so-called time machine itself and fired. There was a brief, blinding flash of electricity and Jo whimpered as her headache suddenly increased to an unbearable intensity. Fortunately, her pain was short-lived. She blinked to clear the stars out of her eyes and saw that smoke was curling from the top of the device itself. Professor Gooder was nowhere to be seen.

The Doctor was across the room in an instant, wafting smoke away with his hands and straining to see the displays beneath.

'Gooder tried to destroy the control pad,' he explained grimly as Jo joined him, 'to keep us from seeing where he has gone.'

'Then the time machine does work?'

'It does something, all right. But without a detailed examination, I can't tell precisely what, and there's no time for that.'

'What are you doing?'

The Doctor's hands were a blur across the switches and levers. 'I'm following Gooder.'

'What, blindly?'

'There can't be any danger, Jo, or else he wouldn't have gone himself.'

'I suppose not,' she said doubtfully.

'But, just in case, I want you to wait outside.' Jo opened her mouth to argue, but the Doctor gave her a sharp look. 'I haven't time to argue, just go!'

Jo went. But she paused on the threshold and looked back at his tall, gaunt form as he stood and took a deep breath before throwing what had to be the final lever. A rebellious impulse rose within her. It was all very nice that he was concerned about her, but she worried about him too. She had to go with him. He might need her.

She pushed the door shut, even as the Doctor pulled the

lever, and he turned, startled, at the sound of it. He had time only to groan, 'Oh, Jo!' before it started.

Even without the dubious benefit of a Time Lord's brain, Jo could feel the pressure of past and future converging upon her thoughts. An adolescent Jo-Jo Grant was screaming in her face. An elderly Josephine was offering kind advice. There were dozens more, all trying to warn her in their own way. But their voices merged into a meaningless cacophony and their presence only caused her pain. She sank to her knees and could only imagine how much worse it must be for the Doctor, with who knew how many lives to torment him. That dreadful moment seemed to last an eternity and she thought the voices might never end. At last, though, they did.

Too late, Jo realised what they had been warning her about.

'I wondered when you might come to see me.'

The Master smiles, to the Brigadier's irritation. His expression suggests that he has won already. He lies back on his simple prison bunk, hands clasped behind his head, a picture of casual confidence.

'The Doctor and his young friend have been missing for – what is it? – four days now.'

'If you know where they are –'

The prisoner winces, as if disgusted by his visitor's impatient bluster. 'Oh, Brigadier, of course I know where they are. Even a reactionary dullard such as yourself could have worked out that much. The question is, what do I get in return for the information?'

'What you'll get,' the Brigadier barks, 'is a longer sentence if we don't find the Doctor and Miss Grant!'

The Master responds with a rich, mocking laugh. 'I wasn't under the impression that you were planning to ever turn me loose.'

'And I,' rumbles the Brigadier, 'was under the impression that you could serve out every day of a multiple life sentence.'

A shadow of disquiet passes over the Master's face. The

Brigadier smirks inwardly, but then the shadow is gone. 'Nice shot, Brigadier, but let me assure you, some day, somehow, I shall have my freedom. Now, you can restore it today and have the Doctor's freedom in return. Or you can wait until I make my own arrangements and have nothing.'

He is perfectly relaxed again now. He even closes his eyes to signal that the conversation is over. The Brigadier seethes. For a second, he considers the possibility of beating the information out of him. But that would have no more effect than screaming and ranting. It is painful for him to admit it but, in the end, he has no choice. 'Exactly what do you want?' he asks gruffly.

The Master opens one eye, and amusement tugs at his lips. 'Why, Brigadier, are you intending to make me an offer?'

Somewhere, somewhen, the construct existed. Perhaps everywhere and at all points in time. Or nowhere. And if anyone could have peered inside with human sight, they would have seen that a confrontation was taking place.

'Like lambs to the slaughter,' said Professor Gooder. No longer nervous, his voice was smooth and confident, with more than a hint of ridicule. He removed his dark glasses.

As the Doctor helped the unsteady Jo to her feet, he stared into the Professor's green eyes and recognised the mind behind their depths.

'The Master. I should have known!'

'Indeed you should, but you did not. As ever, Doctor, you didn't think, and your impetuousness has led you into my trap.'

The Doctor's eyes narrowed. 'This isn't just a disguise, is it?'

'Why no, Doctor, this is something far more ingenious.'

'Mind transference.'

'Ah, I thought you might put two and two together, once you stumbled upon my lab. Yes, Doctor, Gerald Gooder has been growing in a nutrient tank since I established the Freedom Corporation thirty years ago. I obtained the raw material from

Earth's future. In fact, Miss Grant, I should congratulate your race on its developments in genetic research. Quite remarkable, and utterly without conscience. I'm beginning to see why you're so besotted with humanity, Doctor.'

'So you have your freedom, after all.'

'Not quite, Doctor. Not yet. It takes a great deal of effort to control Gooder's body, especially at such a distance as this.'

'Where are we, exactly?' Jo pitched in.

Gooder's lips – the Master's lips – twitched with restrained humour. 'Ah, I'm glad you asked me that, my dear. We are in a pod designed by the people of Arbrocknel to house their most dangerous criminals. The original occupants are long since dead, of course. Arbrocknel's system of confinement is foolproof. We are outside the known dimensions. Any attempt to breach the wall will expose you to the fatal ravages of the Time Winds. There is no hope of escape. Now you, Doctor, can learn what it is to face all your lifetimes confined to a prison cell.'

The Doctor scratched his cheek awkwardly, avoiding Jo's eyes. There was no point in engaging the Master in banter. He had already won.

'You won't get away with this!' cried Jo, sounding defiant although her voice was trembling.

'My dear Miss Grant, I already have. But fear not. You, at least, will have to endure only one lifetime of captivity.'

'Hold on a minute!' Jo turned to the Doctor, who could almost see cogs working in her brain. 'There has to be some way out of here. Otherwise how is the Master planning to escape?'

Their captor erupted into laughter again. 'Your naive friend has much to learn, Doctor.'

'Doctor, what does he mean?'

'I bid you farewell,' said the Master with a smirk. 'I hope you enjoy your imprisonment as much as I have enjoyed mine.'

Then Gerald Gooder's eyes rolled back into their sockets, his legs buckled and he collapsed like a puppet with its strings cut. The Master had taken the easiest route out of the pod: he had withdrawn his intelligence from Gooder's hollow shell. The Doctor's one consolation was that his foe was now trapped in his own body, at Stangmoor. Each Time Lord had taken the freedom of the other.

The Master enters the Freedom building, the cornerstone of which he himself laid in 1936. It was the first action in a complex and far-reaching plan. Now, ignominiously, he is returning under armed guard. Brigadier Lethbridge-Stewart is determined not to take his eyes off his prisoner. He has brought along no fewer than six aides to back him up. He will need many more than that.

It is a shame, the Master thinks, that his mind-controlled army were unable to free him, but they did arouse the Doctor's curiosity. Plan B, though, is going perfectly. He strolls down the corridor, hands behind his back, displaying his nonchalance. He recognises one more of the attendant soldiers. It is Benton. He leans towards the sergeant conspiratorially, indicates the Brigadier with a jerk of his head and whispers, 'Is he usually so paranoid?' He smiles and chuckles under his breath when Benton studiously ignores him and marches on.

They reach the room in which the time machine is housed. For it is, indeed, a machine that can harness the forces of time, if not in the manner that the Master, as Gooder, has claimed. Even to the Brigadier, the device does not look impressive.

'Is this all you've got to show us, man?' he snaps.

'Have patience.'

The Master could spring the trap now, but he has always had a flair for the dramatic. He waits, enjoying the taste of anticipation in the air. He flexes his fingers over the controls of the machine. The Brigadier raises his revolver.

'If you're planning to touch that thing, I want a detailed explanation of what you intend to do with it first.'

'My dear Brigadier, you know as well as I do what a waste of time that would be for both of us. You wouldn't understand a word.'

'All the same.'

'Very well.' The Master sighs and throws up his hands, faking resignation. Then his voice hardens as he turns to his invention and raps, 'Omega.'

The Brigadier's face is an eye-popping caricature of alarm as the machine judders into action. He swings his gun to cover it, as if that will do him any good. The Master could disarm him here and now, but there is no need.

'What are you... Stop this at once!' the Brigadier orders.

The Master just laughs. Waves of solid time energy are sweeping across the room, across the building, across this pathetic planet. The Master's head aches with their passing, but the effect upon his captors is far more severe.

The UNIT men are becoming younger. They seem to know this, but are incapable of doing a thing. The Brigadier's eyes are unfocused. He is no longer even aware of the Master's presence. His hair grows longer. His moustache disappears, even as his uniform becomes newer and then spins away into the fabric of which it was made. He has regressed to infanthood now and he expresses his frustration in the only way that remains to him. He cries. And then he is gone.

The Master smiles to himself, as the very building around him disappears in the blink of an eye. He is standing in a field, watching as trees shrink back into their roots. As a Time Lord, only he remains unaffected. And the machine. He crouches beside it, reaches into its stem and pulls a small blue cube from its inner workings. A multitude of red lights blink on the console. The Master's grin grows broader as he stands and slips the vital component into his pocket.

The final phase of his plan is proceeding perfectly. It is time for him to leave this world, at last. Time to reclaim his freedom.

* * *

At first, Jo doesn't dare to believe it. The construct is filled with the familiar sound of arthritic engines, but she half suspects her ears, so accustomed to silence now, of deceiving her. She leaps off her bed and rushes into the grey room that she and the Doctor have designated their living area. The lifeless body of Gooder is still sprawled in the corner, its eyes open as if mocking them. She feels like sticking out her tongue at it in triumph. For, against the opposite wall, the best shape in the world is blurring into existence. The shape of an outdated police call box: the outer shell of the Doctor's incredible ship, the TARDIS. And if Jo has a trace of doubt left, it is dispelled by the joy that illuminates the Doctor's face.

Somebody, somewhere, can still do something.

The Doctor's expression, as they walk through the doors and into the impossibly large, white room beyond, is almost reverential. The hexagonal console is alight. It hums softly, as if welcoming back an old friend. The Doctor walks around it and runs his hand across its surface.

'They've given it back,' he says, his voice barely more than a whisper. 'They've given it all back.'

'The Time Lords?' guesses Jo. 'Your people have sent the TARDIS to rescue us?'

'More than that, Jo. Much more. They've restored it to full working order. They've returned my knowledge of time travel. They've given me back my freedom.'

At this moment, to Jo's surprise, an alarm klaxon blares out from the console. A red bulb flashes insistently.

'What is it?' she asks nervously, as the Doctor punches up a series of displays and frowns.

'What's wrong?'

'I knew there had to be a catch,' he mutters. 'A reason for their intervention. They wouldn't have done it just to assist me. They need help to repair their precious timestream.'

'Doctor, what's happening?'

'Earth,' he intones, and the single word sends a chill down her spine. 'The Master has disrupted time; sent it running backwards across the whole planet. Even if the Earth can survive the stress, it will undoubtedly be destroyed when it reaches its own moment of creation.'

'But the Time Lords think you can stop it?' says Jo hopefully.

'They could stop it themselves, if they had half a mind to. But no, they'd rather not dirty their hands. The hypocrites! They exiled me for interfering, but they'll use me to interfere when it suits them – use me and then deny all knowledge of it later. As soon as we've returned to Earth, they'll take my freedom from me again.'

He lapses into a bitter silence. Jo sympathises, but he seems to be forgetting one vital fact. She grows steadily more agitated at the thought of her world's fate, until she can remain silent no more.

'Doctor, what about Earth? Time Lords or not, shouldn't we do something?'

He nods, almost to himself. His lips are pursed, his eyes hooded. He operates the controls, slowly and deliberately. And suddenly he flings himself across the console and bats down an array of switches.

A fanatical gleam ignites in his eyes as the central glass rotor begins to rise and fall. The floor bucks beneath Jo and steals her breath. The TARDIS is in flight. She knows instinctively that it is careening away from Earth. She cries out in horror.

'Doctor, what are you doing?'

'Don't worry, Jo. My people won't allow your world to come to grief, especially not through illegal use of their own technology.'

'But they sent you to do the job!'

'Then they'll have to find another pawn.'

'What if they can't?'

'It's all under control, Jo,' the Doctor insists. 'The Time Lords will just have to intervene more directly than they'd like. It might teach them a lesson.'

She tries to believe him, but she cannot. She trusts him, she really does. But she believes in his abilities; believes he is unique. If he will not save Earth, then who else will be able to?

He catches her pleading look, and she can see how it pains him.

'Look, Jo, the Time Lords have given me back my TARDIS and the ability to use it. If I go to Earth, they'll take all that away from me. My one hope is to outrun them, to slip through the Vortex on random co-ordinates. I can hide from them; begin a new life.'

'What about the lives of everyone on Earth?' Jo's voice is trembling and there are tears in her eyes. 'Billions of people, Doctor, all depending on you to save them. You can't just run away from them.'

'The Time Lords won't let Earth be destroyed.'

'What if they do? What if they're all too busy arguing about politics; about whether they can act or not?'

And a terrible thought occurs to her. She remembers sitting in the prison pod, playing draughts with him. She remembers his unexpected apology.

'I was warned,' he said. 'I knew what lay in store for us and I took the risk anyway... A small chance. I thought it was worth taking, at the time.'

What if he has engineered this situation? What if he walked into the Master's trap, knowing it would lead him here? What if he suspected that his arch foe would threaten Earth, seeking a final victory by destroying the Doctor's favourite planet and murdering his friends?

What if he knew the Time Lords would have to intercede? What if he has gambled his limited freedom on the possibility of regaining time and space, allowing Jo's world to be threatened in the process? What if?

There are too many questions. In the end, only one matters. What happens to Earth if the Doctor abandons it?

'Please, Doctor...'

She is begging him with her eyes. He returns her look, and Jo can see his silent plea too. He has wanted this so badly and for so long. She knows what it means to him, but she can see no other choice. If she could, she wouldn't ask him.

She wouldn't ask the Doctor to sacrifice his freedom.

The Doctor steps out of the TARDIS, struggling to drag his thoughts from a world of regret. Waves of time roll across the planet's ravaged surface and cause his head to throb. He is appalled at the sight of this blasted plain beneath a wounded red sky, and his hearts ache in sympathy. It is worse than he expected. He has done the right thing by coming here.

And yet, where is he? He expected the Time Lords' co-ordinates to take him to Freedom, but though the landscape shifts and changes with each fresh wave, he knows he is at least half a mile away from that building. There can be only one explanation, and the Doctor's theory is soon proved.

A familiar figure makes his way through the ruins, unaffected by the chaos but struggling to remain upright. The Doctor moves to intercept him. The Master stumbles to a halt, and registers first alarm and then dismay at the return of his old foe.

'Doctor!'

'Guilty as charged.' The Doctor smiles tightly. 'You, of all people, ought to know that no cell is escape-proof.'

'You must let me pass.'

The Master's air of calm superiority is threatened. He has mistimed his escape, the Doctor realises. He is fearful of being destroyed along with his victims.

'My ship –'

'Never mind that,' the Doctor snaps. 'I'm more concerned with the people of this planet.'

'Then I suggest,' says the Master impatiently, 'that you attend to my machine while you still have time.'

'I intend to. But first, I want the core.'

The Master scowls as the Doctor holds out his hand. 'You're guessing!'

'Perhaps. But if I'm wrong, then we'll both die, won't we?'

They glare at each other for a long moment. The Master

drops his eyes first. He reaches into his pocket and produces a blue cube. The Doctor beams broadly and moves to accept it. And the cube tumbles to the ground as the Master's hands reach for the Doctor's throat.

The Doctor takes a step back and applies his Venusian Aikido to flip his attacker on to his back.

'True to form, as always,' he tuts, 'and complacent enough to think I wouldn't expect a double-cross.'

The Master growls and squirms and tries to stand, but is knocked off his feet again by a tremor as another wave crashes by. His head impacts heavily with the ground and his eyes close.

'Hoist by his own petard,' the Doctor murmurs approvingly. He himself can barely stand, but he takes the time to bind the Master's hands with a length of rope. As he retrieves the cube, he takes a final look at his fallen foe. 'I'm truly sorry, old chap,' he says, 'but you have left me no choice.' Then he heads for the Freedom building, running awkwardly beneath a blood-red sky, to save a world.

Soon, everything will return to normal. UNIT troops will take the Master back into custody, hopefully before he awakes. He will face many years trapped between four walls. The Doctor can sympathise, more than ever before. For him, too, freedom is a pipe dream. Even had he made good his escape, the Time Lords would have found him eventually. Still, there is a twinge of disappointment as he feels his knowledge of time travel being once more sapped from his mind.

He is as much a prisoner here as the Master.

# GLASS

by Tara Samms

I don't know why I'm telling you this. I suppose it's because I just need to say it out loud, to say it so you know what's been going on, what I've been living through. As to what might happen if it comes back, I really don't know.

There's absolutely nothing special about me. Late thirties, married, one child, just getting on with things. I've never thought very much about anything before these last months. I'm just boring - I'm so, so boring and I've never had ambitions or wanted very much. My husband is a nice, ordinary person and we have a nice, ordinary child. That was all I wanted. And now my husband thinks I'm mad and my child will hardly speak and I just want to know why it happened to me. Why it happened at all, I suppose, but really why it had to happen to me.

I've lived in Cambridge since 1976. That garden out there was nothing but cracked earth then and now look at it. It hadn't rained for weeks, we'd just moved in and we weren't even allowed to flush the loo or have a bath after carting everything in. It seems so long ago now, I can't believe it's only four years. It was a nightmare - we didn't know anyone beyond Alan's - that's my husband's name, Alan - mum. She was getting sick and he thought we should be nearer her and I didn't really mind, you know. I hadn't made much of a go of it in Greenford. I used to work at the hospital, the Central Middlesex, used to clean there. So I wasn't leaving much behind, but I should've known it was a bad move because Alan's mum died a fortnight after we got there. We hadn't even unpacked.

But it was good for my son, Jason. He started school that year and so he wasn't really that unsettled by the move, I mean no one knows what they're doing on their first day, do they? I started at the Smith's along St Mary's Hill, as a sales assistant. I didn't know what I was doing. It was so much nicer, though, being surrounded by all those books and papers. It didn't smell at all, not like the hospital.

So we were all fine, for years, really. Then I saw him.

It was in the window at Smith's. It was just a normal, ordinary day – quite boring, I suppose, but I don't mind that, like I told you. I like it when things are ordinary, I'm happy.

It was just a face. Funny sort of a face, like a boy, but a grown-up boy. Blond hair. Pink skin, really pink, like he'd just come in from somewhere very cold. It wasn't particularly cold that day, but I remember thinking that it was…

Blue eyes. Grown-up eyes. That was what made him not a boy. And his smile. It was horrible… It was an evil smile, like he'd done something, something horrible, and he was really proud of it.

I realised I had a customer and I took for her paper. She was looking at me like I was weird, and she had a kid with her, not much older than my Jason, and I looked at her boy and all I could think of was, 'That's a kid, a proper kid', and I looked back at the window thinking that horrible face would have gone, but he was still there, still smiling. Then some people moved out of the way and I could see the whole window, and I realised it then.

That's all there was, a face.

It was floating there in the glass like a photograph or something. But the eyes moved and it was alive, I could see that. You know when you just go cold all over, like someone's walked over your grave, or whatever? Well, that's what it was like, and it just stared at me, this face, all big in the glass and looking right at me. In Smith's! I wanted to ask someone to look at it, to tell me I wasn't imagining things. I tried to ask a customer – some man it was, kind-looking. But I couldn't say the words. I just looked at him, and he looked at me a bit concerned, and asked if I was all right and I told myself I was being stupid and I said, 'Yes, yes, I'm fine. Sorry.' And every time I looked up, the face was there, and every time I went to ask someone to look at it and tell me what they saw, I just… knew they wouldn't see it, that they'd think I was mad. That they'd look at me the way that man did. I knew they wouldn't see it.

I told myself it would go away, that I'd been overdoing it, because I hadn't been sleeping all that well even then. They're a bit noisy next door – you know, rows and stuff. Either rows or doing it, really noisily. There's no half-measures with them, they're always either shouting at each other or at it. I used to lie there and listen to them and wonder what it was like being them. I still do that. I do it more often.

Anyway, they took me off the till after an hour and I went to the loos. And I sat there, on the loo, thinking I should cry, wondering what I'd tell the doctor and if he'd believe me, and I was so embarrassed. I was ashamed of myself for crying, getting in such a state. Maybe it was someone playing a joke or something, maybe other people were looking at it wondering who it was, maybe there was quite a fuss going on.

I'd pretty well convinced myself, up there in the quiet of the cubicle, that everything was fine. When I went back down to the shop floor, I made sure I didn't look at the window. I just tidied the books and the magazines. That was my area, you see, the mags and the books.

I finished at half-five normally, but a couple of the casual girls finished ten minutes after me, so I waited for them before going out. The window was right by the main entrance, did I mention that? Well, it was, anyway, that's why I couldn't believe people weren't noticing the face or pointing it out.

So anyway, yes, it was there. But it was still looking at me. It wasn't looking in the direction of the tillpoint, it was looking at me. My heart seemed to freeze. You know when you're scared and you get that feeling that every part of you is sinking into your stomach? It was like that. I couldn't even breathe. It was like every last bit of me was having to be frozen just so my legs could work, just so they could get me out of there. Outside.

I didn't look back. I got on the bus with the others and maybe I was a bit quiet as far as they were concerned, but they didn't seem to notice much. Inside, though, I was absolutely frantic. I just couldn't believe any of it had happened. I could see those eyes the second I closed my own. I could see them... I hated it.

And yet, back home, surrounded by... you know, everything that you know, that's yours, it seemed so different. It's funny how we manage to ignore or dismiss things we don't really understand, isn't it? Do you know what I mean? Like they're not there. And I really began to think, 'No, it couldn't be there, it couldn't possibly have been there', and Jason was telling me about his day at school and when Alan got back I started cooking for us all and I actually forgot about it for most of the night, and I slept OK. I remember really holding Alan, and it was OK.

So next day, of course, it starts to get real again, doesn't it? I'm sitting on the bus on my own and I'm dreading it, you know, really dreading it. But I'm almost a bit excited too. It's silly, isn't it? I felt silly. I felt like you do when you're on a blind date or something, I don't know why.

It was still there. I didn't want to believe it, but...it was like, really faint, and when I came into the building it was like someone had turned up the brightness control, or the contrast, whatever. It was still looking at me and this time I actually said, to a new girl who'd just started, 'Oh, look over there', and I pointed right at the face, that horrible little evil face and she just said, 'What?' and I knew then, I knew she wouldn't be able to see it and I just said, 'Oh, they've gone now.' She just looked at me a bit funny and smiled, but I couldn't smile back. I thought, 'I'm losing it here. This is just stupid.' But it floated there, watching me, all morning.

Then I had my break. I was parched, I got a glass of water. And it was in the glass.

It was the same face, just watching me with that smile. The water in the glass was sploshing about, but it was that face, him, just the same. I must've shouted, must've dropped it, because next thing I know I'm up the other side of the staff canteen and I'm just shaking, shivering like a little kid. People came up to me and asked me if I was all right, and Brian from the warehouse sat me down, asked me if I was really all right. I didn't know what I could say, so I just said it was problems at home, and he squeezed my knee and said he understood. Said I should go home. My supervisor said I should, too, and I was just crying then, and the glass was on the floor. Although I kept trying not to look at it, I couldn't help myself. I kept looking, looking away, looking, looking away.

Brian offered to run me back as he was on his break too. He sat me in the car and put the seat belt on me, and he sort of touched me as he did it – do you know what I mean? But I only realised after he'd done it, and I couldn't really say anything, I wasn't thinking about that. He was talking to me as we were going back. I couldn't concentrate on what he was saying I just knew no one would believe what I'd seen and say that I was going mad. And then Brian put his hand on my leg again and he said, 'I understand' again, and then I saw the face in the windscreen.

It was on my side of the car, looking right at me, curved in the glass like it was part of it, so close this time I could see how old the eyes looked. Funny how you always remember eyes, isn't it? I do. I remember the eyes in that face more than anything else. Cold, so cold. Blue and sparkly, like rock with little bits of quartz in it. I'm not good at describing things, I'm sorry, but... well, you just wouldn't forget those eyes. You can't.

Anyway, I lost it. I was screaming, hiding my eyes, screaming, and I could hear the brakes screech, and as we skidded I remember I thought Oh my God, I'm going to go right through the windscreen, right into him, into that face. And I screamed louder and kept screaming, and Brian hit me, he slapped me right round the face, said it was just a bit of fun, he was sorry and that, but it was just a bit of a laugh. It took me ages to work out what he was on about. He just left me on the pavement where we'd stopped and drove away. I had to walk home. He'd told me not to tell anyone, and it felt like I couldn't tell anyone about anything that was happening, anything. I just looked at my feet as I walked home. It was so slow and I was so afraid out in the open, but I didn't want to look up, didn't want to see anything. I felt like I was mad, and I was so embarrassed and worried what Jason's mates would think. How they'd taunt him. Kids can be cruel like that, can't they? They're pitiless. The face looked like that sort of kid, pitiless.

I know I'm going on. I'm sorry. I suppose I'm just glad to be talking about it all.

Anyway, it went on like this for a few days. I had to get time off work, which they were quite good about actually, probably because it was the holidays so they could get a student in quite easily. I told Alan I wasn't feeling well. He started going on about a holiday for all of us, which I knew we couldn't afford and it just made me depressed. He knew something was up, and he was treating me like an invalid already, like I was cracking up. But that was it, I suppose, I was! I knew I was, I just didn't want to know it. Do you know what I mean? I'm so bad at explaining myself.

But it didn't help. Staying at home, I mean. I saw it in glasses in the house so I used mugs. I saw it in the windows, so I kept the curtains drawn. Then I started seeing it in the light bulbs, so I had to light loads of candles. God knows what Jason thought of it all. I think I really scared him. He would be talking to me and I just wouldn't notice. Then I saw the face in Jason's glasses, both lenses, that same bloody face. I just screamed and ripped the glasses off Jason's ears, and I must've scratched him because he cried out and he was bleeding. He screamed, 'You're not my mum', and I threw his glasses after him and slammed the door.

I couldn't even look at my own son any more.

I'm sure the face knew that and found it funny. I just didn't know what I could do, or where it would stop. I was too scared to step outside the room. I locked it. I wouldn't even let Alan in.

This must've gone on for a week. Then the two people came.

One was a doctor, or so he said, calling through the letter box. I didn't believe it. I thought maybe Alan had called one for me, although I'd told him through the door I didn't want to see one. I thought it was a joke, that he was making fun of me, and I was going to ignore him. Then he said something like, 'It's about that face you've been seeing,' and I felt sick. I thought someone must've seen it after all, that I wasn't crazy, and I felt myself about to cry again and I actually opened the door and went out into the hall. I was going to let him in.

Then I stopped. What if it was the face? What if it was the body come looking for the face? What would I see on the other side of the door?

I just stood there for ages, and the man called my name again and I froze. His voice was deep and warm-sounding. I just... I felt it wasn't the face's voice. But I was still scared, scared to death. Then I heard a girl's voice too. 'You can trust us, you know. In fact, you must trust us. We need your help.' It was quite a snooty voice – she sounded quite kind but a bit hoity-toity as well, you know. I didn't know what to do.

Something plopped through the letter box and I almost screamed. Then I saw it was a jelly baby and I started laughing. Couldn't stop. I went and opened the door and there he was. Tall man, brown curly hair, standing there with a huge grin on his face. Blonde girl next to him, with big teeth. Grinning too. She was wearing a really old-fashioned outfit, white and red. Then he strode in and she said, 'Thank you,' and they were both inside, sitting in the lounge.

'Don't go in there!' I shouted, and the tall man, the Doctor, looked at me with big pale-blue eyes. 'Why? Our shoes are clean,' he said, and he smiled again, but I felt sick and I said,

'No, he'll be there.'

'He?' said the Doctor, looking puzzled, and she said, 'It,' and he said, 'Ahhh.' Then they both looked at me and I really didn't know who was mad now, or even if these people were really there.

He didn't stop looking at me, and though he sounded, you know, chatty, I could tell things were serious. 'I know you've been seeing a face lately. You must tell me when you first saw it and how often you've seen it since.'

And I started bawling again, because here was someone who did understand, and while the tall man just sat there looking at me, his friend the girl – I can't remember her name, I've got a complete block about it – she went over and held me a bit, sort of like you would a child you were going to speak to quite... quite sternly, I suppose.

'Have you seen it in here? In the house?' she said, and I nodded. I could hardly speak. 'Everywhere,' I croaked.

'Everywhere?' boomed the man, and he stood up so quickly he made me jump.

'Everywhere where there's glass?' said the girl, prompting me, I suppose. I just nodded again, but I couldn't look up.

'Pretty advanced in its manifestation, then,' she murmured. I remember that because she made the word 'manifestation' sound so romantic, so mysterious.

'I'd say so,' said the man. 'Let's look around. And he just started walking about, holding some big black box with a few dials on it, and he strode right into my bedroom, and I was so embarrassed because I knew it must stink – I hadn't been out of it for days. And I just wanted them to go.

'Get out', I said. 'Get out.' And he turned to me and said, 'Ahh... we really are the only people who can help you right now, so please... let us get on with it, mm?' He smiled and carried on. I just stood there.

They poked around all over the house, muttering things and talking to each other in serious voices, and I began to feel scared again. I'd felt scared for so long, but this was like a different feeling. Maybe because now I almost felt there was hope and I was so scared of losing that feeling.

'Where did it come from?' I asked him, and he turned around and put his head up close to mine. 'It escaped from a carpetbag,' he said, deadly serious, and then I began to realise that this man was crazy too. It was all crazy, you know, and I began to feel sick again, when she spoke. 'He's telling you the truth. It was being held in a big silver sphere that was kept in a carpetbag, to be precise, but that doesn't sound quite so nonsensical, does it, Doctor?'

'Nothing wrong with nonsense!' beamed the Doctor. 'Half the universe doesn't make sense unless you abandon rational criteria.' Those words just tripped off his tongue. 'And where's the fun in that?' added the girl, looking a bit grumpy. I felt she had quite a lot to put up with somehow.

Then she stopped, called him over to the window and opened it. The two of them stood there looking at the back garden and I just felt really detached. I remember wondering when the garden had been weeded last, and realised that it hadn't been done properly since we got here, when all that cracked earth was baking in the sun.

'Would you look at the greenhouse?' he asked me, and I felt a chill down to my feet. I couldn't even move. 'Please,' she added, and she steered me over there.

I suppose I knew what I'd see before I got there. I looked through the opened windows and followed their gaze.

The face was in every pane of glass in the greenhouse. Dozens of faces, all the same, all looking out. Looking at me.

Happy. All of them looked really, horribly happy.

The needles on the Doctor's gadget were flickering up and down the scale, and there were lights flashing on and off. The girl called him 'ostentatious' or something, saying there was no need for all that, all he needed was a simple data screen, and I was thinking, Just what are you doing talking like this? They seemed to think it was all one big joke and I felt angry. So angry. This thing, this thing that had driven me half mad, made me into a wreck, this evil thing, and the Doctor looks at me with big boggly eyes like some drunk and says, 'You have faces growing in your greenhouse.'

And then – for the first time in ages – I started to feel calmer. I don't know why. I just said, 'Look, are you going to help me or not?' and she said, 'Of course we are,' and I said, 'Well, just what are you going to do?' and they looked at each other like they were sharing some special secret and I said, 'Because I'm going to throw bricks through every window in that greenhouse. I'm going to smash that evil little swine's face in!'

But the girl had walked round behind me and she held my arms. Really gently, but holding them tight at the same time. And her friend looked at me quite seriously and said, 'Don't you even want to know its name?' and I said, 'No. No, I don't.' That scared me, the thought of knowing its name. I can't really tell you why, but maybe because it would be like... like I knew it better or something. I can't explain it. And the man, this Doctor, he shrugged and pulled his lips down, and asked me if I wanted to know why it was here.

'Yes,' I said. 'Yes, why is it here?' And suddenly I needed to know that.

I looked at its faces again in the greenhouse and I needed to know what it wanted.

And the Doctor told me the weirdest story, stuff you'd laugh at, really laugh at, if you heard it. Something about this man who'd come to Cambridge in an invisible spaceship and who had a floating ball that was full of people's minds... something like that anyway. The Doctor and the girl had got rid of him somehow, but one of these minds had got out of this floating globe. It had escaped and was looking for a way back into... well, into this world, I suppose. It wanted to live, really live. And it was using me to help it get back. This Doctor told me this thing had an affinity for glass, was using my mind to focus it into glass, any glass.

Anyone out of all these thousands of people and it chose me. 'You're just unlucky,' the Doctor said, but he reckoned that the odds against it happening were so high I'd probably win the pools or something later on. I know he was just saying that as a joke or something, but it did make me feel a bit better. I think I was so screwed up then I didn't know what I was doing.

I was so scared, you know. I mean, this thing had been using my mind to get stronger, to grow. It was smiling at me like I was its mum or something. That face – the Doctor said it got that from me somewhere. I said I've never seen any face like that and he said in the back of my head there were lots of things I'd never seen, that none of us should ever see, and he was sorry this thing from the blackness was looking at me, full of evil and love… some twisted, mad thing trying to live again in a world it didn't belong in. And I was helping it. It's silly, but I just felt really embarrassed. Yes, more than feeling scared, I was ashamed and embarrassed. I was so messed up…You can't know what it's like when everything has been turned upside-down, even things you didn't know were there, everything, upside-down, broken, useless. I felt useless.

The Doctor said there was no telling what harm or damage this creature could do if it was allowed to get into our world. It wasn't the right dimension, or something, it was unstable… I don't know what he meant really, but he wasn't happy. He told me to stay inside, away from any glass, told me to think about something else. I could barely think at all.

The next thing I knew, the Doctor and the girl were out there in the garden. I watched them through the window – it was still open and I could see the face staring at them. It looked really spiteful, peevish. The Doctor picked up a stone, quite a big one, and threw it at one of the panes of glass – I was thinking, that was my idea, he'd listened to me. It shattered, but then the glass sort of… well, sort of came back together. It was solid again, but the face looked angry now. I felt angry too. I think I felt more angry than afraid then, angry that any of this was happening to me. These people were fighting over my greenhouse, for God's sake! It just felt so strange and stupid.

The Doctor walked right up to the face, looked at it in a way I'd never dared – angry, confrontational – then he just looked surprised, and I realised his arms had been pulled through the glass. There was the sound of breaking glass but no sign of any. It was like his body was being pulled into the glass, and I thought, What about the metal frames? And I could see his body crushed against them, and he looked like he was in enormous pain. He was shouting to the girl, and she turned and caught sight of me watching, and I could see now – she wasn't so haughty, she was scared like I was.

'Get out here,' she shouted at me, and I did. I found myself obeying her even though I was scared to death. Maybe I was just scared that if the Doctor went, I'd never know what had happened. By the time I got out of the kitchen door the Doctor had gone. I stared at the face – I'd stayed away from it for so long and there it was. I'd run out to see it and I swear – and it chills me even as I sit here and talk to you – it looked at me like it wanted me, like it wanted me to hold it or something. Holding a face, I know it sounds stupid but I saw something in its eyes… I just knew it was evil and knew that it wanted me. It was hateful – horrible.

'The Doctor's in there!' she yelled. 'Help me with these.' She was trying to pick up bits of the sycamore we'd cut down the autumn before, big spindly, gnarled old branches. They'd been lying in a pile waiting to be burnt. They were all slimy… horrid. 'We're going to push these through its faces. And hold them there! We mustn't let the glass grow back.' And there was such certainty in her voice, you know, I just nodded. She was like a school teacher. I was so scared, but I nodded, and I looked at it with that nauseating look on its faces and I ran up to one and battered it with the stick. I heard the glass crack – then shatter – but the stick was just sucked straight through. 'Hold on to it!' the girl screamed at me, and I was imagining what the neighbours must think, if they were calling the police, if the police came and couldn't see the face and took us away and left the Doctor in there. I wonder if he would see the back of its head from inside the greenhouse. But somehow I knew that each pair of eyes would be turned inwards too, fixing him there under the glass. I thought of the pain on his face as it had dragged him through.

And it made me more determined. The Doctor's friend had shoved a branch through the glass in one pane and part of the wood was splintered against the frame, holding it in place. The face looked so angry, it was furious. I could hear the Doctor shout out and I looked at the girl. She looked back at me and she was smiling – actually smiling, a really brave smile. I managed to break more of the glass, right through its smile I went, and I was terrified it would bleed and I'd be covered in its blood, but there was just this kind of howl, a distant sort of howl... The glass was trying to re-form around the wood but it couldn't. It was trying to spit out the wood, or suck it in, but as I held it there and felt it tugged by whatever was in there, I just kept saying, 'No, no,' like I used to coo to Jason when he was little, and I thought of him with his little glasses and how this face had taken his eyes from me.

Then the Doctor's friend suddenly waved another branch at me and, still holding on with one arm to the wood wedged in the window, I kicked against the bottom pane with my foot, really hard, again and again. I shoved the end of the branch through it, held it there, and it was sucking at this one now too. I just held on, cooing at the faces under my breath, looking as they swam about the panes, looking for clear glass to be whole in.

But the Doctor was smashing the other panes from the inside and the tugging was getting less, and I could see the faces were fading from the other panes, they were gasping in silence, gasping for someone to help them, and I just thought, 'I can't help you, you mustn't be here, let go, it'll be OK, let go,' and I nearly let go myself – of the branches, I mean; I had to shake my head and hold on to them tighter. I really don't know if it had been talking to me or if it was just me after all – do you know what I mean?

It was more or less over then. I had my eyes shut, so I don't know how the faces were looking when they finally went. It bothers me in a way, now. I wish I had been looking, right at the end.

The Doctor seemed fine. He had something wrapped up in his coat, something he wouldn't let me see. He said whatever it was had been 're-creating' itself – or trying to, trying to get into our world – and this was what it had managed to make for itself. It was the size of a sack of potatoes, but it didn't seem to weigh very much. Apparently it had dragged in the Doctor to try and use his energy to grow. He said he could shield his mind from the power in the glass in some way, so it had brought him through, to focus itself on him, to destroy him. But he wasn't complaining. It was as if he understood or something... or even respected it.

But I was so tired by then and the explanations didn't really make much sense. All I knew was they were laughing now, him and the girl. They were laughing like it was all some joke, and I just said, 'Well, what about my greenhouse' and he stared at me with those wide eyes and his big grin and told me to blame it on energetic bluebottles or something. Then he said they had to go, that I'd have no more problems, and that was it – gone out of my door, with whatever it was under his arm, and they left me alone.

Alone.

And I was still so scared. I was so scared I ran from the house into the street, and I must've smelt, and people stared at me, and I still wouldn't look at any glass. I couldn't.

I can't begin to tell you what it's been like since. I can't work. I'm on benefit. The doctor – my GP, I mean, Dr Gellert – says I've had a nervous breakdown. I cried when she said it. I was overjoyed. It sounds crazy but I was... I wouldn't have to tell her the truth. I knew she'd never believe me. I know you don't, not really – it's all right, I don't blame you. I almost think I've made it up myself half the time...

We're waiting to move now. The house has been on the

market for months… I wouldn't let Alan rebuild the greenhouse. Blamed it on vandals. Alan doesn't understand any of this, but I think he's so sick of the way I've been it's either move out with me or just divorce me. He probably thinks it's more respectable for us to move. I don't know… I don't know.

I'm still scared to look at my boy. I'm still scared to look too hard at anything. Because it wasn't a joke, or funny. It was evil, whatever it was, it was evil and it loved me and it wanted me, and I can't help thinking – knowing – I'm going to see it again. See its face, in the window, in the bottom of a glass… There, in the bottom of a glass.

# Mondas Passing

## by Paul Grice

Ben decided he didn't like the hotel room. OK it was warm, providing shelter from the cold drizzle of the early evening, but it seemed somehow claustrophobic despite its agreeable size.

He switched on a wall-light and it shone upward on to the red sheen of the wall, filling the room with a dull, lazy glow that seemed comforting against the darkness encroaching from the window. Crossing over to the bed, he opened his suitcase and took out a miniature bottle of rum. He needed a drink after the long drive down. After all, it was New Year's Eve – New Year's Eve, 1986.

He couldn't believe how quickly the year had gone, moving inexorably towards December, the time it had all happened – or rather would happen. The Zeus spacecrafts had started their launches early in the year. He'd even seen the Snowcap base and General Cutler on the news. Poor old Cutler…

The thoughts sent chills through his whole body. Ghosts from his past enacting events that were really only just happening. How many times had he had the nightmare of the Cyberman advancing on him in the Projection Room? Waking up in a sweat shouting, You didn't leave me no alternative! Hard to explain to the wife… And if it wasn't that, there were the dreams of 'her'. He could hardly tell the wife about that, could he? Of course, he felt guilty leaving her alone tonight, but he just had to be here.

He told himself it was stupid: he knew the Cybermen didn't win in 1986, just as they wouldn't win on the Moon in 2070. Twenty years ago he had helped to save the world he lived in today. Now he was middle-aged and world-weary. His eyes had lost a lot of their cocky self-assurance, and his expression now constantly seemed somehow troubled or slightly hurt.

God, he wanted his youth back. Wanted her. Somewhere at the South Pole around now they were together and he ached for that time. He couldn't be sure exactly when it was; he remembered only that the calendar had said December 1986. But there had been no mention of a tenth planet lately, no reports of any energy drains, so it couldn't have happened yet. Unless it had been covered up. Yeah, maybe –

His thoughts were interrupted by the knock on the door. He froze. This was sooner than he'd let himself dare hope for – he'd only been there himself half an hour. He frantically checked himself in the mirror: oh God... oh God...

'It's the staff,' he told himself, 'checking the room's OK. That's all.' But the knock came again, a presumptuous knock, familiar still after all these years. Breathing in deeply, stomach held firmly in, he opened the door.

'Hello, Duchess.'

'Ben!'

The warmth of Polly's hug surprised him. Maybe she had been dwelling on things as much as he had. Or maybe this was how she greeted everyone now; he hadn't seen her for years... Her hair was still long, and almost the same colour blonde – must be dyed now, of course, he mused. And she smelt the same. That scent had brought so much warmth to the cold sterile air of the TARDIS. She'd kept her figure well, too – better than he had anyway. She was still the same Polly.

'Didn't think you was coming.' Ben's voice came softly, experimentally, into the soft red light of the room. He wasn't sure whether words were appropriate at this moment. The seconds ticked by and he fiddled nervously with the hem of his sweater.

'I nearly didn't.'

'S'pose you couldn't get away from the old man?' The bitter tone was barely concealed.

'He thinks I'm with some of my old girl friends from school

166

on a reunion.'

'You must 'ave him eating out the palm of your 'and.'

'He likes me to be happy.'

'Yeah, I'll bet he does.'

'Ben, don't.' Her tone was angry but her eyes were pleading with him to leave that part of her alone. 'Not tonight.'

He walked over to the window and stared out into the clear, dark night. No tenth planet glowing and pulsing in the sky... 'Course, you might not be able to see it from here anyway, being in the northern hemisphere...

'Is it there, Mondas?' Polly's voice sounded almost childishly timid.

Ben answered with reassuring brashness: ''Course it ain't. We ain't heard nothing, 'ave we? It's been and gone, we sorted it... with the Doctor.'

'Just before he changed... yes.'

She joined him at the dark window and idly doodled on the huff she breathed on to the cold glass. 'Did it ever really happen? Any of it?'

'Guess so, Poll.'

The Moon stared down at them, meeting their suspicious eyes with a baleful glare.

Polly continued, almost dreamily. 'Have we really walked on the Moon?'

Ben looked at her. 'Dunno... How could we have? After all –' He attempted a broad Scottish accent: 'The Moon is up in the sky!'

Polly laughed and sat heavily on the bed. 'Don't be cruel! Poor Jamie...'

Ben laughed too, then tried to sit down next to her without looking too self-conscious.

Polly's laughter faded away. 'I wonder if Jamie's still with him.'

'Probably,' affirmed Ben. 'He'd follow him anywhere. He's stupid enough!'

'Oh, Ben, he was nice!'

'Yeah, he was a good bloke… Wonder how the Doctor is.'

'Wonder what he looks like now!'

Ben grinned. 'Could be down the corridor for all we know!'

The evening passed. Reminiscences of narrow escapes, of lost Atlantis and Culloden, of Roundheads and Selachians, of giant crabs and Daleks seemed to strengthen the bond between them that had been broken for so long. In the background they could hear pumping dance music from the floor below. The laughter and chatter of hundreds of guests, blissfully unaware of the danger their world might be in, living purely for the moment, floated up. It comforted them both when there were lulls in the conversation, reassurance that everything outside was all right – at least for tonight.

They jumped as Ben's watch alarm abruptly sounded. 'Midnight!'

Polly answered him with startled eyes: 'Midnight.'

A mighty cheer battered at them from beneath the floorboards and from down the corridor.

'Adios 1986,' said Ben, smiling. 'We made it.'

Polly looked at him strangely. 'Yes, we did.'

He moved closer.

At that moment there was a sudden noise – something slamming itself against the door.

Ben froze. Polly jumped. It was his wife. Her husband. The Doctor had come to see them. Or it was a Cyberman. Maybe…

Ben cautiously approached the door. There was another bang, this time followed by a loud, insistent hammering. With a warning glance at Polly and a gesture for her to stay back, he threw open the door.

Polly found herself giggling as Ben reeled under the weight of the drunken man who fell into his arms.

'Wrong room, mate. You want down the 'all... 'Ere, you all right? You've 'ad a right skinful…'

The man's attempts at a reply died away into incoherence. Ben steered him out of the room, struggling a little under his weight, then turned him to face the right way and shut the door.

Looking at Polly, he was disconcerted to see the wide grin on her face.

'All the nice boys love a sailor,' she giggled.

Ben looked down at the floor. He felt foolish. He tried to move towards her again, but he knew that the moment had passed. The intensity between them had faded with the old year.

He tried anyway: 'Duchess –'

'It's over, Ben. It's the past.' She smiled, a little sadly. 'We've only just saved the day out there at the South Pole, haven't we? We can't do it again now... not twenty years later.'

She picked up her bag from the bed and moved silently across the room.

'You're going?'

She nodded. 'We can look forwards now.'

'Will I see you –'

Polly shook her head and opened the door. The noise of the partygoers flooded in, as if to emphasise the silence that had deadened the room. Pausing in the doorway, she turned to face him.

'Somewhere out there, Ben, we're still together. Still having those narrow escapes.'

He nodded, dumbly.

'And, Ben...'

He looked up from the floor and into her eyes as she spoke.

'...none of those escapes was any more difficult than this one.'

As the door clicked shut behind her, Ben walked back to the window. 'What a bleedin' melodrama!' he muttered. 'The missus would be in floods if this was a film.'

The Moon was still staring down, white and aloof. 'Don't look so cocky, mate. I've walked all over you.' He forced a smile and reflected on the evening – on Polly, on the passing of his fears.

Ahead of him now was a new year, together with all the promise it brought. Suddenly he felt very tired. It was only just gone midnight and he was tired! He grimaced. 'I must be getting old...'

He closed his eyes. 'See ya in 2070, Duchess.'

# There are Fairies at the Bottom of the Garden

by Sam Lester

Dodo quickened her pace to catch the Doctor. The caped figure had disappeared round one of the endless twists and turns of the tunnel system. Uneasiness rose within her as she thought of being abandoned in this place. She took a deep breath to quieten the approaching hysteria and almost choked. The cloying fumes filled her lungs with the cold touch of death. That's what this place was - dead. There was no end to the decay as she fearfully gazed up at the faintly glowing canopy.

Occasionally she caught a glimpse of unfamiliar stars - the only indication of anything beyond this nightmare. Suddenly, she realised that she'd been thinking she was underground, that the clammy walls were some kind of tomb. But they were on the surface of a planet - a planet where even the air made her sick. Her eyes widened and she began to retch; she had to get away from the looming forms above her and their putrescent embrace.

Her panic was forgotten as she careered into the low form of the Doctor. She hadn't even noticed she'd broken into a run. 'Doctor! There you are.' Relief quickly turned to embarrassment at the sight of the frail figure dusting himself down and casting around for his cane. 'Sorry, Doctor. I don't like this place at all. And with you wandering off –'

'My dear, of course I "wandered off" as you say. This place is fascinating, simply fascinating. The ship has never brought us anywhere quite like this. It must surely be unique. Fascinating. The infinite diversity of life.' The Doctor's words seemed to be aimed at someone other than herself as he turned back to inspect the walls, prodding and sniffing at the dark substance.

'But, Doctor, how can you talk of life? This place is dead.

Can't you smell it? It's revolting.' Dodo would never understand his preoccupation with investigating even the most obvious things. She realised that common sense must be very much a human thing. 'Why don't we just leave, Doctor? This place is horrible: it's cold, damp and I think the stench is making me ill.' She pulled the fur coat the Doctor had given her up around her mouth, seeking reassurance in its touch. She waited for an answer, her dark eyes imploring.

'Stench, my dear? I find it rather invigorating actually. Stop worrying about such things. Look about you and learn. You have a chance to see something none of  your kind will probably ever see.'

In the weak phosphorescent light that the walls afforded, the Doctor's angular features looked jaundiced. An air she would normally have thought of as aloof now seemed uncaring and arrogant. His eyes sparkled for a moment as he regarded her, then he cocked his head in the curious way that she usually found endearing. But not today. She looked up as liquid dripped from the peak of her cap; she pulled it down tight over her short hair, hiding the anger in her eyes.

'There is something very wrong here, you know, Dodo,' he said at last. 'Something most unpleasant.'

'That's just what I've been saying, Doctor. Let's get out of here.' Dodo's relief was apparent in her words. A small smile crossed her lips as she went to help the Doctor up.

'Nonsense, girl. There is something seriously wrong here that warrants my attention. If you cannot see that, then it would appear that the time you have spent with me has been almost entirely wasted.' With that he grasped his cane, turned on his heel and stalked off with an astonishing turn of speed.

It pondered the two broken drones as it patrolled the life. They were the first it had come across for some time. It couldn't understand where the others had gone. The great paths were growing quiet. Like those it had encountered before, these no longer heard or sang the song – they were separate. What must it be like not to be able to hear the song? To scrabble around the paths alone? To be lost?

Perhaps it would soon learn. It could feel the growth within itself – another call of dazzling brilliance. Singing once more of boundless joy and purpose. It knew it was changing, that new paths were being chosen for it. Hopefully it would be soon, then all would be clear again. And the song would be sung.

Shaking off all distractions, it decided to draw strength. It must finish the patrol – and see if the broken drones could be helped. It decided to head towards the nearest of the two, trying to ignore the tiny seed of confusion deep within its core.

Dodo was furious. He had simply left her. Left her alone on a grim twilight planet that stank. She cursed the TARDIS quietly under her breath and wondered, not for the first time, whether she was really cut out for adventure. She had rather a strong feeling that she wasn't – but she certainly wasn't going to admit that to an old man who seemed more concerned with a world of rising damp than with her own feelings. Anyway, she supposed she could stand the place a while longer. After all, what could the Doctor find to occupy himself with for more than an hour or two? Even his perverse fascinations would surely soon founder here.

She took a deep breath and gagged again. Something would have to be done about that. Once the bile had subsided, she checked the pockets of the heavy fur for a handkerchief or scarf – something to at least take the moisture out of the heavy air. On finding a delicate lace square, she brought it to her lips and began to take nervous, dainty breaths. As she pondered whether to follow the old man or merely sulk in the darkness, she leant against the glowing wall.

With a scream she snatched her hand back, desperately trying to contain her revulsion. The wall was soft. She would have said it was alive if it hadn't been so cold and wet. Her mind immediately went back to the feel of dead fish – something that had always turned her stomach. The simple dislikes of a life galaxies and possibly eternities away brought home to her her sense of isolation and her eyes, like every part of this diseased land, became moist. She was alone in the dark on a planet made of dead haddock! She would have laughed, but once more she could feel the dark presence of hysteria at the edge of her awareness.

She needed something to do. If she concentrated on the little things then maybe the greater picture would fade temporarily. So, after a furtive glance up and down the passage, she took off one of her shoes. As her unshod foot hit the floor, a shiver ran up her spine – the stinking liquid went straight through her tights. Pulling the fur even tighter about herself and grasping the shoe firmly in her right hand, she set about the disturbing wall with the improvised tool.

The simple black shoe had enough of an edge on its small heel to begin scraping at the wall's slimy coating. In no time the glowing outer layer had come away to reveal pliant fungal flesh oozing liquid. Where before the odour of decay had been hard to stand, now it was unbearable. Sulphur mixed with the ubiquitous stench of death, bringing more water to her eyes and closing up her throat.

Dodo staggered back, bringing the hanky to her mouth again but still holding the now partly glowing shoe. Her back hit the opposite wall and she allowed herself to slide down it to the floor, not caring about the streaks of glowing lichen attaching themselves to her coat. She put the shoe back on, rested her chin on her knees and attempted to cover her legs with the limited resource of her short skirt. She gave in. Sitting there in a cold stagnant puddle, she attempted to make sense of the results of her brief attempts at investigation.

The walls here were alive. Or rather, they were organic – but without any of the reassuring warmth and essence she associated with things organic. Perhaps it was dying. Yes, the ship had set them down in the midst of a world of disease. So she had been right to want to leave – she certainly wouldn't want to find such death throes 'fascinating'.

Her own thoughts on death harmonised with a quiet lament that she now noticed for the first time somewhere off in the distance. Could the Doctor be moved to song in such a place? Unlikely, particularly as Dodo didn't recognise any of the words, if indeed there were any words. After a moment she realised that this was a song without a lyric – voice as instrument – but containing the essence of a lament. She couldn't identify any particular element, she just knew that the song had a keening, mournful quality. She closed her eyes to see if she could work out where it was coming from. Suddenly, a thump and a splash marked the arrival of something right in front of her. With a start she looked up.

The scream was on her lips before she'd fully taken in the sight before her eyes. Towering over her huddled, hysterical form was a truly bizarre creature. It must have been at least six feet tall, even though it was hunched over and headless. Like everything else she had seen on the planet, it was greeny-brown in colour, dripping with rancid liquid, and it stank. A vivid splash of crimson marked where its face should have been. Four long limbs shot out in random directions, and where they touched the ground or walls wriggling tentacles sprang out, anchoring the beast before her.

More unpleasant than its physical form and dramatic arrival, however, was its song – for it must surely have been the source of the lament. Despite its obvious lack of a mouth, Dodo was deafened as the song changed tone and overwhelmed her. It seemed to come from all around; her head was filled with whole operas of sorrow. In time, the song shifted again and the lament took on dizzying spikes of anger.

Scrambling away in terror, Dodo realised she was still screaming. But she couldn't stop – her head was filled with desperate sadness and undirected anger, as well as her own boundless fear. As she moved away, the creature followed, its extremities unbinding and rebinding in a curious four-limbed gait that kept its headless torso always above her. Unable to get away, she pulled a knee back to kick out at her tormentor, only to find the shaft of the Doctor's cane across the sole of her foot.

His words stung as much as they comforted. 'Don't do that, child. I don't think we want to give the wrong impression.' Then, with a quick smile and a sharp turn of his head, he approached the beast.

Dodo expected the Doctor to grasp his lapels and browbeat the creature into docility; she did not expect him to lay his cane against a wall, stand squarely before the imposing form, say the unlikely words 'Quite beautiful' and then plunge his hands right into its torso. As he did so, he closed his eyes, screwing them up tight, and began to hum a rather soothing tune. After a while the anger and sorrow that filled Dodo's head abated and she allowed herself a sigh. The handkerchief was now soaked with her own tears.

Glancing up at the Doctor, she struggled to her feet. In his Edwardian garb, winged collar and cape, he looked as if he was conducting a bizarre one-man orchestra. Dodo couldn't help giggling, partly from relief and partly from the absurdity of the sight.

The old man's eyes snapped open and he fixed her with the piercing gaze that always unnerved her. 'Never strike out at something just because you don't understand it.' His words came like blows. 'Can't you see that there's something very wrong here?' Then, with a sickening sucking sound, he drew his hands out of the beast and stalked off again.

But this time she wasn't alone. The creature in front of her seemed dazed after the Doctor's intervention. It swayed gently and cast its limbs about in confusion. Its song was no more than a whisper that Dodo had to concentrate to make out. Suddenly, the beast began to shudder violently, with clouds of cloying, sulphurous vapour spewing from rents in its spasming torso.

Dodo held the handkerchief tight to her mouth and blinked

away the new tears the vapour was producing. She decided to approach and see if there was anything she could do, but before she reached her target it was seized by stillness. It seemed totally calm. Then, with a slowness Dodo interpreted as reluctance, the creature shambled away from her, caressing the walls tenderly as it did so.

The Doctor's words, and his preoccupation with this ghastly world, stung Dodo into action. Waiting for him to come back had not proved overly successful, and the creature hadn't actually harmed her, so she set off after the lurching form. In no time at all she was running to keep up, as she was led along passageways and through dark, oppressive tunnels. Once the creature had decided where it was going, it seemed in a desperate hurry to get there, and soon Dodo was following only the sounds of its movements.

More and more stars became visible. The air seemed subtly fresher. A small, bright moon came into view. They were travelling upwards, and Dodo wondered if there was a place on this world where you didn't feel enclosed. She could still see the ghostly forms of the topmost canopies high above.

Struggling with fatigue, Dodo continued her progress. She strained to hear the distant sounds that told her she was still on the right path. As she ran, she noticed the nature of the walls and floor, the very fabric of this unpleasant land, was changing. What before had been eerie glowing lichen and slick darkness now contained increasingly large streaks of glowing crystal – almost like veins, running in all directions and branching off. Colours varied but the essential quality was that of clean light, which became brighter the higher she went, lifting her spirits enormously.

Soon spars ran across the tunnels and passageways, some more than a foot thick, each made of what looked like amethyst. Dodo occasionally had to climb over or under the most awkward of these obstacles. After a final such hurdle, she looked up to see the sky – the whole sky. But though she had longed for the open, her eye was almost wrenched downward

– to the sight laid out below her.

Dodo shielded her eyes as she took in the remarkable scene. Down a gentle slope that stretched for perhaps a mile, myriad colours danced before her. It was as if someone had taken a rainbow and fashioned a landscape from pure refracted light. Here was a land of crystal, a dazzling glade of perfect fragile transparency. Short shards of amethyst and azure formed a delicate uniform carpet from which sprouted majestic flora: sky-reaching palms and broad, low trees – each with gossamer-thin crystal foliage that reminded her of the snowflake cutouts she had made as a child. The branches and leaves swayed gently in a breeze that still carried a hint of the earlier oppressive decay, but the sheer beauty of the vista cleansed that horror from Dodo's mind. Here was beauty in its highest form – a garden for the angels themselves. In her stained and sodden fur coat, she felt unworthy to even look upon such perfection; she just gawped.

A crash followed by the singsong tinkle of falling crystal splinters distracted her. She pulled herself together and reminded herself of her purpose. The creature was further down the slope, lurching through the exotic garden with a lack of respect that could only be due to its apparent blindness. She set off after it, trying not to walk on anything, and continually failing.

As Dodo made her way daintily down the hill, she noticed that the flora appeared to be increasing in size. This time, however, rather than feeling closed in by the massive forms above her, she rejoiced in their radiance, and her mouth was soon bent into a permanent grin. Indeed, staring up into the multicoloured canopy, she didn't notice at first when she entered a clearing; but once she drew her eyes down to check the path ahead, a gasp escaped her lips. She must have hit her head somewhere, she reasoned, or something in the atmosphere was making her hallucinate.

Before her was a fairy grotto. Across a short sapphire lawn, at the centre of a perfectly circular treeless area, grew an exquisite bloom. Keeping low to the ground, it appeared to be slowly unfurling layer after layer of transparent petals. Each layer was a different shade, but each complemented those of its nearest neighbours – it was a faultless exercise in colour co-ordination. But it wasn't the bloom itself which drew Dodo's gasp; it was the creatures skipping across its surface and dancing in the air above like fireflies. They were fairies. They just couldn't be anything else.

There was no recourse to the life. But was it really a choice? It could not be avoided now. The seed of change was within. Now was the time. The decision would have to be made.

She crept across the clearing to get a better look. Definitely fairies. What else looks like a girl with elfin features, has fragile butterfly wings and can sit comfortably in the palm of your hand? Dodo's grin widened. So they were real after all. The tiny transparent creatures seemed to take notice of her and one flew across to investigate. It seemed to be singing a gentle lilting song – a celebration of the beauty around them and its own perfection. As it danced before her eyes, she wondered whether she would ever see anything like this again – or whether anyone would ever believe her. She doubted both.

In time, the crystal form, its wings showing the merest hint of emerald, veered away from her. She turned to watch the tiny creature approach the now collapsed form of the beast from the lower levels. Dodo was completely unprepared when the song once more crashed over her perceptions. Her grin turned to a rictus of pain as primal sorrow, anger and now agony swept over her. Tears sprang to her eyes and she started to sob.

It felt right now. The choice was made. The severance would soon be over and a new song would be sung. A new, stronger song. A new unity.

* * *

179

The dark creature, like a stain on the sapphire lawn, rocked violently and then was still. With a sound like steam escaping, its skin started to split open. The song was now just an expression of pain, as screams replaced the last vestiges of rhythm. Then there was an echoing silence. The regular tinkle of crushed crystal shards made her realise she had been rocking back and forth. Her coat was now covered in what looked like sapphire pine needles. The Doctor was going to be even less pleased with her.

Then thoughts of the Doctor were extinguished by a final triumphal outburst, and her eyes returned to the dark creature. From a hole in the centre of its cracked and steaming torso a tiny bedraggled transparent form dragged itself. Carefully it spread its limp wings, drawing in light and strength from all around, and after a moment it seemed assured and strong enough to join the others around the bloom. As it swooped by her, Dodo noticed that this newborn had a flash of ruby running through it.

She looked back at the broken form of the beast that had terrified her earlier and smiled. Why did the Doctor always have to be so infuriatingly right? 'OK, I admit it, it's beautiful. You were right, Doctor. I didn't understand. It's the most beautiful thing I've ever seen.'

Dodo was suddenly embarrassed at speaking aloud when she was on her own – she really didn't need extra reasons for thinking she was going doolally – so she returned to her examination of the bloom. The layers of petals continued to peel back every minute or two, revealing a new delicate shade that took her breath away. It was not far off being completely unfurled and she wondered what delights would be uncovered then. She folded the battered fur as a makeshift cushion and settled down to wait. Even though she felt tired and dazed, she could still feel her own massive grin. The soothing song of the fairies kept her expectation company.

'There you are, my dear. So, you found something of interest on this world, I see.'

The Doctor's voice shattered her mood immediately and forced her to tear her gaze away from the bloom. He stood at the edge of the clearing, a monochrome elder in the home of youthful colour. His whole posture seemed to shout out disapproval. His cape lent his slight figure substance and his cane was thrust firmly into the sapphire carpet, as if he were staking a claim. He had put his hat back on and, despite its jaunty angle, it seemed to make him even more austere.

'It's all right, Doctor. I understand now. It's metamorphosis – the ugly becomes the beautiful, like you said.'

Dodo had hoped he would soon relent, but the elderly figure seemed to be ignoring her as he strode purposefully across the clearing.

'Metamorphosis indeed,' the Doctor muttered with a scathing shake of the head. He approached the broken body of the fallen creature and stooped over it. He brought a lens to his eye while he prodded the corpse with his stick. Small drifts of vapour swirled around its tip. Dodo wondered why he should find the dark and ugly end of the process so much more interesting than the beautiful result.

'Doctor, look at the flower. Isn't it just the loveliest thing?' she called, hoping to lift his dark mood.

The Doctor snapped up from his examination. 'What? Oh, yes, my dear. Exquisite. Exquisite indeed.'

He seemed to notice the bloom for the first time. Tucking the lens away in a pocket, he approached the unfurling rainbow. Dodo was surprised by the caution that ran through each of his gentle, precise movements. He slowly circled the bloom, staying a good six feet away and examining it from all angles. At last he decided to go in closer.

In one swift movement, the fairies converged on the elderly figure. They buzzed around his sharp features and the Doctor swung at them wildly with his cane. Tiny scratches appeared across his face, as some of the winged creatures made it through his defences. Dodo couldn't understand why the little creatures were attacking him, but she could see the anger in the Doctor's bright, ageless eyes.

He finally got within reach of the bloom itself and gazed down – just as the last of its petals began to curl back. One moment the cane was held high above the diminutive figure, its silver tip glinting in the rainbow glare, the next it plunged down into the heart of the delicate crystal form. Dodo's own scream mixed with those of the fairies.

It was later, much later, and Dodo finally felt able to speak again. She stared at the old man as he fussed around the TARDIS controls. He didn't seem to realise what he had done. She could still see the shattered flower, petals spinning out across the clearing. The screams of the fairies still echoed around her head. She wouldn't forget their elfin faces as the light and life ebbed from them – broken butterflies on a bed of darkening sapphire. The words just spilled out.

'Why did you do it, Doctor? How could you do it?' Dodo was startled how forceful she sounded.

'Why, my dear? Why?' The Doctor started without looking up from the instruments. 'Because, Dodo, there was beauty on that planet. Beauty beyond simple razzle-dazzle and flimflam. A beauty which probably took aeons to evolve, and one which is certainly unique and enriching.'

The column halted its steady rise and fall, and the Doctor activated the scanner control with a flourish. Dodo saw the return of his mischievous grin. 'And because, my dear, I dislike parasitic crystalline entities.'

Confused, Dodo looked up at the screen. They appeared to be in space above the planet – the journey had been too short for it to be anywhere else. Below them, lit by the arrival of a burnt yellow sun, massive shapes moved.

It took a while for Dodo to realise what the huge forms were that gradually came into view, then it became all too obvious. She blushed at her own misapprehension. They were giant flowers in subtle shades of red and green. Vast and impressive.

At the far edge of the world, touching the approaching sun, she could see a dark stain on the surface of one of the great plants. The odd glint of sunlight brought home to her exactly what it was: a canker, a beautiful crystal plague.

A tear rolled down her cheek as took in the sight and listened to the song – the true song that swept outward from the planet. Its delicacy touched her heart. It was a song of joy, of perfect understanding and freedom.

# Mother's Little Helper

## by Matthew Jones

Hatred can be like food: it gives you energy; you can live off it. Maybe because it's easier to be so angry with someone that you could stab them to death or something rather than actually dealing with the hurt they have done you.

Nanci Cruz had been living on hatred for two weeks, three days and – she glanced at her watch – fourteen hours. The exact amount of time since she had stumbled into the girls' toilets at the end-of-term disco and discovered her boyfriend with his hand up the blouse of her best friend.

Ex-best friend. Ex-boyfriend.

Since then hatred was the only way she could face going out of the house. The pain which bubbled beneath the rage continually threatened to erupt, and if it did then she would probably just cry and cry until there was nothing left inside her at all.

She couldn't take anything for granted now. Even window-shopping in the town centre had become like a reconnaissance mission into enemy territory. She was terrified of seeing Susanne or Joe. Or worse, of seeing them together. The image punched her in the guts. God, that would be unbearable. Don't even think about it.

The sunlit lanes of the small coastal town of Southmouth were packed with souvenir shops and tourists. Nanci made her way through crowds, squinting at the sun as she tried to keep an eye out for classmates. Her humiliation at the disco was probably the latest summer-holiday gossip.

Nanci had lived in the town for almost a year; ever since she had emigrated from NYC. Coming to Europe had not been her idea. The move had been instigated by her mother, an almost famous psychotherapist who had been offered a professorship at the sprawling campus university behind the town. Ironically, it had been Susanne and Joe who had liberated Nanci from the isolated and introverted life of a legal alien. English people were so different. Susanne drank pints of cider and appeared to exist on a diet of French fries. Joe even smoked – like, all of the time! No one took exercising seriously here. There was no one to train with at the gym. Since the disco, there wasn't anyone at all.

Nanci heard a shout from behind her – a warning? Someone or something slammed into her and she was thrown to the hard concrete with a yelp. Her knee lit up in agony and her palm stung where it had been grazed on the concrete. Instinctively, she twisted around to see her attacker and began to scramble away at the same time.

She stopped in her tracks as she found herself staring at a young boy. He couldn't have been more than about seven – eight at the most. He was trying to get to his feet, although he looked as disoriented as she felt. Nanci had never seen anyone like him in Southmouth before. His blond hair was neatly side-parted and his clothes were formal and grey. He was even wearing a tie. A small, brown leather box hung from a strap which crossed his scrawny body diagonally.

She sensed that a crowd was forming around them. Her jeans were torn and blood ran from a nasty gash on her knee. The last thing she wanted to be was the centre of attention. She tried to get to her feet, but leaning on her hand only made it hurt more. She cursed loudly. She didn't want to have to deal with this. She just wanted to be at home in bed, far away from people. Suddenly, uncharacteristically, she burst into tears.

Through her tears she saw that the boy was staring directly at her. His eyes were an impossibly golden colour and as bright as sunlight reflected on water. He began to move slowly towards her, reaching out his hand. The expression on his face was gentle and sincere. His small fingers touched hers and she gasped as she felt their warmth slide under her skin and up through her body.

Nanci forgot about the bystanders. She felt as if she were suddenly standing on a beach on a cool evening. Her head filled with the gentle sound of the sea. Out of nowhere she remembered being gathered up into her father's arms after falling from her tree house; remembered him kissing her grazed forehead better.

The warmth – she couldn't think of another word for it – from the little boy slipped around her defences and comforted her hurt. The terrible betrayal she felt at the hands of her so-called friends began to recede. Her anger towards Joe lessened.

She heard the boy give out a cry of alarm and the small hand disappeared: the warm sensation went with it. The pavement slipped back under her feet. She opened her eyes and saw that the boy was already moving away. His quiet, serious expression had been replaced by a look of total fear. For a brief moment, Nanci thought he must have been looking at her and then she realised that he was looking past her, over her shoulder. Confused but still intrigued, she turned to try and see who the boy was afraid of.

A woman was striding towards them, her face silhouetted by the bright summer sunlight. She was wearing a silver lamé cocktail dress decorated with sequins and had cascades of bright blonde hair. Nanci couldn't quite see the woman's face, but her determined pace suggested that she was chasing the boy. Was she his mother? Nanci couldn't get the boy's fearful expression out of her mind.

Nanci was about to rise to her feet, planning to place herself in the woman's path, when Joe crashed back into her mind, like a tidal wave on to a dusty beach. Suddenly, she was back in the girls' bathroom at the school disco, making out the two entwined figures in the corner. She was recognising the ring on his finger as he slipped his hand under the hem of the shimmering blue blouse. Susanne's new blouse. The one they had chosen together. After the emotional oasis the boy had magically provided, it was like experiencing the whole thing again. The pain as strong as the first time. Nanci had to fight to stop herself bursting into tears. She completely forgot about the woman.

'Did you see him?' a man's voice said, coming out of nowhere.

'Wha –'

'The boy,' the agitated voice continued. 'He was here – just a moment ago. I lost him in the crowd.'

Nanci blinked her eyes open and found herself staring at a heavily lined face only inches from her own. She recoiled from the intrusion.

The little man who had invaded her space sighed with resignation. It was an exaggerated gesture, reminding Nanci of a clown. 'Oh, I see that you have encountered him, haven't you, my dear?' the man said, his voice suddenly gentle. He sat down on the kerb next to her, his old black coat riding up around him. It seemed absurdly large on his slight frame.

Nanci had no idea what to say. She was still reeling from… She didn't have words for what she had just experienced.

The little man took one of her hands in his and patted the back of it lightly. After the intimate contact of the mysterious child, he might just as well have been wearing mittens. She took a moment to appraise him. He was quite old, although she wouldn't have wanted to hazard an exact age. His hair was cut crazily into a Beatle's mop and was beginning to grey. Beneath his coat he wore a tatty blue shirt. A creased bow tie was attached to his collar by a large safety pin, the head of which was painted baby blue and was a little chipped. He smelt stuffy and old, as if he had been mothballed for twenty years and had only just been brought out of storage. The smell reminded her of her grandma's apartment in Brooklyn.

Her eyes met his and Nanci realised that she had been staring rudely at him.

'He's in trouble,' the man said quietly.

'Who?' Nanci asked, but somehow she knew the man was

referring to the little boy.

'You've felt his power, haven't you? You know what he can do.'

'I felt... I felt something, I guess.'

'A rare and precious gift. And a much-sought-after prize.' He looked around him for a moment. 'Where there are prizes, there are hunters.' Then, without warning, he leapt to his feet – he was surprisingly agile for a man his age. 'If you help me, perhaps we can save him.' And with that he darted off through the crowds.

'I can't!' Nanci said, even as she found herself hurrying after him. 'I can't help. I've gotta get home. My mom would, like, have a coronary if she knew...'

The little man skidded to stop and Nanci almost crashed into him. He peered at her closely. They were almost exactly the same height.

'Knew what?'

'That I'd gotten involved with something, I guess. She's from New York and is kinda neurotic. She'd go ballistic if she knew that, you know, I'd even spoken to a stranger.'

The man grinned broadly. 'Oh, my dear, I'm not a stranger. I'm the Doctor!'

Nanci found herself grinning. There was something entirely irresistible about him. He couldn't have been younger than fifty, but he had the energy of a toddler.

They spent the afternoon together, scouring the town for any sign of the strangely dressed little boy. When she asked the Doctor about him, he just turned the question back on her, asking who she thought the boy might be and where he might have come from. The only possibilities that came to mind were so ridiculous that Nanci didn't even entertain the idea of sharing them with her new friend.

The sun was low in the sky when they made their way along the seafront. There had been no sign of the golden-eyed boy. It was getting late and Nanci was trying to think of ways to broach the subject of going home. Mom would be getting worried.

A group of Southmouth kids were heading towards them. One of them was leading a dog on a piece of string. A lanky black girl in a blue Adidas track suit, her hair bleached and relaxed, broke away from the group and came bounding up to them.

'You wanna see a miracle?' she shouted excitedly.

Nanci saw that she was missing a tooth.

The Doctor looked amused. 'What kind of miracle?'

'Me mate's dog got knocked down on the crossing. Broke his leg. Only now he's fine. Do you wanna see?'

The Doctor went to pat the dog, but the girl stepped between them.

'Cost you a quid.'

'Ah,' the Doctor began, his face crumpling into a frown. He patted his pockets. 'We may have a problem there.' He began to pull assorted oddments from his pockets, including a child's wooden recorder with a well-chewed mouthpiece. 'Tell me, do you have any idea as to the cause of his recovery?' he asked, gently keeping the conversation going as he searched in his misshapen coat.

'Told ya. It was a miracle.'

The girl had spied a catapult among the Doctor's things. The Doctor didn't miss her interest and offered it to her.

'Brill!' she said, pleased with her new toy.

Nanci watched as the Doctor crouched by the mongrel dog, which licked his hand affectionately. 'There doesn't seem to be anything wrong with him now.'

'That's because the lad cured him, didn't he?' the girl said, her attention completely occupied by testing the elastic of the catapult.

The Doctor stood up. 'Lad? Did you see where he went?'

The girl nodded in the direction of the old pier.

The Doctor smiled gratefully. 'Thank you. And mind where you point that,' he added, nodding at the toy in her hand.

With the children gone, Nanci and the Doctor walked in

silence towards the iron structure of the pier. Nanci glanced at her watch. Her mother would surely be haemorrhaging with anxiety by now.

'Doctor…' she began.

'Tea ready, is it?' he said quietly.

'Yeah.'

They stopped at the entrance to the pier. The Doctor sighed and offered her his hand. 'Well, it was nice meeting you.'

Nanci shook his hand awkwardly. She glanced at the stern shape of the pier. 'It's been derelict for years, you know. It isn't safe.'

He only nodded, a little sadly.

'You don't want to trust what those kids were saying anyway, Doctor.' Why couldn't she stop making excuses for herself? 'They just wanted your money. A broken leg can't heal, like, spontaneously. It's impossible.'

'Can't it? Look at your knee.'

Nanci glanced down. There was a hole in her jeans where she had fallen, a small bloodstain on the frayed material. She felt for the scab which should have started to form by now, but there was nothing. There was no sign of an injury at all.

'There's always something impossible – or at least vastly improbable – going on around you, Nanci. Just around the corner. The question is: are you willing to take a look?'

With that he turned away and began to examine the boarded-up entrance. Quickly finding a panel which was already loose, he prised it away and crawled through. He turned back to look at her once and then was gone.

Nanci turned and hurried home.

Nanci sat at the dinner table opposite her mother and moved spaghetti around on her plate. Recently she hadn't been able to eat a well-balanced meal in front of her mother. It just meant too much to her.

She couldn't get the Doctor's expression as she had abandoned him out of her mind. She knew that she should have stayed and helped. The strange boy had helped her and she might have been able to help him in return. Not getting involved was something – Nanci glanced across the table – something her mother would have done.

Her mother was presently engrossed in a thick hardback entitled *Adolescent Sexuality: Issues in Psychoanalytic Casework. Third Edition.* The title made Nanci shudder. At that moment she would rather have played Russian roulette than start a conversation. She still blushed at the memory of her mother's awkward attempt at a sex education lecture. Nanci had never really recovered from that. Nor, she suspected, had her mother. And anyway, there was no way that Nanci could talk to Mom about her day with the Doctor. A native New Yorker, her mother thought that there was little difference between talking to strangers and loudly demanding to be robbed. Or worse.

Excusing herself with a murmured sigh, Nanci climbed up to her room at the top of the house. Clothes were strewn across the floor. Mould festered in half a dozen coffee cups scattered across the room. She was presently engaged in a major conflict with her mother over her bedroom. Mom had finally refused to continue clearing up after her, telling her that if she didn't do anything about her room, then it could stay as it was. It was a battle of wills and Nanci was still pretty confident that her mother would break before she did. Still, she was dangerously close to running out of underwear.

Nanci's prized possession was a telescope her dad had bought her on one of their semi-regular weekends together. Mom could barely contain her fury over such a frivolous gift, especially when Dad was so often late with maintenance payments. Nanci didn't watch the stars or the surface of the Moon with the telescope. She liked to watch the town, to peek into people's lives as they travelled through the streets. She didn't focus on the town today, though. Instead she targeted the coast, searching out the old pier. At this time of night it was just a black smear on the charcoal grey of the sea. She focused the powerful lens but could make out only the spiky silhouette of the old theatre and the smaller box shapes of the kiosks. She didn't know what she was looking for. There was no way she was going to be able to locate the Doctor in the darkness, so what did she really expect to see?

She gave up, flopping down on the bed and staring at the ceiling. The soft chime of a Macintosh starting up drifted up the stairs – her mother beginning work on another lecture. After the events of the day, normality descended on Nanci like a blanket of asbestos dust. But there was no way she was going to go on to the old pier, she told herself. Mom would have a fit if she found out to start with. And besides, the pier was boarded up with good reason. It was probably over a hundred years old and was really dangerous.

She'd go to bed, read, maybe have an early night.

Yeah, right.

Twenty minutes later Nanci was standing at the boarded-up entrance to the old pier. She was wearing her black 501s and an old checked shirt that she had borrowed from her dad and never returned. In one hand, she gripped a flashlight that she'd liberated from the cupboard under the sink. The pier looked dark and uninviting, its long floorboards old and untrustworthy. Taking a deep breath, Nanci pulled the loose boarding to one side and, after glancing over her shoulder, crept through. The fencing blocked the light from the seafront. Kneeling in its shadow, her immediate surroundings were close to pitch-blackness.

She crept to the side of the pier, found the rail and began slowly to move forward, keeping her hands firmly clamped to it. The further she travelled, the stronger the sea wind felt against her face. The salt in the air made her skin tingle.

Nanci moved a little more confidently through the empty rooms and passageways of the buildings on the old pier. The floor felt sturdy and safe, but she still tested each step she took, probing the ground in front of her before relaxing her weight.

She found them in the ballroom. A low glow escaped from one of the glassless windows. By standing up on tiptoes, Nanci could peer inside. A bizarre sight met her eyes.

The Doctor was standing on the dance floor, arguing fiercely with the woman Nanci had glimpsed on the street when she had first encountered the boy. The woman was still wearing her bright silver dress, although now her blonde hair was piled up on her head. The Doctor was quite a bit shorter than her and had to look up to meet her gaze. The woman was standing in front of him, her hands on her hips.

'But don't you see!' the Doctor was demanding, sounding out of breath and desperate. 'Your pain doesn't just disappear into vapour.' He gestured behind him. 'The boy has to bear it.'

It was only then that Nanci realised the Doctor was standing between the woman and the strange child, who was crouched behind some rotten tables on the other side of the ballroom.

'Honey, that's what I paid my money for!'

The woman's voice was harsh and cold. Nanci recognised the accent immediately. The woman was from the South, probably a Texan.

'You can't just off-load your disappointments and pain on to other people,' the Doctor replied. 'We can only learn anything from our experiences by living through them.'

Nanci wasn't sure what they were talking about. The conversation didn't really make sense. Suddenly she found herself wondering why she had come out of her safe, warm home. What on Earth did she think she was going to do?

Suddenly she had the feeling that she was being watched. The boy was staring at her, an anxious expression on his face. Then she knew what he reminded her of: an evacuee. He looked as if he had just stepped out of one of those old black-and-white movies about the Blitz BBC2 broadcast on the afternoons when the other stations were showing sport. Like the Doctor, he didn't looked as if he belonged to today at all.

Using the rotting furniture of the ballroom as cover, Nanci

scurried over to him. She tried to smile reassuringly, but if he understood he didn't show it. Apart from a slim metallic band around his neck, he looked as if he could have walked out of the bomb-ravaged streets of London in the Second World War. She reached for the band around his neck, but he backed away, his eyes full of panic. Behind the band she could see an angry red burn mark. Nanci grimaced. How had the silver cuff caused such an injury?

Before the boy could shy away further, she reached out and gently touched his face. Nanci wasn't prepared for the reaction. Immediately, she felt his presence within her mind. Only this time it wasn't soothing. Instead, she was aware of a tidal wave of anger, hurt and bitterness within him. She could sense him fighting to contain it, as if at any moment it might come flooding out of him. Shocked, she quickly withdrew her hand.

From behind her, she heard the woman yell, 'Hey, girl! Leave him alone!'

The boy gripped the band around his neck and began to scream, a terrible high-pitched sound. Nanci's mouth fell open in horror as the strange necklace started glowing red.

She whirled around to see the woman marching towards her, a small metal box in her hand. It was clearly the control device for the band. The Doctor was a short distance away, moving forward to intercept the woman. Nanci was closer. Turning her feelings of outrage into motion, she launched herself forward and charged into the woman, hoping to knock the control device from her hand. The tall woman was deceptively strong and managed to keep hold of the device, but they both tumbled to the floor.

Nanci's ears were full of the boy's cries. She tried to slam the woman's wrist against the warped floorboards of the ballroom, but couldn't get the leverage she needed.

'Doctor!' she cried.

But the Doctor wasn't coming to her rescue. He had crossed over to the boy and was probing the lock of the glowing necklace with a small metal rod. He didn't seem to be having much success.

'Get off me!' the woman roared, and tried to wriggle out from under Nanci.

Nanci leant forward with all her weight and managed to pin the woman's wrist to the floor. Out of the corner of her eye, she could see the Doctor give up his attempt to deal with the lock. Instead, he scooped the screaming child into his arms and staggered towards the main doors of the derelict ballroom.

'Device… Short range,' he called out breathlessly. 'Get him to safety.' And then he was gone!

Gone! He'd left her behind.

Nanci was so shocked to have been abandoned that her grip relaxed for a tiny moment. The woman didn't miss the opportunity. Nanci saw the fist coming too late.

And then her lights were punched out.

The first thing Nanci thought when she woke was that she was in one of the aquariums on the beachfront. The single wall of the round chamber was made of thick glass. Outside the ocean floor was spotlit in several places. The movement of the water lifted up small pebbles and sent them tumbling across the sea bed.

On the edge of the lit area, she could see the diagonal struts of the pier. Its legs were completely covered in fluffy green seaweed which swayed in the gentle tide.

Not in an aquarium, then. She was under the sea, only a few hundred metres from the beach. What was this place?

'Welcome to my home,' a woman's voice said, as if in answer.

Nanci twisted around to see a silhouetted figure against the illuminated ocean. Slowly, melodramatically, the lights in the room brightened, revealing the blonde-haired woman. She walked over to where Nanci lay. As she did so, Nanci realised that the woman was much older than she had first thought. The lines on her face looked deeper than before and there were sunken bags under her eyes. Her mass of thick hair had to be a wig.

'You, my girl, have caused me quite a bit of trouble.'

In the quiet of the subterranean room, the woman's Southern accent sounded phoney, like a bad impersonation.

'Good,' Nanci whispered, trying to sound more confident than she felt. 'You're not an American, are you?'

The woman's heavily made-up face cracked open into a smile. 'No. I would hazard a little guess that I'm no more American than your Doctor is English. My true appearance might create a bit too much attention, if you know what I mean.'

The suspicions Nanci had been harbouring since she had first met the Doctor returned. She glanced about her. The decor of the room reminded her of a roadside motel back in the States. At first glance it appeared to be luxurious, but a second look revealed it to have a cheap and characterless air. Rather like the woman herself. Behind the potted ferns and gilded furniture were banks of sophisticated instrumentation. This was obviously some kind of craft. A craft resting on the bottom of the sea.

Nanci swallowed and a chill of fear rose up her spine. Her hand went straight to the cold metal band which had been placed around her neck while she was unconscious.

Jesus Christ!

The woman produced a small metal box and smiled coldly at her.

'Wha – what do you want of me?' Nanci asked, staring at the box.

'Only your co-operation. It's simple really. Your friend has my boy. I'm willing to do an exchange.'

'The Doctor will never agree.'

The woman laughed. 'My dear girl, he already has. He contacted me this morning and agreed to my terms.'

It took a moment for the woman's words to sink in. At least a day had passed since the events on the old pier. Mom was

197

going to kill her! Absurdly, facing her own mother's anger seemed far more frightening than the very real danger she faced at the hands of this overdressed psycho.

'Once I have my boy back,' the woman continued. 'I'll be off this world in a flash. The Doctor doesn't understand… I need my boy,' she drawled. 'He's mother's little helper.'

Nanci thought of the golden-eyed child and remembered the powerful emotions which threatened to spill out from him. They weren't his. They belonged to the woman.

'He's no good to you now,' Nanci whispered. 'He's full. There's too much inside him.'

She must have touched a raw nerve, because the woman snapped at her. 'Nonsense! He's idle, that's all! Won't try!'

'You'll kill him!'

'Listen, honey, I'll kill you if you don't shut up!' The woman barked. 'I think you need a lesson, you little madam.' The woman thumbed a control on the device.

Nanci realised what was happening as her neck began to gently tingle. 'Oh no, please!' she started, and then she was too busy screaming to say any more.

The woman had been as generous with her punishments as she was with her unwanted emotions. Nanci stood on the deck of the saucer-shaped craft as it moved smoothly across the dark water towards the beach. Even turning her sore neck slightly caused the most terrible pain.

The woman stood next to her, holding the box in her hand. Nanci didn't know how she was piloting the craft, but it seemed to know where it was going. The two figures on the beach were clearly visible in the moonlight.

The craft came to halt just before the breakers. Nanci obediently carried the woman the last part of the journey. Despite the time of year, the salt water was freezing, and the wound on her neck burnt terribly whenever it was splashed. She set the woman down on the beach and then knelt in the pebbles, resting for a moment.

'Come on,' the woman snapped, and Nanci obeyed without question.

The Doctor was standing quietly, holding the little boy's hand. He was wearing the same clownish clothes as before, but he looked serious and dignified as he watched them approach. When she was near, he smiled kindly at her. She did her best to smile back.

Nanci listened as the Doctor tried to persuade the woman to leave the boy behind. She wasn't exactly surprised when the woman refused, demanding instead that the boy be returned to her. Reluctantly the Doctor agreed, provided Nanci was freed in turn.

'Very well,' the woman said.

The words sent a thrill through Nanci. She began to stumble towards the Doctor, just as the boy took his first reluctant steps back to his cruel mistress.

'Oh, Nanci,' the woman called in a playful tone. Nanci turned and looked on in horror as the woman lifted the device in her hand. 'Aren't you forgetting one little thing?'

Nanci felt the now familiar tingle spread around her throat. She was paralysed with terror. She heard the Doctor angrily demand that the device be turned off, but the woman only laughed and threw the still-activated control into the sea.

Nanci stared after it as it sailed through the air and landed with a plop beyond the waves. She pulled at the burning cuff with her hands, but it just scorched her fingers. She was going to die, and there was nothing anyone could do to stop it.

'Please!' she screamed at no one in particular. 'Please! No!'

Nanci collapsed to her knees. She felt as if someone had wrapped a two-bar fire around her throat. Something began to sizzle and she realized with a sickening feeling that it was her skin. Her eyes filled with hot, prickly tears.

And then she felt small hands cup her face and the unbearable pain started to melt away. The boy! It was as if his hands were cool balm against her wounds. Through her tears she saw his golden eyes staring down at her. She felt him drain all the heat out of the band, all the pain she had experienced, sucking it up inside him.

Her relief turned to horror as she saw his skin light up with a burning flame. The boy shuddered and staggered back a few steps as he writhed in agony. Smoke belched from the sleeves of his grey overcoat and the collar of his shirt.

From where she knelt, Nanci heard the woman cry out in anger and watched as she staggered over to the boy, unsteady as she tried to walk in heels on the pebble beach. 'You mustn't take her pain,' the woman shouted. 'That's only for me!'

Nanci wiped her eyes and stared at the astonishing sight in front of her. The boy was ablaze. Tiny flames broke away from his body and flickered up into the night. The woman approached him, panic in her eyes, as if someone had just cancelled her prescription.

The boy threw himself at her, grabbing hold of her throat. For a second his whole body flared white hot and then he channelled all the flames through his hands into the body of his mistress. Nanci could almost see all the stored-up hate and regret and pain and bitterness flood out of him. The woman cried out, broke his grip and took a few faltering steps backwards before she exploded, like a puffball, into ash.

The strange dust rained down for several minutes, landing gently on Nanci's hands and face.

Her mother said she was grounded until she was thirty-five. Nanci didn't really mind; it wasn't as if she had anywhere to go anyway. The only thing she was sorry about was that she hadn't been able to say goodbye to the Doctor properly.

Despite the cruelty she had experienced at the hands of the boy's owner, there was not even a mark on her neck. She still hurt inside though. When the boy had saved her from the woman's wrath, he hadn't taken away her own hurt. School was still going to be difficult to face in the autumn. But that was her pain and she could live with it. She sat in her room at the top of the house and watched the people pass by through her telescope.

She saw the Doctor only once more after that. She caught sight of him through her telescope as he strode along the seafront, holding a bucket and spade in one hand and a large ice-cream in the other. It took Nanci a moment to recognise his companion. The boy's dull, lifeless clothes had been replaced by jeans and a sweatshirt, his blonde hair was spiked up with gel. She wondered what he really looked like, what they both looked like.

Framed in the circle of her telescope, the Doctor's weathered face was full of life. Just before he disappeared from sight, he turned and for a moment seemed to stare directly at her. At first she thought it must have been coincidence, but then he grinned and gave a little wave goodbye.

# The Parliament of Rats

## by Daniel O'Mahony

The *Lung of Heaven* was a good ship, solid and reliable. Katr Korzen had served on board for forty years, more than half as captain, and it had remained trustworthy when all else around her proved treacherous. It was because she trusted the *Lung* that she allowed Constantine to take it off course. Lethe's winter was in its third phase and the mist was thick, the pressures of time on their surroundings constant, but the reassuring creak of the ship's hull persuaded Korzen to indulge her navigator.

The crew didn't share her faith. They clustered on deck, muttering tales about gods of the sea and betting on the outcome of Constantine's excursion. Brunner, the priest-physician, looked on from a distance, his hands idly caressing the dull-silver shaft of his staff. His impatience was a little more good-humoured and well concealed.

At the prow, Constantine too was alone. She stood with her back to the others, her arms raised and her palms splayed as though feeling for intangible shapes in the fog. Her antics unnerved the more superstitious sailors, though not quite as much as the translucent images that would flicker round her as she guided the Lung through the ghost mazes of night. She was the smallest and oddest-looking of the crew. Naturally dark-haired, she had used plant dyes to add long streaks of red, gold and green.

'I can see it!' she trilled. 'The box. It's really here.' She turned, flashing her jewel-eyes at the crew. 'It's in the sea. The blue box!'

Korzen was the first to join her at the prow. Constantine stabbed at the sea, at a dark shape half-submerged, just as she had dreamed. A hinged flap hung open, letting in the water – Korzen was surprised that the box hadn't gone under – and a lamp pulsed at its crest.

There were bodies on the surface: two water-bloated humans. Korzen bit her lip.

'They aren't dead,' Constantine hissed sweetly, 'not yet.'

Korzen turned. Brunner was behind her, his incongruously bearded baby face planted in her way. He stammered, trying to speak. She eased him gently but firmly to one side and yelled out to the mate, 'Kill the wind, Mr Harbou, and prepare to receive boarders!'

There were only the two. Harbou trawled for others until the female recovered and told them they were alone. She was another child, barely older than Constantine, but with a hardness in her face that bespoke an experience the navigator had never known. Her name, it seemed, was Nyssa. Her companion, a dust-blond young man, was a doctor. Nyssa didn't know his name.

Korzen wondered what it must've been like for Nyssa to see the prow of the *Lung* carve through the mist like a crusted brine-stinking shadow. She hoped it was intimidating. Everyone deserved that frisson of fear.

They were strange people, which did little for the crew's morale. The man's clothes, heavy with water when he was dragged aboard, were dry a minute later. The box was stranger still. Korzen had stuck her head through the door and paused thoughtfully for a while before asking Brunner to perform a rite of purging and then sealing the box in the hold.

By the evening both survivors had recovered and were well enough to join her and Brunner for dinner in her cabin. It was the closest to opulence that existed on board. She arrived late, as was her habit, to find the Doctor cradling the dome of his head in silent pain. He looked up as the captain entered, but did not stand. Nor did Nyssa, though Brunner wobbled slightly to attention. It didn't matter. Korzen had never enjoyed the rituals of discipline.

'Ah, captain,' the Doctor said. 'I'm sorry if we've caused you any inconvenience…'

Basic courtesy. Korzen knew better than to answer. 'You don't seem too well,' she commented as she slid into her seat and started the attack on her food. She had never shaken off the need to eat fast and furiously against starvation.

'So, Doctor,' she asked at last, 'what exactly had been going on when we found you?'

The Doctor, who was hardly touching his meal, looked up, his face a mask of discomfort and surprised guilt.

'Ah, well,' he said, 'that may be –'

'We're travellers,' Nyssa cut across him bluntly, 'from another planet. The TARDIS, our ship, was –' she paused – 'brought down into the sea.'

Korzen was finding, to her surprise, that the girl was the voice of the couple. She hadn't worked out what the Doctor was yet. Maybe the heart?

The Doctor seemed mortified, embarrassment outstripping his pain. He exchanged soft words with his companion, too soft for Korzen to pick up.

'But, Doctor,' Nyssa said, 'you've always told me that…'

'Enough,' Korzen said firmly. 'We must look rustic, but we know what goes on up there –' She jabbed a hard brown finger towards the ceiling, towards the sky.

'Good, good,' the Doctor said, his voice slipping as his brow creased with renewed pain.

'I think you're suffering…' Brunner made to begin a dreadful-warning diagnosis.

'You need to lie down,' Korzen interjected, rising. She helped the Doctor up, leading him out and through the cramped passages towards the cabin she had set aside for him.

'This is very kind of you,' he murmured, almost an apology.

Korzen watched as he sank into a peaceful stupor. His body wasn't still. So, her guess had been right. He wasn't remotely human.

* * *

'Lethe, this planet is called,' Nyssa told him. She shrugged.

'In one human mythology,' the Doctor explained airily, 'the dead drink from the waters of the River Lethe to regenerate themselves, but are reborn without memories of their past lives.'

'I see,' Nyssa responded, sounding harsher than she had intended. The Doctor was struggling not to seem fragile but he was less practised at disguise than he had once been. He held his head as though it were new and too heavy. The darkness around his eyes betrayed him. He didn't seem to want kindness. Nyssa restricted herself to imparting the scant information that she had learned about Lethe.

'This is an ocean world,' she reported. 'The humans – their descendants – are island-based. Lethe doesn't have the resources to support a high-technology society.'

'So?' the Doctor prompted. Speaking was painful for him.

'So, something else must have disrupted the TARDIS. It might even have been a natural phenomenon. I think,' she added, smiling with pride at her own deductions, 'it could be a localised time-space distortion.'

'Yes,' the Doctor agreed softly, his hands at his temples again. 'That girl, the navigator, the one with the hair. I think she must be a time-sensitive, steering a course through striations in the time-fields on this planet. I can't imagine someone like Korzen tolerating her otherwise. She was the one who tracked us when we crashed. We owe her our lives.'

Nyssa breathed heavily. The cabin's air seethed with hissing dust.

The Doctor lapsed into silence, his fingers steepled in thought. Nyssa guessed what he was mulling over, in the easy moments between pain. If Constantine was time-sensitive – and she was, beyond doubt – then she could only be the outcome of slow generations of exposure to unfixed time.

The Doctor had more than generations behind him. The distortion was in his eyes, his slumped posture. It was in his head and it was eating him. He was more of a time-sensitive than Constantine could ever be. Nyssa had never thought of the Doctor as a good navigator.

'Do they know about it?' the Doctor mused.

Nyssa wasn't sure whether this was a question for her or a carelessly slipped thought.

'I don't think so,' she said. 'They need sensitives to travel long distances, but... They react to it, they don't understand it. Brunner was telling me –'

'I think he likes you,' the Doctor said absently.

Nyssa clicked her tongue and stared at him, wondering what to make of this. She wasn't deceived by the youth of his new body. When she had first met him – when he was another man – he had been packed with resentful energy that anticipated age even as it crept across him. His regeneration had weakened him badly.

'When Korzen took you away,' she began again, 'Brunner was telling me a bit about his mission. He's chartered this ship. Apparently he's an agent of the Lethean rulers. He didn't say that much. He's very shy.' She almost said secretive but checked herself.

The Doctor gestured for her to go on. His hand sank after the effort.

'His masters are on a crusade against superstition,' she reported. The approval in her voices – real and inner – was warm and thoroughly Trakenite. 'Brunner is trying to stamp out the worship of a sea deity called the White God.'

The Doctor's thin lips twitched. 'A bit difficult for one man.'

'The interesting thing,' Nyssa continued, 'is the legend of the *Parliament of Rats*. It's a pirate ship that supposedly captured the White God, who cursed them –'

'As gods do.'

'– and they sailed into the fog a hundred years ago, never to be seen again. Brunner is trying to find the ship to expose the legend.'

'Do you think he'll succeed?' the Doctor asked. His voice was alert, despite his condition. He already knew her answer.

'If the *Parliament of Rats* is temporally displaced, then the chances of anyone finding it are negligible.'

'What are its chances of finding us?' he asked wryly.

Any answer was pre-empted by Korzen, who rapped sharply on the door before entering. Her face seemed carved from the same wood as her ship, not at all softened by the dark sweep of her hair, and her eyes flickered, constantly watching. 'I should warn you that women are not allowed in men's cabins during the night,' she said.

Nyssa's quarters proved to be a cramped bunk room below deck whose walls ached with the knowledge that there were only thin planks holding back the ocean and death by drowning. It was already occupied.

The wounded Doctor was a solid rock compared with Constantine. This was the first time that Nyssa had been close to the navigator. Before, from a distance, she had been a splash of colour, brilliant enough to illumine her grim environment. At close range she became drabber, the natural tone of her skin and the grime of her clothes deadening the streamers of her hair. She was still liquid, though, smiling dreamily.

'Hello, Nyssa. Would you mind doing me up?'

Constantine's wrists were strung from a coil of rope. Another knot, round her ankle, was already tightened, digging into her flesh. Nyssa felt sick.

'This is my idea.' Constantine could have been talking to herself. 'I might hurt myself if I walk and dream together. I might turn metal-baby blue, precious white metal on my lips where it won't rust. What's that called?' she murmured.

'Platinum,' Nyssa murmured.

'That's right, Nyssa of dead Traken.'

At that, Nyssa found herself pulling the knot as tight as she could. Constantine squealed between giggles, then fell asleep soon after, strung up like a side of cold abattoir meat.

Nyssa stripped off the sackcloth that the crew had given her and clambered on to the top bunk. The mattress was a living thing, stuffed with straw and insects. In the space before she slept she pondered what she had learned about the planet Lethe. But it was not her problem, she knew. Not yet.

The Doctor wore his new body like a scar. Since his regeneration he had become both less and more concerned by the worlds he travelled through, both distant and protective. What was going through his head? The question kept her tense and awake for a while. When she eventually slept, she dreamt of the death of planets and of an oblivion that ate through suns.

Constantine howled. Nyssa jerked upright and peered over the edge of the bunk. She saw that the girl was scrabbling at the coarse rope bindings, her wrists raw and bleeding as she struggled. Her eyes were transfixed; her mouth twisted.

'There is a black ship!' Constantine howled into her face. 'The rats are coming to eat our eyes! Out! Out of the fog!'

'It's in your dreams.'

'Oh, yes,' Constantine crooned, 'but not for much longer.'

The navigator's clothes stank of urine. Nyssa almost gagged.

'All right,' she murmured, 'you can tell Korzen. I'll take you.' Still dozy, she set to work on freeing the grinning, shrieking girl.

The Doctor usually slept easily, when he bothered to, but in the creaking wood cage of the *Lung of Heaven* he couldn't manage it. The pain in his head made him drowsy but kept him from sliding into oblivion. Fear too kept him awake. Nyssa's guess about time fractures had been right, but that kind of distortion shouldn't have a physical effect.

Unable to settle, he left his cabin. The ship rocked gently and he rocked with it. He felt as though he were flying as he moved, the seething floor an illusion beneath his feet. He wasn't sure who to turn to. Not Nyssa, who would worry. Not Korzen, who consciously isolated herself. Not any other member of the crew, who would only tolerate him at best.

He also discounted Constantine, with whom he had so much

and so little in common. Time Lords and time-sensitives did not mix well, the one rigid, unemotional and certain; the other fluid, volatile and transient.

That left Brunner, who was a physician and held out the hope of a painkiller that might not burst his hearts.

Brunner's cabin was a mess, strewn with papers and clothes. The man himself was gone, though his bedcovers were ruffled. The metal staff he had clasped all through dinner was lying across his bed.

The Doctor's head burned. There was no one here to help him. He considered waiting. It crossed his mind to clear up. Something was wrong with the room. It wasn't simply a mess – it was a parody of order and demanded his attention. He lifted the staff so he could sit and think. It flared silver-white, an ice blaze rising along its length and searing his eyes. The metal coiled and writhed in the warmth of his hand, a steel serpent waking.

No, he realised. Not steel.

His hands opened. The staff, dull again, leapt across the room and clattered into the corner. Violent fear overcame his pain and he careered out of the cabin, making for the deck.

The air outside was white and soaking and made the world invisible. In the fog he smashed into a passing body and reeled.

'Doctor,' Korzen said silkily. Her hard, mocking features solidified out of the mist. 'You're looking much better.'

'Captain,' he blustered, 'you must tell me what Brunner is doing on this ship. I'm afraid he's putting us all at risk.'

'Yes,' she said, 'he is.'

She knew, then.

'What is he doing?' the Doctor insisted.

'I believe,' Korzen responded haltingly, 'that he is the appointed official God-killer of the Autarchy. He roots out and destroys rivals to our own precious Om. He's good, I'm told, at his job.'

A horn blared out of the night. The Doctor started.

'I remember this,' Korzen whispered. The mist softened her words further, making them almost inaudible. She was shaking. 'I'd hoped he was wrong.'

Still trembling, she shot a look off to one side. The Doctor's eyes followed. The wet-cotton mist was easing where they looked, thinning into a white film over the night. A line of a denser darkness cut across the sky, a shadow mass ploughing the ocean, bearing towards them. It was another ship, though the mist stripped it of its outline, turning it into an oncoming chunk of shapeless night.

Korzen shuddered, a hand fluttering to her face. 'We should go below.'

The Doctor nodded, but she was already away, darting down a gangway, the wooden steps rattling as she went. The Doctor followed her, recognising the tension urgent in her body.

'Captain Korzen,' the Doctor called, following the bobbing smear of an oil lamp in her hand.

'Yes?' Her voice came from somewhere ahead.

'The other ship, is it the *Parliament of Rats*?'

There was no response beyond a concentrated, deliberate smash and the splitting of wood. Then her voice came again.

'There's been a Captain Korzen on the *Lung of Heaven* since before the *Parliament* disappeared,' she said. 'I'm the last. I want the name to die with me. But not today. Catch.'

The light flew at him. He caught it in both hands and held on though it burned his palms. Korzen came out of the gloom, spectral in the flicker and stink of the oil flame. She had a gun, an automatic pistol. It was, the Doctor guessed, a working antique.

'May the White God deliver us from evil,' she said, 'or grant us some little mercy. Amen.'

The Doctor's lips twitched. Now he understood.

The *Lung of Heaven* heaved under the impact.

The ship's walls lurched sideways and flung Nyssa to the floor. She had been helping Constantine along the passageway, but now the navigator caught her, tucking stick-thin arms round her shoulders and lifting her clear.

'The black ship,' Constantine said, bitter and satisfied. Her seaweed hair drooped over her face. She pointed at a nearby porthole, where a hard mass of black wood was visible, thumping patiently on the *Lung*'s hull.

'They could have smashed us to bits,' Nyssa observed, still calculating even as she nursed her bruised ribs.

'They don't want to,' Constantine purred. Her face swam before Nyssa's as though it were a reflection in water. 'They'll be boarding now. The rat men,' she added, making an odd twitch with her free arm.

The ship's hull beat with a tattoo of thumps. A dirty palm flattened on to the thick porthole glass, sharp nails scratching for an entry. Nyssa recoiled. Constantine's grin was a ragged score on her lips.

They moved on quickly, leaving the invader to scrabble fruitlessly on the outside of the ship. Meanwhile, the Lung's crew had blossomed in the passages and the going became heavier as muscular, alert bodies surged around them. Obviously everyone knew about the black ship now.

Harbou pushed through the crush, pulling a passive Brunner in his wake. The little priest was calmer than Nyssa had seen him before, the blackness of his clothes wasting into the night. One thing gave him away – the fluster of his fingers round the head of his staff. His lips twitched, a silent prayer.

Harbou's eyes were frosted and still. Nyssa shouted questions at him, but he shrugged them off. He was concentrating on the situation in hand and wanted the civilian insects kept together and out of the way. Nyssa turned her attention to the priest, seeing a fat, smug smile on his face. His head rocked from side to side. He was awake and dreaming.

'We have a weapon,' he said cheerfully. 'It is the truth.'

Nyssa realised then that Brunner was mad – madder than Constantine, who had slumped to the floor in a fit of giggles. The sailors were clattering on to the decks, their boots stamping over planks that were Nyssa's ceiling. She wondered for the first time where the Doctor was. He would be either in the thick of the action or far beneath it, lost in a problem of his own. That would turn out to be the important one, she guessed.

There was shooting in the distance, muffled by thick layers of wood. Nyssa suddenly wished that the Doctor was here.

A human shape emerged from the gloom and shambled towards them. Constantine sniggered and Brunner stared confidently. Nyssa dug her teeth into her lower lip. It was not the Doctor. It was nothing like the Doctor at all.

The boarder was a tortured man. Nyssa was intrigued rather than shocked by his deformities. A cold kernel of curiosity forced her to study the gargoyle architecture of his skull with interest rather than disgust. He had one jaundiced eye, while the other was pierced by sharp bone fingers. Layers of skin that rotted scentless and hung on his shuddering bones. His flesh was red and sore – but clean, Nyssa realised, and undiseased. A necklace of pulsing sacs hid his collar and shoulder bones. His hair was combed neatly over his mottled scalp. He had a gun. And it was pointed at them.

There were others, all with guns, all with treacherous bodies. None tried to speak, which was a blessing. As they herded their mute captives on to the deck, Nyssa found herself brooding over their deformities again. Exposure to temporal radiation, she guessed, from charting a ship through the time winds.

'I'm not very good with people,' Constantine confessed at her ear, but was silenced by a gun-butt.

Most of the *Lung*'s crew were on deck, men kneeling in line for prayer with their palms clapped impotently on their heads. The pirates of the *Parliament of Rats* shone glaring beacons at them that cut the fog. Behind them, moored off the prow of the *Lung*, was the dark *Parliament* itself. Nyssa didn't bother following its outline but concentrated on its texture. It seemed a stain of dark matter from under the surface of the white world.

There was no sign of Korzen or the Doctor. She spotted Harbou kneeling with the rest of the crew and broke ranks to address him. He turned his head to regard her with baleful, fish eyes.

'We surrendered,' he said, 'as the captain would have wanted.'

He might have spat then. He left arm was slashed open, but if he was in pain he wasn't showing it. Nyssa looked closer, but before she could get near him a large alien hand snatched her hair and dragged her away. The fingers were wet-hot and waxy on her scalp. More molten fingers picked her shoulder and shoved her away from the praying, bleeding mate. She slumped back on to the deck.

'Not captain,' slurred her attacker. His voice came from the muffling collar of his long jewelled coat, from beneath the brim of his gold-trimmed tricorn, from the hole where his face was hidden. It was a male voice, but with a breathless quality that seemed mockingly feminine.

Nyssa guessed from his elaborate costume that he was in charge.

'Want *Lung* captain. Want Korzen.'

Pale in the shadow of his own ship and the hug of the translucent mist, he was pathetic. Nyssa wanted to giggle. She wanted to take the muffler from his face to see what it was like, to see whether it was more or less decayed than those of the rest of the crew.

'In Captain Korzen's absence,' Brunner called, unusually clear and authoritative, 'I take full responsibility for this ship.'

The captain of the *Parliament of Rats* stamped a foot and snorted impatiently. He raised a gnarled finger to the shadow of his mouth. 'Priest,' he grunted, dismissing him. The finger swayed, pointing tentatively at Brunner, at Constantine, at Harbou, before stabbing confidently at Nyssa.

'God-food,' the captain said. 'For White God.'

He tried to laugh, but the milky rasp died away in a cough.

The captain was dying. All the pirates were dying. Suddenly unable to fear them, Nyssa realised how pitiful they were, how tiny. They were more like parasites on the body of the *Lung* than its conquerors. The black, obliterating bulk of the *Parliament* suddenly seemed more forbidding than its puppets.

'Captain.' Brunner stepped forward, moving determinedly alongside Nyssa. He no longer seemed insane. The confrontation had lent him steel. The pirate had noticed as well and hobbled closer. Brunner flinched, though barely, and drove the hard point of his staff on to the deck.

'Priest,' the captain hummed.

'Yes,' the priest acknowledged.

There was a game going on here that Nyssa couldn't fathom.

'God-food,' the captain sneered.

'Yes,' Brunner responded evenly. He touched Nyssa's shoulder. 'Instead of her,' he added.

The captain's finger rose again and twitched. 'As well,' he rasped.

'Instead,' Brunner repeated, but it was too late. The *Parliament*'s other puppets were already detaching themselves from the fog to take them, their skin glistening and their lamps hissing. Nyssa felt flesh on her hand and recoiled, but it was only Brunner, squeezing her fingers into his own podgy grip.

'Don't be frightened,' he whispered.

'I can't,' she replied, shaking her head frantically as her lip twisted. 'How can I be frightened?'

'Feed to White God,' their captor snarled, his finger now jabbing at the shadow hull behind him. 'Feed to the rats.'

For an hour they hid in the hold, in a tight compartment between bulkheads that Korzen had no difficulty in locating in the dark. She had extinguished the lamp as soon as they heard the first thumps of boarders leaping on to the hull. The Doctor could see her smile in the dark as a crescent of white with

215

gold flecks. She had extraordinarily keen senses for a human.

They were silent as the boarders combed the hold. Only when the last footfalls had died away – leaving just the natural stretch and yawn of the *Lung*'s timbers – did Korzen take the pistol barrel from between the Doctor's ribs and let him speak.

'Don't you think your crew might need you?'

'They've orders to give up the ship. No violence. It was Brunner's idea.'

'And Brunner's paying?'

There was no answer to that, beyond the hiss of her breath and the soft rustle of her hair.

'Then why are we hiding?' the Doctor asked, innocently, without force.

'Because I'm the captain,' she said, 'because I'm Korzen and because Brunner doesn't know what that means. I'll give him enough time to get on to the *Parliament*. Then we can go.'

'Good,' the Doctor murmured. 'I'm getting cramp.'

'Lucky you're a doctor then,' was the last he heard from her until she decided it was time to go.

As she expected, there was a pirate guard at the hold. She levelled her gun and shot him before the Doctor could protest. A black flower bloomed half-way up the pirate's corkscrew spine and he fell. Korzen strutted callously away. The Doctor, appalled, knelt by the body. His eyes misted over, softening the sight of death and the deformities that the pirate had carried in life. The corpse was odourless and seemed to deflate as its brine-blood gushed on to the deck. Curious, the Doctor put his hand to the dead flesh and found it soft and rippling.

Somewhere far away, Korzen was shouting, her voice rattling through the skeleton of the *Lung*. The Doctor left the dead pirate leaking outside the hold and set off after her.

'Pym!' Korzen was calling. 'Captain Pym of the *Parliament of Rats*!'

He arrived in time to see her being hauled through a deck

hatch by string-thick but powerful arms. She saw him flit from the shadows and offered him a confident grin. Something about her manner made him hold back until after her boots had vanished through the gap, as if it were a command. Only then did he struggle up the short steps after her. He poked his head cautiously through the deck, glancing from side to side to make sure that none of the boarders could see him.

The pirates were clustered around Korzen, but not too close. She was forceful and determined and they were too brittle to stand in her way. She strode through the subdued, crouched forest of sailors towards the deck-heart. Here the swaddled but imposing figure of the pirate leader was waiting. This, the Doctor assumed, was Captain Pym.

'You Korzen?' Pym growled. His voice was too sticky-sweet to convey menace and his rival seemed unfazed. Although he couldn't be sure, the Doctor imagined a stern, sympathetic smile had settled on Korzen's mouth.

'Yes.' She shrugged. 'The last.'

'Korzen!'

'By right of conquest,' said the woman, fervently. 'It's my right to be captain.'

A muffled snigger rose from the captain of the *Parliament*. His crew's mauled bodies rippled uneasily. Korzen stood, figurehead-still, at the centre. She was a caged animal, tense and savage and patient. It was hard to guess who was in charge at the heart of the deck.

'Hi down there.'

Constantine's upside-down head dropped out of the sky before the Doctor's eyes, her vermilion-gold-jade hair streaming deckwards, her crescent-moon face blocking his view of the confrontation. She was smiling so thoroughly that, inverted, it turned into a fierce and crooked scowl. Hungry eyes glittered and the Doctor had the unnerving feeling that she was looking at many things more than him.

'This is exciting, isn't it?' she babbled. 'This is what she wants.'

217

The Doctor tried to shush her.

'Don't worry. They won't pay us any attention. I know. They're all a bit mad after all the time in the black, black ship. I know,' she insisted.

'I want to hear what she's saying,' the Doctor hissed.

'Oh,' the girl mouthed, eyes flashing frantic apologies. Her head bobbed out of the way, but the Doctor couldn't forget the orbital presence over his head and its childish, excited breathing.

The two captains were the centre of everyone's attention now. The sailors of the *Lung* knelt round them in sullen prayer. The sailors of the *Parliament* were a cluster of humble penitents. Korzen had grown larger, it seemed, or the fog had opened to make more room for her. The other captain was diminished, shrinking into the folds of his coat. Korzen was suddenly the more monstrous.

'I... know Bori Korzen,' Pym coughed, almost in apology.

'Dead, long dead,' Korzen said plaintively, 'with rust through his heart, like his sons and their sons.' Her voice was too calculated to be genuine.

Pym pushed his invisible head into the malformed cradle of his fingers. 'Hundred years,' it slurred from behind its mesh of thin skin and bone.

Korzen nodded. 'A hundred years.'

The pirate captain swung his head from side to side and the Doctor caught a hint of its shape; not much, but enough to raise doubts and questions. He craned his head up to find Constantine still beaming down at him.

'There'll be fighting soon, and blood and blood and blood, and it will be joy –' she kicked the last word into a squeal.

The Doctor forced out a hard glare. 'Where is Nyssa?' he asked.

Constantine raised her little fingers to her teeth, where they picked awkwardly. This was a bad sign.

'You take,' Pym was saying, his crooked fingers picking at the bullet hole on Korzen's coat. 'You make us free again?'

'Where is she?' The Doctor's eyes scanned the ranks of sailors, the backs of two dozen shaved heads. There was no sign of Nyssa's ample brown curls. Nor, for that matter, could he see Brunner.

'Yes,' Korzen said, far away and meaningless. 'I make you free.'

'Where is she?' the Doctor barked into the waif's guilt-swelled face.

Korzen's hand came up and it was full and spoke and the top of Pym's head came away in a scarlet-spattered shower.

Constantine quivered and her mouth opened. The explanation poured out and the Doctor's hearts froze.

A scattering of the pirate crew sagged, as if resigned to death. Korzen put bullets into the closest, then ducked behind the still-staggering cadaver of her first victim as his more belligerent comrades returned fire. There was ample meat left in Pym's body to stop their shots. They were slow and clumsy and open, while Korzen, quick, lithe and protected, took out more of them. As their guns fell, the *Lung*'s crew snatched them and joined their captain in a bloody rout. Constantine watched and cooed.

The Doctor paid little attention. He was already running for the edge of the deck, for a line across the water, for the obsidian bulk of the *Parliament of Rats*.

The pirates blindfolded them when they were taken aboard the *Parliament*. Nyssa felt certain that she would remember her path through the invisible labyrinth but the journey proved too complex and too long. She began to suspect that she wouldn't live to have her sight restored. She was surprised when the blindfold came off. Brunner was still with her, blinking in the wan light of the *Parliament* below decks. His staff was an awkward baby in his arms. The pirates had tried to take it from him but had given up when unable to prise his locked fingers from its shaft.

Their captors led them down into the bowels of the ship and placed them together in a cabin whose walls were smeared with weed and brine and worse. Their escorts left quickly, a dissatisfied pinch of silence round them as they lurched back through the cabin door. It locked before Nyssa could reach it.

She glanced round their cell, seeing no furniture and no decoration except for a stretched mirror against one wall. The reversed Nyssa she saw there paced and brooded, barely containing her energies. Brunner's mirror counterpart seemed wispy on the surface of the glass. The genuine article was imposing and dominant by comparison.

She shrugged. What now?

'Why aren't you scared?' Brunner said simply.

She stared at him. He took a practised step backwards.

'You look scared,' he said, 'except in your eyes. It doesn't convince you, does it?'

She shook her head. 'The Doctor doesn't understand.'

'I might,' Brunner said easily.

The Doctor had been right. He did like her. Even so, she had to think carefully before answering.

'I'm tired of being frightened, that's all. I feel exhausted by it all. I've seen too much, I've lost too much,' she finished in an expressionless tone. 'I've been wrung dry.'

Brunner nodded, a scrawny fringe of black creeping over his domed head. He seemed gentle and pathetic and funny, and she laughed at him. He didn't seem to mind. He seemed no more frightened than she did.

Behind her the mirror growled.

Brunner's eyes gleamed. The staff came forward in his hands.

Nyssa turned. Her reflection was melting into Brunner's. The mirror Nyssa became a strange sharer of ghost flesh. Their false bodies seeped together and their heads locked into a single skull. If she showed any distress, it didn't register on the face of the glass. Her reflection grinned instead, with half a mouth and one blazing eye. The colour smeared to the edges of their body, leaving them bleached.

The surface of the mirror pulsed and bulged. The monocreature at its heart was stepping forward, struggling to become free.

'The White God,' Brunner said calmly. The staff was rigid in his hands.

He's going to fight it, she realised.

The passion was naive but determined in his features. Nyssa made for the door, rattling its handle but finding it frustratingly solid.

'Don't worry,' Brunner warned her, the calm insanity easing back into his tone. It was in the staff. He carried his madness round with him as his weapon. 'It can't stand against the truth,' he added blithely.

Nyssa dealt the hard door a thump from her shoulder, but it held fast.

… I knew that he was going to go wrong. I knew it I knew it I knew it, but I didn't see it for a long time because I was watching all the shooting and all the things on the deck with the blood. I made the blood all myself. Maybe that's why it was a bit strange.

I don't know who he is, even when I looked in his head I couldn't see everything because he has a huge mind, I don't know how he fits it all in a tiny head. They call themselves Time Lords, his people, which is funny. I don't know who he is really. Being a doctor is a disguise. I saw the clowns when I was a girl with my sister at my side and he was one of them. A parade! A parade of clowns!

He thought about me while I was thinking about him. Snap! But he's right.

He can't see, the Lord of Time can't see. Time smashes to bits, crash bang. He can't see on the *Parliament of Rats* because he was right, because we are different. He belongs in a straight world of sense and order and I am giggling, dribbling, drooling down a maze of things possible. It must have scared him, to be in those passages lost. I might have warned him not to go.

But he was worried about Nyssa, who might be hurt and is kind.

So when the fighting was getting boring because blood and guts everywhere are boring, especially when you've only made them up yourself, I sent a bit of me across into the ship, floating through the maze of time and death to catch him before he turned blue as the sea in second summer.

He was on his knees and he was crying and I've heard crying like that before. He looked at the bit of me I sent him. I must have been an angel to him, floating in the air in my halo with my head twisting. Or something like an angel but not an angel.

'I can't see,' he said and he was crying.

Actually I'm not sure if he saw me at all.

'I can't find her –' oh, he was begging – 'I can't find my way.'

So I gave him my hand because he made me sad.

'It's that thing…' I said, 'the opposite of bad. I can show you the way.'

A trail of flailing membranes followed the White God, umbilical cords that linked it to the dense silver mirror that spawned it. Nyssa slashed at the nearest and severed them. The god was undisturbed. It grew and sang as it grew, a babble of many voices bleeding into one. There was no menace in it, but she knew it would consume them dispassionately once they were in reach.

It no longer had their shape, or any shape. It was white, perfect and unstained, and terrible. Framed against it, pale Brunner seemed dusty by comparison, every textured line of his skin visible against the immaculate white. He struck it ineffectually with the point of his staff and bristled with frustration when this had no effect.

'Truth!' he cried, striking pointlessly again. 'Truth and order!'

Nyssa rattled the door again, helplessly. The key was still in the lock, but out of her reach. She lost interest in the effort. There didn't seem any point.

Brunner skipped backwards to avoid the encroaching crush of the creature. He inclined his head away, appealing to Nyssa with baffled eyes.

'It isn't working,' he said, stumbling numb over the words.

Nyssa took the staff from him and flexed it.

'What's it supposed to do?'

'It's worked before,' he said blandly. 'It should kill it. It should kill it so thoroughly it would never have existed.' He turned his head to the god, which was wide and large enough now to push them against the wall, a breath away from physical contact. Brunner's face blanched in the blaze, the whiteness enhancing his hatred and revulsion.

'Abomination,' he spat brutally and cast his head down, expecting the end.

Nyssa looked away from him into the swollen incorporeal god, finding it less appalling than Brunner did. He suddenly seemed distant and pointless, stripped of all his life and sharp humanity by the clarity of the being that unfolded before them. The god-light caught every one of his wretched tears and set it sparkling. She had more – wanted more – in common with the god than she did with Brunner.

She put her fingers into the outermost edge of the glow. To her surprise they remained cold, solid and uneaten. It wouldn't harm her, even as it absorbed her. Braving a moment's blindness, she stared further into the depths and saw a cosmos forming in its heart, nebula dust coalescing into suns and stars spitting forth new planets and new life.

Not a god then, but something close, something better.

A white hole. A womb breeding universes.

'No,' the Doctor's firm voice said at her ear, 'it isn't that either.'

His sudden appearance broke the allure and she pulled her undamaged hand free of its light. His young face was a worn crag and his eyes were stinging red. He had the key in his hand, the door framed behind him and Constantine's eager head bobbing carelessly over his shoulder.

She was grinning and pointing wildly into the maelstrom.

'Wow!' was all she could say. She said it again and again.

The Doctor put his hand on Nyssa's shoulder.

'Come on,' he said. 'I'll see to this. Constantine will show you the way back to the *Lung*,' he added coolly. 'Korzen should have the, uh, the pirates under control by now.'

His face wrinkled, revealing a deeper pain than a headache.

Brunner was already making for the door, retreating from the slow forward creep of the white hole. Nyssa's eyes stabbed at him, making him a coward. She felt bad about that later, but not yet, not quite yet.

'Could you leave the staff?' the Doctor asked. Brunner nodded and laid it on the floor as the Doctor continued, 'I don't think it works the way you wanted. I think it's amplifying all this.'

He cast his eyes to the floor, where the mundane metal stick lay, then into the light, staring unblinking into the fierce white firestorm.

'Will you be all right?' Nyssa asked, clutching protectively at his shoulder.

'Oh yes,' he replied brightly. 'There's no danger here. Just history.'

Brunner and Constantine were already shuffling her out of the door. The last she saw of the Doctor before it closed, trapping him in the cabin with the roaring hungry White God, was him leaning to pick Brunner's staff from the floor. He was ancient, his false young body hurting as he bent, but he wasn't feeble. His eyes had been vital.

Constantine skipped ahead, her vibrant colours leading them easily through the dark guts of the *Parliament of Rats*. Tears sparked unwanted in Nyssa's eyes. They left fat smears down her face. Brunner tried to comfort her, squeezing the bones of her hand.

'He'll be all right,' the priest-physician whispered. 'He said it.'

'Yes,' she said, 'I believe him. I believe him.'

* * *

Call me the Doctor. (He speaks to the staff, the living metal in his hand.)

My lord?

It was you in my head. It was you who brought down the TARDIS.

My lord (says the staff). When I sensed you close I had to reach out. We were conceived as the ultimate defence for Gallifrey and we served well. It was not our destiny to be abandoned like roadside trash. We need orders, my lord.

I'm sure you do. You weren't the only thing the Time Lords left behind.

No, lord. Lords, like yourself, did great things on this rock but they are now gone to dust. Such is our destiny. Oh, lord, it is wonderful to touch the clean purity of your DNA. These human creatures smell. Their flesh stinks. They are not like us.

No, they aren't.

It is demeaning to be a slave to them and their callow whims. I structure. I rationalise. I find weaknesses in the fabric and bind them tight. And they confound me. They use us to pursue crusades of superstition. We did not do that. They use us to shore up their own empires. We did not do that.

No, we didn't, of course.

And their children have fed on our trash-relics and grown into beast things like the female who has tormented us. They are unclean in space and they become unclean through time. AND IT IS OUR FAULT!

Yes, there's no need to shout. This 'White God' is of your creation?

We were made to draw it from the structure. It is a living thing, a white hole, from the old times, when such things were allowed. We can barely control it. It stands on the threshold of the event horizon and will become too real soon. Give us orders and we will push it back into the shadowlands, where it will not exist.

Now, that's fascinating. You know, white holes also contain the event horizon. Theoretically, this is –

Lord, there is no time.

Hardly. There's too much. I can't do much about it.

My lord, I must have orders.

Very well. Dissolve. Unbind your DNA. Cease to be validium. Everything you created shall become water and spread out across the world and forget.

You cannot order me to die!

I can. Isn't that terrible? I would do anything to be free of that.

My lord?

I would lie. One day I might. But not to you. You can't be fooled.

No, my lord.

Then obey my orders.

Yes, my lord.

I'm sorry.

Yes, my lord Doctor.

(And the staff turns to water and dribbles through his fingers.)

Korzen was helping Nyssa clamber over the rails on to the *Lung* when the ebony hulk of the *Parliament* was broken open and began to blast streams of dark water across the sea. It had drifted too far to strike the *Lung* but the howl of the gushers shook her, as if her god was screaming in pain.

Murmurs on the deck behind her made her turn. The piled bodies of the boarders were dissolving into frothy salt liquid.

In her arms Nyssa was struggling as she saw the *Parliament* dissolve.

'Doctor!' she howled. 'Doctor!'

Korzen hauled her aboard and let Brunner help her. The priest would be kinder, she knew, but she offered a smile of bitter encouragement.

The Doctor was already out of the door when the White God split open. The walls of the *Parliament* were breaking apart before he was in the corridor. The ship's timbers crashed around him, no less violent or heavy for coming in torrents of water. He tried to throw himself out of the way but the water came relentlessly and smashed him down. The *Parliament of Rats* sank round him. Invisible weights pulled him into the smothering dark as his clothes and skin were drenched. The thick salt waters of Lethe clutched at him. He conserved the air in his body as he sank, his instinct to survive overruling the yearning desire to open his lungs and swallow and forget.

It would be easy to float away.

Calm hands dropped on to his shoulders and seized and pulled upwards – or downwards, he could hardly tell. Legs kicked powerfully into the water at his back. He broke the surface of the water sooner than he had expected. Constantine's drenched head broke through the water soon after, close enough to be made out through the thickening mist. Her hair was matted on to her head, revealing the crude, lumpy shape of her skull. Her teeth scored her face. She spat ocean.

'Why?' the Doctor gasped as his breath returned. 'Why did you do it?'

'You're a nice person,' she said, floating unconcernedly with her face projecting through the scum-surface of the sea. 'I wouldn't let you die.'

'No.' He kicked to stay afloat.

Constantine looked playful and ashamed. 'You mean, the pirates and the god and the ships and everything?'

'Yes.' He kicked again. His legs were ice cold and softening.

'It was what everyone wanted,' the navigator purred. 'Korzen and Brunner have so many gaps in them. I filled them a bit, just a bit. The staff helped. I could make it do so many things by thinking. There are so many unmade worlds I can see that I can make. I took the ship from one. Oh, and the god, the god came from a huge empty world, a great big sucked-hollow world!' She clapped, setting a spray of water fluttering into the mist.

'You shouldn't do things like that,' the Doctor warned, the ice water sloshing over his chin. 'You're virtually rebuilding the universe from the foundations up and you shouldn't be able to. It was the staff that gave you the power.'

'I didn't make the staff, my lord Doctor,' Constantine mewed. Cramp stabbed through the bone and muscle of his legs.

'I never did a thing for myself,' Constantine whined guiltily.

'No.'

A horn blared out of the fog, not the animal howl of the *Parliament* but the real call of the *Lung of Heaven*. Turning his head, the Doctor saw it. Its prow was a shadow visible through the veil of the mist and as the sound of the horn died away, the Doctor heard calls from the distant deck.

'There! He's there! I can see!' Constantine's voice.

The Doctor kicked round to confront the woman in the water, in time to see the multiple bodies flickering round her outline, in time to see the water seethe to fill the gap as her body-form collapsed into nothing.

He lay silent, cold and thoughtful on the surface of the sea until Korzen herself came down to help him out.

The *Lung of Heaven* sailed into port five days later. By that time Nyssa felt she was on a new ship. Korzen had changed – slightly. Nyssa noticed that she talked more openly with Harbou and the crew, and a closeness had crept into their regular meals with Brunner. One morning Nyssa caught her smiling without irony or rancour. That was a good morning. The tenor of the ship changed with its captain. At one meal Korzen had spoken of the strength and security she drew from the tiny sounds of the *Lung* around her and had been mildly surprised when both Brunner and Nyssa understood.

Constantine had locked herself away. She stood at the prow on difficult days and turbulent nights, guiding the *Lung* with curt, barked orders. She spent the rest of her time in her cabin and said nothing. Nyssa watched her on the deck one day, surprised by her coldness. The colour was bleeding unattended from her hair.

The Doctor too had retreated into his cabin. Nyssa visited him occasionally but only once asked him when they would be leaving. He looked at her with ancient, contemplative eyes and sighed. 'When I make up my mind,' he said.

He didn't confess his problem to her until the night before they sailed into port. She had to coax him, but as he spoke she realised how much he needed her to help him make the decision.

'It's not our problem,' she said, as he finished.

He nodded. 'It is. The Time Lords made her, or their wreckage did. She understands what she can do, even without the staff. She…' He caught a glimpse of Nyssa's sceptical, spiked expression.

'I made her,' he insisted.

'So what are you going to do?' Nyssa prompted blandly.

'I think we have to take her with us,' he said. 'If she agrees.'

Nyssa gave a grim nod, silently pleased.

With Korzen's permission they went to Constantine's cabin the following morning to ask the girl. Nyssa had left her bound and remembered the waif's hostile and intelligent face peering out from under her shock of hair. The rope was still locked tight around the bunk when she returned, but the navigator herself had melted into air.

'Should we search the ship?' Nyssa asked.

'No,' the Doctor responded. 'Somehow I don't think there'd be any point.'

He looked at his hands – at his flat palms – as if they were dirty and repellent. His voice was dull.

'This isn't our problem,' Nyssa said.

'No.' The Doctor shook his head wistfully. 'Not any more.'

# Rights

## by Paul Grice

The metal walls clamped down around her. A soft iridescence bathed her wide eyes and gentle filaments brushed softly at the thick crumples of grey skin around them. A pearl of water threatened to drip down the corrugated ripples on the side of the fat face, until the rotating pad whipped it from the eyelid precipice.

A gun-shaped device hummed and throbbed inside the split stomach, vibrating and making soft, gentle, sucking noises. The metal walls held every fragile, spindly limb in place, some in clumps, others individually. The thick lips parted and the mouth gaped open as a low wailing moan, like some kind of distorted whale song, echoed round the sterile room.

The Doctor looked up sharply. 'She's not unconscious?' His eyes were fixed on the grim face of the Chief Clinician, who quivered there, shaking his large head.

'Our race knows nothing of the unconscious, Doctor. And to be unaware of something so intimate, so integral, is unthinkable.'

'He turned back to the machine room. There were no leads, no wires, nothing to suggest control of any kind. The way the machine chugged and vibrated, one might almost have thought it was laughing.

'Is she in pain?'

The Chief Clinician sighed. 'Of course there is discomfort. But she will be thinking of the greater good, of the sacrifice all who are able must make.'

One of the lolling eyeballs rolled towards the viewing mirror, as if it could see through the silver to the faces beyond.

The Doctor did not acknowledge the remark. He just stared

straight ahead, seemingly unaware of the twitching, uncomfortable creature by his side.

With a quiet hum a gap in the far wall appeared and widened. Like an incision into the clean white of the room, the deep red of the corridor outside bled in for a moment as a slim, brown-haired girl in a denim trouser suit stepped softly inside. By the time she had turned round to see if her escort had entered with her, the wound had healed and she was alone. Raising an eyebrow at etiquette on this planet, she paused to take in the medical centre.

In two adjectives, it was vast and white. Her journalistic mind niggled at her to find something a bit more descriptive, but what chiefly struck her was the contrast made by her best friend, standing with his back to her, leaning over a rail. In his dark red jacket and long scarf he looked ridiculously out of place, a riot of colour where none should be. His brown hair was a mess of curls, and for a facetious moment she wondered if their bald Farrashian hosts were at all jealous of him. They hovered around the room, looking at the walls as if transfixed, stroking whole sections with their wispy tendril arms as if they were alive and in pain, constantly milling about as the mass of legs supporting each of them moved to a constantly changing rhythm, while their linen-swathed torsos remained strangely still.

'Come on, Doctor,' she thought. 'I'm sure these people are just as lovely as you say, but they give me the creeps.'

As if reading her mind, a Farrashian technician turned to look at her suddenly, making her start. She tried to meet the mournful gaze in the big saucer-eyes but instead found herself, as usual, gazing at the blubbery skin of the face, which was like a huge wizened balloon full of water.

'Doctor, can't we just go home?'

'Hello, Sarah,' called the Doctor, without turning round. 'Stay where you are. I'll be right there.' He looked back at the Chief Clinician. 'What happens to this woman after you've finished with her?' His low voice was rich and deep, but there was no warmth in it. The Farrashian met his gaze, rising a little as if slighted.

'She will go to the rest bay with the others.'

'Barren?'

The pale alien tilted its big face, as if trying to discern what emotion had made the voice become hoarser, so that it was almost a whisper now.

'Possibly.' The fish-like mouth barely moved to articulate the word. 'But she is not of social standing.'

'And if she isn't – possibly,' continued the Doctor, his voice hardening, ignoring the latter part of the Farrashian's reply, 'she goes through it again?'

'Of course.'

Sarah coughed. 'I've had the guided tour,' she called over. 'Is this where you indoctrinate your interior decorators?'

The Chief Clinician stared at the two humanoids in some consternation. Watching the Doctor squash a battered brown felt hat on top of his curls and stride purposefully over to Sarah, he shuddered at the loping gait of the two long legs. Without another word he turned back to the female Farrashian encased in the metal carcass. Some minutes later his delicate ears informed him that the walls had opened and closed again to let the two visitors out into the blood red of the corridor.

'Things are bad here, Sarah.'

The Doctor had taken her outside the medical centre and they were now sprawled on the marble steps around the Farrashian City Square. It was a huge, wide-open space flanked by the distinctive spiralling glass buildings that comprised the architecture on Farrash, with a large, waterless fountain nearby. Sarah just couldn't get over the size of the pavements and walkways. At least twelve feet wide, they could still only accommodate two Farrashians walking together as they bobbed about their business. She watched them, greeting each other in their dance-like manner, spinning and weaving subtle, intricate patterns. They were unsettling – ugly even – but they had a weird grace that was undeniably beautiful.

'What do you mean?' She lay back in the twin sunshine, smiling at the black spaghetti shadows the buildings cast so sharply on the ground. 'They all seem quite uptight here, but you can't blame them really – I bet they lose patience just doing up their shoelaces.'

The Doctor spoke over the end of her sentence: 'They're dying.'

She turned quickly to look at him, but his face was hidden beneath his hat.

'Dying?' No reply. She pulled off the hat and he just stared at her, his pale blue eyes unsquinting in the strong sunlight. 'Oh, Doctor, stop acting like this.'

'Like what?'

'Like the moody alien.'

'Well, aliens do have moods, you know. It isn't a human preserve.'

She realised that he was looking past her now, at a large crowd of Farrashians bobbing round the corner. These ones wore vivid blue tunics, and as they began to fill the square a low moaning that hurt Sarah's ears started up.

'What's wrong with them?' she asked.

'It's a protest, I believe,' said the Doctor.

'You sure? It'll take them all day to chain themselves to the railings.'

The Doctor finally relented and smiled, absently. When Sarah spoke again, struggling to make herself heard over the low, distorted moaning that was getting louder and louder, her voice was earnest. 'What is it, Doctor?'

Before the Doctor could reply, a Farrashian detached itself from the crowd and called out angrily. There were forty or fifty of the creatures thronging about now and gradually a chant began – ragged at first, then stronger and clearer.

Starting to feel scared, Sarah reached out for the Doctor's scarf.

'"Babykillers"?'

The Doctor sighed. 'They're a people with problems –'

'Doctor, they're heading straight for us!'

The crowd was beginning to whirl and heave and flutter up the steps towards them. The huge fish-eyes were slanted in anger as the chant grew more and more urgent.

The Doctor rose to his feet and stood protectively in front of Sarah as together, facing the massed Farrashians, they backed away.

Put on the chain. Put on your dignity. Quickly now, meet them, show them you're not afraid. You're not killing babies. You're harnessing the essence of their lives so that a race can continue to live. That is good. Quickly now, meet them, answer them. Let them answer for themselves, are they saving lives, a planet's life?

Put on your dignity.

'And can any of you say, "I am saving lives, I am saving a planet's life"?' The Leader paused impressively and his chain of office tinkled slightly in the warm breeze.

'There is no proof, no proof at all that your twisted work is saving anybody's life!' came the angry rejoinder from the front of the mob.

'Fraal,' proclaimed the Leader, shaking his huge head from side to side, 'we know there is an answer. Let us find it! Leave us in peace!'

'Not until you leave women in peace! Not until our babies are our own again!' The crowd roared supportively. 'Then we are saving lives!'

Sarah and the Doctor were standing to one side. She looked at him. 'Is it true, Doctor?'

'Yes, the Farrashians are experimenting on their own foetuses.'

'But why?'

The Doctor shrugged. 'They're desperate. Almost a century ago something happened to that sun there.' He waved in both

235

suns' general direction. 'It began giving off a new strain of radiation – one that caused mutagens in the Farrashians' blood. Their sperm count began to decrease dramatically –'

Sarah was impatient. 'So why kill babies?'

'– amongst other things,' continued the Doctor, as if she'd never spoken. 'That sun has become a killer. They've got about three or four hundred years.'

'Until what?'

The Doctor turned to her and stared. 'Extinction.'

'We don't want to live in a body animated by dead babies!' cried Fraal, to a resounding cheer.

'That's the alternative?' whispered Sarah.

'An alternative,' replied the Doctor, his voice almost drowned out by the angry rumblings of the crowd.

'That machine –' Sarah broke off in shocked realisation. 'It was inducing labour?'

'No. It was aborting the foetus and snaffling it up for later use.'

'How can you just –'

It is a symbol, a symbol of your dignity. With it round your neck, they would never dare touch you, would not presume to argue, to –

'Fraal, stay back! I warn you, Fraal, for our planet's future!'

'Maybe it's your brain we need to animate our new plastic people!'

Remember your dignity. Don't fluster. Don't fluster. She's trying to intimidate you. Remember your dignity –

'There is nothing further to be gained from this ridiculous display –'

It was then that the grenade landed. About the same time Sarah spotted the troops.

A thick gas seeped from the egg-shaped bomb, yellow and evil-smelling. It cast a shadow over the marble of the square as the Doctor waded into it. What was he doing? Helping out the woman, Fraal, or – No, he was shielding the Leader. One of the women – they were all women, that must be why they dressed differently – was hitting the Doctor with her wispy arms, and he was going to – Yes, he'd fallen down, into the yellow smoke, as the Farrashian troops, sporting huge grey gas masks, poured into the square. They held things that looked like cattle-prods and they were buzzing blue electricity round the legs of the women, who froze and stumbled, rolling down the steps, colliding with each other.

She ran to help, was hit by the blue buzz, fell as well. Down and down the marble steps, and how hot even the stone was, and a wispy arm pulled her up with frightening strength and carried her away, out of the yellow smoke and out of the square, the sound of a herd stampeding, and where was the Doctor, and how could he... how could he sanction...

'That's not going to get anyone on your side, Leader.' The Doctor was sitting in a plush office sipping a glass of brown liquid. Disappointment was heavy in his voice as he spoke: 'How could you sanction that?'

'The gas is unpleasant, but otherwise harmless. The prods only stun. Feeling will return.'

The Doctor rubbed his legs through his checked trousers. 'Bad feeling will return. Feeling aimed right at you, Leader.'

'I am saving this planet.'

The Doctor slammed his glass down on the table. 'Waffle! You're pinning the hopes of your planet on a long shot that might just work.'

The Leader's wide eyes narrowed a little. 'We are sanctioning the work of others. Professor Delemet and his automaton. We even allow Fraal's research into her ludicrous movement device.'

When the Doctor said nothing, toying with the end of his scarf, the Leader tried hardening his voice, leaning easily but precariously forwards on his crinkled legs.

'Why did you come here, Doctor? The Bipeds stopped

visiting our world a long time ago, when our suns were young.'

The Doctor met the Leader's gaze with equanimity. 'Perhaps it's for the sake of your sons we've come again.'

'Come again?' Sarah looked blankly at Fraal in the Bortia Dwelling Centre gardens.

'Two-legged people like you haven't been seen for centuries on Farrash. Some of the outer Biped Colonies used to trade food with us, but they packed up and moved out long ago. We don't matter. We're nowhere! No one can even be bothered to invade our planet!'

Sarah thought of the Earth Colony delegate who should have been attending the Farrash Future Ratification but who was too busy relaxing on Deladus III. 'It won't even make the last item on the 23.00 news,' he had said. 'I'll just fudge the report.' Trust the Doctor to borrow his credentials and go along instead. Trust him even more, she reflected bitterly, to tell her nothing of what was going on and to arrive two days early. In fact, don't trust him at all. She roused herself when she realised Fraal had come to the end of her little rant.

'You might think yourself lucky. Some of us are sick of being invaded!'

'Lucky.' The word, while shrill, fell glumly from Fraal's round mouth. 'Lucky to be dying. No one will miss us. No one will be brought to account for the murder of our babies.'

'Tell me more about that,' said Sarah, absent-mindedly reaching for a notepad that wasn't there. 'Just what is going on around here?'

'Our form –' she gestured at herself with a wispy arm – 'will soon be unable to function in the new biosphere. Harmful light from the sun will kill these bodies.' (Remember journalistic bias, Sarah told herself, she doesn't sound too well informed.) 'The Leader has spent a long, long time working on a new shell for us, on a process to take our minds and place them in identical bodies. "Strong bodies that will survive!" he says.'

'So where's the catch?'

'We were proud to make as many babies as we could. We paired with the dwindling number of fertile men many times. The Leader claimed our foetuses were being cryogenically frozen for the future, to ensure our race would survive.'

Sarah watched as Fraal bobbed about, shading her eyes under the sparse foliage of a curved tree. There was something unsettlingly foetal about the Farrashian herself.

'But you don't have cryogenic technology.'

The Leader sighed again, toying with his chain of office. 'No. The Bipeds left some technology but it was alien to us... not our way. We had no wish to study it. It is in a museum.'

'So you lied to your people.' The Doctor drew his head up close to the Leader's. 'Why?'

'We knew there would be resistance, and that time was running out for our people.'

'And what they wouldn't know wouldn't hurt them. It's not the first time, I suppose. Carry on.'

The Leader rustled to his many feet and bobbed out from behind his desk. 'I'll show you, Doctor.'

'Our babies start with a brain. They are conscious from the moment of conception in a simple way. As foetuses, from our brains, we grow our bodies, our arms and legs.' She smiled joyfully as she spoke of it, and Sarah found herself smiling too. 'There is a story that the very first Farrashian was so impatient to be born she grew many legs to carry her away from the womb of our Creator.'

Sarah looked at Fraal's legs, twenty or thirty of them twitching or stroking each other or batting against the soft earth. 'They're incredible.' She looked up and wondered if she was being impolite. 'Your legs, I mean.'

'It is natural that you are jealous,' said Fraal sympathetically. 'Only having two yourself.'

Sarah opened her mouth but could find nothing to say.

'We would surely go mad were we in a frame such as yours – so cramped, so stunted. What kind of life do you have, poor Biped?'

Again her mouth opened, but looking at her cuts and bruises and wondering what the Doctor was up to, Sarah almost found herself agreeing.

'In here.'

The Doctor peered into the gloom, then blinked as the guard pressed a button and light flooded down. The Doctor discerned a fallen figure in the centre of the room and dashed over to it.

'Get help!' he said, examining the limp Farrashian, cradling its head and looking intently for some sign of injury. 'I said, get help!'

The Leader looked smug as he ignored the Doctor's angry hissing. 'It's not alive, Doctor. It's a shell.'

The Doctor turned back from the Leader to the prostrate body in his arms in disbelief. 'But –'

'It feels real, it looks real and, with the help of our children, it will help us live for real. Live, Doctor. Really live!'

'So what are you doing?' asked the Doctor, rising to his feet. 'Preparing a castle for a bolt of lightning?'

'We must be free to move, Doctor!' cried the Leader, agitatedly bobbing and scuttling around as if to prove the point. 'How can we exist without physical sensation.'

'But can't they simulate your bodies' natural movements?'

Fraal sniffed. 'I'm sure they could make Biped machines with ease. But Farrashian movement cannot be reproduced by motors and parts. We are born with that skill.'

'So that's why!' Sarah was on the scent. 'They take your babies from you to study how they know!'

'No. They take our babies, suck them from our wombs as soon as they can and pulp their heads. They squeeze their little brains like damp sponges and scoop up the drops for their – their – stupid, half-alive, motor-propelled corpses!'

'That's horrible!' spluttered Sarah. 'It's your right – your right to say whether or not you have your own baby.' Her voice rose in anger, but Fraal looked confused, in a supercilious sort of way.

'No one disputes this, Biped. The women are volunteering. They have been duped by the Leader's promises. But when they stop volunteering the Leader will take our babies, I have no doubt. Take them!'

'Take them. Do please, go on.' The Doctor was offering a couple of grimy sweets in the plam of his hand to the Farrashian scientist, who shook his head.

The Doctor shrugged and pushed out his lower lip. 'So, you can harness the personality of the subject but never the motor functions?'

'Never,' affirmed the scientist. 'A few twitches. Nothing else.'

'Understand this, Doctor,' said the Leader with a hitherto unrevealed passion. 'Your two legs give you limited movement. You are cramped, constrained, inexpressive.'

The Doctor grinned cheerily, popping the sweets into his mouth as he did so. 'You don't miss what you've never had!'

'Precisely, Biped… Doctor. Do you think that a race such as ours could be reduced to inhabiting such a constrictive, easy to balance form as yours?'

The Doctor pulled a face. 'No wonder you have so few visitors, if that's how you charm them.'

'No computers, no equations, can simulate the complexities of our dance.'

'Oh, I'm sure they can. You just haven't found them yet.'

'We have found something better – and something instantly available.'

The Doctor sat down in the large plastic chair and swung his long legs on to the desk.

'Ah, yes, the elixir you distil from each foetus, some kind of –' he smiled bleakly – 'motion potion, can interact organically with the artificial nervous system.'

'That's correct,' said the Chief Clinician. 'And once we harness the mental force of the individual as well, we can project it into this body, a symbiotic shell.'

'As long as you can keep topping this up.' The Doctor tapped the little phial of liquid with the toe of his battered boot, much to the alarm of the scientist.

'We have been culling for some time.'

'But you must have had enough to experiment with for some time now. Can't you replicate it?'

The scientist, the Chief Clinician and the Leader just stared.

'You mean you haven't even tried?'

'To give birth at present is simply to condemn to death. In any case, in only a matter of years all uncontrolled breeding will be ended. We shall farm the foetuses until all viable sperm is exhausted and our race is truly barren. Then –' and the Leader held his chain of office – 'we will enter the next stage of our evolution.'

'Evolution.' The Doctor shook with fury. 'Evolution? You slaughter your children for the right to exist in a shell?'

'An animate shell, Doctor,' said the Leader, calmly, 'one that bears the hallmark qualities of our race, one that will learn and plan and philosophise, one that will go on.'

'To do what, hmm? What will it go on to do?' The Doctor pushed both hands deep into his pockets, wide eyes staring in defiance.

'We will survive.'

The Doctor's face assumed a weary expression. 'I've heard that one before.'

The creature was frightened. It wailed pitifully as the woman scrabbled with the knife around its neck, missed, fell in the mud. The creature pulled away again, long snout stretched out in front of it in desperation, eyes bulging, but the others closed in with large sticks and hit its various legs until they broke. Its screams mingled with Sarah's outraged voice.

'Stop it, for God's sake! What are you doing? Stop it!'

One of the women wiped yellow beads of fatty sweat from her brow, her arms resting on the beast's flank as her friend finally slit its furry throat and stopped its struggle once and for all.

'The Leader,' she gasped through the round flappy mouth, 'has turned his back on animal experimentation.'

'But you haven't.' Sarah closed her eyes, feeling sick.

'Our resources are few, but we have a small science unit that is on the verge of a breakthrough.'

Fraal wafted over. 'And an ally in the next town who raises funds to buy the beasts for us,' she added proudly.

'But your ally is not prepared to slaughter them, I take it?'

'The animal cannot be dead too long.'

'Then what about humane killing?' Sarah just couldn't get over the lack of compassion among the women.

Fraal leaned over Sarah and spoke the words as if explaining to a simpleton. 'It is an animal, Sarah. It has no feelings. Not like we do.'

'But it has legs like we do,' giggled the woman as she wiped some blood from the blue plastic of her tunic.

'Almost,' said Fraal. 'The weight balance is completely different but –'

'I'm sorry, Fraal.' Where the hell was the Doctor? Why hadn't he come looking for her? 'I want to go back to my friend. It was kind of you to look after me when I fell, but –'

'I can spare no one to take you back,' said Fraal, turning to leave in the same direction as the women hauling away the freshly slaughtered beast.

'I'll find my own way, but I really have to go.'

'You are a female, Biped. You belong with us. And soon you will come with us to the City Square once again.'

Sarah couldn't help looking over Fraal's shoulder at the bloodied hulk of the beast receding into the distance. By the time she'd pulled her eyes away to look at Fraal, the Farrashian had turned away.

'What happens then? Another demonstration? And where will that get you?'

'The support we have garnered from some quarters of the population has won us a place on the Ratification Assessment Committee. It is our last chance. And your presence will lend further credence to our cause.'

That wretched Ratification Assessment Committee! Sarah tried to muster some dignified response. 'We are impartial observers, the Doctor and I. We cannot be seen –'

'Your friend the Biped is on the side of the Leader. You will be on my side.'

Sarah stood there glaring at Fraal, who had sucked in her cheeks in an expression Sarah could barely guess at. She figured it was better that way.

'You will be on my side.'


The Doctor strode softly around the red corridors in the evening gloom. Sarah was safe in an encampment a few miles away from the city. He had been shown photographs from government observation cameras and, apart from looking more petulant than usual, she'd seemed fine. The guest-delegate communal debating chamber was empty save for one or two creatures studiously consulting their briefing notes. The Doctor nodded politely. He felt genuine embarrassment as well as anger that so few races cared enough to try and help these people. The Farrashians were quietly dignified about their predicament. From the outset they had made it clear they would never abandon their world, would accept no charity and brook no outside interference.

That was probably just as well, mused the Doctor, as he came across the delegates' relaxation suite. Wide seats, a huge table laden with different foods and drinks under a transparent protective canopy, impeccable white linen. He wondered how the Leader would amend his speech tomorrow when faced with addressing a practically empty gallery of observers. Or how the caterer would feel as his magnificent dishes came back barely touched. He tried to imagine the cold knots of fear in every Farrashian delegate's stomach, in the Leader's own. The foetal research, impressive though it was, clearly had a long, long way to go.

'We will survive.' How many times had he battled with the aftermath of that basic, essential desire? Would he one day find himself pitted against legions of artificial Farrashians, the tiny child inside them twisted to hatred, war, the acquisition of power to replace the loss of everything... everything Farrashian about them?

Tomorrow, with all the research groups planet-wide in attendance, a final course of action to shape the destiny of Farrash would be decided upon. Or had it already been decided? That old cliché found its way into his head: how would history judge them at this moment?

He picked up a soft white roll of some doughy substance and idly pulled it apart as he headed for his room.


Sarah thought about escape. But where to? The next day they would take her straight back to the Doctor anyway and he would see her moral predicament. Oh, but what predicament? Maybe she was on the side of Fraal and the women. Surely she ought to be? But that poor animal... maybe she should break away and form an Animal Liberation party, and sod the lot of them.

They chased balls in her dreams, running with red setters and collies, spindly legs propelling them with that funny balletic grace across her old school playing fields. She woke several times with a fearful start (where am I who are you where's the Doctor) and found herself staring at a translucent Farrashian eyelid, stretched tautly across the big eye in soft sleep. The lights were on all night. Farrashians do it with the lights on. When's morning coming? She felt a pang of guilt at her desperation for the Farrashian suns, a whole race's death knell, to reappear. Then she remembered the animal. She thought of the children. She remembered Fraal sucking in her cheeks as though consuming ice-cream through a straw. Then she thought of the Doctor, floppy felt hat on his head with a cheery wake-up grin plastered over his face.

Then all thoughts blurred into a grey soft centre as sleep tugged her back into the darkness. She idly wondered how she could fall asleep whilst feeling so afraid.

'It's good to see you, Sarah,' said the Doctor, grinning as widely as she'd ever seen. He awkwardly knocked her arm, as if he wanted to hold her but had no idea how to go about it – like a worried father scared of holding a new-born baby. In fact, Sarah couldn't help feeling a little embarrassed at the Doctor's sudden delight, taking in the tight-lipped faces of the Farrashian delegates as they filed sombrely into the room.

'Judgement Day,' breathed Sarah.

The Doctor pulled an apple from his pocket and bit into it, chewing thoughtfully. After a few moments he offered the apple to Sarah. She declined, as did no small number of Farrashians sidling past. Shrugging, he plonked his hat on Sarah's head and gestured over to the guest-delegates' enclosure, offering her his arm.

'Thank you, kind sir,' she murmured as they shared a smile. Again she felt a pang of guilt, her personal relief at being reunited with the Doctor outweighing her concerns for the conference ahead and its ramifications for this race. To be honest, she was tired, sore and wanted out. Back to the TARDIS and to somewhere fun.

She felt impatient just looking round the room – featureless, grey, like an echoey great lecture hall. A large, long metal slab of a table stretched from wall to wall. No chairs. No windows. No sunlight.

Then she took in the Farrashians as they shuffled and swanned their way to the table, peering with those giant goldfish eyes at nameplates, gliding round each other before sitting on a cluster of legs, arranging the others out around themselves.

'No,' she murmured, smiling sadly to herself, 'I can't see you wheelchair-bound somehow.'

'Hmmm?'

The Doctor was taking in the scene himself, blue eyes wide and alert. Sarah wondered if Time Lords saw things in the same way as humans. Didn't dogs see only in black and white?

The animal again, legs splintering.

She realised Fraal was staring fixedly at her from the speakers' portion of the table, her blue tunic polished and shiny. Feeling the strength of that gaze, she couldn't help wishing that there were more guest-delegates enclosed here with her.

'This is so horrible, Doctor.' Sarah grimaced. 'Can't you help them?'

'Of course I can.'

Sarah was astounded, but soon found her voice. 'Well, then, why don't you just –'

'Why don't I make the plains of Africa abundant with food and water so that millions of doomed souls can survive? Why don't I cure the common cold so that 3 million working days can be saved every year? Why don't I wake up the reptiles that once ruled your world so that their race can thrive and yours be wiped out?' The Doctor was looking thoughtfully at the table filling with delegates, his voice level and emotionless. Then he turned to Sarah and smiled a sad, toothy grin. 'I'm just performing in the play, Sarah. I don't write it.'

Sarah scowled. 'And you don't care about the supporting cast? Look at you, you're observing. You're just sitting there observing, like you're at some dreary press conference –' Sarah suddenly drew a breath and hugged her legs. 'Or like a Time Lord. You're doing just what they do! Observing! You're doing just what you despise them for.'

'Have you finished?' The Doctor's tone had turned irritable. Then he adopted a loud stage whisper. 'They're beginning.'

It seemed to go on for ever. Delegates pored over figures and calculations and results of interminably weird experiments. Sarah was reminded of the days she used to spend people-watching in train stations, except those people all looked more or less the same and so it was just too boring. In contrast, one of the visiting alien delegates kept catching her eye – or rather, she kept catching its eye, a wobbling protuberance that was focused on her more than on events round the table, the scratchy voice of the translator-com rattling from a device clipped to a huge flappy ear. The Doctor had remained staring straight ahead. Sarah wondered if Time Lords' buttocks were at all sensitive to hard plastic seating, then decided not to pursue that train of thought.

She was suddenly aware that Fraal was speaking. Then she realised that Fraal was pointing at her and raising her voice.

'That alien, there, in the box, a woman, she knows we are right. We are right to want to save our babies! Everyone must know what we are fighting!'

'Delegate Fraal,' blustered the Leader, 'if our race is to survive we must, regrettably, be prepared to push aside certain... hysterical notions of ethics –'

'Hysterical?' screeched Fraal hysterically. 'You squander lives to try and extend your own, lives that have barely begun –'

'Delegate Fraal, the progress we are making more than justifies –'

One of Fraal's assistants piped up in a high-pitched bobbling wheeze of a voice. 'Progress? Your progress is negligible. Admit it. You had hoped to present your hideous shell of a body today to these aliens.'

'We have such a body!' retorted the Chief Clinician, stung. 'We have –'

'You think we will jump into your fake body, knowing our children have died to make it move?'

'They live on in the body, Delegate Trisst, they commune with the mind and will accompany the host for ever.'

'Wretched pomposity!' Fraal's voice was a twisted scream as she wobbled about like a macabre jelly on her trembling legs.

'Please!' The Doctor was standing, arms raised in a calming

gesture, staring round at the suddenly hushed hall, speaking clearly in impassioned tones. 'Please. Listen to yourselves. The issues you are facing –'

'Enough, Two-legs,' snarled a small, fat Farrashian pushing forwards through the astonished delegates. 'The issues are ours and we have solved them through machinery!'

'This mad scheme again, Delegate Delemet. You persist, yet surely you can see we have exhausted all avenues for computer simulation.' The Leader's eyes looked red and watery, and he was breathing deeply.

Sarah tugged on the Doctor's scarf to pull him back down. 'So much for the observer,' she whispered.

The Doctor said nothing. He waved her into silence as the new contender continued.

'You reckoned without my genius!' Delemet cried with a leering smile. 'Enter!' he called behind him, then turned back to the table. 'Let the future usher itself into our rescued lives!'

The doors to the hall were slammed back as a huge, glittering machine kicked out with hideous strength. A good twenty feet tall, streaked with thick brown oil and with no discernible features, it wobbled about noisily in a ghastly approximation of Farrashian movement. A high-pitched rustle of anxious voices spread around the room.

'Of course, as advances in technology occur, our new bodies can be smaller –'

Delemet never finished his sentence, as a mechanical steel hoof from his creation smashed with horrific speed through his head. A pale slush rained down on the delegates nearby, who screamed and yelled as the faceless machine began to move, high-kicking, rolling and vibrating further into the room, advancing remorselessly on the quivering Farrashians in its path.

'Get out of the way!' screamed Sarah.

Her cry was aimed at the panicking, screaming aliens as the machine weaved about the room. As for the Doctor, she saw him rush into the fray, hurling delegates to one side, to safety. Then he was floored as a piece of splintering wood from the vast table caught him across the face. The machine was whirling out of control above him.

Fraal made a desperate attempt to rescue her small prototype movement mechanism from the floor, where the Farrashian stampede was threatening to shatter its display case and turn it into so much tin foil, but she was being knocked further and further away from her life's work, and nearer and nearer to the robot. Wide eyes narrowing, she caught hold of one end of the Doctor's scarf and hauled him out of the machine's path.

A hole in the floor was punched through by a gleaming steel hoof where the Doctor's head had been seconds before.

'I'm grateful –' began the Doctor, but Fraal still had hold of his scarf in her flimsy hands, and she spun him round by it, sending him reeling. He was scrambling to his feet when Fraal tugged sharply and he fell back to the floor, directly over the movement mechanism.

'Guard that, stupid male Biped!' she roared, smiling in satisfaction as two terrified Farrashians ran over the Doctor to escape a flailing mechanical tendril.

Sarah had made her way round to the back of the hall, staring with fear and revulsion at the grisly scene. She had been trying to get to the Doctor, but she had lost sight of him in the chaotic rush of Farrashian bodies. Eventually she had decided she'd be better able to help him if he was injured by staying alive herself, and so had ducked down behind the wreck of the Leader's large ceremonial plastic chair. Where was the Leader? Why wasn't he leading his people to safety?

Then she saw him. The machine was sweeping the floor with his struggling, gurgling body, impaled on the end of one of its wobbling metal legs. Sarah gave a low moan, then gasped as the hideous metal monster smashed into the pale concrete of the wall, battering its body against it repeatedly until, with a crash that echoed and re-echoed around the devastated conference room, a giant hole appeared in front of it. Without stopping it pushed through the gap in the wall, glowing iridescent in the

250

fierce sunlight that flooded into the room like an evil spotlight as it fell out of sight and landed with a resounding crash.

In the comparative silence that remained in the room after the creaking and grinding of the gears that propelled the machine had gone, Sarah ran across to see what had become of the robot, terrified it would somehow return. Peering into the aggressive light outside, she discerned it far below, shattered across the great square. The Leader's body lay upturned in the vast waterless fountain, legs splayed about like skinny petals on a fat pale flower.

Shuddering, she turned to look for the Doctor through the chaos in the room. Weeping Farrashians shivered in floods of tears or paced about, bodies bobbing up and down, almost comical in their distress. She felt her own tears welling up and wished, wished so hard that she wasn't here and that they had never come.

'I know, Sarah,' said the Doctor, suddenly by her side and shocking her from her reverie. She burst into tears and grabbed hold of him, burying her head in his chest. 'Don't tell me you thought I was dead again?'

She looked at him. His coat was torn and there was a nasty bruise developing on his forehead, but his grin was as wide and as bright as ever, even in this carnage. He pulled out Fraal's mechanism from his coat and scrutinised it.

'She was going down a blind alley, I'm afraid,' murmured the Doctor, pulling his lips down in an expression of sadness.

'Was? Where is Fraal?' Sarah stared around her with growing concern.

'Give me... my baby... Biped.'

Pulling herself along towards them by her wispy forearms was the battered Farrashian woman. One of her eyes was closed and leaking a sticky fluid. She scrabbled about like a flailing beetle until she was on her many feet, then she straightened herself up and took back the motor unit from the Doctor.

'As you can see,' she gurgled quietly, gesturing at the shattered conference room, at the panicked, the dead and the dying, 'there is only one way forward for us now. My way!'

'And now the end is near...' muttered Sarah. 'Fraal, I'm glad you're all right, but don't you think you should give it a rest, just for a minute?'

'Rest? When every moment I delay a baby's life is harvested for –'

'Then I'd get over and join the Doctor there with the others,' interrupted Sarah. The Time Lord had already gathered a small group of Farrashians about him – Sarah recognised the Chief Clinician and the Deputy Leader, and from their sashes she guessed the others were government officials as well. 'He's already trying to sort everyone out.'

Fraal squawked, then bobbed over at speed to the party. The Doctor held one finger up to his lips in a gesture of silence when he saw her arrive and, to Sarah's astonishment, Fraal said nothing.

'This has been a terrible day,' whined the Deputy.

'Yes... yes, it has,' concurred the Doctor.

He was interrupted by the Chief Clinician. 'Our Leader – dead! What chance do we have of a future now?'

'Well, perhaps it's time to recognise the other groups working to save your planet,' said Sarah, quietly joining them, pursing her lips.

'Yes. Your Leader called this meeting to formulate a future strategy, to listen to ideas.'

'He wasn't listening –'

The Doctor plonked his hat on the end of Fraal's waving arm and she was silenced, staring at it as he continued. 'So embrace his plan, but progress it. Think about it – a government committee sharing research, working in harmony with itself,' added the Doctor. He looked around the solemn, battered group. 'Work together. Trade ideas. Pool your resources. Learn from each other's mistakes.'

Fraal looked at the Doctor's fist, clenched as it was to convey a fighting spirit, then at the others. 'You would let us use your facilities?'

The Deputy Leader shifted uncomfortably. 'We could perhaps discuss this further at the next meeting of congress. First, we must arrange the send-off for our Leader.'

'And you will stop the foetal experimentation?' Fraal hopped off after the weakly protesting Deputy as the delegation moved away.

Sarah looked around the room. Medical help had arrived and the room was being cleared. She frowned at the thought of the Farrashian Leader having a 'send-off'. Farrashians sitting round a relative's house with limp sandwiches and sausage rolls didn't really seem all that likely.

The Doctor, whether by coincidence or design, answered her unspoken questions. 'They'll send the Leader off into space, now. It's their custom.'

'Custom?'

'Yes, sealed in a casket along with a constantly transmitting recording that will announce the story of his life and the manner of his death.'

Sarah considered the Leader's skewered body in the square below. 'That's no way to be remembered.' Then a thought hit her. 'How long do Farrashians live for?'

'A good two hundred years. That one was Leader for over a hundred.'

'Around the time the research began?'

'Yes,' said the Doctor, smiling. 'He'll go off into the stars now, the poignant message of his life going out over and over again...' They began walking from the room. 'He'll be out of this sector in ten years, reach a whole new galaxy in fifty.'

Sarah scuffed her shoe against a deep red wall. 'What if he hits something?'

'Perhaps he will. Or perhaps... perhaps out there there'll be someone who'll be moved by his story.' He smiled quickly at her. 'Someone who can help.'

'Can we come back? Can we give it two hundred years and see?' asked Sarah as they stepped out into the cruelly bright sunlight.

But the Doctor was out of earshot, striding off on his long legs, already way ahead of her. To her right, in the fountain, the sun had already baked the Leader's blood into the stone.

# Wish You were Here

by Guy Clapperton

The most obvious question was what in the five galaxies he thought he looked like. Janis Carma was well travelled enough to have had her mind opened to a variety of extravagant costumes but this one took a bit of swallowing.

Starting at the bottom, the shoes were normal enough, she supposed, although the red spats were rather unusual. Yellow trousers with black stripes she could take too – the stripes were presumably there to conceal the rotundity of the wearer. But with that waistcoat? Of course, there was nothing intrinsically wrong with a checked red waistcoat, even if its occupant did show signs of being about to burst out of it at any second, but not with that pale-blue cravat with the white spots! As for the coat, well – one lapel was pink, the other yellow, the collar checked and the rest predominantly red, with cuffs to match the trousers. The whole ensemble was truly shocking.

The fact that the stranger responsible for thrusting this appalling vision upon her was smiling – he probably thought serenely, but it just looked plain daft to her – at a rose, of all things, did little to improve her opinion of his sanity. He looked at the rose encouragingly, sniffed a little, and nodded at it.

Janis could stand the performance no longer. 'What are you doing?' she asked, as politely as could be expected of someone convinced she was talking to a complete lunatic.

'Communicating with a rose,' he said, as if this should be obvious.

Janis had started backing towards the door almost before she was aware she wanted to be anywhere but here.

* * *

This was getting to be a bore. He was definitely following her. Fair enough – she wasn't shy and, despite being over forty, she'd looked after herself and was attractive. But normally she could shake off unwanted admirers. She'd increase her pace, look determined and, not to put too fine a point on it, they'd clear off. Not this one, though. He didn't seem to realise that she was moving any more quickly than usual. His strides were long enough to keep up with her without any apparent effort and, from the look on his face, he seemed to be finding the exercise positively stimulating.

'Ah, the rose…' he declared conversationally, but in a voice that could have reached the back row of a hall full of people. 'Quite remarkable. A species that appears to survive on beauty alone. Of course, humans see so little of its beauty. Did you know that if you were an insect on Earth you would see this rose completely differently? Insects – at least those that use pollen – can see ultra-violet light. Flowers look completely different in ultra-violet, even more breathtakingly beautiful. I, of course, can identify 170 different levels of the spectrum…'

Had he noticed she was running now? He somehow still seemed to be walking. She couldn't stand much more of this.

'Insects are attracted to the rose because of its dazzling appearance, and so pollination takes place. Mankind, with its much more limited visual appreciation, cultivates the rose for aesthetic purposes, creates new strains… The rose survives – and thrives – simply through its ability to give pleasure to others.'

He smiled a broad, thin smile.

'It's a bit like you Thetrans, here on Nestra.'

'Look, mister…'

'Doctor.'

'Look, Doctor, I'm sure you're a very nice person and all that –'

'Thank you.'

'– but if you don't mind, this is where I leave you. I'm here for a quiet holiday, nothing else, so if you'll excuse me…'

The strange man looked only marginally disappointed. 'Of course,' he said, gesticulating around the narrow marble stairway they had now reached. 'Make the place your own. Have a nice day. Do what tourists usually do...'

Her relief was almost palpable. The last thing she needed was to be bothered by some crank banging on about botany when she had work to do. She turned and started to make her way out.

'It's just that I'd have sworn you were here as a Thetran agent, armed to the teeth and trying not to look as though you had a tracer implanted under the index finger of your right hand.'

Janis stopped dead. She would have sworn that the blood literally stopped flowing around her body for a moment.

'Just a hunch.'

She turned to face the Doctor very, very slowly, only to be greeted by the ample acreage of his disappearing back.

'I'll be in the coffee lounge if anyone wants me,' he added, turning round with what was no doubt intended as a winning smile.

The lounge was undeniably hideous. The Doctor was well aware that some people considered his taste poor, but whoever had been responsible for the last few redecorations here ought to think seriously about their vocation.

Presumably they'd started off with the notion of doing something vaguely in period. Earth, Britain, late Victorian – one of the Doctor's favourite eras as long as no one made him go to the dentist. The picture rails, the dado rails, the massive ceiling rose and the skirting boards, they all made sense.

Although it was too big for an ordinary tearoom, being more like a ballroom in its dimensions, that was understandable given the number of people who came to Nestra on holiday. The tables, presumably some sort of imitation mahogany, were solid and the chairs were comfortable. So quite why anyone had painted the walls that particularly virulent shade of bright pink was anybody's guess. As for the woodwork – lilac-mauve gloss – it didn't bear thinking about. The Doctor shuddered briefly, then turned to smile and wave at some of his fellow patrons, pallid and pasty lot that they were. They waved feebly back as if the effort might make their arms drop off. The effect would have been comical if he hadn't suspected the reasons. His reverie was interrupted by the clearing of a throat and a familiar sensation at the back of his neck.

'We need to talk,' said Janis. 'Where can we go that's quiet?'

The Doctor looked around. 'Here?' he ventured. 'And put that gun away. I wouldn't want to have to disarm you. You might get hurt.' Ignoring the blaster completely, he stood up and, with exaggerated courtesy, pulled out a rather elegant Queen Anne chair for her to sit on. 'It's a fake, of course.'

This she had not anticipated. When she pulled a gun on someone, the general idea was that they should act a bit scared – throw up their hands, maybe try to run, start whimpering, whatever. Her new companion just wasn't responding in the right way.

'Waiter!' he boomed.

Janis felt herself shuddering at the noise again. She realised that she was still holding her gun, and suddenly this made her feel oddly self-conscious rather than confident. Gently she lowered herself into the proffered chair. This was not how the day was supposed to pan out, and somehow she had a nasty feeling that things were only going to get worse.

'OK, good buddy, what can I do you for? Nice threads, but then that covers a lot of ground. Say, you cover a lot of ground too. Maybe you ought to get moving. I hear they're about to tear you down and put an office block in your place.'

The stilted voice came from a little besequinned droid that had just appeared at the Doctor's left elbow. Janis felt strangely as if she were losing her grip on reality. The Doctor, meanwhile, was doing his best to fix the droid with a look of contempt.

'I suppose, you metal moron, that is what passes for wit in your transistorised cranium?'

'Sure thing, bub. Okey-dokey. There is only one thing worse than being talked about and that is not being talked about. Life, don't talk to me about life.'

The Doctor leaned sympathetically towards Janis. 'Don't let the poor little thing worry you. It's his programming, but then you know that. In order to engender a relaxed and calming atmosphere in this pangalactic Pontin's, the Thetrans decided that the servitors ought to engage in a little light banter with their guests. Unfortunately, their idea of humour is somewhat limited. They seem simply to have raided the archives for a few overworked catchphrases and thrown them all together, regardless of context. Now, why am I telling you all this?'

'I come from Barcelona. I speak English. I learn it from a book,' the droid suddenly announced in an appalling Spanish accent.

'Two cream teas with extra scones. And extra tea and extra jam,' the Doctor snapped. 'And extra cream!'

Apparently happy now, the gaudy automaton trundled away, muttering something about this being another fine mess someone or other had gotten him into.

Janis looked at the Doctor again. Although he had not changed his clothes and his blond, curly hair was still unruly, he suddenly looked less the clown. It was his eyes, she decided. Whereas before it had been easy to look past him, now his eyes had a searing quality. They seemed to be looking through her, and yet there was warmth there too. He wanted to know about her, she felt. Of course, it could be a trick. Best to play it cool.

'What gave me away?' she asked, with a toss of the head that was rather too theatrical to be convincing.

'Body language,' he replied, easing his ample girth back into the comfortable chair he had found for himself. 'I, for example, am sitting here, relaxing. That is how I am able to dominate. It's a natural position for someone who is in charge. You, on the other hand, have been poised for action ever since you arrived here. This –' he threw out his arms expansively, as though he had a whole audience to address instead of one individual – 'is a holiday camp, nothing more and nothing less. And there you were, pacing around the place like a caged beast. No, you're not on holiday.' He stopped, realising that the manic droid had returned again.

'Just one Cornetto,' he piped up tunelessly. 'Tea for two and two for tea...'

The droid somehow managed to be totally out of tune by the same degree with every note without actually slipping into any identifiable key. He deposited rather tired-looking scones, jam and milk on the table, and left a teapot full of brown liquid that smelled of stale teabags just next to it, before trundling off with a final 'Y'all enjoy now.'

The Doctor busied himself pouring the insipid liquid into the barely clean cups, trying to look enthusiastic.

'So,' he said eventually, 'what's the story?'

What indeed? There seemed little point in witholding anything from him since he seemed to know so much already.

'You're right,' said Janis.

'Invariably.'

Ignoring the interruption, she took a sip of her tea and grimaced. 'I'm a Thetran. We run Nestra as a business venture.' The last two words were almost spat out. 'We're having problems with our bookings.'

'So you sent a spy to your own holiday camp?'

'That's... That's right,' she replied, somewhat lamely.

'Yes. Yes, I suppose it is,' said the Doctor. 'Although my information is that your problem is more to do with the fact that the people who book themselves in so very rarely seem to come out again.'

She shifted uncomfortably and told him the story of how a scientist named Korriklimm had built a set of leisurebots known as Lakksis to run Nestra as a holiday paradise for offworlders.

As the explanation continued the Doctor began to grow more and more impatient. 'Yes, yes, look, we all know about the Thetrans and their legendary hospitality to other species, their total love of and dedication to everyone in the Ragnar system, but... Sorry, do you mind if I ask what precisely you are laughing at?'

Janis tried to straighten her face, but failed miserably. 'I'm sorry,' she spluttered. 'Obviously our PRs have done a cracking job, but... dedication? Love? For those plebs?'

She motioned towards the other people in the room, who had finished their refreshments but seemed too exhausted to move. They looked more like patients at a sanatorium than holidaymakers. Even the Doctor, who prided himself on finding something endearing in every life form, give or take the odd citizen of Skaro or Telos, had to admit they seemed an unattractive bunch. Something here didn't add up.

'And yet,' he started, as the small gaudy droid came to tidy the table, humming what sounded as though it might once have been 'Hi ho, hi ho, it's off to work we go'.

'And yet...' He tried again, louder: 'And yet...'

The servitor looked up at him. 'I say, Jeeves, the old banjolele not annoying you, is it?'

The Doctor gave his best glower – one of his better expressions with this face, he thought. 'The banjolele, the singing, the enforced bonhomie, I am fed up with the lot. Now, cut it out – and stop twinkling those wretched soothing colours at me. I'm immune!'

The grass-green glow emanating from the metallic slave ceased immediately, as did the whale song that had surreptitiously started up.

'Gee, ya only hadda ask...'

Had the Time Lord been in a more fair-minded mood, he would have admitted that the table was cleared so unobtrusively after his outburst that he quite forgot the little servitor was there.

'As I was saying,' he started again, 'the Thetrans have been running the leisure syndicate for over five centuries. I understood that your whole economy was based on services rather than manufacturing, to the extent that your stock exchange even has a separate listing for intangibles.'

'You're right, and we hate it,' she spat. 'Tourists... Can you imagine what it's like having to run around at the beck and call of whichever barbarian species decides it needs you at any time of the day or night?'

The Doctor had never looked at things in this light before, but actually the complaint did resonate with him.

'Fetch this, do this, do that, or else our whole employment infrastructure will go out of the window. We've become too dependent on the service industries, as you say. We don't produce anything ourselves, so we end up serving these – these slobs!'

The Doctor gazed around the room again. Slobs did indeed seem an appropriate, if unpleasant, word.

'OK, but you still haven't told me what's going wrong.'

The droid was taking a long time to get rid of the teacups, she was thinking. Stupid idea, trying to make 'cute' little servobots only to have them clear tables. She suddenly realised the Doctor was still talking.

'Everyone can regret the turn their society is taking. And certainly an element of rebellion can be healthy. But I don't understand what you're doing here.'

She breathed in deeply amid the clatter of cutlery. 'The mistake came in asking Korriklimm to automate the process. He'd based the whole robotic servitor race on his unique experiential technology, which enabled the droids to learn from real-time input, actual events they witnessed, rather than depending on standard scripted responses. We first knew something was going wrong when the families of people who had stayed here started contacting us because their relatives had not come back. Then our requests for information went unanswered.'

'I see,' said the Doctor. 'And that's when Korriklimm went missing.'

'Yes, that's – Hold on. How do you know that?'

'Oh, sources.' He gave a dismissive wave – exaggeratedly so, she thought – as if to make her think he was covering something.

'Well, since you know already, yes. He agreed to come and look into things and –'

And that was the last you or his family saw of him, the Doctor silently added. And that in turn was why Manta, Korriklimm's life partner of twenty years, had asked him to look into things. An old friend needed help...

He became aware that Janis was still speaking.

'... So they sent me in under deep cover since the direct approach had failed. The only problem is knowing where to start.'

'What? Oh, I'd just enjoy the holiday if I were you. I don't expect there's much of a problem. These things happen. Old Korriklimm's probably stopped off for a cream tea or something.'

No, Doctor, he thought, that wasn't very convincing. You've already shown an interest, so she'll never fall for it. Never mind, it's done now. She was standing up, the body language registering distance and alienation. He sat back in his seat, trying to look satisfied and relaxed.

'There's a very major problem here,' she said, suddenly suspicious. 'And, for all I know, you're part of it. You're to keep your distance.' She had started backing away. Only minutes before she'd felt she could trust him totally and yet suddenly he was trying to stop her doing her job. It was all very baffling. 'I'm leaving now. Don't try to follow.'

'Perish the thought,' he replied, nodding towards the table. 'Don't forget your blaster. It wouldn't do to have an unarmed master spy, after all.'

Cursing under her breath, she reholstered the weapon and stalked off. This time it was the Doctor watching her retreating back.

The droid captured her within ten minutes.

* * *

The Doctor continued to wander, mentally as much as physically. He had no particular aim, nowhere particular to go, and he eventually found himself in the souvenir gallery – an indoor selection of shops under a glass-domed ceiling, all selling the same garments, picturemails, soundcards, talking histories in 100,000 languages on the same disk and old-fashioned paperback books for the grown-ups. The usual tat and rubbish, he thought, fingering a plain black T-shirt with the most discreet of souvenir logos sewn into it by hand. He admired his own outfit in a handy mirror. Nothing to match this anywhere in the galaxy, he mused proudly, and smiled to himself.

'Exterminate! The Doctor is an enemy!'

The voice came from nowhere and everywhere at once and he found himself instinctively ducking behind a display of artificial Gannukskin coats.

'Ha ha ha, I thought it was you!' came a boisterous voice.

Tall, thought the Doctor. Unduly loud, generally pleasing demeanour, something of an ego about him, but no... it wasn't one of his previous incarnations. 'You don't remember me, do you?'

'Of course I do, I mean, I... er...'

This happens all over the galaxy. A person decides to get away from it all for a few days and what happens? They bump into someone they know! Given the length of the Doctor's life, in spite of the fact that several of his incarnations had been somewhat prematurely curtailed, he had met more people than most, so it was only natural that he should have forgotten a great many of them.

'It's K'Tarth! K'Tarth from Jovanna!'

Of course, now he remembered. He started making appropriately polite noises. Jovanna, where he'd set right that minor skirmish with the dictator who wanted everyone to wear red in memory of his lost bride. This had seemed a reasonable enough request, except that the Jovannans had a defect in their visual physiognomy that meant if they saw too much red they became blind. He'd sorted that one out with an intergalactic dating agency and a swift bit of matchmaking, if he recalled correctly. And that's where he'd met K'Tarth, the chatty young man who had wanted to see the universe. Of course, like any responsible Gallifreyan, the Doctor had tried to talk him out of it immediately, describing the horrors he might have to face – and the young idiot had become hooked.

'So, K'Tarth, what brings you here?'

'Same as you, I imagine, holiday. It must take it out of you, going around saving the universe and righting wrongs all the time...'

'... righting wrongs all the time...'

The speaker crackled a little but the meaning was clear enough. This other visitor was a potential contaminant and, for the good of the rest of the community, must be eradicated, the droid's circuits told him.

Lakksis didn't have to reach for the liquefication button. It was imprinted into his control circuits. Rather like the failsafe, which kicked into gear at that moment. Logically, the Doctor had been identified as a disruptive element, but as this was so far unproven, the thing to do was question him.

The droid set off in search of the Doctor.

'Hey, man, what is that?'

K'Tarth, only recently arrived, had not yet seen their robotic host, the design of whose casing made the Doctor's choice of garments look positively conservative. His reaction was therefore understandable.

'K'Tarth, meet the manic machine that does most of the work around here. It's called Lakksis. Whenever you want anything, this little chap seems to be right there at your elbow.' There was a sarcastic edge to his voice. 'Lakksis, meet K'Tarth, an old friend.'

'Howdy pardner, how you doing?'

The Doctor winced. He loved the planet Earth and he

enjoyed America, the country that had produced Mark Twain, Norman Rockwell and Scott Fitzgerald, not to mention Peri. But why was it that so many preprogrammed automata looked to the States for inspiration and emerged as simplistic stereotypes talking in hideous sub-Wild West drawls? Lakksis was only the latest in a long line of tin cowboys the Doctor had encountered.

'Say, Doc, what say we mosey on down to mah hide-out? There's some folks down there who wanna talk to you and all.'

The Doctor stared at the ground as hard as he could but it resolutely refused to open up and swallow him.

'If it's all the same to you, I'd rather –'

'But, gee, it ain't all the same. No sirree, it ain't the same at all.'

A metal claw made a grab for the Time Lord's coat. The Doctor ducked and ran, K'Tarth close behind him. They were already half-way across the marbled courtyard before they realised they had no idea where to go.

'In here!'

The Doctor had spotted a service door of some sort, lurid green with the phrase 'Do not enter' picked out in telemetric writing – a universal communication system that used telepathy to overcome language barriers. Closing his mind to the message, the Doctor dragged K'Tarth through the door.

The corridor behind the door must have been built for robots. There was no way a human would be comfortable in here, he realised, as he hunched his back and inhaled the stale air.

'Where to?' asked K'Tarth, who seemed in an absurd way to be enjoying the experience.

The Doctor found an auxiliary corridor even as they heard the little droid behind them.

'This way', he suggested. 'He'll expect us to move outwards, so we'll make our way inside the complex instead.'

Presumably the piping in the cramped passageways they

were traversing was part of the heating system. It was dark down here, mostly because there was no need for light, and the Doctor and K'Tarth kept burning their hands on pipes they couldn't see. It seemed to bother K'Tarth a good deal less than it did the Doctor, but then, that was the young for you. Take a child, knock it over and it'll stand up as though nothing has happened. Take an old... take a mature Time Lord and it was a different matter, naturally.

The Doctor crept along, painfully catching his breath, aware that he might be heard at any time. Oxygen was short – no need for air conditioning when the intended inhabitants didn't breathe.

He could hear K'Tarth's footsteps behind him. He could hear his own breathing. But that was all, so at least they had lost the little droid. Now all they needed to do was find a way out.

Their search didn't take long. It was K'Tarth who spotted the doorway. They might be less safe in the open but they wouldn't survive down here for any length of time.

The Doctor soon realised they had stumbled into some sort of infirmary, but what was wrong with all these people? He and K'Tarth were surrounded by rows and rows of bodies in beds, bloated and yet, judging by the pallor of their skin, the watery lifelessness behind their eyes, strangely undernourished. Some were hardly able to move under their own bulk.

'Doctor...' came an appallingly familiar whisper.

'Korriklimm? Korriklimm, is that you?'

'Help me...'

The room was spacious, gleaming white and immaculate, although there was something pungent about the air.

The Doctor rushed over to where he believed the voice had come from. It was Korriklimm all right. Enormously overweight, lips trembling, anaemic, probably diabetic as well, and obviously receiving no treatment.

'Korri...' The Time Lord knew it would be best if he stayed calm, but he felt his anger rising. 'What has happened here?'

'My... my fault, my friend... Get away...'

The invalid looked up at something and the Doctor realised too late that he was staring directly into the lens of a monitoring camera, no doubt with one of Lakksis's aides on the other end.

As the Doctor turned to talk to K'Tarth, he was aware of a sudden sluggishness in his movements. K'Tarth lay slumped on the floor next to him, already unconscious. By the time the Doctor's legs gave way he knew that the air was being gassed. But with what, and was it lethal?

'Are you all right?'

A familiar voice, but one he'd not known for long. A woman. Janis... Janis Carma, master spy, expert. Huh! Calls herself an expert, so how come she's tied up, then? Oh, hang on, so am I.

The Doctor was slowly coming round. Regaining awareness, his mind limped into focus along with his eyes. He was in a workshop of sorts, held down by some pretty rusty chains that looked as though they'd been used for packaging a long time ago. The bolt that held them together didn't look terribly solid and had started to corrode.

He could either wait for his head to clear or make a break for it now, then figure out what had happened to him. Three things militated against his making a break for it. First, the presence of Janis. Granted, she'd got herself into this, but he couldn't just leave her here. Second, the presence of Lakksis, the little waiter droid, who suddenly looked a great deal less irritating and amusing and now appeared downright menacing instead. Third, the presence of K'Tarth, lying unchained on a table next to the Doctor, with his shirt undone to reveal a chest full of electronic gadgetry.

'I said are you all right?'

'What? Oh yes, yes, I'm all right, yes, no question. Erm... Lakksis?'

'Hiya, kid. How's tricks?'

'Tricks is fine. It's my friend K'Tarth I'm concerned about.

He seems to have turned into an artificial life form while I was sleeping.'

'Hey, neat, ain't it? Y'see, your actual friend never visited Nestra as such. We took a telepathic scan when you arrived and built him for ya.'

With the same technology they use for the multilingual door signs, the Time Lord realised. Very clever.

'We had a feeling a schmuck like you'd land up in trouble, so we put a tail on ya, 'specially when we heard you talking to the dame.'

So that was how it had been done. Smart, he had to admit. Leave a potential troublemaker alone until he actually makes trouble – you never know, he might not do any such thing, and you don't want to go making work for yourself. Then when you think his troublesome instincts have been aroused, follow him until you're sure. Try taking him in for polite questioning, and when that doesn't work... The Doctor shook his head. There was something more important than this. Something – the hospital! Those people, the illnesses...

'Now listen to me, you metal maniac. Just before I was gassed I was in what I can only call a mortuary for the nearly dead.'

'Whuzzat? Oh, right, the infirmary.'

'Call it what you will, those people need treatment and they need it fast. You may think I'm a troublemaker, but I am still a doctor. I need to know what exactly you are doing for them.'

'Cheez, what a scuzzball. We're lookin' after them, ain't we? That's why they're in the infirmary!'

'But they're still ill! Including your creator, Korriklimm!'

Lakksis paused, as though considering something he didn't understand. 'Y'know, it's kinda strange, but poor old Korri has been looking sorta under the weather lately. Then he keeps asking for some injection or other –'

'Insulin,' put in Janis. 'He was diabetic. I remember it being mentioned when he was briefed before coming here.'

'Yeah, right. Only I ask whether he likes injections, and he smiles and says no, so I don't give it to him.'

Rage, followed by bewilderment and then a glimmer of understanding shot across the Gallifreyan's brain. He looked at the small droid, which wouldn't administer anything unpleasant to anyone, and said, 'I see. This is a holiday complex, so nobody is allowed access to things they don't like.'

'You got it, bub,' the robot replied happily.

'And if someone likes, let's say, cream teas, they get lots of them, whether they ask for them or not, and they don't get anything that doesn't appeal to their sweet tooth. Then they get ill.'

A pause from the droid. 'Y'know, a lot of them do end up a little pale. Then they start asking for stuff I know they don't like. And that's when –'

'That's when you know they're ill, so you have to consign them to the infirmary.'

If Lakksis had possessed the necessary mechanisms to smile, he would have done so. 'Right! Anyway, gotta go, people to see, teas to serve, ain't nobody here but us chickens...'

The droid scuttled out of the claustrophobic quarters, leaving the Doctor plenty to think about. It was suddenly all so simple. The robot had not been programmed to understand the consequences of its actions, and could see only the pain and displeasure on the faces of his victims – or patrons, indeed, because he truly believed he was working in their best interests.

'Now do you believe there's a problem?'

The Doctor had almost forgotten Janis. He tested the chains. Flimsy. Rusty.

'I always believed there was,' he replied, throwing his weight against his chains, feeling them stretch and snap. 'And I don't mind telling you, I was more or less right about what was actually happening.'

'But you said –'

'I said not to worry about it or do anything, because it's the people who worry or do something who get fingered as troublemakers. Any droid overhearing us at that tea table would have realised that at least one of us needed to be captured and tamed. How long did it take them to pick you up? Five minutes? Ten?'

She remained silent, unsure whether to congratulate him or thump him for his smugness.

'They weren't certain about me. But I let myself down with that replicant. Oh, come on –'

He made a great show of snapping her chains too, and she had the feeling that he was deliberately making it look like hard work.

'Let's get ourselves out of here.' He put his head around the door. 'No, he's left it unguarded. He thinks I understand him so I won't run away. Metal imbecile...'

Lakksis was as happy as a series of bio-emulator circuits held together in polycarbide armour can actually be. He'd expected, no, really expected, that there would be more trouble over this Doctor fella turning up out of nowhere. He started assimilating the new data: 'not always a problem', he ingested, and felt deeply satisfied by the surge of information passing through his memory banks. Maybe the Doc had some sort of programmable intelligence like his own. It was always possible.

He continued clearing the coffee cups in the great hall, turning down requests for greens, carbohydrates, cough medicine, anything that might be unpalatable or unappetising. What an illogical species, he mused. One woman had even had the strange idea that she ought to be cut open, insisting that she was suffering from something called appendicitis. Strange thing to want. He'd sent her to the infirmary straight away and restrained her for her own protection. The only problem was those feeble packing chains he had to use. The place hadn't been set up as a prison colony, he was programmed to understand that, so naturally there weren't any strong chains specifically designed for holding prisoners, but even so you might have expected them to provide something for emergencies.

He started to make his way back to the lab in which he had left the Doctor and Janis. They were nice guys. They just had the wrong end of the stick. At least, so he'd thought until the Doctor showed he actually understood pretty well. He trundled along some more. Maybe he and the fella in the funny clothes would become friends. Lakksis had never had a friend before but he'd picked up from the humans that they must be really great things to have.

He noticed that the corridor along which he was moving needed cleaning. Such things didn't usually bother him, being only a droid and all, but if he was going to have a friend, well, he'd have to cheer the place up a little. In time he reached the lab door and prepared to greet the flesh-and-blood being he was beginning to consider his soul mate.

The room was empty, the Doctor and Janis long gone. But why? This was crazy. What could they want to do that involved avoiding little old Lakksis? What had he done? He just didn't understand. Had they deceived him? Or were they playing a joke, one of those human things? Maybe they were behind the door and – no. They were nowhere to be seen.

If robots could cry, Lakksis would have done so.

Janis had been surprised when the Doctor went off by himself again. Surely he could see that it made sense to stick together. Reluctantly she'd agreed that he was probably on her side, if a little misguided. As they left the laboratory she had been all in favour of using some of her high explosives to, how could she put it, lighten the tin skunk's capacity to take any more captives. And what had he said? No, I think I'll go and have a little chat with him. A little chat! People had died here. People were still ill and suffering and he wanted to talk. She could see him now, dodging shadows and moving cautiously in the corridor just ahead.

Well, that wouldn't be a problem. If the Doctor wanted to find the rogue robot that was fine by her. And when he'd done so, she'd blow the metal mutt's head off.

A dejected droid, looking even smaller than he usually did, opened the door to what he liked to call his office. It looked more like a workshop than anything else, although the desk in the middle was identifiably intended for paperwork. It was frustrating and all, not being able to sit on the chair behind the desk, but it made him feel a little more human, more lifelike. And you never knew, one day a visitor might come...

'I did try knocking, but there was no one in,' said the Doctor. 'I hope you don't mind.'

'Doc... you came back... just like Lassie in the movies!'

The Time Lord did not wince this time. He'd been mistaken for Earth species often enough, so one more time wouldn't make much difference. 'Yes, I came back. I thought we might have a little talk.'

'Right, right, a little talk. Gee, it's great to meet someone who wants to listen... ah... what shall we talk about?'

'Oh, robots, humans, rampaging injustice, unintentional homicide, that sort of thing.'

Lakksis settled down. This was going to be one humdinger of an evening.

Janis eventually saw through the trick, but she was too late. She'd followed the loud-suited idiot, then he'd vanished around a corner. She saw him in the distance and he didn't move. So she waited.

And waited.

Patiently.

No, really.

Patiently.

He still wasn't moving. OK, so what? He'd seen her and was biding his time. He couldn't be sure. She could wait him out. He'd have to move soon. He'd get cramp. Or she would.

273

A minute. Two. Three. That's enough, she decided. Quietly, and preserving some sort of cover in case he decided to get up after all, she approached. Stealthily, she drew closer. Fifty yards, forty-five. Strange, that hair looked more like a mop than it had done before. Forty yards, thirty. No! She hadn't fallen for that old... Twenty yards away now and she was running...Yep. The coat, a hanger, a mop, just far enough away so she couldn't make out what was going on.

Damn him! Damn him damn him damn him...

'And yet some suffering can lead to good,' the Doctor was saying to his sceptical automated audience. 'Look, what do I do if I have toothache?'

'Uhh... you go to the dentist.'

'Absolutely. And the treatment hurts.'

'Right... so you don't go to the dentist.'

'Yes, you do, if you've got any sense. Because by going you'll stop the pain. Now, what about if you break a leg? That hurts if you're flesh and blood.'

'Right... so you go to the dentist and it hurts some more.'

'Yes... What? No. No, you don't have to go to the dentist if you've broken your leg.'

'So broken legs prevent toothache? Say, what sorta sucker d'you take me for, Doc?'

This was exasperating. It was obvious that the Thetrans didn't like tourists, otherwise they'd have programmed their droids properly, thought the Doctor. Korriklimm's initial program had been promising, but he hadn't bothered with further development work. Of course, the droid could learn, but only in a linear fashion. This meant going through every possible permutation of fact, regardless of how obvious it might seem to a sentient being with even the slightest inkling of how to apply principles laterally. It should have been imprinted into the initial program.

'We'll start again. Sometimes humans are damaged through no fault of their own.' He thought about the cream cakes he'd been consuming earlier and reflected guiltily on his waistline. 'And sometimes they unintentionally inflict harm on themselves. Then they require treatment that they may not enjoy but know will ultimately do them good.'

'So they'll ask for something that'll be unpleasant?' Lakksis sounded stunned. 'And that's not a major psychosis? But, mercy me, this is terrible! All those people I restrained, all those ill people who aren't getting the treatment they need, all the... all the runaways I... I had to deal with them, I didn't know, I...'

'It wasn't your fault.'

The Doctor relaxed. He was getting through at last. He hadn't realised quite how tired he'd become in the process. The thing about it was, though, there was no one to blame except the Thetrans, and what crime had they committed? Set up a business and not anticipated some of the technical difficulties that ensued? He considered whether anything could be done to prevent this whole absurd situation arising again.

The blast was deafening. It was also unexpected.

Later, the Doctor would wonder why he hadn't seen it coming. If he could find Lakksis, so could she. She was quite old enough and experienced enough to trace a simple target, and his delaying tactic was never going to hold her for long.

He opened his eyes as the dust cleared and the ringing in his ears subsided. Where there had been a desk, there were splinters of wood. Where there had been shelves, there were holes in the wall. And where there had been Lakksis, there was a heap of tangled metal wreckage.

'Well, Doc...' A choked voice from an electronic synthesiser, halting and weak. 'That's another fine mess you've gotten me into.'

It was time to go. The recriminations had been predictable and the arguments that followed unwinnable, the Doctor understood that. Lakksis had been only metal and animated circuits. Korriklimm and the others had received the necessary treatments and the families of the deceased had been contacted. The demise of one enterprising, misguided droid was a small price to pay. But what a waste. He thought of Kamelion, K-9 and other automata for whom he'd developed a fondness. Who was he to decide what was alive and what wasn't, and what was worth preserving?

He approached the TARDIS on the outskirts of the complex sadly. As he drew closer he was dismayed to see Janis Carma, now in full military get-up, standing beside it.

'I really don't think we have anything left to say to each other,' he began.

For some reason her face was welcoming and she smiled as she spoke. 'Oh, I think we do, Doctor. I've brought someone to meet you.'

'Frankly, I'm not in a sociable mood.'

It had only been a robot, he told himself again, and a dangerous one at that. Dangerous through none of its own fault...

'Nyaaa, what's up, Doc?' came a familiar mechanised voice.

The Doctor hesitated. He turned. The chassis had been redesigned and was a little more streamlined, the colouring was, if anything, even more hideous, but the whole was recognisable.

'Lakksis?'

'Lakksis-2 to you, good buddy. They re-engineered me from parts of the other guy, but we're real similar inside. You oughta come and see us some time. You look as though you could do with a holiday.'

The Doctor very nearly smiled at that.

Janis beamed at him. 'These things cost money. You didn't really think I'd have destroyed a perfectly workable droid without attempting to salvage at least some of it?'

He shot her back an equally charming grin. 'Yes,' he said. 'Yes, if I hadn't argued, I think that's exactly what you would have done.'

With that, he was inside the TARDIS and away.

Wheezing, groaning, that sort of thing. Whatever you called it, it was noisy if you were standing right next to it, like Janis was. Had he made it louder just to aggravate her headache? She wasn't sure. She put a hand to her brow.

'Headache? Tense, nervous headache?' the Droid inquired.

'Something like that.'

'OK, babe, the Doc told my bro' all about this. You need to suffer a little so you can get better. Maybe the dentist. I have a drill attachment right here...'

'No, wait!' She was suddenly aware that her arm was being held securely, uncomfortably and against her will.

'No need to wait, Lakksis-2 is here right now. You won't like it, and it'll hurt you more than it hurts me...'

Janis struggled uselessly as the drill drew closer to her mouth. Then Lakksis-2 paused and she was uncomfortably aware that she was being scrutinised, as though he were remembering something that had happened a while ago. Then he started moving the drill towards her again and, if she hadn't known better, she'd have sworn that his painted smile had grown broader. Broader and colder.

'Say, I remember you,' he said. 'Didn't you kill my brother?'

The drill was getting closer. Closer. Closer...

# Ace of Hearts

by Robert Perry and Mike Tucker

**6.45 p.m.**

'Mother, stop it!'

Kathleen Dudman snatched her gaze from the door and back to the table, where her daughter was laying out plates.

'But he's late!'

'So he's late...We've got three hundred ex-Wrens turning up in an hour. Here.' Audrey Gale dumped a pile of crockery into her mother's arms. 'Plus I'm not happy with Dorothy's baby-sitter...'

'She'll be fine.' Kathleen began tossing china on to the table. 'Anyway, if your Harry hadn't gone running off to that football match...'

'Rugby, Mother...' Audrey's voice grated. 'It's the Five Nations.'

Around them in the dusty church hall tables were laid, bunting hung, chairs put out. Two elderly men struggled to hang an obstinately flapping banner – WRNS ANNUAL REUNION DINNER: 1971 – over a makeshift stage.

Kathleen frowned.

'They'll not be needing a stage if he doesn't turn up...'

'He'll be here, Mother!'

'And why you agreed to put him up...'

'I'm on the committee and we've got a spare bed. Now can we get on, please?'

She bustled through the door. Kathleen's gaze followed her.

'I can't bear people who're late. At my age I can't be doing with hanging about,' she called after her daughter. 'He can't have any sense of time!'

**7.20 p.m.**

The Doctor pulled his pocket watch from his waistcoat and checked it again. He'd travelled the universe, bent the very time stream to his will, but getting from Perivale to East Acton by London Transport without being late seemed to be impossible.

Paying for his journey had been a trial in itself, since the one thing he'd managed to arrive early for was decimalisation. The ticket-seller had looked with bewilderment at the collection of coppers he'd been offered – new pence? – and threatened to call a policeman.

The Doctor had eventually made the platform in time to see a train vanish into the rain-drenched February night and to hear the announcement that the Central Line was experiencing delays due to a signal failure at White City. A train had eventually arrived but its progress had been painfully slow and sporadic. They were just outside North Acton – only two more stops to go – when it ground to a halt again.

He snapped the watch shut and thrust it into the pocket of his jacket, feeling the comforting shapes of his spoons. He'd been practising for weeks. He gazed out of the window into the dark winter evening. He could see the faces of his fellow passengers reflected in the glass. Sad. Tired. Defeated.

He pulled the spoons from his pocket and clattered them cheerily.

The woman opposite him pulled her newspaper up in front of her face.

The Doctor sighed. He had a feeling this was going to be a very long journey.

**11.05 p.m.**

All in all, the evening had gone well, Kathleen supposed, although she couldn't work out whether this had been by accident or design. The little man had bounded on to the stage

– late – and dropped his spoons. Attempting to pick them up, his trousers had split. Nervous, embarrassed titters around the hall. Juggling plates, he'd dropped more than he'd caught. Audrey had been frantic, as the plates belonged to the Mothers' Union. But gradually unease had given way to laughter – open, happy laughter.

When he'd offered to saw a woman in half, most of the audience had squealed in apprehension, and no one had volunteered. His bird impressions had attracted an eerie and slightly alarming response from high in the eaves and attic spaces of the old hall – flutterings and warblings and a thin rain of dust and heaven knew what else. And then, by way of a climax to the show, the unsteady WRNS banner had come loose and sailed down on top of him.

He'd reminded Kathleen of Tommy Cooper.

So why was she edgy around him? Something about him nagged at her memory. In the car on the way back from the performance, his manic energy had given way to pensive silence. She had sat behind him in the back seat, afraid to look at him, afraid he was aware of the phantom fears in her eyes.

When they had arrived back at the house Dorothy had been crying upstairs. A thin, persistent wail. The little man's eyes had snapped to the ceiling and stayed there. He had excused himself hastily and asked to be shown to his room.

Only when he had retired did it occur to Kathleen that no one had thought to ask him his name…

### 2.50 a.m.

The door of the nursery opened and the Doctor slid into the room, wincing at the protesting hinges. He tiptoed over to the crib.

'Ah, there you are. Hello, Ace.'

The baby cocked her head and looked at him, wide-eyed, unsure of the stranger. Her brow creased and she drew in a breath, ready to cry out. The Doctor swiftly dangled the end of his scarf into the crib, waggling his fingers and making bird noises. The delighted baby caught hold of the scarf, gurgling contentedly.

She pulled down hard and the Doctor's chin cracked on the edge of the cot. He tried to extricate his scarf from Dorothy's grip but she immediately squealed in protest.

'This isn't exactly how I wanted to talk to you.'

He paused, suddenly uncomfortable. There were things he wanted to say. Things he thought would be easier said to the baby than to the teenage Ace.

She had trusted him – and he had betrayed that trust. More than once. He had seen how vulnerable she was beneath the angst and the bovver boots. He had played with that. Gabriel Chase. Fenric. And he would do it again, he knew.

He stared down at the baby.

'I... I just wanted to say...'

Dorothy met his gaze.

'I'm sorry...'

The baby released her grip on the scarf and yawned. The Doctor stepped back from the crib.

'Forgive me...'

## 3.10 a.m.

Kathleen Dudman woke with a start from the dream that always came when rain beat on the windows. The dream that had haunted her for nearly thirty years. A dream of razor claws and storms. Of running, desperate to save her baby.

The baby.

Dorothy.

Suddenly she was concerned for her granddaughter. Rising painfully from her bed, she donned her dressing-gown and crossed the landing to the nursery.

A look of concern swept over her face. The door was ajar. She peered into the room. Dorothy was asleep, curled up.

Kathleen was about to pull the door shut when something

caught her eye. The photo of Dorothy on the dresser... She entered the room and picked up the little gilt frame. The photo was gone. In its place was a playing card – the Ace of Hearts.

She pulled the card from under the glass, puzzled.

Suddenly a noise drifted in from outside – an alien trumpeting from somewhere in the night. This was the noise she had heard many years ago, just before her recurring nightmare had started.

The face of the little entertainer suddenly clicked into place in her memory and she stared down at Dorothy.

'Ace...?'

She gently scooped the sleeping child from the cot and gazed through the window. Rain lashed against the glass, but she knew that tonight she would sleep soundly. The noise that had heralded the start of her nightmare would also herald its end.

The ghosts of the past could rest. She had to attend to the future.

# The People's Temple

by Paul Leonard

## PROLOGUE

Two children on a beach, long, long ago, both of them young enough to believe in magic.

One is the bear cub, round and heavy, rolling, confident, his nose into every tumbled rock, his feet into the freezing grey surf as it sucks over the pebbles, his blue-green eyes tracking the misted red cliffs for paths that can be conquered. The other is the young deer, long-limbed and fragile, uncertain, awkward, uncomfortable on the rough edges of the rocks, jumping back from the cold, aggressive sea, terrified of falling from the high cliffs that his friend insists on climbing. But they are friends, even so, because Bear Cub makes Young Deer feel useful, and Young Deer makes Bear Cub feel brave.

Today, they are building a miniature temple of stones. It doesn't look much: two lines of upright pebbles in the dry sand just above the reach of the waves. But the pebbles are special. Those on the left are smooth and squat, those on the right tall and angular, this marking the difference between the principles of Earth and Sky. Young Deer spent most of the morning looking for the right stones. He's the son of the clan Priest, and he must get this baby Temple right. It's even aligned according to the Rule of Stars, facing north-east towards the approximate position of the midsummer sunrise. But now it has been spoiled. One of the stones has fallen, the victim of a scrawny seagull searching for food.

Although Young Deer is angry, he doesn't show it. The stone can always be put back in place. But before he can act, Bear Cub is running across the temple, knocking one of the other

285

stones over as he goes.

'I'm going to catch that bird and kill it!' he says, though the gull has already flown away and become indistinguishable from a hundred others, riding the wind, half obscured by the mild, steamy drizzle blowing in from the sea. When he realises that the bird is out of reach, he runs back up the beach towards the winter settlement, a straggling collection of thatch-topped huts built inside a high stockade above the river.

'Stop!' calls Young Deer. He doesn't want to be left alone on the beach. Without his powerful friend to protect him, he might be set upon and beaten by the gang of boys who call themselves the Bear Men. But he doesn't want to leave the beach, doesn't want to leave his temple half built because of this one accident. He starts to run after Bear Cub. 'Stop!'

Bear Cub half turns, dancing on the spot as he shouts back to his friend. 'I'm going to get my bow! I'm going to shoot that bird!'

Bear Cub's father won't let him shoot gulls on the beach – the chance of losing an arrow is too great. But Bear Cub doesn't remember this, in his anger and impatience. Young Deer does. He always remembers, when Bear Cub forgets. This is another reason why they are friends.

'I've got a better idea!' he yells.

In fact he hasn't, yet, but he knows that if he thinks quickly, he can probably come up with something more exciting and immediate than shooting a seagull.

Bear Cub doesn't stop his dancing on the spot, but at least he doesn't run off. 'What? What is it?'

'My father,' begins Young Deer, still thinking. 'When he does the sacrifices –' yes, yes, this will work '– he can substitute one animal for another. If the gods call for the sacrifice of a boar and the hunters can't catch one, he'll kill a goat instead. So we could kill something else instead of the seagull. You could get a fish from one of the pools –'

This is an inspiration. Bear Cub never tires of showing off his speed and skill, catching the slippery finger-sized fish with a single swoop of his net. Young Deer is hopeless at it; they always get away from him, even when the pool is almost dry.

It works. Bear Cub is already trotting back, his eyes alight, a huge grin on his face. 'I can go one better than that!' he says.

He always can.

'I can take a baby seagull from one of the nests on the cliff!'

Young Deer feels a thrill of anticipation. This is reckless, brave, interesting. It's something he couldn't possibly do; but if his friend does it, then he will share in the glory.

'Right,' says Bear Cub, reading the answer in his friend's face. 'I know a path that will get us there.'

The stone is upright again, stained with the young bird's blood. The flock are still screaming overhead, but they've given up diving at the two boys. Probably they know that the bundle of guts and bloodied brown feathers is no longer alive. But Young Deer was afraid of them, diving like that, even as he carried out the sacrifice.

Bear Cub wasn't afraid, of course. In fact he quite enjoyed the thrill of it, swatting at the screaming white bodies, collecting a couple of long, perfect wing feathers. He's already thinking that he'd like to catch an adult seagull, alive, so that it can be sacrificed. He's not sure what will be achieved by this, but it should be fun trying. And he could mount the long feathers in a headdress afterwards. He picks up a stone and lobs it at the flock.

Young Deer, for his part, is thinking about his temple. It won't last: if nothing else, the sea will demolish it with the next high tide.

'We should build a temple on the sheep pasture,' he tells Bear Cub.

'Why?'

'Because it'll last longer. In fact –' Young Deer is thinking again – 'a circle would be better, because circles have more power. Like the Great Temple.'

'The Great Temple's made of wood,' observes Bear Cub.

'Yes, but we could make a little one. Of stone.'

Bear Cub's eyes light up, as the idea hits his brain and germinates. 'Or we could make a big one! As big as the Great Temple, but made of stones!'

He begins looking around the beach, as if he hopes to find suitable stones now and drag them upright himself.

But this time it's Young Deer who goes one better.

Not just 'as big as' the Great Temple, but the Great Temple itself. Rebuilt in stone.

He can see it now: the inner and outer circles, the totem-carved wooden posts replaced by stones. If the stones were big enough, and if the pits they stood in were deep enough, then nothing could knock them over. It would be the most powerful temple in the world.

It would last for ever.

He turns, looks not at the sea but at the land: hunched, enormous hills, framed by red cliffs, crowned by the brown winter skeletons of trees. He feels a wild excitement, as the image of the stone Temple in his mind superimposes itself on the land.

If he can make this happen, he will have made something as huge and eternal as the land itself.

He will be immortal.

'Come on,' says Bear Cub impatiently. 'Let's go and find some really big stones. I'll get my brother to help us move them if you like.'

But Young Deer stops his friend with a raised hand. 'No,' he says. 'If we're going to build a proper temple, there are things we need to do first…'

He's thinking of a sacrifice, of course. To obtain the blessing of the ancestors. But even he doesn't realise how many sacrifices will be needed.

Not yet.

# I

'Doctor?'

'Mmm?'

The Doctor was propped up in his favourite armchair, feet on a stool, reading. A red mug of cocoa was on the arm of his chair, and Sam was cradling another one in her hands. In her lap was a book: a glossy, old-fashioned, rather heavy, hardback book.

'I want to see Stonehenge.'

'What century?'

Sam grinned. She liked the way that the Doctor was never, ever, taken aback – and usually managed to go one further. 'When it was built. It says in this book that no one will ever be sure how they moved the stones.'

The Doctor glanced up. 'Magic.'

Sam was surprised, but did her best not to show it. 'Did it work?' she asked, as casually as she could manage.

'No. They had to use ropes in the end.' The Doctor grinned at his little joke, then went back to his book.

Sam was disappointed. More disappointed than she'd expected. She hadn't really believed that there was any magic in an old stone circle, but –

'There's no magic then? No –' she glanced down at her book – 'meeting of ley lines, no "Natural Temple of the People"?'

The Doctor glanced up sharply. 'I didn't say that. But magic isn't usually very useful. "Any magic sufficiently advanced becomes indistinguishable from technology." And no fun any more.'

'Shouldn't that be, "Any technology sufficiently advanced…"?'

'Yes,' said the Doctor. 'That's another way of putting it. Did you know that Henry James believed in ghosts?'

'No,' said Sam. Then, well aware that the Doctor, given half a chance, would start on a digression about how he'd met the novelist at some function in 1872, or suggested the ending of one of his novels, she added quickly, 'But I'd still like to see Stonehenge. When it was new. When people used it as a temple.'

'Are you sure about that? It was the Late Stone Age, you know. There were a lot of very nasty ceremonies involved. I don't think you'll like it. "Megalithomania", I believe one archaeologist called it.'

Sam sighed. 'Haven't we had this conversation before? You don't try to keep me from seeing things just because you think I won't like them, OK?'

The Doctor met her eyes.

She didn't look away.

He took a deep breath. 'OK, yes, if that's the way you want it.'

He got up, his mug of cocoa in his hands, and walked towards the console.

## II

'Pull!'

*Like oxen.*

Dorlan felt the ropes bite into his chest as the group of them hauled on the stone in the near-darkness. He put all the strength he had into the task, leaning into the ropes. His feet slipped on the muddy ground, made slick by the endless rain.

'PULL!'

*They'll work you like oxen, on that temple of theirs.*

Dorlan risked a glance over his shoulder. The stone hadn't moved. But in the light of the flames it seemed to dance against the black sky, like an angry spirit – the spirit of evil, perhaps.

Dorlan shivered. He was sure this was the biggest stone yet. Somehow, in the rain and darkness, they had got it into the pit that had been dug for it, and now it stood upright, but tilted. All that remained was to pull it to the vertical – always the hardest part of the job.

'PULL!'

*They'll slaughter you when they've finished, like an ox that can't work any more.*

Fighting his exhaustion, Dorlan made himself pull again: the aching whip-scars on his shoulder reminded him what would happen if the stone didn't move this time. From the corner of his eye, he could see the Bear Men standing, waiting, staring at the stone.

*It will be better to die, my son.*

No, it won't, thought Dorlan fiercely. He remembered his father's face, twisted in rage and pain and humiliation, and the spear wound that he had received in the battle bleeding each morning and finally swelling until his father, black-faced, had died in agony, leaving Dorlan, barely a man, chief of a conquered people.

But it *isn't* better to die. It *isn't.*

He yanked on the rope, almost slipping again. 'Come on,' he gasped. 'PULL! We'll get this thing built for them yet, and then we'll go home! PULL!'

There was a ragged cheer. Dorlan felt the weight on his shoulders increase, the weight of responsibility. His people still believed in him. If he told them to pull, they pulled harder.

But it was no use. The ropes bit, Dorlan's feet slipped in the mud, the stone didn't move.

Dorlan looked across at the fires, at the children whose job it was to keep them burning. He saw his sister, Saffen, run up with some dry wood, eyes blinking furiously in the smoke, swaying a little as she stood and fed the flames. She looked at the limit of her strength.

Like Dorlan. Like every single one of his people, man, woman and child. When had any of them last slept?

The Great Bear, the king of these Bear Men, was insane.

'Why aren't you telling them to pull?'

Dorlan became aware of a shadow standing over him. He looked up, saw antlers shifting in the flame-light, and the shadow of a man's body. Deer hide, with the hooves still attached, swaying like charms. The click of bones, deer bones from the necklace he wore.

Shalin: the Deer Man, the magic-maker. Dorlan shivered. Even though Dorlan had never seen him hurt anyone, the Deer Man was somehow more frightening than his master. His bright eyes, his constant talk of numbers and rotations and elevations and plans and circles, his 'southern mysteries', as he called them, made him seem both more and less than human: a god, but not a kind one.

'It isn't working,' he told Shalin, trying to keep his voice from shaking. 'We haven't the strength to do it. Perhaps if we rested –'

'There isn't time!' snapped the Deer Man. 'There are ten more stones waiting at the end of the Great Avenue, and they must all be laid before the solstice ceremony can be held. That's ten days away, so it's one stone a day. Understand? And this is yesterday's stone – so it must be done tonight.'

Dorlan shut his eyes wearily. It didn't make sense. None of it made any sense. Working in the winter, in the rain, was stupid enough. Working all night was pointless. Everyone would be too tired to work in the day. And why by the solstice? Even the Deer Man wasn't pretending the temple would be complete by then.

'I'm going to try something,' said Shalin suddenly. He was standing in front of them now, an antlered silhouette against the fire-lit stone. He was moving his fingers above his head, the long, dead legs of the deer hide swaying from his wrists. Dorlan recognised the gestures: counting, he called it. Another of his southern mysteries.

Finally, Shalin seemed satisfied. He moved to one side of the team, near to where Saffen still stood, weary, by the fire.

'I want everyone from here –' Shalin stamped on the ground with his foot, then danced across to the other side of the team – 'to here, to pull when I say "bear". Then I want everyone from here to –' he danced again, the antlers swaying in the light, the necklace of deer bones clicking – 'over here, to pull when I say "deer". Understand?'

Dorlan was fairly sure that what Shalin was trying to do wasn't going to help. If all the men pulling together couldn't move the stone, how could half of them do it? But he knew better than to argue. He watched, still confused, as Shalin separated the two teams, until each was at an angle to the stone. The ropes shifted, dripped water.

At last Shalin walked forward, taking a place between the two teams. The rain was heavier now, threatening to douse the fires. Dorlan could hear the water hissing as it hit the burning wood.

*Like a snake.*

Yes, father, thought Dorlan dumbly. It's probably an omen. But what can I do?

'Deer!' shouted Shalin.

Men pulled.

'Bear!'

Dorlan pulled, felt the stone move slightly. Or had the rope just been a little slack?

'Deer!'

Pull.

'Bear!'

Pull.

Another slight movement. This time Dorlan was sure that it was the stone shifting. Perhaps the Deer Man's strange plan was going to work.

'Deer!'

Pull.

'Bear!'

The rope went slack. For an instant Dorlan thought it had broken. Then he heard Shalin yell something in his own language, his voice high and panicky. He heard earth breaking, a huge popping sound, a crack of wood and a grinding of stone.

Dorlan struggled to turn around, clumsy in his harness. He saw the stone tilting – no, falling – towards the fire and the children.

'Saffen!' he shouted. 'Run!'

But the hammer head was already slamming into the fire, and burning fragments were flying in all directions.

One of the children screamed, and went on screaming.

Dorlan shrugged off his harness, ran through the tangle of slack ropes and confused, frightened people towards the fallen stone. He almost fell twice in the slick mud. The screaming had stopped, but Dorlan could hear a gasping, gurgling sound which was much more frightening.

'Dorlan!' Saffen's voice. 'Quick! It's Marin!'

Her best friend.

He reached the stone, scrambled around it, almost burning himself on the smouldering fragments of the fire. On the far side, Saffen was standing, her eyes wide, staring down at a shape in the shadow of the stone.

Dorlan approached, saw that the shape was Marin. As his eyes adjusted to the dim red light, he made out the child's head, her arm, part of her chest.

The rest was buried under the fallen stone.

'She's dead,' Saffen informed him expressionlessly. 'I'll tell her mother.'

Then she turned on her heel and walked away.

Dorlan knelt down, put a hand in front of the girl's mouth, but Saffen was right: there was no breath. He felt his heart pound, his muscles tense in helpless anger and frustration. Marin had been a happy, healthy child. In time, she would have made a good wife, a good mother of many children; and he knew she had been learning the hide-stitching craft that was her mother's. Now she would stitch no hides, marry no one, be mother to no one, and Dorlan's people would be the worse for it.

He hit his fist against the grey stone. The shock and pain jolted him to his feet, his head buzzing with anger.

'Why did this happen?' he yelled. 'Who did this?'

At his words, light burst around the long side of the fallen stone, the strong light of lanterns burning with rendered oil.

A huge man stood there, careless of the still-smouldering ruins of the fire around his feet. He was dressed in the hide of a bear, with the long, shaggy winter fur still attached. A square plate of gold burned on his chest and below that a dark belt held the bronze dagger and axe of the man who called himself Great High Supreme Chieftain and King, Lord of All the Lands and All the Peoples.

Coyn. The Great Bear.

Two of his Bear Men stood on either side, one with a flare, one with a raised axe. They always stood like that, ready to kill anyone who approached their master without permission.

'Who did this?' said Coyn suddenly, repeating Dorlan's words, his eyes on Dorlan's face. 'You know, I was about to ask that myself, but you said it first.' He took a step forward. 'That must be an omen. Don't you think so?'

### III

'That's it,' said the Doctor, pointing straight in front of them. 'The Temple of the Great People of the Bear.' He flashed her a bright grin. 'Known to some later humans as Stonehenge.'

Sam looked, but she wasn't quite sure what he was pointing at. It was still only half light: grey clouds raced in the wind and the air was full of a thin, cold drizzle. Worse, Salisbury Plain in the late Neolithic appeared to be a built-up area. From the edge of the forest where she and the Doctor were standing, Sam could see two large clusters of rotund wooden huts with thatched roofs, each encircled by a high wooden stockade. There were other, more distant stockades that she couldn't see inside, and several individual wooden buildings, mostly circular, some quite large. She also counted at least a dozen mounds that were obviously artificial. The two biggest were the size of small hills and capped with trees. There were quite a few standing stones, one of them surrounded with something that looked almost like modern scaffolding, none in anything that resembled a circular pattern. And everywhere there were artificial banks, lines of posts, brown strips on the earth that Sam first thought were roads, then decided might be fields of some sort. Everything overlapped everything else: fences crossed fields, rows of posts ascended to hulking longbarrows. The half-light added to the sense of mystery and confusion. Sam realised that it was probably before sunrise; despite all the buildings, she could see no people about.

She admitted defeat at last. 'Which one is the temple?'

'The big one. Low. Flat. See the stones rising above the stockade? Those are the trilithons. I think they've got three of them up already.'

Sam looked again, saw a shadow of grey. Yes. One of the stockades, on top of a low earth bank. It was about a kilometre away, and seemed to enclose a roughly circular space. It was hard to see inside, in the poor light – they weren't really far enough above the structure for that. But now she was sure what she was looking at, Sam realised that she could just see the flat tops of grey stones inside.

She felt her heart hammering with excitement, and set off across the muddy ground, dodging tussocky grass and loose stones, letting the Doctor tag along behind for a change. A black, bony dog ran out of a derelict-looking hut, barked at Sam as she passed, then sniffed the air and howled.

'Sam!'

She looked over her shoulder.

'Come back! You're going the wrong way!'

Sam looked around at the dark landscape, confused. She had been looking at the right place, hadn't she? 'You said it was straight ahead!'

'Yes, but we have to approach it properly.'

Ah. 'This is respecting their culture, isn't it?' she said aloud. 'We're guests on their land, so we have to follow their routes.'

But the Doctor had already marched off along a line of carved posts, almost directly away from their destination. Sam could see now that it ended in another stockade surrounding a longbarrow. Two grey stones were just visible at the entrance, standing like guards with a carved wooden lintel between them.

'This is one of the ceremonial routes,' the Doctor said without looking round. 'There were five others we could have taken, according to the season, but –' he looked round and flashed her another brilliant smile – 'I think you'll agree when you've seen it that this is the pretty one.'

Sam was still grinning to herself when they heard a man scream.

'Who did this?'

Coyn's question was an animal growl, the call of an angry bear. He twisted Dorlan's arm again, and again Dorlan screamed with pain. He was sure that the arm was already broken. He could feel the wrongness in the way it moved. And the pain, as if a knife were cutting the flesh away from inside…

He looked up, his eyes misting, and saw his sister hiding her face in her hands, sobbing.

'The rain did it,' he said, wishing that his voice sounded more like a man's, less a boy's half-choked sob. 'The rain – it fell –'

'This didn't happen because of the rain! The pit was deliberately weakened!' Coyn twisted the broken arm again. Dorlan gritted his teeth, but the scream escaped. His vision blurred and he felt tears trickling down his cheeks. The shame was almost worse than the pain.

Dorlan became aware that another face had appeared in front of him. A face painted with red and white clay, in the curved lines of the Deer Man. The look in his brown, deer-like eyes was curiously sympathetic. His glance kept sliding sideways, towards Coyn, who was pacing up and down beside the stone that had fallen. There was fear in that glance.

'You didn't do it, did you?' said the Deer Man quietly. 'But you know who did. Now tell me, and I'll mend your arm, and you won't have to work again, and your sister won't have to work –'

'No one.' Dorlan's teeth were chattering.

'Give him a name, Dorlan,' said the Deer Man, his voice no more than a whisper. 'Any name, it doesn't matter who. If you don't he'll just kill you, then somebody else, then somebody else…'

Dorlan felt a wave of faintness. For a moment he was floating above the Northern Waters, the place where his people had lived before they were conquered, and his father was speaking to him again. But he couldn't understand the words.

He heard shouting, and opened his eyes. The Deer Man's dark face, still peering into his. And the voice of his father's brother, Teln.

'Stop this! The stone fell because of an accident, anyone can see that!'

The sound of a blow, a grunt of pain. A woman's scream.

Dorlan tried to sit up, was surprised when the Deer Man helped him. He saw his people crowding forward in the half-light, the Bear Men standing with their axes and spears at the ready.

Responsibility.

'Stop it!' he called weakly, his voice catching in his throat.

The shouting went on.

Dorlan fought the pain, made himself take a deep breath. If they tried to fight now, they would all be killed.

'Stop it!'

There was silence. The Great Bear, who had been standing with his men, turned slowly and looked down at him.

'I'm the chieftain. I'll take responsibility for this,' said Dorlan weakly. 'Kill me – do whatever you want – but leave the rest of my people alone.'

Coyn laughed, laughed so hard that his necklace of bear's teeth rattled. 'Dorlan! It's good to see such bravery from the son of the man I killed. It shows that you have the true spirit of a warrior of your people. And do you know what?' He took a pace forward, leaned down and put his face so close to Dorlan's that the young man could smell the rotting meat on the king's breath. 'I'm going to accept your courage and respond to it in kind. You're going to die for this.'

For a moment, Dorlan simply didn't believe him.

But then the Great Bear stood up and shouted, 'Bring the drums! Bring the masks! We're going to have a sacrifice! Here! Now!'

The Bear Men started to move, heavy feet splashing in the pools of water that lay all over the muddy ground.

Dorlan watched, his body shaking, and slowly realised that the insane king was serious.

He was going to die.


'Come on, Doctor. We've got to do something to help those people.'

As soon as they'd worked out that the screaming was coming from the temple itself, Sam and the Doctor had hurried across the open ground between the posts and the earth bank that surrounded the temple, scrambling over a fence, through a muddy ditch, and squeezing between a line of tall posts carved with animal totems.

But now the Doctor had stopped dead, staring ahead into the growing light. There was only a narrow muddy ditch between them and the embankment.

The wind gusted, and Sam could hear chanting, the regular beat of a wooden drum.

'That can't be right,' muttered the Doctor. He pulled a watch out of his waistcoat pocket and consulted it, then looked up at Sam, an expression of consternation on his face. 'I think we've come at the wrong time. We should go back to the TARDIS. Now.'

Sam stared at him. He was deadly serious.

'No,' she said simply. The sound of her own voice surprised her. She met his eyes. 'You're going to tell me this is some sort of ceremony. But that scream wasn't ceremonial and you know it. That was someone being –' she searched for a word – 'violated.'

'Sam,' said the Doctor, his voice low, 'I made a mistake. I

thought this was a safe time for you to see the temple, but it obviously isn't. We have to go.'

'But it isn't a ceremony! It isn't part of anyone's culture, it's –'

'Sam! Sam! How can you know what is and what isn't a ceremony four and a half thousand years before you were born? I know. Believe me.'

Sam took a breath, then turned away from him and jumped across the ditch.

'Sam! No!'

She stumbled on the far side, half falling into the filthy water. Looking back, she saw the Doctor standing against the brown streaks of fields and the dark shadows of trees, his hair dancing in the wind.

'I'm going to find out what's happening,' she said. 'I won't interfere, not if it's a real ceremony.'

Even if people are being killed?

Well, she'd deal with that one when she got there.

She scrambled up the far bank, her jeans soaked to the knee, her sweatshirt covered in mud, her nose full of the stomach-turning smell.

In front of her was the stockade around Stonehenge. It wasn't very tall and she'd have been able to climb over it quite easily if it hadn't been topped by savagely sharp spikes. The wood was also thickly embedded with sharp fragments of bone, of pottery, even of stone. Through the narrow gaps between the posts she caught tantalising glimpses of stones, fire, people's faces.

The drum was beating again, single, slow beats. Someone was shouting – no, chanting.

The Doctor was right. This did sound like a ceremony. Could she have made a mistake? For all she knew the screams had been someone injured in an accident, and this was a healing ceremony.

Well, she was going to take a look anyway.

She began jogging as quietly as she could around the bank,

taking care not to slip on the wet grass. Seeing a gap ahead, she stopped, crouched down and shuffled forward the last few metres.

When she peered over the edge, she found herself looking into the eyes of a man.

He was huge, his head almost level with Sam's feet despite the two-metre-plus height of the bank. His hair was a thick black bush, braided at the sides. For an instant, he just stared at her, his eyes wide with amazement. Then he hefted a copper-tipped spear and levelled it at Sam's chest.

She was trying to think of something to say when, from the corner of her eye, she saw the Doctor trotting towards the entrance across a muddy wooden bridge, a smile on his face, a hand extended towards the guard.

'Good morning,' he said. 'I'm your local Betaware representative. I hope this is a convenient time to call on you.'

As soon as the Doctor started speaking, Sam saw the big man's gaze turn away from her and she started moving. The way he wouldn't expect her to move. Down, forward, towards the spear – and then ducking aside, scrambling down the rough, slippery grass behind the giant and into the open space beyond.

She could see stones ahead. Stones, people – and two more enormous men in bear hides, with copper-tipped spears already pointing in her direction. Behind them, a crowd of people in furs and brown leather, most of them staring at her, wide-eyed and afraid.

Ancestors, she thought desperately. They believe in Ancestors.

'I'm the Ghost of the Great Mother,' she proclaimed. 'Make way for me.'

Amazingly, it seemed to work. The spearmen were frowning, confused, but they were letting her through. And the crowd behind simply scattered.

She could see the stones ahead. Newly cut, smooth-sided, glossy with rain. She walked through the outer ring, saw that it was only half complete. Lying across the middle of what would be the circle was a fallen stone, one end surrounded by churned-up earth. On top of it stood a deer-like alien.

No. Hang on. Remember what century you're in.

It was a man, wearing an antler headdress, a deer hide, and a deer mask. He was holding a long bronze dagger.

Below him, held down against the fallen stone by two of the huge spearmen, was a young man. When he saw Sam he struggled and tried to say something, but she couldn't make out any words.

Sam looked from him to the Deer Man and back again. 'I am the Ghost of the Great Mother,' she said quietly, 'and I demand to know what's happening here.'

'Who are you really?' the Deer Man asked. His voice was shaking slightly, but Sam couldn't tell whether it was in anger, fear or simply surprise.

'I am who I am,' she said simply. 'Give me the knife.'

For an instant she thought he was going to do it. The hand holding the knife started to move, cautiously. But then the man froze.

Behind Sam, another voice roared, 'No!'

She turned to see a huge man in bearskins stepping through the gap between two stones. He carried a wooden staff and wore a breastplate that looked like solid gold. He stared at her without any fear at all. In fact, he seemed to be amused.

'I am who I am too,' he said. Then he strode up to her and grabbed her arm in a painfully tight grip.

Sam felt a lurch of panic, but managed to restrain her instinct to struggle. She had to make it look as though she was in control, even if she wasn't.

She looked up at the man with the knife and the antlers.

'This ceremony is wrong. You know it's wrong. You must stop it now.'

'Or else what, woman?' said the man holding her, twisting her arm painfully.

'The Spirit of the –' what had she called herself? – 'Great

302

Mother will –'

There was a loud bang and the sky went red.

Even the big man was frightened this time. He released Sam's arm and drew a spear, then just looked up in awe.

'The sun!' bawled someone. 'The sun is angry with us!'

Sam grinned. She could see the bright red ball of the flare overhead, the trail of white smoke behind it.

Good timing, Doctor, she thought.

For the first time, she noticed that the young victim's arm was broken, the bone protruding from the skin. Blood leaked from the wound.

The flare died, leaving relative darkness. Quickly, before anyone could get over their surprise, she marched the few remaining metres to the centre of the Temple and grabbed the victim.

'Come with me,' she said.

He didn't move, instead staring down at a point about half-way along the side of the fallen stone. With a shock, Sam realised that he was younger than her, perhaps about fourteen or fifteen. His blond hair, a complex pattern of braids, had become tangled, drenched with sweat.

Sam heard the big man bellowing at someone and she pulled again at the young victim.

'Come on!'

At last, he seemed to get the point and let her lead him away.

Coyn hadn't understood, as usual.

Shalin had seen the man dressed in summer green even before the explosion and the light. He'd seen the aura of confidence and power around him too. The woman wasn't important; she was just carrying out his orders.

As soon as the light faded, Shalin left the fallen stone and Coyn's abortive sacrifice and jogged towards the stranger. Everyone else was screaming, struggling to get out. Even the Bear Men seemed afraid and confused.

Shalin wasn't afraid, exactly. Instead, he felt a curious sense of anticipation. As he drew closer, the stranger saw him and their eyes met.

'Ah, just the man I wanted to see!' he said.

'Yes,' said Shalin. 'I think we should talk.'

He approached the man, lifted his antlered mask away from his face – then brought the sharp wooden chin of the mask down on the Doctor's head.

'You –' began the Doctor, his eyes rolling.

Shalin hit him again and watched with satisfaction as the Doctor dropped to the ground.

Once they were through the wall of sarsens, Sam could see that everyone was crowded around the entrance, shouting, panicking, trying to get out. Some had climbed the bank and were struggling to climb the razor picket on top. She saw a woman with blood streaming down her face.

They were terrified.

She looked around for the Doctor, couldn't see him.

'Listen, everyone,' she cried.

Slowly, the shouting and confusion subsided.

'If you let me go from here with this man, I'll make sure the –' what could she call it? – 'false sun doesn't come back. OK?'

The young man was now leaning against her, stinking of sweat and panic. She could hear his breathing: ragged, slow. He must be in shock, about to collapse. She'd never get him to the TARDIS.

'No!' That bear-like roar again. 'Keep her here!'

Sam heard heavy footsteps behind her and hauled the boy off towards the entrance at a run. People scattered in front of her. She ran through, crossing the muddy wooden planking that bridged the ditch.

She heard the Great Bear roaring behind her, then another voice calling him. She heard the young victim's breathing, now coming in big, unstable whoops.

He's going to faint. Doctor, where are you?

She stared around the dawn landscape, the brown

causeways, the dark barrows, the criss-crossing lines of posts.

But the Doctor was nowhere to be seen.

Coyn stared down at the strange figure on the ground. There was a bruise spreading across his face where Shalin had hit him.

'You say this is their leader?' he said to Shalin.

'Yes, I'm sure of it. He has the real power. The woman was his tool. Perhaps she is his wife, or his acolyte.'

Coyn was pushing at the bruise on the Doctor's forehead with the toe of his boot. 'He's just a man, wearing strange clothes.'

Shalin watched the Doctor breathing, watched the strange shine on his cloak. Coyn must be aware of the special nature of this man, but he probably thought it would look weak to show his fear. Very well, then, he would play to the other aspect of the Doctor's power.

'He made the sky red,' he observed. 'That's a trick we could use in war.'

'Yes.' Coyn's hand descended on Shalin's shoulder. 'Your thinking is as clear as it ever was, my friend. Find out how he did it, so that we can do it too. Kill him afterwards, unless you think we need him. I'm going to see if I can find the other one.'

Hefting his spear, he nodded at his escort of Bear Men. They set off through the old south entrance to the temple at a fast trot, scattering the crowd before them.

Shalin watched him go.

'Kill him afterwards.' Did Coyn respect nothing?

Shalin knelt down by the Doctor's side. 'Wake up,' he said quietly. 'We can have that talk now, I think.' He glanced up at Coyn's party, disappearing through the entrance. 'In private.'

# IV

Dorlan's strength was almost gone by the time they reached the edge of the eastern wood. He stared at the dripping fringe of the trees, aware that his body was swaying despite all his efforts to stand still. His legs trembled and his arm was a burning mass of pain and sickness.

His rescuer looked back. 'Come on! It's not much further!'

Dorlan still couldn't understand where they were going. All the land here belonged to the Great Bear and his people. They knew all the trails.

'We'll need to get much further from the temple to be safe,' he said.

'Save your strength for running,' said the woman. 'I know where we're going. You'll be safe. There's food and water, and we might be able to fix your arm.'

Fix? Dorlan knew that broken limbs could be splinted. With luck, he might be able to use his arm in the future, at least for light tasks. But he knew he would never use a bow again. If he survived at all.

He looked back at the confused, misted landscape, striped and distorted by the Bear People's endless causeways and monuments. Two of the Bear Men were still in pursuit, though they were some distance behind. But they knew the land, and had endurance. How much longer could he and Sam stay ahead?

His rescuer grabbed hold of his uninjured arm. Even that contact made him wince.

'Come on!'

She kept saying that. He wished he understood where they were going.

They jogged into the shelter of the woods, quickly straying off the obvious paths into an area dense with beech and oak, where the ground was thickly littered with wet leaves. The woman held on to Dorlan's arm, perhaps worried that he might fall.

Then, ahead, he saw a totem post, higher than a man, square, with the girth of a tree. It was made of wood, stained in a blue pigment. It was covered in carvings, mysterious grid lines, and huge, straight-edged jewels. Dorlan had never seen anything like it before.

He stopped, shivering.

'Who are you?' he asked the woman.

She ignored his question. She was touching the surface of the post. For the first time Dorlan had time to really take in her strangeness: the clothing, her impossible bright-red cloth on her legs, the sea-blue cloak, her shoes apple-blossom white under their coating of mud.

'Your clothes are the colours of flowers,' he said. 'Are you a spring spirit?' It hadn't occurred to him before that she might not be human. He'd never met a spirit. But he had been about to die...

Ahead of him, a door opened in the totem post. Light streamed out into the dim winter forest. The woman stepped inside and vanished.

He heard her voice from inside. 'Come on!'

Dorlan hesitated. It was obvious that the door led to some other world. So his rescuer wasn't human; which meant she might do anything. Perhaps he was already dead and this was his first test in the spirit world. But he didn't remember dying, he didn't feel any different, and this was nothing like any of the stories he had heard.

And his arm hurt. Surely it wouldn't hurt so much if he was dead?

He stood, shivering, uncertain, his legs unsteady beneath him. Then he became aware of sounds behind him. Steps in the forest, the tread of heavy men trying to be quiet. The Bear Men.

Then the woman was in front of him again, a concerned expression on her face.

'All right,' she said. 'Take my hand. I'll lead you through the door.'

Dorlan realised that he hadn't any choice but to go along

with her.

Inside, the space and light made him blink. And the air was warm. Warm and dry like a summer's day. He looked around, saw a carved hearth with a few small lights burning, but there was no fire, no smoke. The immense space around it was filled with totems and things that might be tools. Many of them, like the woman's clothing, had the bright colours of flowers and fruit. Others looked like metals.

Dorlan gaped. He hadn't known that there was so much metal in the world.

The woman – spirit? – was calling out, 'Doctor! Doctor! Where are you? I need your help with –' She turned to him. 'What's your name?'

'Dorlan. Who are you looking for? Is he a man, dressed in strange clothes like you?'

The woman laughed: light, gentle, almost a girl's laughter. But she was at least as old as Dorlan.

'Yes, that's him,' she said. 'Everyone thinks his clothes are strange, wherever we go.'

'There was a man dressed in the green of leaves at the temple.'

'You saw him?'

'He was lying at the feet of the Deer Man when we left.'

'Lying at his feet?'

Dorlan sensed her sudden fear and immediately felt afraid too. He looked nervously at the door behind them, but it was shut. Could the Bear Men force their way through?

The woman had advanced on him. 'What happened to him? Why didn't you tell me?'

'I didn't know he was your friend. I didn't know anything,' said Dorlan miserably. 'I still don't. I'm sorry.' He felt his body begin to tremble: the shaking sent a bolt of pain through his arm. To his shame, his eyes misted with tears.

'I'm sorry,' he repeated. 'Are we going to die?'

The woman sighed. Now she looked much older, as if a burden had descended on her shoulders. And Dorlan knew why. Responsibility. She had saved his life: now she was responsible for him in this strange world.

'I don't want to be a burden to you,' he said. 'If there's anything I can do, tell me. I am a chieftain of my people; I have been trained in many skills.'

She met his eyes, then put a hand out and touched his shoulder softly. He knew then that she wasn't a spirit, however strange her world.

'Don't worry about it,' she said. 'The Doctor will be OK, he can look after himself. Come on, let's see what I can do to fix up your arm.'

'Are you a god?'

'Ah, I wondered when you'd get around to asking me that one. No, sorry, I'm not. I haven't even got his phone number any more.'

The stranger flashed Shalin a disconcerting smile. The Deer Man wondered what a 'phone number' was. Some kind of totem?

'Good,' he said aloud. 'I knew that of course, but I wanted to see if you would lie about it.' He met the Doctor's eyes, paused to let his remark sink in. 'Now, how did you make the fire in the sky?'

The Doctor propped himself up on one elbow and looked around the hut. His eyes rested for a moment on the place where one of Coyn's Bear Men stood, the southern bronze of his axe gleaming in the daylight seeping in through the hides hung over the entrance. Then his gaze moved on to the totems of the conquered tribes laid out on the wall, each one splashed with the brown, faded blood of one of their warriors killed in battle. Finally, he looked at Shalin again.

'What an interesting collection! You haven't got the Mountain Lake People yet, I see. I suppose they're on next year's conquest list? Or the year after? You have got lists, I suppose? You look like the kind of man who makes lists of the people he kills.'

'I don't kill them,' said Shalin. 'Warriors kill. I am the Deer Man.'

'Oh, so when you had the knife poised above that young man out there, you were just trying to frighten him, were you? Or was it a game? Follow-the-knife?' The Doctor stood up, brought his face close to Shalin's. 'How about guess-where-I'm-going-to-stab-you?'

Shalin jumped backwards, and at the same time the Bear Man leapt away from the door, axe raised.

Shalin saw that the Doctor had no knife and signalled the Bear Man to stay where he was. The stranger didn't even seem to have noticed the threat: his eyes were still fixed on Shalin's, full of accusation and anger.

'Yes, I can see, you're a coward. Most people who kill from lists are cowards. I almost prefer the other sort.' Now he did glance at the Bear Man, who was still hovering with his axe. 'At least you know where you are with them.' He relaxed, stepped back from Shalin. 'Come on, Shalin, I'm not giving you any fire in the sky, so you can forget it. Why not just let me go?'

Shalin started at the use of his given name. How had the stranger known that? It was obviously another indication of his power. And his power meant –

'I have my own reasons for talking to you,' he said.

The Doctor just looked at him.

Shalin gestured to the Bear Man to wait outside. When he was gone, he said quietly, 'You are the only man I know who has more power than Coyn.'

'And?'

Shalin shook his head. 'Coyn is insane. He wants the stone temple completed in his lifetime, in his honour. He wants to be a god in the afterlife.'

The Doctor nodded. 'The Pharaoh syndrome. I've met it before.'

Shalin didn't understand the Doctor's words, didn't care much. This was the first time he'd been able to unburden himself about Coyn to anyone for years.

'He wasn't always like this. To start with, it was just a dream. To rebuild the Great Temple in stone. But first he killed his brother, so that he could be chief, and then he conquered the Sacred People, who lived here, so that we could do what we liked with the temple. Then Coyn wanted stones from everywhere. "It has to be the greatest Temple in the world," he said. "We want stones from all over the world." He wanted sarsens from the Old Temple Plain – so we had to conquer the people there, kill half of them, build trackways, drag the stones three days' walk across the land. He wanted stones that were "already holy" – so we had to conquer the Hill People across the water. Doctor, he just doesn't understand that there are any limits. He's going to destroy every hearth in the land – in all the lands – just to build this temple.' He lowered his voice. 'And he surrounds himself with those Bear Men – they're not even our people, don't even speak our language. He got them from the south somewhere.'

'Yes, that must be difficult. But it's quite common with those sorts of people. Importing strangers as personal guardians. I remember the Emperor Caligula…' He trailed off, staring at the entrance to the hut.

Shalin looked round, nervously, but nothing moved. He turned back to the Doctor. 'I need your help.'

The Doctor took hold of Shalin's shoulders, looked into his eyes, a clear, blue, disconcerting gaze. 'Have you seriously tried talking to this Coyn?' he asked.

Shalin shook his head. 'We've been friends since childhood,' he said. 'But he doesn't listen any more.' He almost added: he never did, then thought better of it. The Doctor would probably accuse him of lack of foresight, and he would probably be right. Coyn's flaws of character were, after all, obvious.

'Well, I'll talk to him, then,' said the Doctor. He let go, started to turn away.

But Shalin grabbed hold of the Doctor's arm. 'It won't work,' he said. 'I've tried. There's only one way to stop Coyn…' he whispered. He touched the bronze dagger at his belt. 'I want you to help me to do that.'

He had to be indirect. He didn't want to risk using the word 'kill'. The Bear Man was still outside. He might hear. He might understand.

'Certainly not!' said the Doctor. 'There's been enough killing around here already.'

He snatched himself away, but before he could reach the hides covering the doorway, they were flung back from outside and daylight flooded in.

'Stranger!' Coyn's voice.

Shalin felt his body freeze with terror. How much had Coyn heard?

'You are clearly a powerful man, Doctor,' Coyn went on, striding towards them. 'I believe I can come to an arrangement with you. But there's something I must do first.'

'No!' cried the Doctor, 'You don't understand!'

Shalin started to turn, felt a powerful fist thud into his back, pitching him forward. He saw the Doctor staring, an expression of horror on his face. Then he saw the long shaft of the spear protruding from his own chest, the copper blade covered in blood. The pain bit into him and he tried to scream, but his breath was gone. He fell to his knees, then the ground seemed to roll upwards and hit him.

He heard the Doctor's furious voice: 'He didn't really want to kill you, Coyn! He was just afraid of you! This could all have been sorted out!'

Then the Doctor was kneeling over him. His face seemed to glow from within.

So he was a god, after all.

Shalin wanted to ask where he would go after he died, whether he would be punished for what he had done, but his throat was clotted with blood.

The Doctor's hand touched his face, and he died.

# V

Sam wasn't sure whether she'd set Dorlan's arm properly. She'd done her best, following the instructions in the TARDIS medical kit. It had provided her with X-rays, and had told her where to grip, how much pressure to apply, but it couldn't set the bone for her. It looked all right, but...

Dorlan hadn't quite lost consciousness. Painkillers from the kit had helped, but Sam suspected that sheer determination, and not a little sense of wonder, had kept him from fainting. Even when the fluid cast from the kit had been crawling over his bruised skin, he'd been staring, bug-eyed, around the console room: mostly at the console itself, but also at the library shelves, the record collection and the VW Beetle still parked in a corner, all of which he seemed to regard as equally marvellous.

Now the cast had set and he was holding the Doctor's empty cocoa mug in his left hand, turning it over and over. 'I've never seen pottery so fine,' he said. 'It's so smooth, it's like a stone in a river! And the colour!'

The mug was post-office red. 'It's the Doctor's,' said Sam.

'The one who made the sky red?'

Sam nodded.

'Is red his sacred colour, then?'

Sam managed to suppress a giggle, then saw that Dorlan was smiling at her anyway.

'He hasn't got a sacred colour,' she said, grinning back. 'I think he just likes colours in general.'

She walked over to the console, switched on the viewscreen, looked outside. One of the Bear Men was still standing guard: the other had gone, presumably to fetch reinforcements. Well, let them try to get inside the TARDIS.

She noticed that Dorlan was staring anxiously at the screen.

'They're not inside, are they?'

'It's only an image,' said Sam. 'I control it.' She turned it off.

Then she met his eyes and said quietly, 'Dorlan, why were you going to be killed?'

She listened as he told her, asking questions now and then, feeling her sense of outrage grow as the story of injustice, conquest and slavery built up. So this was how Stonehenge had been built – stones dragged across the countryside at the cost of lives, slaves digging pits at the point of spears. Suddenly the stones didn't seem magical any more. Not when the secret of their building was human misery and death on this scale.

'We're going to do something about this,' she said at the end. 'Your people can't go on suffering like this.'

'What can we do?' asked Dorlan. 'Do you have spears here?'

'No. No weapons. This is the TARDIS.'

'If there are no weapons, how can you oppose Coyn?'

Sam thought for a moment. There had to be a way to convince Coyn that what he was doing was wrong – or, better, that the gods were against him.

Suddenly she thought of something. It was so obvious that it was almost funny.

She grinned at Dorlan. 'Wait here! I think I know a way!'


Coyn, chieftain of the Bear People, and in addition the Great High Supreme Chieftain and King, Lord of All the Lands and All the Peoples, stood on the embankment around his stone temple, looked at the lowering grey clouds, at the lashing rain, and scowled. The day had been bad from the start: the fallen stone, the strange visitors, the aborted sacrifice. And now his friend was dead.

And he, Coyn, had killed him.

He had known it was coming, this death. His old friend had been too powerful for too long. But he hadn't thought that it would come so soon.

And he hadn't imagined it would feel as terrible as this.

He saw some of Dorlan's people peering at him from outside the embankment. He waved his spear at them and shouted. Even though they were almost at the limit of a spear's throw, they still cowered. He waved the spear again. They turned and started to run away.

Shalin had always said, 'Make them afraid of you, and then they'll do what you want.'

'Perhaps you should have been more afraid of me, my friend,' he muttered.

'He was afraid,' said a voice behind him. 'That was the problem with him.'

Coyn turned and glared at the Doctor, trying not to show his disquiet. The stranger had been able to creep up on him, unheard. That should be impossible, especially in those strange, heavy shoes. Whatever he was, the Doctor had powers that were beyond anything Coyn understood, or wanted to understand. He wondered if it was the stranger's power that had caused the stone to fall in the first place. If everything that had happened today had been a demonstration of that power.

Well, there was only one way to find out.

'I should kill you, too,' he said, letting the spear fall so that its point was level with the Doctor's chest.

'But you're afraid,' said the Doctor, infuriatingly calm.

Coyn shook his head. 'Not afraid.' To show weakness in front of this being would probably be his last mistake. 'But it's clear that you have power, or at least some useful tricks. Your people must have power too. I'd rather bargain with you than invite their anger.'

'Yes, and it's a shame you didn't think of that before killing Shalin, isn't it? I mean, what do you think his spirit's thinking about you now? Not to mention his Ancestors.'

Coyn shuddered. 'I keep feeling the spear going through my friend's body. I keep wishing it hadn't happened. But he said he was going to kill me. And he was going to use your power against me.'

The Doctor shook his head. 'I wouldn't have let him do that. But have you wondered why he wanted to kill you?'

'I don't need to know why. No one threatens me.' Coyn pushed his face close to the other man's, tightening his expression into a mask of anger.

This usually terrified men, but it had no effect on the Doctor. All he said was, 'That's it exactly. No one's allowed to threaten you, are they? To question you, to argue with your judgement? You want this temple finished in your lifetime. You keep coming up with grander and grander schemes, most of which are absolutely impossible, and you don't care how many people die to get things done.'

The Doctor's anger was clear, his eyes seemed to be ablaze with it. Coyn stood back, feeling his heart thud in his chest.

'Do you think the only way to stop me is to kill me?' he said at last.

The question had to be asked. If he was going to die, he wanted to know that it was coming.

The Doctor waited a while before speaking, still looking into Coyn's eyes, as if he were measuring something.

'Maybe,' he said eventually. 'But I'm not as precipitate as you.'

Coyn looked over the Temple, along the great ceremonial way that led to it – two high banks of earth, topped by lines of totem posts. 'Shalin was going to place stones along those banks,' he said, pointing to them. 'He said it would increase the power of the temple. You say that I only cared about the temple, Doctor, but it was Shalin who told me what was needed.'

'You blame Shalin, he blamed you... Look, don't you think it's time this obsession with stones and power stopped? People are dying because of it.'

'People die anyway. It's the afterlife that matters.' He raised his voice. 'I will be a god!'

'Shalin said that too, did he?'

Coyn frowned. Did everything he believed in come from Shalin? He'd never thought of it that way. His ideas were his. But they had to come from somewhere...

'Look,' said the Doctor, interrupting his confused thoughts. 'Why don't you try something? Release the boy, Dorlan, and all his people. Escort them home, with whatever food you can spare. Don't use conquered people any more. There are plenty of your own people who would work on the temple willingly, in the slack season.'

'Shalin says –' began Coyn. Then he realised what he was saying. 'Shalin's dead!'

Coyn turned away from the Doctor and walked along the bank, staring into the temple, into the rain, not sure whether he was thinking, or acting, or just mourning his friend.

A bird landed on one of the stones. Brown and white. For a moment Coyn thought it was a baby seagull, but then he saw that it was a hawk.

Sacrifices, he thought. Who told me that there had to be sacrifices? It was you, my old friend.

Well, now you've joined them.

At last Coyn returned to where the Doctor stood, waiting.

'I will free Dorlan's people,' he said. 'I will ask my own people to work on the temple, and see what happens, until the winter solstice next year. After that time, I will be free to make my own decisions once more.' He paused. 'In return, you and the woman you brought will leave my land, and never return.'

The Doctor met his eyes. 'Accepted,' he said, then added quietly, 'Maybe no one has to kill you to stop you, Coyn. Maybe you just need good advice.'

Dorlan looked at the strange object that Sam had called an 'aerosol can'. It was like a pot – a long drinking pot – but there was nowhere to drink from it. It was cold in his hand, and it looked and felt as if it was wet. But in fact it was dry – it left no moisture on his hand.

Its strangeness was frightening, but Dorlan wasn't going to show that fear. Not in front of this woman who had helped him. He told himself that the 'cast' on his arm was just as strange, and it didn't hurt him – it did just the opposite.

'Turn the button on top so that the arrowhead points away from you,' instructed Sam. She was standing with a sheet of white material in her hands, spread out across the front of her body.

The material looked like a sort of cloth; she'd called it 'paper'.

Dorlan looked down at the can he was holding, at the knob of finely ridged bone-like material on the top, and saw the arrowhead. It was a tiny, intricate carving, which must have taken many hours of work. There were many things like it in the hearth-place that Sam called the TARDIS; Sam had yet to explain where all the people were that laboured to make these things.

'The arrow's pointing away from me,' he told Sam.

'Right. Now press the button.'

Dorlan pushed. The hissing sound made him jump, even though he'd heard it when Sam had used the aerosol. Determinedly, he held on to the thing, watching as the white sheet in front of Sam turned blue.

'Turn it a little as you spray.'

Dorlan turned the can, watched a blue stripe form on the paper, creeping towards the edge. He turned the can a bit more –

'Ouch! Careful!'

Sam danced out of the way as the blue colour spread to her hand and her shirt. She was grinning, but when he turned the can towards her deliberately, and made as if to press the button again, the grin died.

'No! It's not that funny, Dorlan – you've really got to be careful not to spray it at anyone. Especially not into their faces. You could blind someone.'

Dorlan nodded. 'It's powerful?'

'Well, it's dangerous,' said Sam.

'And it will make Coyn let my people go?'

'It's a matter of showing them that you have power,' said Sam. She was loading the other cans into a backpack. The carved tops showed their colours: sea-blue, sky-blue, green, orange, yellow – there was even one that shone a little like gold.

With the aerosols packed, she turned to him. 'If Coyn wakes up tomorrow morning, and the whole temple's covered in stuff like this –' she gestured at the white sheet, covered in coloured paint – 'he's going to realise that you've got some powerful friends. With any luck he'll think we're gods, especially after the Doctor's display yesterday. Then he'll think twice about doing anything to the Doctor, and about keeping your people in slavery.'

Dorlan wasn't sure about this. Coyn was a determined man, insanely determined. The magic paint alone might not be enough. But… He looked at the aerosol he was holding, remembered what Sam had said about it being dangerous to the eyes. She had certainly got out of the way quickly enough.

Yes. It might work.

Sam was standing by the hearth now, fiddling with a small, brightly coloured tube. A flame lit near the end of it, and for the first time in the TARDIS Dorlan smelled smoke.

'A distraction,' she said. 'If it worked for the Doctor, it should work for me.'

Dorlan nodded, though he didn't understand.

She touched something on the hearth, and there was a sound like a stick breaking. Dorlan felt a breath of cold damp air, turned to see that the TARDIS doors had opened. He could see the back of the Bear Man standing guard outside.

Sam ran past him, the sputtering torch in her hand.

'Geronimo!'

Dorlan wondered why she was shouting. This wasn't the way to achieve surprise. He could see the Bear Man staring in through the door, startled and confused.

But that wouldn't last long.

Dorlan started to rush forward, lifting the aerosol.

Then lightning struck outside: a flash, an ear-splitting bang. Dorlan guessed it was Sam's device and ignored it. The Bear Man was more alarmed and looked over his shoulder, but quickly looked back again. He saw Dorlan and raised his spear.

'Dorlan!' yelled Sam. 'Get back! I'll close the door!'

Just for a moment, the Bear Man's gaze flicked to her. In that moment, Dorlan jumped, dodging the spear, pressing the knob on the aerosol and aiming the tiny arrow at the Bear Man's eyes.

They were looking at Dorlan when the paint hit them.

The Bear Man grunted, brought his hands up to his eyes. The spear fell, brushing Dorlan's hip. He made a grab for it, missed. From the corner of his eye, he saw the Bear Man trying to draw his bronze dagger, one-handed, the other hand still tearing at his eyes.

He was starting to scream, a surprisingly high wail of pain.

'Dorlan! We'll have to wash that out of his eyes!'

Dorlan wondered what Sam could possibly be talking about. They needed to kill the Bear Man, not wash his eyes. Perhaps she didn't like killing: women usually didn't.

He had the spear now, though he'd had to drop the aerosol. It was heavy, but his muscles were strong from all that hauling on stones, and he managed to lift it with his good arm.

'No, Dorlan!'

Dorlan knew that he couldn't afford to listen to Sam. He drove the spear clumsily into the Bear Man's side.

The man screamed again, but Dorlan wasn't sure he'd done any real damage. He'd never killed a man before. The spear was heavy, the bear hide thick and tough. Dorlan tried to pull the spear back for another go, couldn't.

The Bear Man grabbed the weapon and wrenched it out of Dorlan's grasp. He held on to it, feeling his way along the haft to the point embedded in his clothing. Dorlan could see some blood there, but he was sure it wasn't enough.

'Sam!' bawled Dorlan. 'You'll have to help me!'

But Sam was shouting something about having found some rope, something that didn't make any sense. She was trying to get close, which was dangerous. The haft of the spear was flying around as the Bear Man tried to pull it loose.

Then Dorlan saw the bronze dagger. It was half out of the scabbard. He kicked out, catching the top. The big man felt the impact, but Dorlan was back out of range by the time he'd responded. It was clear that he couldn't see: his face was covered with the shiny blue pigment.

Suddenly, the dagger clattered to the floor.

Dorlan dived in, grabbed it, reached up and stabbed the man in the base of his throat, where he wasn't protected by the thick leather of the hide. He was rewarded with a gout of blood as he withdrew the knife. He jumped back, to avoid the flailing arms and legs of the dying man.

'Don't kill him!' shouted Sam.

'I already have,' said Dorlan, puzzled by her strange behaviour. She seemed so knowledgeable in other ways. Had she never seen anything killed before?

The Bear Man crashed to the floor, half-in and half-out of the TARDIS. He was still breathing, but they were the broken gasps of a dying animal. Satisfied, Dorlan pushed the bloodied dagger into his belt, lifted the spear with his good arm. Then he put it down and grabbed the pack of aerosols, awkwardly shuffling it on to his back. They weren't as good as knives or spears, but they were still weapons, and they were all he had. His people could use them.

'You'd better stay here,' he said, looking at the white-faced Sam as he picked up the spear again. She was obviously going to be no use in battle. 'Keep the hearth for your kinsman. I will tell him you are here when I find him.'

Then he stepped over the Bear Man and ran into the forest.

The short winter day was almost over when Coyn's party reached the fringes of the wood. The light of the lanterns carried by the Bear Men threw long shadows across the leaf litter and the pale trunks of the trees. Coyn thought he saw a glimpse of red deerhide in the weak, shifting light of the flames.

He shivered. Shalin had often walked in this part of the wood, gathering his herbs and potions. What if his angry spirit walked there now?

But the Doctor simply went in, unafraid, and Coyn had no choice but to follow. He waved the Bear Men after him. The

Doctor led the way, though the Bear Men with them also followed the trail that had been left earlier, reading the marks on the forest floor by the light of their lanterns.

At last they came to the Doctor's totem place. It frightened Coyn: a blue colour he had never seen before, dark as an evening sea, carved and set with squares of glass. It seemed somehow alive in the light of the flames.

One of the Bear Men called out. 'Here!'

Coyn turned, followed the voice, and saw the man's body on the ground, stained with dark blood. The trail led to the Doctor's totem.

Coyn whirled round to face the Doctor, in the same movement pulling his bow from his back, loading an arrow.

'No! Coyn! Sam wouldn't –'

Coyn took aim at the Doctor.

'It doesn't look as if your companion is interested in making agreements, Doctor.'

'She wouldn't deliberately kill anyone,' said the Doctor quickly. 'I'm sure this man was killed by someone else.'

'He was my kinsman and now he's dead!' roared Coyn. 'And it's the doing of your woman!'

But, as usual, his anger had no effect on the Doctor. The stranger spoke calmly. 'Even if that was true, we're just going to have to stop her, Coyn. Before she does any more damage. That's all.'

'You're going to have to stop her, Doctor,' said Coyn quietly. 'If you don't, our agreement is over. I will kill both of you.'

Gasping for breath, Sam crouched on the wet grass. A few metres away, across a ditch, was the stockade surrounding the Great Temple. Once she'd realised that the Bear Man was dead, she'd run as fast as she could in the fading light, pushing her way through lines of posts, wading through a stinking ditch, almost falling into an unexpected hole in the ground, hidden in clumps of long grass.

And she was too late.

Dorlan was standing by a gap in the fence. Behind him were some other people carrying crude weapons – wooden stakes, sharp-edged pieces of broken pottery, lumps of stone. Some of them had aerosols. Two were carrying spears – which probably meant two dead Bear Men. She could see some huts inside a stockade burning, people throwing brands at unseen attackers.

One of Dorlan's people shouted, pointed, and Dorlan looked down.

'Sam!' he shouted.

'Don't kill anyone else,' she shouted back. 'Please.'

'Why not?' Dorlan's puzzlement was obviously genuine. 'If we don't, they'll kill us.'

His people were already piling through the broken stockade towards the stones of the temple.

'If you kill any more of them the aerosols won't work!' she yelled after him, but she wasn't sure he'd heard.

Sam saw more Bear Men running across the plain from a nearby settlement, carrying lanterns and weapons. Some stopped, knelt. Arrows started to fly.

Shakily, she sat down in the grass.

The Doctor was right, she thought. I didn't understand. Dorlan is no better than Coyn.

I haven't helped anyone. I haven't even saved anyone. I've just started a war.

VI

Dorlan watched as his father's brother Teln and the other hunters slammed the last piece of wood down into the crude barricade across the entrance to the temple. He heard the whoop of arrows in the air, saw them rain down around the stones. There was a clatter of arrowheads bouncing off the hard surfaces, then silence.

'This isn't going to work!' hissed Teln. 'We can't escape from here. And we can't fight – there aren't enough of us and we haven't enough weapons.' He gestured round at the small band of hunters. Three had spears; the rest just had sticks, and the aerosol cans from the TARDIS.

Dorlan lifted one of the cans and sprayed a long plume into the air. 'This will destroy their strength. It's a sort of magic of Sam's people. We have to spray it on the stones, and they will believe that their gods have turned against them to favour us. She said it would work.'

But here, now, away from Sam and the strange magic of the TARDIS, that didn't seem so convincing, even to Dorlan.

Teln was shaking his head. 'I still don't believe it. But now we're here, there's nothing else to try.' He glanced around the darkening enclosure, as if afraid that the stones might come to life.

Dorlan knew that he had to get the magic working quickly. He walked to the nearest stone and sprayed a trail of red paint across it. Slowly, the others began to follow suit. Lines, squares, axes, the zigzag water sign of the Northern River People, all blossomed on the stones in the failing light.

Then Dorlan heard a woman's voice, shouting.

Sam. He could see her for a moment, scrambling over the stockade on the top of the embankment, silhouetted against the light – light from the lanterns of the Bear Men who were climbing the bank behind her.

'They're attacking!' shouted Sam again, unnecessarily. An arrow flickered past her, then she dropped, rolled down the bank, ran across the grass. 'I can't find the Doctor, I don't know what to do –'

Dorlan could hear wood cracking as the Bear Men forced their way through the barricades.

'The paint!' he shouted at Sam. 'Why isn't the paint stopping them?'

Sam gazed at him, bewildered. 'What?'

'You said the paint would stop them. That it would make them think their gods were against them.'

'It... you mean –' Her face twisted. 'Not until they see it!

We've made our point – we've got to get out of here!'

Dorlan turned, saw that the Bear Men, many more than the hunters, had already shut off both entrances and were advancing, some carrying spears, others bows.

'There's nowhere to run,' whispered Dorlan.

An arrow landed between him and Sam, almost hitting her left foot. She jumped, looked around, seemed to realise what was happening.

'There must be something –' Dorlan began.

But he saw the answer in the fear on her face.

There was a yell from behind him. Turning, he saw a hunter on the ground with the massive shadow of a Bear Man above him. A spear came down and Dorlan heard the wet crunch of the man's ribs breaking.

He realised that it was Teln.

The Bear Man looked up, and for a moment Dorlan thought he was next. Then he realised that the man was looking over his shoulder.

A roaring sound filled the air, great waves of it, getting steadily louder.

Sam's face lit up. 'It's the TARDIS! It's the Doctor!'

Dorlan turned, just in time to see the strange, blue totem post materialise in the pit where the stone had fallen that morning.

The door opened and light flooded out. A huge figure emerged from the totem post, his golden breastplate glinting in the strange glow.

Coyn.

And behind him, the antlered figure of the Deer Man, his eyes pools of shadow in the dark wooden mask.

'Your gods have deserted you,' muttered Dorlan.

'The King has returned,' said the Deer Man, 'and we must all abide by his judgement.'

# VII

Sam stared, open-mouthed, as Coyn beckoned her forward.

'Woman who travels with the Doctor,' he said, 'did you start this rebellion?'

Sam thought for a moment. If she said 'No', then the King might blame Dorlan again and would probably kill him – if not now, then as soon as the Doctor left. If she said 'Yes', he might want to kill her...

But the Doctor wouldn't let that happen. And she could see the Doctor's trousers and patent leather shoes projecting from the bottom of the bloodstained Deer Man costume.

OK, then. She was going to have to take the blame. It wouldn't be the first time.

She stepped forward, until she was only an arm's length from Coyn. She had never been this close to him before, never realised how physically powerful he was. He could almost *be* a bear. Her head was barely level with the top of his breastplate; a necklace of teeth was in front of her eyes.

She felt physically weak with fear.

'I – uh – did it,' she made herself say. 'It was my fault. Dorlan's innocent.'

Coyn smiled.

Sam felt herself growing angry. She wasn't going to let him get away with it like that, just because he was bigger than she was. Quickly she said, 'Dorlan's people should be free. What you're doing is unjust –'

The blow was totally unexpected. Sam didn't even see Coyn's arm move. Her head jolted sideways, and she was falling, hitting the hard mud floor of the temple precinct.

Coyn's face appeared in front of hers, terrifyingly contorted. 'One of my people has died because of you!'

Sam opened her mouth, tasted blood. Coyn just carried on talking.

'I would kill you, but your friend is powerful and he doesn't like killing. For the same reason I will spare Dorlan and his people. But you will suffer a punishment. You will help the other women dress the bodies of the dead, for the rites of the Ancestors. Then you will leave my land and never return.'

After a moment Sam stood up slowly, shakily, half-expecting another blow from Coyn. But he was walking across the mud, his shadow growing longer and fainter as he moved away from the TARDIS. She saw him speaking to Dorlan.

She turned to the Doctor. 'Why did you let him hit me?'

'I didn't know he was going to do it!' whispered the Doctor. 'Coyn is a very powerful man, Sam. And he's ruthless. He's already killed one person today. You'll have to go along with this.'

'We could just go.' She looked longingly through the open door of the TARDIS.

The Doctor stepped aside, but then said quietly, 'If we do I'll be breaking my agreement with him. He'll kill Dorlan. He might kill all of them.'

Sam hesitated. She felt the first pulses of pain from the bruise that must be forming on her face.

'Come on, Sam, it's not so bad. You won't have to do anything much. You don't know how. Just watch. It might even be interesting.'

Sam shuddered.

Then, behind her, she heard Dorlan whooping with joy, shouting, 'We're free! My people are free!'

And she didn't really have any choice at all.

VIII

'I know how Dorlan felt now.'

'Hmm?' The Doctor looked up from his book. One of the console room clocks chimed behind him, a strident repeated trill like a bicycle bell.

Sam waited until the noisy clock had finished before continuing. 'He said he felt responsible for his people. He said he felt responsible for Teln's death.'

'Yes, well, people who are chiefs and the like often have a very high sense of personal responsibility. Individual people, when they're any good, are often better than committees. I can remember a chat I had with the Emperor Hadrian once. He wasn't a bad chap, a very good administrator in fact. He was going to build a wall along the Rhine, as well, you know, but –'

Sam realised that the Doctor was changing the subject again. She didn't want him to.

'I feel responsible for Teln's death.'

The Doctor stopped his Roman ramblings mid-sentence, and stared at her. 'Why?'

His surprise looked almost genuine, but Sam knew it wasn't. 'I started it, didn't I?' she said. 'The revolution, the war. No one would have died if it hadn't been for that.' She wanted to say more, but to her annoyance found her throat clogging up with tears.

'Oh, Sam!' And the Doctor was kneeling by her side, a buttercup-yellow handkerchief in his hand. 'It wasn't your fault.' He put an arm around her, began dabbing rather ineffectually at her face. 'Let's get you a cup of cocoa, then you can go to bed, have a rest, and you'll feel all right in the morning.'

'No I won't!' snapped Sam. 'I've killed at least two people today!'

The Doctor took her hands, looked at her with a serious expression on his face. 'No, you haven't,' he said. 'Dorlan killed one, and the others were killed in a battle that Dorlan started. What you told him to do might even have worked. It's not your fault he didn't listen.'

Sam took the handkerchief, blew her nose. 'You told me not to interfere. I shouldn't have.'

'Yes, well...' He looked down and fiddled with a button on his jacket, as if testing to see whether it was loose or not. 'You did what you thought was right. There would have been a battle of some sort, sooner or later. Coyn was mad, or nearly mad. Dorlan was strong-minded and determined. Dorlan and

328

all his people would probably have died before the winter was out – or fought their way out.'

'If Coyn's nearly mad, how do you know he'll keep to the agreement you made?'

The Doctor looked up at the infinite ceiling of the console room. He didn't speak for a while.

'I don't,' he said finally. Then he patted Sam's hand, and smiled. 'We could stop off and look, if you like. Say ten years down the line. Or twenty.'

Sam thought about it.

'I'm not sure,' she said finally.

The Doctor went back to his chair and picked up his book.

'Well, think about it. Some day, perhaps.'

'Some day,' echoed Sam. 'Perhaps.'

# EPILOGUE

One old man is sitting on a stone, a flat, low stone in a cleared space among many other stones.

He comes here every day that he can now. Every day that his strength is enough for him to leave his hut and be carried here. He sits facing the north-east, facing the place where the sun will rise next midsummer day.

He will not live to see midsummer day, and he knows it.

His attendants are young men. They do not remember the time of Shalin, of the conquered peoples. They know only that this old man with his golden breastplate and worn, faded bear-hide cloak once ruled the world. They think he is here to glory in his temple, the great work to which he dedicated his long and tempestuous life.

The sound of antler picks chipping away soil drifts in over the walls of the temple precinct. Outside, the people are working on a barrow grave for Coyn, said to be the greatest such monument ever built.

But Coyn doesn't care much for any of that. Not now.

The sun bakes the stones and the heat rises in waves. Flies buzz in the short grass that rings the stones. A bird sits on one of the totem posts at the entrance. But Coyn sees none of this.

He looks north-east, not at the place of the midsummer sunrise, but at a slight depression in the ground which is all that remains of the pit where he had been going to place the great stone on that terrible night, so long ago. The stone that killed the girl, on the day that he killed his oldest friend. He has never placed a stone there and now he never will: the inner circle of the temple will remain incomplete, for all time.

Shalin's monument.

But that isn't why Coyn looks at the remains of the pit. He isn't regretting his life, any more than he's celebrating it. The time for all that has already gone, now that each breath is so hard.

He's remembering the magic. Not the power of it, which was all he thought about at the time, but the magic itself. A totem post that appeared and disappeared, and contained a world inside it. And the man inside that world, a stranger with strange powers. The only man who ever gave him good advice.

So each day, the Old Bear waits, drawing painful breaths in the baking sun.

He's hoping to see the magic again, one more time, before he dies.

# About the Authors

**Simon Bucher-Jones** nearly became a man of mystery by failing to get this biog finished. Nothing else about him is mysterious, much to his annoyance. Born Simon Jones, he married Sarah Bucher and they joined surnames. He is 33 and works as a systems development manager for the Home Office. He has a 21-month-old daughter called Morgan. This is his second published short story (the first, 'The Spidermonger' appeared in a small press magazine). He has also written two novels.

**Jonathan Blum** is the first American to write a *Doctor Who* novel; his wife (as of January 1998), Kate Orman, was the first Australian. Together they wrote the Eighth Doctor novel *Vampire Science* and the forthcoming *Seeing I* (June 1998). *Model Train Set* is his first solo commission. In the rest of his life, Jon designs software, directs videos, and spends far too little time playing with his *Lionel* trains.

**Guy Clapperton** has written for radio and TV, including *Spitting Image*, *Doon Your Way* and *Bits from Last Week's Radio*, as well as the *Newsrevue* cabaret on stage. He previously contributed to the short-story collection *Decalog 3*. He is also a journalist and has contributed to *The Times*, the *Daily Telegraph*, *Punch*, the *Guardian*, the *Oldie* and more computer publications than he likes to admit to, except when he's talking to his bank manager.

**Paul Grice** was born during *Terror of the Autons*, something he regrets missing to this day. Whilst his profession is systems analyst for a major high street retailer, his true vocation is as rock god axe wizard in top pop band Shortlist, expected to be big some time in the next century. He lives with Tricia in Ealing, and has also been published in *Playdays* magazine.

**Matthew Jones** has variously been a criminologist, a university lecturer, a film critic, a counsellor and a receptionist in a dating agency. He lives in east London and writes lots of things.

**Paul Leonard** is the author of five *Doctor Who* novels, including most recently *Genocide*. He lives in Bristol, in a flat full of books, magazines and many unread pieces of paper, which might hold the secret of eternal life but are more probably telephone bills. His next *Doctor Who* novel, *Dreamstone Moon*, is out in May 1998.

**Sam Lester** feels his life so far is infinitely boring and surely of no interest to anyone – but with his moral fibre now almost entirely rotted away, he has high hopes for the future.

**Steve Lyons** has written for and about numerous literary icons, from Spider-Man to Captain Kirk to Emily Bishop. He co-wrote the bestselling *Red Dwarf Programme Guide* and the not-so-bestselling *Doctor Who – The Completely Useless Encyclopedia*. He is responsible for six Doctor Who novels (and some short stories).

**Paul Magrs** was born in Jarrow in 1969. His first living memory was of Linx the Sontaran's head deflating at the climax of *The Time Warrior*. Chatto and Windus have published three of his novels, most recently *Could it be Magic?*, and his first collection of short fiction, *Playing Out* is in Vintage paperback. He lectures in English Literature and Creative Writing at the University of East Anglia.

**Daniel Patrick O'Mahony** was born in Croydon, south London, in July 1973. He has written for small magazines on a variety of subjects, including regular book reviews for *Vector: The Critical Journal of the British Science Fiction Association*. His two *Doctor Who* novels were *Falls the Shadow* (1994) and *The Man in the Velvet Mask* (1996). He lives in Hampshire and has delusions of grandeur.

**Robert Perry** and **Mike Tucker** met at a comprehensive school in South Wales in 1977, and started writing together shortly afterwards. Now that people have actually started to commission them, they have decided to live on opposite sides of London. They have written for Marvel and Virgin and their *Doctor Who* novel, *Illegal Alien*, was published by BBC Books in 1997. Their next novel is *Doctor Who: Matrix*, to be published in late 1998. In their 'solo' careers Mike is an effects designer for the BBC and co-author of *Ace!* with Sophie Aldred, and Robert has written for, and toured with, veteran rock band The Enid.

**Evan Pritchard** lives alone in a small cottage in Somerset. Happy to research every moment of human history in detail so intimate that it transcends the purely anal, his lust for knowledge is second only to certain primal urges he would rather keep secret. He feels *Doctor Who* ended for him when William Hartnell left the part, and does not believe in an afterlife.

**Tara Samms** was born in 1971 and has watched far too much television all her life. Unlike every other author she has ever known, she is entirely happy with her job and doesn't seek to write full-time; she is a life model for several art schools in London. She has two dogs and dreams of immortality.

# OTHER BOOKS AVAILABLE FEATURING

## THE EIGHT DOCTORS
### By Terrance Dicks

The Eighth Doctor embarks on a hazardous journey to regain the memories of his past selves – and gains a new travelling companion, Samantha Jones…

## VAMPIRE SCIENCE
### By Jonathan Blum and Kate Orman

The Doctor and Sam come up against a vampire sect in present day San Francisco. Some want to co-exist with humans, but some want to go out in a blaze of glory. Can the Doctor defuse the situation without bloodshed?

## THE BODYSNATCHERS
### by Mark Morris

The deadly Zygons are menacing Victorian London, and only the Doctor's old friend Professor Litefoot can assist the time travellers in defeating them. But why are the Zygons stealing the bodies of the dead?

## GENOCIDE
### by Paul Leonard

The Doctor and Sam arrive on Earth only to discover humanity never existed – the Tractites are the rightful masters of the planet…

# WAR OF THE DALEKS
## by John Peel

The Doctor discovers the body of Davros, ruthless creator of the Daleks, on board an old salvage vessel deep in space. But why are a party of Thals, the Daleks' sworn enemies, so desperate to revive him?

# ALIEN BODIES
## by Lawrence Miles

The Doctor and Sam attend a very special auction that has attracted a number of aggressive alien bidders – and the relic going to the highest bidder may change the Doctor's life forever…

# KURSAAL
## by Peter Anghelides

Kursaal is a pleasure world – or will be if it isn't destroyed during construction by eco-terrorists. Arriving on the scene, the Doctor soon links a series of strange murders to the last remains of the long dead Jax, an ancient wolf-like race…

# OPTION LOCK
## by Justin Richards

Landing on present day Earth, the Doctor and Sam are soon embroiled in a deadly conspiracy to start a nuclear war. But what do the conspirators really want – and how are they linked to a secret society almost 700 years old?

# LONGEST DAY
## by Michael Collier

A sinister device is buried somewhere in the time-swept wastes of the unstable planet Hirath, and a bloodthirsty alien race will stop at nothing to retrieve it. Sam discovers that even the Doctor cannot always win…

Other *Doctor Who* adventures featuring past incarnations of
the Doctor:

# THE DEVIL GOBLINS FROM NEPTUNE

## by Keith Topping and Martin Day

(Featuring the Third Doctor, Liz Shaw and UNIT)

Hideous creatures from the fringes of the solar system, the deadly Waro,
have established a bridgehead on Earth. But what are the Waro actually
after – and can there really be traitors in UNIT?

# THE MURDER GAME

## by Steve Lyons

(Featuring the Second Doctor, Ben and Polly)

Landing in a decrepit hotel in space, the time travellers are soon
embroiled in a deadly game of murder and intrigue – all the while
monitored by the occupants of a sinister alien craft…

# THE ULTIMATE TREASURE

## by Christopher Bulis

(Featuring the Fifth Doctor and Peri)

The Doctor is embroiled in a bizarre expedition on the planet
Gelsandor, in search of the fabled treasure of Rovan Cartovall…

# BUSINESS UNUSUAL

## by Gary Russell

(Featuring the Sixth Doctor and Mel)

Discovering the Brigadier has gone missing, the Doctor investigates. He
soon comes up against SenéNet, a sinister multinational company with a
deadly agenda…